A STAR IS BEING BORN.

A MOVIE IS BEING MADE.

A FIFTEEN-YEAR-OLD GIRL WILL BE LAUNCHED AS AN EROTIC SUPERSTAR.

HER NAME IS BELINDA BARSTOW.

Bursting with the drama, dreams, legends and ruthless realities of a rarefied world, *Belinda* takes you behind the scenes of a major motion picture studio at a crucial turning point in film history. Peopled by the fabulous and fabled darlings of the movie colony, *Belinda* is a rich, raw panorama of jet-set life, the stunning sequel to Mary Loos's glittering bestseller *The Beggars Are Coming*.

Bantam Books by Mary Loos

THE BEGGARS ARE COMING
BELINDA

BELINDA

Mary Loos

BELINDA
A Bantam Book / May 1976

Published simultaneously in the United States and Canada

Bantam Books are published by Bantam Books, Inc. Its trademark, consisting of the words "Bantam Books" and the portrayal of a bantam, is registered in the United States Patent Office and in other countries. Marca Registrada. Bantam Books, Inc., 666 Fifth Avenue, New York, New York 10019.

PRINTED IN THE UNITED STATES OF AMERICA

Contents

Cast of Characters

BELINDA BARSTOW. A classic beauty destined to become a superstar at fifteen.

JEFFREY BARSTOW. Belinda's father, the matinee idol who laughed, loved and drank his way through a world of fantasy.

JESSICA BARSTOW. Belinda's brassy, beautiful, wheeling, dealing mother.

CLAUDIA BARSTOW. Belinda's aunt, confidante and acting coach—the stunning, ruthless star of *The Beggars Are Coming.*

FERGUS AUSTIN. Hollywood's most powerful tycoon.

DAVID AUSTIN. Heir to Titan Studio.

MAX ZISKA. The Viennese genius, director of *The Oracle,* starring Belinda.

JOHN GRAVES. The dashing young British actor who plays opposite Belinda.

PERICLES NIADAS. A Greek billionaire who'd pay a fortune for Belinda.

POWER, MONEY,
SEX, GLAMOUR, FAME—
THEY IGNITE THE MEN AND WOMEN OF
BELINDA'S HOLLYWOOD

I

HOLLYWOOD:

1949-1956

1

Jeffrey Barstow was depressed. He sat at the desk in his study, ignoring the beauty of the California morning, which he usually cherished as his own. Beyond the French doors, the gleaming green leaves of honeysuckle with their fragrant little yellow bugles, and the distant sun-filtered splendor of sycamore, tree fern, and glimmering pool were lost to him. He felt he would not see them very much longer.

Absently he picked up a globule of amber, which his father had given him when he first trod the boards at Drury Lane. As he fondled it, he remembered that long-gone evening; only a Barstow would have the gall to play Hamlet at the age of thirty-eight and let his eighteen-year old son play Fortinbras. But Chauncey, temporarily throwing away his native bottle of Irish whiskey, did it.

Both father and son, being Barstows, had an incandescent handsomeness, but the sudden backstage raves about Jeffrey's glowing youth and cameolike beauty had irritated his father.

After the performance, he had closed his dressing-room doors against intruders and sycophants and had handed his son the smooth, translucent golden amber sphere. As long as young Jeffrey could remember, it had been his father's talisman, from theater to theater, always set among pots and brushes of his stage makeup.

"It's time for me to give you this, son," said Chauncey, "just as your grandfather Philip handed it to me when I took over *his* spotlight. I will tell you the same thing he told me: 'Just study this, son, when you think you're on the path to glory.' "

"Thank you, Father," Jeffrey had gasped, astonished that it was his.

"Don't thank me, you little son-of-a-bitch. Giving you this is my way of saying, as my father did to me: you're on your own."

His father gave him a quick buss on the cheek, grasped him by the shoulders, spun him around, shoved him out of his dressing room, and slammed the door.

Jeffrey studied the amber. It had become his talisman. And now he looked upon it as an old friend, his hands having polished it these fifty odd years.

He rubbed it on the sleeve of his shabby cardigan, which, like himself, was a relic of London theater days. Charged with negative electricity, the resin gathered several bits of lint. He held it to the light, his face contorted into a sudden expression of distress. He tried to check himself, but he knew his emotions were too palpable these days.

He suffered from what he saw inside the smooth nodule. Once it had been a conversation piece. Now, as time had caught him in its maw, the trinket saddened him. For it reminded him of his life.

Looking into it, he realized anew what his father had tried to tell him. Inside it, imprisoned forever, was the ultimate moment of two insects, wings atilt. They had not quite touched, trapped in the resin in paleozoic ages during a spring mating season, frozen for an eternity in their perpetual striving, millions of years before the dawn of man.

Jeffrey felt in a way that he had become a further counterpart in evolution to one of these tiny imprisoned insects, their wings still bravely unfurled, attempting to reach the moment of fusion for which they had been created. Poor little Isoptera, he mused.

Never, he felt, had he reached a moment of any complete fusion. He peered up at the photographs that lined one wall. Jeffrey Barstow, of course as Romeo, Hamlet, François Villon, Sydney Carton, Lorenzo the

Magnificent, Petruchio; Jeffrey Barstow as anything but Jeffrey Barstow, in half a century and more of posing, posturing, donning the carapace of men more heroic than he, men who had been created from the minds of Shakespeare, Ibsen, O'Neill, Shaw. Then to the frenetic images churned out of the option-fevered skulls of the hacks of Hollywood.

None of these roles, with the exception of the one in Gustav Jones's *April in the Flesh*, had been close to his goal. And ironically, that had been because Jones had limned him in his own abject eclipse, which he played magnificently at the time he considered the nadir of his life. That led to his renaissance in Hollywood and to the one thing in life that meant anything to him.

He looked at the framed picture on his desk. There she was, the miracle, the child of his loins. It had taken a corrupt doctor, an ambitious bitch wife, incredible hormone and tincture of cantharis to produce her. Seven-year-old Belinda, named after her beautiful great-grandmother. This new Belinda had blue eyes, framed with doubly thick dark eyelashes, not unlike those of his sister, Claudia. God forbid she should have such a life, spawned of silent movies, the most of her the worst, a, quote, movie star, unquote. He looked at the picture closely. The child's blond hair tumbled over her slim shoulders. He felt she looked more like him than Claudia, but she was Barstow all the way. This thought nourished what little spirit was left in his wasted life.

But on reflection he could not say Belinda was the only one who meant anything to him. There were two others he loved, although they had been heartaches for many years.

He slid open his top desk drawer and pulled out several pages that he had torn out of magazines. One worn picture was from *Town and Country*. In a jaunty pose, mallet on shoulder, was a young man sitting his polo pony gracefully. The caption read, "David Austin, son of Fergus Austin, head of Titan films, and grandson of Simon Moses, late founder of the noted film company, had just been made captain of the Stanford polo team. He rests between chukkers on his Argentine pony at Kaliolani Park polo field in Hawaii."

Jeffrey looked at the peaked hairline, the tight flat ears, the widely spaced eyes, and classic nose. The young man looked so much like the picture of himself at that age on the wall next to the desk, that he wondered that anyone could not know this was his natural son.

Then he lifted up a picture from a recent *Tatler*. Here was his David, eight years later. He was a man now, his face angled and serious. He was shown in a reception line at a command performance in London, introducing a Titan film star, Leslie Charles, to Queen Elizabeth and Prince Philip. The caption blurred before his eyes: "Her Majesty Queen Elizabeth and HRH Prince Philip greet film star Leslie Charles, introduced by David Austin, late of the American OSS, stationed in London during the war. Mr. Austin, heir to Titan studios, has established European branches of the studio at Shepperton, in Rome, in Madrid, and is planning film sound stages to be built in India."

Jeffrey held the picture at arm's length, so he could see it better, as he had many times. He wondered what had happened to the joyous, outgoing boy he had met on the Santa Monica beach, the day his heart had ached to embrace him, to tell him he was his father. What had happened since the carefree polo-playing lad had become the severe man in the *Tatler* picture?

He swung his chair around to the shelves behind him. Face-to-face he stared at the treasures in his room.

He grimaced into the shining curve of a yachting cup, making him look out of shape, like the mirrors at the fun houses on the old Venice pier. And then he saw her reflected, standing by the desk. He swung around, instinctively, to slip the pictures of his son, David, back into the drawer. But it was too late.

"Well," said Jessica, "you needn't bother, Jeffrey. You don't think, for God's sake, that I don't have a duplicate key to your little treasure trove. And you don't think that I don't know about David?"

He stared at his wife. She wore a white bathing suit, her splendid body tanned and oiled to perfection, her auburn hair brushed against her shoulders; her green eyes looked at him coldly. She picked up the picture.

He reached out to snatch it from her, but she pulled her hand away.

"Don't be foolish," she said. "*I* knew he was your son before Fergus Austin did."

It took a moment for this to sink in. Jeffrey half-rose from his chair, and then sat back helplessly.

"He . . . he knows!"

"Yes," said Jessica, "Fergus knows. I told him. As a matter of fact, his wife, Esther, told me. How she caught Fergus with your sister, Claudia, when they were on location. Right on the floor, like animals. And how she came to you, and spent the night."

Jeffrey stared at her, swallowing. It was true. She did know.

Seeing the contempt in her face, he stared balefully at her.

"Why did you marry me?" he whispered.

"Why not?" said Jessica.

"Because you always loathed me," he said. "Tell me, what was your game?"

Looking at the hatred in his eyes, she bent forward, creased the picture with two long nails, and set it neatly on the desk.

"Because it was David I really wanted. Your bastard son. Yes . . . as a matter of fact, the very day I married you, Fergus broke it up in the most horrible way. And that's when I told him the truth, that David was not his son, but yours. He wouldn't believe you could father a child. So I had to prove it to him. That's why I married you and had Belinda, if you must know. Although I never thought I'd make it. It took Dr. Wolfram, with all his skills and hormones, to get one last sperm out of you."

Jeffrey stared at her. Then he looked at the picture of his daughter on the desk.

"Oh, God," he said, "how could anything so beautiful come out of anything so hideous?"

"Remember," said Jessica, "I didn't bring it up myself. You asked."

He closed his eyes. He couldn't bear to look at her. In a moment he heard the door close. And as he sat trying to fit the pieces together, he heard the splash in the garden pool as Jessica began her precise thirty laps, her morning routine to keep her figure in shape. It was like everything she did—calculating, meticulous, and, to him, without any inner meaning or passion. So that was why she had no longer been Fergus Austin's mistress and executive secretary and had eloped with him. He had always wondered why. Now he knew.

Finally he opened his eyes, picked up the picture of David that Jessica had creased, smoothed it, and held it up beside the framed picture of Belinda. The two of them; his children.

He took out an envelope, a piece of stationery, and scribbled a few words. On the envelope he wrote, "For my sister, Claudia, when I am no longer here."

He took the amber off his desk, polished it once more, peered at it, and suddenly, without any warning to himself, he began to weep. He stuffed the amber into the envelope, and wiped off the flap with the tears that were wetting his cheek. He sealed it and put it in the drawer.

He wiped his eyes with his sleeve, and shook his head. Despising his weakness, he went to the French doors. He opened one. A wisp of honeysuckle waving in the light breeze brushed against him. He reached up, pulled it from the vine, and inhaled its fragrance.

"They underestimate me, Esther," he said. "The time has come."

Slyly he peered toward the pool. Jessica was still stroking her way to perfection. He moved as quickly as he could on his edematous feet. In Jessica's dressing room, her clothes were all laid out, her purse packed for her coming trip to the beauty parlor.

He fished in it. Sure enough, several twenties, a ten, two fives, and assorted change. He pocketed them and rushed to his room.

He changed quickly into a gray sport suit, knotting a

Sulka tie with shaking fingers in his haste. He tucked dark glasses in his pocket. He rushed to the butler's pantry. For years no one had ever expected he'd been looking for a car key. And there it was, on the keyboard, the sacrosanct key to the Rolls-Royce given him twenty years ago by Titan films when he had won an Oscar, and kept in prime shape for any previews or social functions that might have been planned. Like himself, it was a classic.

He snatched up the key, and warily rushed out into the motor court.

Pedro, his Mexican gardener, waved at him, as he always did. Jeffrey peered down the driveway and saw that the gates were open, for Pedro's truck, with a load of potted begonias, stood at one side.

He slipped into the garage. There was Jessica's standard Cadillac coupé, the station wagon, and the Rolls, in polished perfection.

He slid into the front seat, turned the key, and tried to start it. It made a hideous sound, he thought, loud in the morning silence; the garage seemed to make it echo. It died. It hadn't been turned over for so long. He tried again. He was clumsy about shifting gears. He had forgotten that the goddamned car was so complicated. He tried again. It started.

Jessica suddenly appeared. Nothing escaped her. She had heard. She was dripping wet, her cap still on.

"What do you think you're doing?" she yelled. "Get out of that car!"

For a split-second he had the wonderful vision of running her down, but he couldn't move the damned thing. Where in hell was the brake release?

But as she approached him, he realized his chance. She was on the wrong side, thank God, for the right-hand drive. He slid out of the car, ran swiftly toward the gate, God knows how, his legs aching, and before she or Pedro realized what he was doing, he was in the gardener's green Ford truck, had switched on the ignition, started it, and taken off, curving over the driveway, ripping up turf, and speeding away with begonia pots crashing out of the open tailgate, as he sped down the street.

He veered up a side street, pulled over to the curb under a tree, and stopped to catch his breath. No one had followed; he was safe for a moment. He got out of the car, closed the tailgate, and then sat, shaking his head, trying to clear his brain, wondering exactly where he was and how he was going to get where he had to go.

Perhaps this truck was better than the Rolls. It was a disguise. No one would ever suspect who he was. He fished out his dark glasses, took his coat off, pulled his tie loose; it was now or never. He pulled into a gas station, and while the truck was being serviced, asked the young attendant how to get to Pasadena.

◆◆◆◆◆◆◆◆

How fortunate, thought Jeffrey, that he had been an inmate of Las Cruces Sanatorium so many times, drying out.

The institution was an exclusive catch bag of southern California's misfits, mental or alcoholic. As one of its most renowned past residents, he knew every pathway in the garden of his alma mater. Parking his truck at the side, he realized this was the time of day that Esther Austin would be sitting near the latticed grape arbor, under a sycamore tree, swinging gently in a garden glider, while her nurse went to check what was on the luncheon menu, and sneak a cup of coffee before she returned to get her charge. She knew, as everyone did, that Esther was usually in a dream, and would rock comfortably until she was moved by the whim of someone else.

It was Saturday, the day that her busy husband, Fergus, could get away from running Titan studio and would come in the early afternoon to pay his weekly visit, so her blond hair was brushed and combed into curls around her pretty, lineless face. It hardly seemed possible that her son, David, was almost thirty, for time, like life, had escaped her these years. She wore a pink dress, which reflected a becoming glow on her fair face.

Jeffrey approached her cautiously. He was terrified. He had not seen her for years, this woman who after one night of love had given him a son. She looked beautiful. Everything was falling into place. He spoke softly.

"Esther," he said, "I told you we should have run away from them thirty years ago. And I've come to get you."

"That's so nice."

Incredible, Jeffrey mused; this woman thought of him so much that she canceled out his reality. Even now, when he spoke to her, she was blocking out his voice for the dream of his voice.

To his distress, he saw a middle-aged nurse coming along the arbor walkway. It was too late to hide behind a tree. He decided to brazen it out. Thank God she wasn't Esther's nurse. Jeffrey took off his sunglasses and waved at her jauntily; he'd seen her before.

"Oh, hello, Mr. Barstow," she said. "I haven't seen you for years. I didn't know you were here again."

"You can always count on that!" he said with a grimace.

She giggled, self-conscious in front of a movie star, and went her way. Thank God, a fan, he thought.

"Now, my darling," he whispered, as he helped Esther to rise, "we're going to do what I told you long ago we should have done. Come along, my love."

He helped her up. The motion seemed to jog her. She looked up at him, it seemed, for a moment, startled, but accepting him.

"My love," she echoed.

As for Jeffrey, remembering that night so out of context with anything he had known gave him courage.

He seated her in the truck. Shrewdness had to be his ally, to make up for time and cirrhosis. Often when he had been recovering from his alcoholic bouts he had roamed the rear of the Las Cruces property where trucks disgorged supplies. He had often seen gardeners bringing plants and equipment in the back way. When you lived in this limbo, any incident was an event.

He put on his dark glasses and drove cautiously past the service entrances, grateful that he was in the gardener's truck. The Rolls-Royce would have been a giveaway.

Cautiously he drove through downtown Pasadena, over the Arroyo Seco bridge, with the Rose Bowl beyond, where once—it must have been a million years ago—he was cheered as grand marshal of the Rose Bowl Parade; through Glendale, past Los Feliz, and finally on Wilshire to the Pacific Coast Highway, nervously peering behind him every time he saw a motorcycle or a police car.

◆◆◆◆◆◆◆◆

It took the nurse fifteen minutes to discover that Esther Austin was gone. It took another twenty minutes for the nurse who had seen Jeffrey Barstow to hear about it and identify her companion. Five more minutes to put the picture together. The panicked nurses rushed to the director, Dr. Lindstrom. A scullery helper remembered, when the word got out, that a green truck he had never seen before had passed by the kitchen windows with a man, and a woman in a pink dress in it.

Frantic calls to Fergus Austin were to no avail. He was on his way to his weekly visit with his wife. He arrived an hour later.

Tall, spare, and nervous, his reddish hair peppered with silver, Fergus entered Las Cruces. A receptionist stopped him with the message not to go to his wife's bungalow, but to go directly to the executive offices, Dr. Lindstrom was waiting to see him.

Now what? thought Fergus, hating the place. What unpleasant memories. He remembered particularly as a young man getting Jeffrey Barstow in and out after drinking bouts. And also Claudia, Jeffrey's sister, beautiful, provocative Claudia, the first woman in his life, the first Titan star.

And then, reaching back most painfully, he remembered the beginning of Las Cruces, his wife's breakdown after David had been born, when Dr. Lindstrom, a young psychiatrist then, had taken her over, and explained to him all the tragic symptoms of schizophrenia, and alerted him about what her future would be.

Now Fergus was middle-aged, Lindstrom was the elder doctor, Esther had spent a generation away from life while Fergus had slowly taken over control of the whole Titan studio. Esther did not even know that her father, Simon Moses, had died, and left the path open to Fergus.

So what could it be? Maybe something new? More shock treatments to help Esther? News that she might come home?

His thoughts were divided. In one way, he hoped Esther could be cured. In another, he wished fervently that the doctor would never tell him she could come home.

As he walked into the room, Dr. Lindstrom adjusted his steel-rimmed glasses and tried to give him a smile. Dear God, how was he going to tell him? Lindstrom had disliked Fergus Austin for thirty years. For his brusque attitude and overtipping the staff. For his lack of real humanity toward his wife. For the coldness that seemed to wrap him in ice when he looked at her. For the patronizing way he visited her, without any affection. And now he was forced to tell this man something that could destroy his whole sanatorium.

He got to the point.

"Mr. Austin, nothing like this has ever happened in this institution. Your wife has disappeared. She was driven away, as far as we can find out, in a Ford truck, in the company of Jeffrey Barstow."

Fergus stared at him as if he were insane.

"What are you saying?" he asked.

"I said," Lindstrom repeated, "your wife has been driven away by Jeffrey Barstow."

"It's impossible," said Fergus. "Jeffrey Barstow is a

very sick man. Everyone in town knows he has cirrhosis of the liver. He just couldn't function."

"He did," said Lindstrom. "The whole thing is incredible. If Mr. Barstow had not been considered a patient by the staff, it never could have happened. Believe me, her nurse was away from her only five minutes to order lunch."

Fergus faced Lindstrom, his lips white with anger.

"For almost thirty years," he said, "I have trusted you, paid you a fortune, and you let this terrible thing happen. You should not have even allowed that man to speak to her."

"But they knew each other," said Dr. Lindstrom.

"They did . . ." said Fergus bitterly, "indeed they did."

"We tried to reach Mrs. Barstow," said Lindstrom. "She was not in. We left word with the maid for her to call back. She had gone someplace to pick up her daughter at a birthday party. Do you wish to speak to her when she calls?"

The doctor was puzzled at his violent reaction.

"Under no circumstances! Take care of it yourself. Just find out what make of car he was driving, and the license plate. That's the least you can do."

"Shall we call the police?"

Fergus paced to and fro angrily.

"By no means!" he screamed. "Do you think I want it all over the front pages that my wife has been kidnapped by that maniac Jeffrey Barstow! Think of the scandal. My God, what kind of a place do you run?"

Dr. Lindstrom spoke in a calm voice.

"I have to tell you something, Mr. Austin. If you don't calm down, you're going to be a patient here yourself. I have had the opportunity to see a great deal more than you of your wife these last thirty years. What a lonely woman. No one seemed to care to come visit her. Although your short visits have been constant, obviously they were lip service. And often, when Jeffrey Barstow was here, I would see him talking sweetly to her. Sometimes he picked her a flower or read a verse to her. And when he did, it was her best therapy. She reacted, and seemed to be happy."

"No one told me about this. She was here to be protected, not exposed to a drunkard," said Fergus.

"He was not drunk when he was here," said Lindstrom. "And I have one more thing to say to you."

Fergus looked at him angrily.

"This was no kidnapping," said Lindstrom. "Apparently she went of her own free will."

Fergus stared, at a loss for words.

The phone rang.

Lindstrom, answering, put his hand over the receiver. "It's Mrs. Barstow. . . . Hello. Mrs. Barstow, I've been trying to reach you. Dr. Lindstrom here, from Las Cruces. Do you by any chance know where Mr. Barstow is?"

There was a short conversation on the other end.

"What kind of a car was he driving? . . . A green 1946 Ford truck . . . your gardener's. Could you get the license? . . . No . . . Mr. Barstow isn't here. But, Mrs. Barstow, Mr. Austin is here right now, deeply disturbed. It seems your husband picked up Esther Austin and drove her away with him. Have you any idea . . . ?"

Lindstrom lifted his eyebrows. Even Fergus could hear wild laughter over the phone. After a moment Lindstrom cleared his throat and interrupted.

"Mrs. Barstow, this is very serious. Mrs. Austin is a mental case, and your husband, under certain conditions, is none too stable. We will have to inform the authorities."

He listened for a second and then hung up. He looked at Fergus, puzzled.

"That's a very strange woman," he said. "She laughed her head off, then said, 'Let the poor bastards go,' and hung up."

Fergus took a cigarette out of his case, snapped it nervously shut, clicked his gold lighter, and puffed at a cigarette. Lindstrom noted how yellowed his fingers were from chain smoking.

"What do we do, doctor," he asked, "get in detectives?"

"The expense to cover the state would be terrific," said Lindstrom. "It would not be possible to cover every road. I think we need the police force."

"That means the papers would be on our necks," said Fergus.

Lindstrom noticed how his hand shook as he smoked.

"It would be bad for both of us," said Lindstrom. "Would you risk waiting twenty-four hours, to see if he doesn't come back with her? His means and mind are not what they were twenty years ago; they'll have to surface. I think we'll hear from them. Are you willing to take the chance?"

Fergus looked at Lindstrom eye-to-eye. Each one thought the other one was cold. And each one had a great deal to lose. For Lindstrom, it was the reputation of his sanatorium. For Fergus, it was his pride.

If and when Esther and Jeffrey were found, most likely a private payoff could be arranged. How many of these he had handled over thirty-five years at Titan studio!

He nodded.

◆◆◆◆◆◆◆◆

Driving along the Pacific Coast Highway, south, Jeffrey talked to Esther as if they were both in complete control of their escapade. His feet hurt, for he was not used to driving, and his edema was such that he had to kick off his English fox-embroidered slippers. The swelling of his abdomen caused him to unfasten his belt.

"In the old days," he said, "I would have had a suite for us at the Coronado Hotel; but in this truck I fear that we must change our plans. We would have driven up in my Rolls, and dined in our suite, and I would have read the most beautiful love poems in the world to you. How many times I thought of you in my loneliness. Ah, listen."

He bent his head toward her and whispered, " 'My beloved spoke, and said unto me, Rise up, my love, my fair one, and come away. For lo, the winter is past, the rain is over and gone; The flowers appear on the earth. . . .' "

The car veered over the center line, and the honk of a horn awoke him to reality. He jogged sharply back, and she leaned against him. A truck passed by, the driver cursing angrily at him.

He took off his dark glasses; the shadows were lengthening.

"Thank heaven Mr. Gideon carries our poetry in almost any hotel room," he said. "Bless Solomon for getting in the right book."

She looked up at him placidly, her hands folded. She smiled at the sound of his voice.

He drove into a gas station. While they were filling and servicing the car, he rushed to the men's toilet. His bladder was not what it used to be. Whatever happened, he had to keep himself in form for this adventure. It was difficult to equate his circumstances—an old sick man in a stolen truck, his companion an insane woman.

He led Esther to the ladies' room, opened the door, and let her in, standing by, concerned, waiting to see if she could handle herself. The attendant looked at him sharply as he peered in.

"It's okay," he said, "my wife's just a little unsteady."

The man smiled and signaled that he understood the frailty of women.

He bought two Cokes out of a machine, and brought her one, as she settled into her seat.

"We'll still spend the night by the sea," he said, "and we'll watch the moon on the water, and we'll go where they'll never think of finding us. Never."

When he got back in the car, he leaned his head back. He felt giddy. He forced himself to sit straight.

"We'll have a good meal when we get there, and I'll buy you wine, my love. . . ."

It was nighttime when they reached the international

border to Mexico at Tijuana. The traffic was heavy, people going down to Baja for a weekend in the shabby glaring streets of the honky-tonk border town, alive with screaming vendors, people selling paper flowers, greasy food, cheap watches on boards, gaudy clothes, sombreros, tawdry floor shows, girls, boys, jumping beans, plaster crockery.

Jeffrey parked, got a boy to watch the car and clean it with an oily rag, and then led Esther to Caesar's café. They had to stand in line. She was docile, did anything he said. He held her hand, and once when he let her go, he was pleased to see that she clutched it again.

An old waiter recognized him.

"Señor Barstow," he cried out, "it's been so long since you were here. Welcome!"

He rushed off to call the manager. In a moment, a group of middle-aged tourists moved in on him. They were of an age to remember him. Suddenly they grabbed menus, cards, anything for autographs, shoved him pens and pencils; one snatched a button off his shirt for a souvenir. They were hot, screaming, excited, pressing. Esther put her hands to her ears and began to whimper.

"Oh, God," said Jeffrey, "let's get out of here."

He pulled her outside, and they dashed for the truck.

He tried to make light of it. "That's fame!" he said.

There was nothing to do but go on. He followed the bumpy road out of town past the forest of cardboard shacks and poverty to the clean shoreline toward Ensenada. It seemed as if the trip would never end. He was hungry, thirsty. He saw, gratefully, that Esther had fallen asleep, her head on his shoulder.

What have I done? he thought. How am I going to handle this? He parked the car, took his jacket, and covered her from the sea breeze. At least the evening was not too cool. He breathed deeply, the salt sea air a tonic.

He recollected that somewhere along the road was a

little pink hotel. If he could only keep awake. His legs ached. His belly hurt.

Finally he pulled into the little *posada* near the La Misión turnoff.

He woke her up, smoothed back her hair. "Here we are, at last, it's going to be fine."

He led her inside. A few people were sitting drinking around a fireplace. A guitarist was playing, and several people sang. Jeffrey pulled out his money; he handed the sleepy desk clerk a folded five-dollar bill.

"I want a room facing the ocean," he said, "and dinner served in my room, for two. The best you've got, and some wine."

The young man looked at him. A tired old man. A sleepy woman. Well, you got them all.

"The dining room's closed," he said.

Jeffrey handed him twenty dollars.

"The dining room has just opened," he said regally, using his sonorous voice and pulling himself together with the Barstow panache. Then, looking toward the fireplace, he saw that look again; a middle-aged woman had recognized him and held one fat arm out, pointing, her mouth open in surprise. He quickly maneuvered Esther outside, and signaled to the clerk to get them to their room.

The room was not too bad. As in many Mexican hotels, it had two double beds and a small bed for large traveling families. But there was a balcony atop the rocky cliff with two deck chairs, a tile-topped table, and pots of geraniums overlooking the sandy beach below, and a sea that was silvered by a waning moon. The sound of the surf and distant guitar music was just right.

He settled Esther on the balcony and looked around the meager room. In the bathroom was a thick toothbrush glass and a candle in case of power failure.

On the terrace she was placidly looking at the moon.

"It isn't all it could have been, my darling," he whispered, "but with you, it's everything."

He lit the candle and set it on the table, picked some of the geraniums, and put them in the bathroom glass as a centerpiece. Then, rushing back into the room, he opened the drawer of the crude night table, and to his joy, found a Bible.

Squinting, because he did not have his reading glasses, he fished through the pages, holding the book close to the flickering candle, and found what he wanted.

"Solomon wrote this for us," he whispered, and read, " 'O my dove, thou art in the clefts of the rock, in the secret places of the stairs, let me see thy countenance, let me hear thy voice; for sweet is thy voice, and thy countenance is comely.' "

He looked at her, his eyes welling with tears. How beautiful, how sweet she was, how serene her face.

" 'Thy countenance is comely,' " she whispered, looking at him.

He closed the book, gazed out upon the ocean, relishing the soft sounds of the waves, as they sucked at the sand below the cliffs. For a moment his mind whirled. What was he doing here? Where was he? And then he looked back at Esther, smiled at his foolish thoughts, and said to himself: You are home, because she's here.

◆◆◆◆◆◆◆◆

In the morning, the chambermaid knocked. There was no answer. Later the waiter came to pick up the tray that was in front of the door in the corridor. The bottle of Santo Tomás wine was empty. The totoava dinners had been partly eaten. But there was no answer at the door.

About one o'clock the maid informed the desk clerk that someone had better check that couple who came in late.

At two o'clock the desk clerk knocked on the door. There was no answer. He got the passkey and with a feeling of foreboding opened the door.

Esther was sitting on a deck chair that had been brought into the room. Her hair was hanging in disorder about her face, but she was smiling. On the bed lay

Jeffrey. His mouth was open. A great gush of blood had fallen from it onto the pillow, and down one arm.

The desk clerk let out a gasp. He whispered to the chambermaid to call the police. While he was waiting, he saw that the man was still alive. And he shivered when he saw the woman, staring happily at the bloody man. He went through the pockets of the man's coat and found the credit cards made out to Jeffrey Barstow. He thought the name sounded familiar, but he couldn't place it.

The Mexican police *jefe* was an old hand. He not only knew the name, he had bailed Barstow out of the *cárcel* several times in years past. He knew what to do. He called Titan studio.

"My God!" said Fergus. "Don't move anything. I'll fly down to San Diego and meet you. Get an ambulance . . . or a hearse."

"He ain't dead," said the *jefe,* "but we'd better get him out pronto before he dies. I've seen it before with these alkies—they just explode. But you know how tough it is to get a body out of Mexico."

"How is . . . the . . . the lady?" asked Fergus.

"She's not at all shook up," said the *jefe*. "She just sits smiling at him, blood and all, and says 'thy countenance is comely,' over and over."

◆◆◆◆◆◆◆◆

Whether Jeffrey died on one side of the border or the other was something that only the *jefe* knew, but money in his pocket kept the secret. And he did not especially feel guilty, because his compadre on the American side had an equal wad on his hip. The sere, redheaded gringo who had the plane waiting took the woman in the pink dress by the hand. Everything was in proper order.

The *jefe* was not too surprised to see that Señor Austin had a nurse with him, because he had already figured out the lady was *loca.*

Esther was returned to Las Cruces. The nurse who had been away when her charge escaped was fired. Dr.

Lindstrom put a double watch on Esther, but it was not necessary, for Jeffrey Barstow was dead.

All Hollywood paid proper respect to Jeffrey. His sister, Claudia, was called back from London.

The older fans of Hollywood remembered what dazzling stars the brother and sister had been in the early days of Titan. But at fifty-six Claudia was no longer the flawless beauty remembered from lush days, even though her petite, trim figure and double-lashed eyes showed the beauty she had been.

In the previous year she had startled the town when she made a comeback with her independent film, *Quest for a Key*. But since then she had cross-collateralized another film. This meant she had reassigned the rights from her first picture as collateral for the money she borrowed for the second.

Claudia had garnered an Academy Award for *Quest for a Key*, but that was about all that was left, save an opulent wardrobe. In the tradition of Hollywood, one shattering failure had reduced her to the status of a has-been. Again Claudia was on her uppers.

She still had a trickle of dollars coming in. She would have come back to pay respects to Jeffrey if she'd had to work her way across on an ocean liner.

Jeffrey, her brother, was the only person in her life to whom she had really related. They had always fought and scrapped, and rejected each other, and made up. He had deplored her long relationship as Simon Moses' mistress, not on moral grounds, but because he believed she was wasting time on an older man.

"But I love him," she had said.

Jeffrey had lifted one of his eyebrows, as he often did when she puzzled him.

"When," he said, "are you going to learn that the act of sex is not going to get you close to anyone. You are just fooling yourself if you believe that."

"But he really takes care of me," Claudia had said.

"Well, that's different." He had sighed. "No one ever did that for me, really."

"I would," she had said.

He looked at her. "I believe you would."

And that was about as close to spoken affection as they ever got. But she remembered now, and her heart bled.

Ignoring expense, Claudia took the first plane.

Jessica invited Claudia to breakfast before the funeral. Of course, they would attend as a family. She told her how Jeffrey had died in his bed upstairs, sorry that he had wasted his life so long before being married and having Belinda. She brought in a charmingly invented postscript about Jeffrey leaving a last fond message of love to his sister before he peacefully perished. Pure bullshit, thought Claudia. Jeffrey never talked like that!

At this moment Effie came into the room. She shook hands warmly with Jeffrey's sister. Claudia looked at her black beauty, the compassionate brown eyes with purple circles of sadness around them, the trim figure, and remembered how Jeffrey had told her that Effie was a gem, more than a maid, a kind, warm person in his lonely days.

Effie seemed to avoid the glance of Jessica as she proffered Claudia an envelope.

"He meant this for you, Miss Claudia," said Effie. "This was in his desk when I cleaned up, marked to be given to you."

Effie's eyes brimmed with sudden tears. Claudia felt more affection and love for her brother in this woman than she saw in his widow. And she also noted Jessica's little flicker of resentment as Effie handed her the envelope, as if it were something that might never have come to her hand, save that Effie had insisted.

"Oh," said Jessica, "of course it *must* be for you."

Claudia noted the flash of irritation that was quickly concealed as Jessica graciously waved the gift into her hands.

Being an actress and onetime movie queen, Claudia spotted Jessica's behavior for what it was. This was Jessica's third-act curtain as a young widow. She would get more attention today, due to Jeffrey's demise, than she would perhaps ever have again.

Claudia knew Jessica had been Fergus' mistress, and

she had long been suspicious that the letters she had sent to his office had been jettisoned. The polite responses to her from his secretary had hurt her in her hard days in London.

She took the envelope, and was about to open it when Belinda entered. The child rushed up to her aunt and put her arms around her.

"Oh, Aunt Claudia," she said, "I wish you had been here!"

Claudia stared at her, overwhelmed at her beauty.

"Belinda didn't see her daddy at the end," said Jessica. "They took him away at night. Belinda was asleep."

"What time did they take him?" asked Belinda.

"I really don't know," said Jessica. "Oh, I guess one o'clock in the morning. Now, don't bother your aunt with these details, dear. Brush your hair once more. The car is waiting, and you know your father would want you to look your best.

"Forgive me," said Jessica. "I must get ready." She left.

Belinda, her hands on her hips, looked at her aunt.

"I was up at one o'clock," said Belinda. "My dog Sarge was sick. I don't think Daddy ever was here. Something's fishy."

Claudia's eyes widened. Was this ever a Barstow! Her cameo face, impudent, with lifted brows, wide-set eyes, the classic widow's peak that showed even with her blond hair tousled, and the stance, so sure, so graceful. Suddenly her eyes brimmed.

"Oh, Aunt Claudia, I loved him so. He was so sentimental, so . . . so silly, and so . . ."

She waved her arms, trying to find the word.

"So debonair," said Claudia, her own eyes brimming.

The two embraced. Belinda looked up at her.

"That's the word," she said. "I love your eyelashes. I wish mine would be like yours."

"They will, dear," said Claudia, "they will, when you put this much mascara on them, and I'm going to get it all over my face."

She fished for a handkerchief.

Jessica called Belinda from upstairs.

"Oh, damn," said Belinda, "I've got to go fix my hair."

She bounded away, and Claudia patched up her face, smiling. For an eight-year-old she certainly had a lot of Barstow showing.

She opened the envelope; surprised, she clutched the familiar amber talisman in her hand.

> Dear Claudia:
>
> I have decided to escape this bitch, come what may. I'm running away with the one I love. No matter what, for time is fleeting. Cherish this talisman of mine, dear sister, and when Belinda is ready to take off on her own, give it to her. If she's ready, she'll understand. And as I said on the beach when we were together on her sixth birthday, look after her. She sure as hell is going to need you someday. Hike your tights and keep the torch lit for me.
>
> Your loving brother,
> Jeffrey

Effie came in to clear the table. She still walked as regally as she had when Claudia first knew her, when she had come to work for Jeffrey years ago. Claudia took her hand and squeezed it.

"Oh, Effie, thank you for getting the note to me. What will it be like without him?"

"It'll be empty, Miss Claudia. Mighty empty." She flashed an affectionate little smile at Claudia.

"I sort of kept that note to myself until you came. I didn't want nobody to interfere with it."

"I get the message," said Claudia, "and thanks. It was very personal. And it's a good thing I got it."

"I figured," said Effie. "Well, I'd better get my dress and hat on. Mrs. Barstow's going to let me sit in front with the driver."

On the way out, she turned to Claudia with a soft smile. "Faithful retainer and all that! Just hope God lets me stay with that child."

Claudia wandered into the living room. The shaded

gallery looked out on the garden and pool. Tree ferns, hydrangeas, camellias, gardenias, all the things Jeffrey loved, which had nourished him before his arteries turned to coral.

She was elated, somehow, that Jeffrey had escaped. Whoever could have been his companion? And where did he go? And how did he die? It was obvious from his note that he wasn't at home.

It really didn't matter much, she thought; she just hoped he'd had a ball. If she could, she'd like to take off with someone she loved the last day of her life, whenever it would be. People weren't always so lucky.

It would be strange not to have Jeffrey around to talk to, to drink with, to bitch with about Fergus and the studio. But that was all gone.

Oh, Jeffrey, she thought. Why do I wait until it's too late to tell you how I loved you? Do you feel it, brother, lying there? They say your casket's closed. I dread to imagine why, but I'm glad, for I remember you as ever beautiful. When I looked at you, I saw part of myself. There were such great, glorious things about us. And such great, wrong things. Strange, I'll see you again on the screen, and you'll live for me, because of that damned mesh of celluloid which enslaved so much of us; you'll be alive on film, and I'll have to remember. . . . If I had to do it all over again, you're the one I would want to be with most. You were the talent, the inspiration, the guiding light, even if I was too stupid to understand. I wish I had listened to you. I wish you had listened to me. . . . I wish . . . Oh, I wish . . . But I'll try to make up for it with Belinda. I'll work it out somehow. . . .

Fergus wouldn't be at the funeral. He was in New York.

Small wonder, she thought. He certainly wouldn't come to the funeral of the man who had married his mistress.

She hugged her purse, delighted with the last message Jeffrey had flashed her. It was almost as if he were here, sharing a last laugh with her. In her pain of bereavement there was a little nudge of amusement.

She knew the pain would go, and the remembrance of him would be sustaining.

So she was bolstered and prepared when Jessica came downstairs. Her wisp of veil with its wide black chiffon border was stunning. She pulled on her gloves. Claudia figured she knew how damned good-looking she'd be when the vulture photographers moved in, as they always did at a Hollywood funeral.

Claudia adjusted her own little Paris hat, looked in a Venetian mirror on the way out, and decided she looked pretty good herself. Her black hair fitted her head in a caplike swirl, her Molyneux suit was smashing. Even Jessica cast a sidelong glance, and Claudia could have sworn her Hattie Carnegie didn't look quite so good to her suddenly. . . . What rotten things to be thinking when you were going to your brother's funeral.

"What," said Jessica suddenly, a flash of annoyance on her face, "was that . . . ah . . . message that Effie handed you?"

"It was just a little note from Jeffrey," said Claudia, "about his . . . plans."

"Plans?" said Jessica looking at her sharply. "What plans?"

"Oh," said Claudia, waving it away, "just holiday plans. We always wrote each other nonsense, you know. And that lump—it was that piece of amber. We always had it around."

Jessica looked slightly relieved.

"I never cared for it myself," she said. "Those bugs in it! But if you like it, I'm pleased you have it for a souvenir."

"So am I," said Claudia, relishing the moment. Oh . . . if only she knew what was in that note!

Belinda came downstairs. She wore a navy middy suit and coat, socks and Mary Janes, and a brimmed hat that sat back on her blond head.

Claudia realized it was proper for a little girl, but already she could imagine her longing to get out of the uniform. She was too beautiful to be boxed in tradition.

"I want Sarge to go, too," Belinda said suddenly.

"Are you out of your mind!" said Jessica. "Dogs don't go to funerals!"

Effie came in, dressed in a dove-gray suit, with a smart gray beret. She carried the dog.

"What are you doing?" said Jessica, shocked.

"He's just going to sit in the car, Miss Jessica," said Effie. Jessica glared at her but rushed ahead.

"Just keep him out of sight," she said.

Claudia noticed that Effie and the child shot each other conspiratorial glances. They had won.

Hori, the chauffeur, who had been in Manzanar the war years, was back again to serve his master's house this sad day. He stood at attention, doing what he must do out of respect.

"There's so much to do," said Jessica, as the car started. "Everyone's coming by later. The cook's making sandwiches, and I suppose, Hori, you'll have to tend bar." She turned to Claudia. "Seymour Sewell's meeting us at the church. Leave it to an agent not to miss anything. So many things to think of."

"Yes," said Belinda, turning to her, "don't forget the main thing. Daddy's dead."

She began to cry, and Claudia took her hand.

"Now, now, sweetheart," she said, "Jeffrey would want you to play it well. I know it isn't going to be easy."

She tried to hold back the tears in her own eyes. Clutching her bag, and the message in it from Jeffrey, which comforted her, she glanced at Jessica, and grudgingly respected the fact that at least she wasn't shedding crocodile tears.

Jessica sat cool and pale, ready for the onslaught. She knew Fergus wouldn't be there, and she gloated at the reason. After all, she didn't care. It ought to hit every paper. The three Barstow women, a solid front, all of them beautiful. What a triumph.

Claudia glanced at her and saw the shadow of a smile. It angered her. Well, anyway, she thought, Jeffrey, old boy, at least you got rid of her.

2

◆◆◆◆◆◆◆◆

Fergus Austin settled into his flying bed on the DC-6 and recollected wryly that the airplane seemed to be not only his second home but also his refuge. For a few hours he was in an enforced limbo and had time to avoid the telephone and analyze the disasters he had to face in New York. And there were many.

He had attended the very private meeting of studio heads at the Hillcrest Country Club right after the war. This had been the beginning of the deluge that was now flooding every stratum of Hollywood.

In his briefcase he had a top-secret dossier of Titan personalities and properties that had the red hex on them. In other words, they were accused of being tainted with the curse of communism. And he was going to have to tell Abe Moses and the board how many projects were now unusable. It would cost the company millions.

In addition to several up-and-coming actors who had been expensively groomed for stardom, he would have to jettison four important directors and eight ace writers as soon as possible. (Writers were always suspected commies, because they loudly held forth on all political subjects in the commissary, being authorities on everything.)

But the greatest loss of all to Titan was the schedule of current films in which some of these personalities were involved; these would have to be scratched or suspended. Also there was a shelf of properties ready for production that would have to be replaced immediately, for the scripts were written by men in shadow, on the suspect "gray list," just one step above the obvious "blacklist."

Dropping the options of the current offenders was Fergus' least problem. The taint of the whole studio's product in the last several years would cost Titan its profit. Fergus knew that Abe and all the board would light on his head when he explained the situation, blaming him personally for allowing the "reds" to infiltrate the studio.

In 1947 the stir had been caused by various groups: the Motion Picture Alliance for the Preservation of American Ideals, which was witch-hunting Communists and hiding some pro-fascists behind its rich skirts; the Committee for the First Amendment, middle-roader do-gooders who got stuck with the antics of the leftists who later became the Hollywood Ten; and the Association of Motion Picture Producers, led by Eric Johnston, who had the hard task of being asked to pick the bad apples out of the current harvest, after the cider was made.

The whole economy of Hollywood and the salaries of thirty thousand workers were at stake when the House Un-American Activities Committee began to get front-page space. The Motion Picture Alliance breathed information to J. Parnell Thomas, the committee head. Protests about the destruction of civil liberties filled the air. On the other hand, Paul McNutt, acting as Producers' Association counselor, advised Fergus of the danger of using a blacklist, saying it would be a conspiracy without warrant of law.

Fergus had been confounded. He had not had much time for politics. He had abhorred Roosevelt's cutting down of private income, he had been distressed by Hoover's phlegmatic personality. He had shaken hands with many politicians and a few statesmen. But his basic interests were incestuous—the Titan studio.

Although he deplored the function of the Un-American Activities Committee as a Salem witch-hunt and an invasion of the picture industry, he knew it was necessary to go along with it for survival. As a representative of management, he sat through endless committee meetings and reports far into the night. He hoped it would blow over soon, with the elimination of a few of the most militant radicals.

And then the bombshell fell on the town. The speech which Johnston gave in New York at the end of November, 1947, known later as the Waldorf Statement, was a complete reversal of his earlier stand. As the Los Angeles *Times* had put it a few weeks before, Mr. Johnston was chiding the Committee on Un-American Activities for smearing Hollywood. Now, a month later, he said of the Hollywood Ten, "their actions have been a disservice to their employers and have impaired their usefulness to the industry. We will forthwith discharge or suspend without compensation those in our employ, and we will not reemploy any of the ten until such time as he is acquitted or purges himself of contempt. . . . On the broader issue of alleged subversive and disloyal elements in Hollywood, our members are likewise prepared to take positive action. . . ."

And in this last statement lay the problem. The ten whose red party cards were exposed took their legal chances. But the people on the fringe, who had appeared at benefits for this country or that group of orphans, were suspect. And young and old, without any record being made of the reason, found themselves unemployable, cautiously ignored by those who previously had sought their talents. Sitting it out, wondering what had happened to their careers, they had no recourse or protection.

Even those who appeared as witnesses were suspect. The lovely Viennese actress Mady Christians, who had just come to America from the bloodbath of Europe, put her hands over her ears after listening to the discussions.

"You don't know what is happening," she said. "I saw it in Europe. First artists are silenced, then the press, then comes dictatorship. God help this wonderful country if it begins here. It happened in Germany. It happened in Russia. No matter which side you are on, it is necessary you should be heard."

There was no way anyone could be cleared, once an

accusing finger was pointed. The damage was never repaired. Several committed suicide rather than face a bleak future, for in the arts, unemployment meant death in life; there was no way to make a living if one was on a blacklist, or even a gray list.

Fergus, irritated at the interference of these witch-hunters in his world, knew as well as anyone the reason for the sudden switch. Wall Street backers had sixty million dollars tied up in picture companies, and because they were afraid of public opinion, the telephone wires connecting the two film capitals whispered orders that never would be written, only acted upon.

So, he thought, now he was stuck, trying to make better pictures with untalented goddamn middle-roaders. Everyone had a list, and crank calls from all sides came in every time a picture was released.

Stool pigeons darkened the skies, naming Communist members, hoping to protect their money and their prestige. Yet others refused to squeal on their friends. Friends became enemies. Confused people switched sides. Some fled to Mexico and Europe. Others wrote under assumed names. Studios demanded clearances before giving anyone a job. And some of the proud who were innocent of belonging to anything more subversive than the YMCA refused to sign clearances on moral grounds, and sat at home broke, alone with their morality. Nobody cared.

But to Fergus this was all a matter of juggling of personnel, distressing, and complicated, yet what he was facing in New York was much more serious to Titan studios. It was the ending of the world he had forged with Simon Moses for so many years, since he had come out as a green kid on that long train ride with Claudia.

Practically, at the moment, however, he thought of Jeffrey. As Fergus had checked his name off the studio lists, although he felt relieved to have his mortal enemy in his coffin, and knew Jeffrey had long outlived his usefulness, he realized how the ranks were thinning. Most of the box-office stars who had helped save Titan, along with sound, had now grown old, or perished, or drifted off into oblivion. And the newcomers, unless they were truly stellar, like the young sexpot Martha Ralston, who helped bring back mammary-gland popularity in the khaki eclipse of World War II, were not as negotiable as the stars of early years.

They just don't make stars like they used to, thought Fergus.

He had arranged his New York meetings to coincide with Jeffrey's funeral. The publicity department had a florist scout clusters of orchids, to be set in an enormous star of red roses. It was fitting tribute to a star who, although he had caused the company a great deal of anguish, at the same time had garnered them millions.

Fergus would have walked to New York rather than confront Jessica. He could imagine her in stylish widow's weeds. And the idea of meeting Belinda Barstow chilled him. He had heard she was a beautiful child, with long blond hair, who already wore the Barstow beauty like a nimbus about her. He feared he would not only see reflections of Jeffrey, and of Jessica, in her, but also see an unmistakable kinship to David. He seethed with anger every time he thought of how he had raised David as a beloved son, to discover that Jeffrey was his natural father.

He was relieved that David had exiled himself to the chores of the new wave of international filmmaking, using up frozen foreign currency to help salvage Titan's economy.

As he flew over the United States, looking down on the sluggish expanse of the Mississippi, Fergus remembered that just now, as a few words were being said over Jeffrey's coffin, he was flying over the same spot where he and Doc Wolfram had flown to collect Jeffrey from the black brothel in St. Louis to receive his Oscar twenty years before. Although life had seemed so complicated then, he realized it had been incredibly simpler, and the patterns, however annoying, at least were more personal. It had almost been a jousting tournament that the cleverest, strongest men might win. Now it was a mass of technical and business complications presented by distant experts.

Besides the activities of the House Un-American Committee, Titan had a second problem with the Federal Trade Commission. For years the company had siphoned off product into their own theater chain. Block booking could be set up for as far as a year ahead. The unimportant pictures, the weak films, and the boo-boos were pushed into economic success by the important films. Stars came into their own, as the power of their films forced exhibitors into buying every studio picture in order to get the cream of the crop.

Now Fergus, along with Abe Moses, was facing a complete divorcement of studio product and theater chains. The Federal Trade Commission investigations had revealed the collusion of the powerful theater chains, secret agreements that had attempted to force the independents out of business.

Commissions, commissions! The trouble they were bringing to the industry!

The fact that pictures would have to be very good to be sold was much more than pride in his product. Fergus knew as well as anyone could that picture making was not a formula. Films had to go on unknown elements, the strangest chemistry of story, director, actors, and production, which could sometimes make a "sleeper" a moneymaker and turn an epic film into a colossal economic disaster. Magic could not be anticipated.

He recollected how he and Simon Moses had fought in the old days, to be able to make pictures without getting their heads bashed in by itinerant goons hired by the powerful trust. And he realized that now Titan was in the same position as the trust. Titan had been a monopoly, with enough power to show its product in its own houses, and keep out the struggling independents. But that privilege was going to be taken away. If the worm was going to be cut in half, Fergus wondered which part of it would crawl away and sprout anew, and which might curl up and die.

And that was not all. Already Americans were beginning to buy a new source of entertainment. With prices soaring, and the new rash of war babies tying up families, a new element had come into the American home. It was television, and although it started with only sports events, variety shows, and foreign films, many stayed at home with their fascinating electronic theater.

Today films had to be blockbusters, stars were beginning to see their original contracts with studios run out, star personalities suddenly becoming corporate assets on their own, with lawyers and agents taking over. This was hitting the Titan interests right in the solar plexus—the studio facilities, which were so costly.

Fergus, having been in Hollywood so long, still envisioned New York as it had been in the days when he was a young man, his future before him. And now, in spite of irritations and battles that had passed in between these years, his hostilities seemed to dissolve. He wished that he could be stepping off a sooty hot train and picking up Claudia, swinging her silly tasseled purse, with her dark curls bobbing around her heart-shaped face. He wished he could see handsome Simon Moses in his new shirt with real French cuffs, and the gold comedy-tragedy-mask cufflinks that were so proudly worn. He wished he could go into an elegant restaurant with shaded candle tapers, not with canned music but real music of another era; he wished he could watch Claudia's pleasure as she helped Mr. Moses order an elaborate meal. He would have time to look around the room and see the dramatic Belasco and Zukor, enthusiastic young De Mille, and Lasky, Griffith, and delicate Lillian Gish, and pretty Mary Pickford, and a cute little brunette scenario writer, Anita Loos, and he wished they were all planning their onslaught again, full of excitement and dreams.

Instead, everyone was fretting about the canned pictures that were now performing in people's living rooms. The business was in such a state of flux that nobody knew what would happen next.

Fergus would check into the antiseptic Waldorf Towers and look over the changing skyline of a new

New York. From then on, his whole pattern would be enormous board of directors' tables, each nervous man doodling away his own frustrated energy on a blank pad. The bankers would have the say, and as they listened to dire forebodings, the Titan brass would all agree, having little choice. Then they would shake hands in pecking order, and eventually all go back to the corners from whence they came, to see how they could put together the puzzle and make economic sense out of it. The businessman must now pretend to be an artist, and the artist a businessman.

◆◆◆◆◆◆◆◆

In a week, Fergus was back at his desk in Hollywood. He knew that he would have to face even more drastic cuts than he had done in times of previous distress. Many old hands would go. No longer would there be a permanent roster of writers and stars as there were in the old days. Films would now be commissioned by financiers, and he would have to set each one up as an entity by itself. There was going to be no comfortable theater chain to take his product willy-nilly.

Harriet Foster, his secretary, buzzed him. He recognized the deep-throated gurgle in her throat, one of delight, which usually meant something was going to happen that didn't particularly please him. He did not like to have other people make choices of what he was going to be enthusiastic about.

"Oh, Mr. Austin, Miss Barstow is here to see you."

He was torn between pleasure and annoyance. What did she want?

"Send her in," he said.

But before she entered, he thought of the fact that once again funerals had brought them together. He remembered the day of Simon Moses' funeral years ago when she had come to say good-bye to him. Simon had been a family man, and the fact that he had died in Claudia's arms at their hacienda retreat, revealing the fact to the public that she had been his long-time mistress, had caused a scandal that had ruined her career with Titan.

But today half the people on the lot had never even seen Simon Moses, the founder, and if she came to call at the office, it meant she wanted a favor.

When she entered the room, for a moment he forgot they were in their fifties. She was still beautiful, her black-lashed blue eyes dazzling. Her makeup was cleverly applied; it should have been—she had been doing a sketch of herself as she once was, over and over again, for all these years.

As usual, she had on a clinging silk suit. She was dressed in a Paris fashion too chic for Hollywood, and perfume wafted around her like her own little personal cloud.

She lifted up on her tiptoes and kissed him, as she always did.

"Oh, Fergus, I'm so glad to see you!" she said.

Her resonant Barstow voice hit him in the gut as it always had. He put his arms around her and held her a moment.

"You always do something to me," he said.

"Well, before I go back to London," she said, "I intend to do more. When do I have an evening with you?"

"You could have arranged that by phone." He grinned. "Why don't we have dinner tonight. Romanoff's, Chasens?"

"I'd rather have dinner at your house," she said, "and we could walk on the beach, and I could look in on my old beach house. You know, I just sold it to some rich Texans. It gives me a pang to think I don't own it anymore. It supported me for a while in London. But I couldn't keep it up. And with Jeffrey gone . . ."

Her voice dwindled sadly.

"I'm sorry," he said. "It all must be very hard for you."

He saw she was stifling a sob, and decided to change the subject.

"What are you doing at the studio?"

He could always tell when she didn't want to give a direct answer. She had a way of looking over his shoulder as if she saw a fly on the ceiling.

"Oh, just saw some old pals, and I dropped by to say hello to Laura Gold in the story department."

An alarm went off in Fergus' head. She and Laura hadn't been such close chums.

"Well, that's nice."

She looked at her tiny Cartier watch.

"Oh, it's almost five-thirty. Why don't you have a drink with me later at the Polo Lounge at the hotel?"

He smiled at her.

"All right, and then you'll have dinner with me. If it's not too nostalgic, we will take a walk on the beach and see your old house."

"I'd love it. Time marches on, doesn't it, Fergus?"

He saw how sad she was about the loss of her brother. He put his arm about her as he saw her to the door.

As she left, he looked out the window. He saw her rented limousine below waiting for her. He noticed that on the way out she had picked up a large manila envelope, which looked like it contained a script. He finished the day's work, sat through routine daily rushes, and in spite of himself, looked forward to meeting her, figuring damned well there was an angle.

They had a ceremonial drink at the Polo Lounge at the Beverly Hills Hotel.

Then he drove her along the familiar curving Brentwood area on Sunset Boulevard.

"How was New York," she asked, "and what happened?"

"Same old rat race," said Fergus. "Last year was a peak year of pictures. But now, aside from this rotten commie scare, everyone's tuned in to Uncle Miltie, British movies, football games, and political conventions. I'm afraid of that electronic theater, Claudia."

"If you can't lick 'em, join 'em," said Claudia.

"Also," continued Fergus, ignoring the unpleasant thought, "there's the bugaboo of divorcement. Theaters and studios separated by government decree. Claudia, the life we knew may be obsolete."

Claudia shivered.

"You know, Fergus, I've decided I'm never going to get old. I won't allow it."

Fergus patted her hand. "Let me know how you work that out," he said.

At his house they dined by candlelight and drank a fine wine. Old Primo, the cook, was getting so blind that he set each plate down an inch from the table with a clatter, but Claudia laughed at it when he was out of the room.

"The only good servant in town is Effie, at Jeffrey's house," she said. "She'll probably stay for Belinda, but God knows how she stands that ice-cold Jessica."

Suddenly realizing what a gaffe she had pulled, mentioning his ex-mistress, she jumped up. "Let's go for our walk on the beach!"

It was a mild starstruck evening.

She pulled off her shoes and stockings on the veranda and ran bare-legged in her blouse and skirt, out on the sands, to the dark tideline. Fergus kicked off his shoes and joined her.

"Oh, Fergus, look how that new breakwater has made the tideline recede. Remember when our houses almost had their feet in the water? It's all changed."

They walked along the waterfront. Houses of the famous. Shearer, LeRoy, Zanuck, Hearst-Davies, Claudia's little house. For a moment she stood looking into the lighted windows. There was candlelight at the table. People were sitting, dining and laughing. A light shone upstairs. She looked at it wistfully.

"Remember," said Claudia, "when the depression hit, and you came to see me, we thought we were all ruined, and I took your last five hundred dollars, and you made love to me right up in that room. That was a good night."

Fergus caught her in his arms.

"This is a good night," he said.

She reached up to him, put her arms around his

neck, and kissed him, her mouth moist and her tongue finding his.

"My house is a few steps away," said Fergus.

"I have another idea," she said.

She led him into the garden gate of the house she had once owned, past the swimming pool, and to some little side stairs that led to the upstairs balcony.

"Are you out of your mind!" he said.

She put her hand over his mouth. "Shut up, and follow me."

Astounded at her, he followed her up the stairs. The door to the upstairs hall was unlatched. Below, they could hear music and conversation.

She led him into the bedroom. She had sold the house furnished. Her large bed was in the same place, the room newly decorated, but it was still very much hers.

She closed the hall door softly.

"You're crazy!" he said.

"Shut up." She laughed.

Before he could stop her, she had wriggled out of her suit and scanty lingerie. And when she came to him, naked and laughing, the idea was so preposterous—making love in somebody else's house while they were dining below—that it stimulated him. In a moment they were on the bed, and the excitement and danger of their audacious act triggered them both. He fell into her as passionately as he had almost twenty years before in this room. It was Claudia, the beautiful, the mysterious, the unique he claimed, and he was Fergus, the boy she introduced to sex so long ago in New York when their world was very young. At the end, they clung for a brief moment, heard laughter downstairs, and quickly got into their clothes.

Claudia smoothed the bedspread, they unlocked the door, which made more noise than they thought it would, they heard somebody come to the stairwell, but got out the side door and tiptoed down the outside stairs in their bare feet.

He looked down at her fondly.

"Claudia," he said, "you are the craziest woman in the world. I love you!"

He proved it again when she stayed with him the night in his house.

By the light of the morning, when Fergus dressed to go to the studio, Claudia stepped naked into his shower.

He could not help but notice that without the blinders of liquor and sex, she was far from the young beauty he had known. Her body was being clutched at by gravity. Her breasts were still small and round, but they had slipped lower on her rib cage. Her little belly was not quite as firm, and the waist and buttocks could not possibly have retained the firm contour of her youth. Even with the beauty of her eyes, the eyelids were slightly heavy, and a little puff at her chin, when she did not hold it high, revealed the marks of age.

Looking at his own image in the mirror, the silvering hair, and the hard lines that a thin-skinned Irishman often gets about the neck and chin, he was ashamed of criticizing her even in his mind. For her age she was superb.

They breakfasted on the terrace, Claudia gazing at the old Santa Monica pier and the new breakwater beyond.

"It wouldn't be a good shelter for Jeffrey's or Simon's yacht, would it?"

"They don't have them much, anyway, these days," said Fergus. "Everything's changed."

When they drove to the Beverly Hills Hotel, he was puzzled. She hadn't mentioned what had been on her mind.

"What were you doing with that script?" he asked. "I saw you, Claudia."

She looked up at him, smiling.

"You're so smart. Laura Gold lent one to me. I'm returning it. Don't fret! I wanted to see what Titan was up to. Fergus, I have news for you."

"What is it?" he asked suspiciously.

"I have decided I'm coming back to Titan. I read

your script *Catherine and Peter.* I want to play Catherine the Great. I would be perfect for it."

Fergus looked at her, astounded. "You're out of your mind. The Catherine in this version is a young woman. We are thinking of Martha Ralston for it."

"Martha Ralston!" said Claudia. "Why, Fergus, I'm ashamed of you. She has no style. Catherine is regal. I must do it."

Fergus turned into the hotel driveway. There were several cars in front of him.

"Claudia, you know how I feel about you, but don't fool yourself. You're not an ingenue anymore. You are a mature woman, beautiful, but mature. I know how old you are, so don't be foolish with me."

She looked at him, hurt and angry.

"I have a classic face. I kept my body beautiful. I weigh the same as I did when I was your top star. And I can act. That little blond bitch doesn't know how to get across a set without an intercut."

"She's got youth, Claudia. You know I'd have loved to have seen you play it if you had youth."

There was a moment of silence.

"Would you let me do it if I were younger?" she finally said.

He patted her hand, as the car inched slowly forward.

"Of course I would. You know that. No one would be better."

"When are you going to make it?" she asked.

"In about six months."

"Six months," she whispered.

The car pulled up to the canopy. The doorman opened her door, saluting.

"Thank you, Fergus," she said, kissing him. "I'll be seeing you."

"Of course," he said. "Before you go back to London. Look, I didn't mean to hurt your feelings. We must be realistic."

"Yes," she said quietly, "we must be realistic."

She rushed away. He looked after her. He had hurt her feelings.

In the afternoon Fergus called her at the hotel. He had been a little rough on her, and after all, they had just spent a memorable night together.

The telephone switchboard girl informed him that Miss Barstow had checked out.

◆◆◆◆◆◆◆◆

Claudia had escaped reality all her life. She had flown on what she considered a magic carpet, aided by her beauty and her career, which had led her into a continuing world of make-believe.

She had sustained her ego by the flattery and adulation that went with a succession of motion pictures and attendant sycophants.

But now she faced a time of truth as she studied herself and looked into the mirror. True, the gleanings had been slim these last few years, but always before she had managed to pull herself out of the quagmire. Not so, now.

Her brother, Jeffrey, was gone; she had no one to fall back on. She grieved, missing him; he had always been her takeout in lonely or troubled times. For the first time, she was really alone, and the little she had left of a fortune to make her way was terrifying.

She could not sit in a rose-lighted dressing room and apply cosmetics against a candlelit evening. She saw herself painfully glimpsed in mirrors, street windows, and people's eyes.

Somehow she had hoped that Fergus would let her test for Catherine the Great. Her skills and her charisma would prove she should play the role; they could just doctor the script a little, and make it take place in Catherine's more mature years. But his blunt refusal shattered her. If he had said, "We'll see," she would have been satisfied.

The sale of her heavily mortgaged house had not brought her much money. The California curse, termite and dry-rot repair, replacement of windowsills and metals that were eaten into by the salt sea breeze, painting and refurbishing, putting in a new pool motor, heater, lawns, and updated kitchen equipment, had cost her thousands. She could not linger around Hollywood in an expensive suite at the Beverly Hills Hotel, or rent a house at going rates and staff it, as suited her image.

As for Jeffrey, he had left her only some minor keepsakes. Perhaps the thing she liked the most was that chunk of amber, for it was a pledge for the future and a tie in to his daughter, Belinda.

Before she checked out of the Beverly Hills Hotel she stepped out on the terrace of her room. In the bright sun she looked at the shining piece of amber, those insects preserved in their tiny perfection forever. Then she held a mirror up to her face.

In the brilliant sunlight, each furrow, each line, each hollow seemed to show her a road map of anno Domini and broken commandments.

Damn it, she thought, if those wretched bugs could be preserved, perhaps there's a way for me. It would take some doing, but she could investigate.

It was not difficult to discover ways of rejuvenation. It took only several visits to the Sauna Club massage parlor on Sunset, where people of all ages and sizes had gone since the early days. Scraps of conversation drifted over the partitions. She set her course, sifting her needs and economy to the situation. Obviously she could not go to the new cellular-therapy clinics in Europe, nor could she afford the exclusive ministrations of such posh places as Elizabeth Arden's Main Chance, which would cost at least a hundred dollars a day.

A surge in the youth cult in California had brought all sorts of experts to Hollywood.

Her first move was a visit to a gabled old house on upper Franklin Avenue. There a white-haired, fresh-faced woman, Madame Gerard, accepted guests for a stay of several weeks who would pay to have their faces peeled with a buffered phenol base. This carbolic-acid burn was born in agony, taped onto the face with tiny bandages, erupted serum, and finally, after the tapes fell off, was powdered until a thick scab formed. After several weeks, when the scab dropped off, this chemosurgery revealed a smooth, babylike face. Provided, some medical authorities whispered, the patient did not get keloid problems that made the skin blister like frozen bubbles, or permanent pigment discoloration, or scars, or a damaged kidney from phenol absorption.

Thinking of the dazzling entrance she would make into Fergus' life and Titan studio, she listened to the blandishments of Madame Gerard, signed papers absolving the management from any mishap, and moved into a dormer room in the old-fashioned mansion, wondering if she was signing a death warrant.

She was sedated with morphine. Her face was dabbed with acid. She awoke to a sea of pain, suffered through several days of agonizing second-degree burns, smothered with Demerol, sipped her food through a straw because her face was too thick with scab to move her lips, and waited, looking out on the Hollywoodland sign on the hills, her face in a mask, wondering if she would ever be able to see anyone again.

No liquor, no cigarettes, not even the passing refreshment of a gourmet meal. Between sedations she thought that if it did not all come out well, she would kill herself.

At last the scabs peeled away. Her face was beet-red, but it was oiled every day, and finally she looked in a mirror and saw that she was beautiful. It was a joy to apply makeup, to be able to trace her lips in a bow as she had done as a young actress, to be able to put makeup on her lids without looking owl-eyed.

And then, in her quest for perfection, she knew that her body could not match the face. Her waist must draw in, her breasts be more firm. The skin on her arms and thighs needed toning.

The answer was the rolling hills and vineyards at an inexpensive spa in Mexico. It was in Tecate, across the border from San Diego. A Hungarian and his young American wife had settled and built a cluster of cozy little houses. It was rugged, exercises were mandatory—early-morning walks, a pool, a gym, and experts on body fitness. Again rigorous, a vegetarian diet, no-

nonsense regime, early to bed and to rise. A beautiful hideaway, and a road to rejuvenation.

She protected her new baby face with large hats and wigs, and with Fergus' amazement as her aim, even avoided the Saturday night debauches of some of her fellow curemates who went into the nearby village for margaritas, Guaymas shrimp, and the local crusty buttered bolillos. It was a Spartan life for an Athenian.

◆◆◆◆◆◆◆◆

Harriet Foster always twittered when Claudia Barstow appeared. But this time, she stood, mouth agape. There she stood, svelte, her face glowing, looking as beautiful, Harriet thought, as anyone who had come into the office. Even Martha Ralston, the new sex object, the lush white hope of Titan studio.

"Oh, Miss Barstow . . ." she finally gasped, "you look just gorgeous!"

"I'm just fine, thank you, Harriet. Is Mr. Austin busy?"

"You know he'll always see you."

She buzzed, and Claudia heard Fergus' "Send her right in."

It made her feel good. She'd bowl him over.

As she entered the room, he rushed to her, put his arms around her, and then pulled back.

"My God," he said, staring at her, "what have you done! You . . . you look . . ."

He stopped, astonished.

"Years younger?" she asked.

It was worth the pain, the money, and the loneliness to see the look in his eyes. She had it made!

"Well, I did it, Fergus," she said. "You know, George Cukor used to say that actresses were in league with the devil, they'd do anything to get a role."

He looked puzzled.

"What role?"

"You said if I looked younger you'd let me play Catherine. That no one would be better."

He sat down at his desk.

She took a chair opposite him.

"But, sweetie, that was just a hypothetical comment. We never even discussed it further."

She could feel herself getting cold.

"But, Fergus, you can see for yourself. Test me. You don't know what I went through. Physical agony. Not to mention no food, no drinks, no cigarettes."

He stood up, disturbed.

"Claudia, there's nothing I can do about it. It's out of my hands. You look absolutely gorgeous. But . . . but the New York office insisted."

"Insisted on what?" she said.

"On Martha Ralston."

"She's . . . set?"

He nodded and lit a cigarette. He offered her one. She shook her head. "You said six months."

"Six months to shooting. We're working on preproduction now. Wardrobe, wigs, fittings. Tests."

"In my day," said Claudia, "we got a scenario and an old car. I threw some clothes in a bag, and we were off. You remember that. Now that stupid bitch Martha Ralston has to have months for wardrobe and tests."

"Claudia, things have changed."

"You have changed," she said, getting up, tight-lipped. "Once you were my friend. You cared. Now you're part of a heartless machine. Everything's impersonal. There's no heart in this place anymore. You're all fodder for a New York brain."

"Claudia," he said, "please. What can I do?"

She arose and looked out of the window at the busy studio below. All of it once a part of her. Her early successes had helped create it. She tried not to tremble.

"Well," she said, "well, forget it. I should have known. Everybody in this business knows how old I am. And nobody cares about me."

"Claudia . . ." he said.

The tears began to flow down her cheeks. She couldn't help it.

"Sorry," she said, "since I've had my face peel, I have this trouble."

He took his handkerchief out of his pocket and handed it to her.

"No thanks," she said. "I use Kleenex, it's more antiseptic."

The buzzer rang.

"Miss Ralston is here to show you her court dress," said Harriet Foster. Claudia heard the same star enthusiasm in her voice that she used to get.

"Have her wait a moment," he said.

He turned to Claudia.

"I'd like to have you meet her."

"In a pig's eye, you bastard," said Claudia. "Just get me out of here through the back door."

She rushed for a side door, and Fergus hurriedly opened it and let her out.

◆◆◆◆◆◆◆◆◆

Claudia sat at the phone in her little apartment on Havenhurst. The Beverly Hills Hotel, of course, now was too rich for her purse. It was a lovely day, the plants and flowers and tile made the courtyard seem like Mexico. This was a good day to patch up a quarrel.

"Fergus," she said, "I'm so sorry I was upset. You know we are too long friends to let a thing like this happen. I want to see you. I guess I'll be leaving for London soon, but I couldn't go without saying goodbye."

She waited a moment. He wanted to patch it up, of course. She knew he'd be delighted.

At last the voice came back.

"Claudia, how very kind of you. I'm afraid I can't make it. You know, as much as I'd love to, I am so tied up with studio problems I just don't have time for social evenings."

She was speechless. Was it possible that Fergus would reject her, Claudia, the excitement in his life? She had always had him at her beck and call.

"I don't believe it," she gasped. "I just don't believe you'd say this to me, after all—"

She heard a buzz over the phone.

"Claudia," said Fergus, "I'm sorry. I have to sign off right now. I have a long-distance call. I'll try to get back to you later."

"Don't bother, you bastard," she said. "It'll be a long day when a Barstow gets snubbed by a go-betweener like you."

She hung up.

All day she awaited his call. He had said he'd try to call back. But there was no call.

In the afternoon she received a large bouquet of red roses. In the box a note: "Dearest Claudia, please forgive me, I'm under such pressures, I know you'll understand. Affectionately, Fergus."

Kiss of death—flowers to a has-been. Rejection. Well, life will just have to go another way. She tried to look at the roses as a beautiful bouquet, but they irritated her so much she threw them out.

For several weeks she called up agents and saw directors and actors she had worked with. They were all polite, charming; she garnered a few lunches and fewer dinners. Conversation all reverted to the past, to the glorious golden days of Titan. To fun times, rich days. Too many anecdotes about her brother, Jeffrey, which only brought on the hollow pain of his loss, and her loneliness. There were no suggestions about the present or the future. The subject was gracefully avoided.

She could not afford to stay on. The hell with Hollywood. Her therapies had cost her so much that she would barely be able to get back to London with enough money to eke out an existence until she found something to do.

Before she left, she called Jessica. After a wait on the phone, Effie told her, obviously embarrassed to say it, that Mrs. Barstow and Belinda were out of town.

The next day Claudia saw Jessica in the distance, at Schwab's drugstore, around the corner from her apartment.

Claudia got away before she was seen.

Complete blitz. Adios Fergus, adios Jessica Barstow,

adios little Belinda, God help you. Farewell Titan, and that tower that still stood pointing like a rocket in the sky, with the logo's angry fist holding bolts of lightning that were being extinguished by time and tide. Adios Hollywood, whatever you are.

3

In 1956 only the citizens in the film world in Hollywood who cherished their folklore memories remembered that Jessica Barstow had been only a secretary, that her past had been clouded even before she had married a man who had been long senile from drink. And as for the Barstow name, there was just a little girl, and, oh, yes, a has-been star, wasn't it an aunt, Claudia, who lived in London, giving voice and diction lessons?

Jessica was relegated to the position of a widow without social standing, money, or power, and in Hollywood, that was the kiss of death.

Jeffrey's greatest legacy, had he known it, was that Belinda remembered him with love. The little Yorkshire, Sarge, was the creature she cared for the most in her life, for the dog was the connecting link with her father.

The mortgaged Barstow hacienda, a style of bygone wealth that was becoming increasingly rare in Hollywood, was sold; and with it, memories of a great carreer passed into limbo, save for picture historians and diehard Barstow buffs. Furnishings, paintings, and social connections dwindled for Jessica.

At last an apartment furnished with remnants of antiques and paintings was all that was left to Belinda to show that Jeffrey Barstow had sired her.

That is, all but her personal beauty, and the Barstow voice, and of course, the little dog, now settled into maturity of nine years. And Effie, who came daily to keep house for Mr. Barstow's family.

One fateful April day had begun like most. But now, in the afternoon, the slanting sunlight fell through the slats of the venetian blinds and crosshatched the dark waxed floors and shaggy rugs in Jessica's living room. Two empty cocktail glasses drained of their martinis glistened dully in the rime of smog that filtered in with the sounds of late-afternoon traffic on South Palm Drive.

Scattered on the marbleized coffee table was a welter of corrected manuscript pages, cigarette stubs, and a strapless brassiere.

Outside on the street corner there was the squeal of brakes and the snakelike hiss of a pneumatic door as the school bus disgorged its cargo. From upstairs came a female cry of irritation, followed by a male groan of protest and the frantic opening of a bedroom door.

Down the stairs rushed Jessica. She clutched her silk kimono, belt dragging in one hand, nude to the waist. She wore a panty girdle of flowered elastic. Her long, slim legs were naked. Her gray eyes were slitted in annoyance.

She struggled into the sleeves of her robe. As she tied her belt, Sarge came from the kitchen and danced about on his hind legs, reaching his paws up at her, long hair hanging over his bright brown eyes. He almost tripped her.

"God damn you, Sarge!" she said, rushing to the living room, snatching up her brassiere, and shoving it with the two martini glasses into a cabinet. "Get the hell out of my way!"

The bell rang, two sharp distinctive rings.

Why does it have to happen to me? she thought. That damned high-school bus, early for once. Bad timing. . . . Bad timing. Like being born in Smackover, Arkansas, which has to be on all my identification. Like having to carry the horrible family name of Klopfinger, when my mother's maiden name was Carrington. Like the chance I lost to marry the richest, best-looking man in California, and I liked him. Like having to marry one of the world's greatest matinee idols and stars. *Only* (har-har) he happened to be sixty-two, a drunk, and senile. Like having the best figure in Hollywood, and getting involved with that selfish son-of-a-bitch Fergus Austin, who couldn't take me out in public. Like having Belinda come home from school right now on Effie's day off, when I'm about to climb into the most important hay I've rolled in for years. . . . Somebody's going to grab this Max Ziska fast, now that he's back. He's a gold mine. And he doesn't know yet what's happened in this town. Jesus, right now he thinks *I* can help *him*. . . .

Jessica went to the door, snatching the dog leash angrily off the hall table. She opened the door a crack and peered out, holding it fast with one foot.

"Belinda, how many times have I told you not to ring the doorbell like that?"

"Sorry, Mom," said Belinda, unchastened.

"I have a terrible headache," said Jessica grimly. "Take Sarge out for a walk around the block. And go by the drugstore and get me some bromo."

"I'll need some money," Belinda said.

"Charge it," said Jessica testily, "and take your dog for a long walk. He hasn't been out all day."

"Okay, Mom."

Jessica started to close the door, then had an afterthought.

"You can get yourself a soda."

"Oh, no," said Belinda's sweet voice, "if you've got a headache, I'll come right back."

"Don't bother, dear," said Jessica.

But Belinda had run off quickly with the dog and turned out of sight past the front apartment.

A man passed, turning to stare at the young girl. Tendrils of blond curly hair were blowing against her cheek, and her ponytail fell in a cascade over her shoulders. She could tell by the way he glanced at her that he saw the new thing; under her sweater, her swelling breasts bounced as she walked, and the nipples pointed upward.

Piqued by his raking glance, she stopped short.

"Bastards," she muttered to her dog. "Why are they all doing that, all of a sudden?" She pressed her lips together. What's the matter with the whole thing? Mom's got a man upstairs again. That's where all this ends when you grow up. Hot. Sweaty. Why do they do it?

Did Mom think she was square? That scent of man and woman was like something out of the center of the earth. It was like smelling cigarettes when you didn't smoke, and smelling liquor when you didn't drink. It had to do with that dirty line in Shakespeare that all the kids read, "the beast with two backs." It sounded pretty awful.

What man did Mom have up there now?

Often, when she was younger, after her father died she would peek through the crack of the door at a mussed-up bed. And usually, next day presents arrived, champagne, or perfume, and sometimes flowers and candy, records and books, and those fancy baskets that came with all those itsy-bitsies of cocktail-hour snacks, looking lush and full on top, but underneath a disappointing mass of shredded colored cellophane. Inevitably, if the gifts continued, it would mean that Mom would squander money on new resort clothes and say she wanted to get away for a little change.

Effie would stay on. She would treat Belinda to a movie, or if it was warm, drive them to the State Beach in Santa Monica, and sit on a big towel, while Belinda swam.

It seemed to be a pattern. Sometimes after such a trip, when Belinda came home from school, Mom would be sitting, waiting. . . . Mom looked at her absently.

The next day she would be nervous. Once she saw her mother pick up the phone and jerk it so hard it came out of the wall, and the phone company had to come and fix it.

So Belinda would sit in the quiet apartment, where there was no music and no ringing phone, or take Sarge out for walks as often as she could get away, while her mother brooded.

And now, would it be this all over again?

She looked down at the dog, who, as always, met her eye-to-eye, seeking any message she sent.

"C'mon, Sarge," she said, "let's go to the drugstore fast, and hurry home and screw everything up!"

The girl and the dog ran fast, but the traffic signal changed. They came to a sliding halt, Sarge looked up at her, his shoebutton eyes glowing through shaggy golden bangs.

"I love you, too," said Belinda.

◆◆◆◆◆◆◆◆

Max Ziska and Jessica sat side-by-side on the sofa, fresh drinks before them, both lying to each other and themselves.

"You are what I knew you would be," he said, kissing her hand, "with that beautiful body I used to watch, of all places, in that studio commissary, as you walked to your table."

Jessica smiled.

"And what a miracle that, aside from this"—Max waved his glass in a wide arc encompassing her body—"aside from this beauty, still as lovely as it was so long ago, you have the influence to help me."

God, thought Jessica, don't let him know. . . .

"We must keep very quiet about it until your first screenplay is updated," she said. "You are too valuable."

"Of course," he said, looking down modestly.

Max needed her. It wasn't too late. Perhaps that script *The Oracle,* with the power of his genius and the other scripts that he spoke of, would get her back *in* again.

"You have to learn, Max, what has happened since you were here. Stars and star-makers are no longer under contract to the mother studios. Metro, Fox, Titan, Paramount, Warners, Columbia, all of them *beg* independents to release through them. Subsidiary companies that split the profits, and help fill their sound stages, and pay their . . . their armies of employees.

Can you imagine anyone like old man Moses, or Fergus, cutting a melon!"

Max shook his head.

"It seems incredible that any Augustus Caesar would share the laurel leaves."

"It's like the Hungarian omelet recipe . . ."

Max made a face.

"First, you steal an egg," he said, resigning himself to the old wheeze.

"First, you steal a story," said Jessica, "or you grab it quickly, before the major studio sees it. That's why you can't trust agents anymore. They won't even try to sell a client's story they might purchase for one of their stars. They get first grabs. And script is king. With a good, well-developed screenplay, you can get, beg, or borrow the greatest acting and directing talent."

"And I have six magnificent scripts," whispered Max.

Jessica could almost feel the hackles rising on the back of her neck. She knew him, and she knew.

She pitched on. "I would only tell you this because I know you will work—with me. Now I know why I didn't take a studio job. It must have been intuition."

"No more serfdom," he said, shaking his head.

"You are so *right,*" said Jessica, running her hand along his forearm. "Why, do you know, recent box-office champions—*The African Queen*, Bogart, Katharine Hepburn, John Huston; *High Noon*, Gary Cooper, Grace Kelly, and Fred Zinnemann; *A Streetcar Named Desire*, Marlon Brando, Vivien Leigh, Gadge Kazan—every one of them either independent, or splitting that so-called melon. All that talent. Available. Why?"

He pulled his arm away reflectively.

"Through story," he said. "I see now. Stars, writers, and directors don't have to be slaves. Talent is asking for what it wants."

"Talent is calling the shots," said Jessica, "and it has since Mr. Selznick paid Mr. Mayer a million and a percentage on *Gone with the Wind* to borrow Mr. Gable. Stars couldn't *wait* to be free-lance! Mr. Mayer hadn't a clue of what he had started. It was the first death knell of the studio system he had worked so hard to create!"

Max shook his head. This was all a new world.

"And do you know, that last year *Gone with the Wind* was one of the top money-makers, in reissue!"

Max raked his white hair with his two hands.

"So, for God's sake, Max, don't show your scripts to anyone."

"Excepting you," he said.

She suspected irony, but forced his hand.

"Excepting me. Because not only do I know where the body is buried in certain circles, I know what stars are free, and when options come up. I also know how to help you update your material, without any second-rate collaborator getting ideas, and spilling."

"You have a point," he said.

The doorbell rang. Jessica answered it.

"Hi, Mom," Belinda said.

"Come in, dear," said Jessica sweetly, putting on a company voice. Already Belinda knew this guest must be something special.

"Belinda, this is Mr. Ziska. Max, this is my Belinda. Max was an old friend of your mother's and father's a long time ago."

Belinda looked at his thatch of curly white hair, fine-spun and unruly, and the dark brows and piercing brown eyes. This was an odd one. Oh, of course! Maximilian Ziska, the man she had seen in her father's bound movie scripts. Glossy eight-by-ten production stills had been inserted at the beginning of each sequence. Ziska had been a bright-eyed, black-haired man then, and she had studied the pictures, wondering how it must have been to see her father take his direction. The photos had revealed their mutual interest and involvement with each other.

"Hello, Mr. Ziska," she said. "I've seen you in my father's scrapbooks when you directed him and my Aunt Claudia."

"Belinda spends too much time poring over those old books," said Jessica. "She stays up too late. But what can I do? She's Barstow to the bone."

"A night bird," said Belinda, smiling.

Ziska's surprised glance panned up from the floor like a moving camera shot, starting with her slender feet in patent pumps, her long, tanned legs, a short navy-blue pleated shirt, and shapeless pullover which could not conceal her delicate body, broad-shouldered, on up into her face, opening like a bud. Her red lips formed a full mouth, her short nose glistened like clean porcelain; and those blue eyes, pale and liquid, were set in double black lashes like her Aunt Claudia's. Shockingly, she had the Barstow widow's peak, exactly like her sire. The resemblance was uncanny. He knew he was seeing Jeffrey Barstow's last and greatest performance.

"Max," said Jessica's voice from far off, "who do you think she looks like?"

"Like Helen of Troy," he said.

Pleased, Belinda gave him her hand, but Sarge began to yap. She pulled her hand away.

"Oh, shush!" said Belinda, laughing. "Pardon him, Mr. Ziska. His name is Sarge—Sergeant Yorkshire—and he can't help being jealous, you know."

"I can't blame him," said Max sincerely.

Belinda looked into his brown eyes. They were soft. She suddenly wanted to charm him because of her father. She again turned on the voice she was just discovering. Max recognized it. It had the unforgettable timbre that her aunt, Claudia Barstow, had been blessed with long ago.

Belinda held up the dog.

"Papa gave me Sarge," she said.

Max was surprised, "Your *father* gave you the dog?"

"Oh, yes!" said Belinda. "My sixth birthday! Eight years ago."

Max said warmly, "He was a gifted man." And he was suddenly depressed that he had drunk, and smoked, and fornicated on the afternoon that this glorious young creature had walked into his life.

"A dividend?" asked Jessica, brashly blotting out Belinda across the room with her crystal cocktail pitcher.

"Thank you, my dear, for the most charming hospitality," he said, "but no. I must be going. I have many rewrites on *The Oracle* to do, thanks to your advice."

"Sweetie, you'd better get Sarge's dinner out of the fridge," said Jessica.

Belinda sauntered into the kitchen. Max's eyes followed her carefully.

"Glad I helped you," said Jessica, pouring herself a martini. "Max, your script is really magnificent. It's just that colloquia and certain technical terms have changed through the years you've been away. And the work of Maximilian Ziska must be perfect."

"Of course," said Max, "no one knows better than you what pleases Fergus Austin."

Little do you know! she thought with a shudder. She quickly drank off half the cocktail. Belinda came back into the room. Max noticed a quick flash of resentment on Jessica's face, which she immediately overlaid with a determined smile of affection.

He kissed Jessica's hand and bowed to Belinda.

As he left, he bitterly reflected that thank God she couldn't know he didn't have enough money to take the three of them to dinner at Barney's Beanery.

Loathing the fact that fate had stolen years from him, diminished his value as a playwright and director, and put him economically at the mercy of strangers in a new world, Max clutched the corrected pages of his script and cursed the nature that split him.

The old, old story. My gonads, and my poet's soul battling for supremacy every day, and me, the loser, between them.

Max walked along South Palm Drive with a jaunty step. The ridges of pain where his toenails once had been were gone. The well-worn paths of thought that had traveled so endlessly through the bloody trails of Warsaw, the cellars of the Braunhaus in Munich, the stinking nightmare of Dachau, and the freezing fields leading to Switzerland. The white agony of years in a mental institution, leading back slowly to the endless corridors of hospitals. The memories of eight operations and three years of skin transplants were all gone. He was grateful that Jessica had not seen the jigsaw puzzle of skin stitched on his back, or his prison tattoo.

Then he was ashamed. For it was not Jessica who had soothed him, nor was it the aid she would give him in properly presenting his screenplays in this terrifying new world.

It was this child Belinda, with virgin eyes that seemed to be staring out of the memory of an old sinner, Jeffrey Barstow, who had stirred him into a startling, instant euphoria.

He recollected the incredible drama of his last meeting with Jessica over fifteen years ago, was it? Yes, one of those nightmare eve-before-Christmas Hollywood times. A night, he reflected, that had ended the life he had meticulously constructed, almost as unequivocally as death.

That night, puzzled and angry, he had struggled with two burly studio policemen and had been thrown out on the street and kicked into a rainy gutter—he, with his ten-thousand-dollar-a-week contract, because Fergus Austin had thought he was having an affair with his mistress, Jessica.

He had picked himself up in shock. What was he doing, he thought, here in this ego-glutted, insane place, when the tragedies of thousands of his own kind in Europe were daily occurrences? This was not for him, this place. Not with what was happening in the world.

He had taken the first plane he could get, and then the first boat, and gone back to the land of his beginnings. He had walked, knowingly, into the torture of mind and body that had taken years to end.

And now he felt, at last, a release. Not because he was back again in this strange scene of his earlier triumphs, not because his animal hungers were sated. But because he had experienced beauty; nourishing beauty for the first time in many years.

At such a shrine, as a young man, he could have made worthy offerings. But now, even though he was old, with a body that had been tortured, and with no power or funds, at least in such a presence, perhaps he could again kindle the dormant poet's wellspring of joy, that bursting tide of inspiration that had slept so long. Perhaps he could feel again, live again, and dream again.

Standing on a corner, before stepping into the flow of traffic, Max paused. How strange that his footsteps had led him to meet this child, Jeffrey Barstow's daughter. Jeffrey, whose house he had rented when the actor's years of barnstorming had left him almost penniless before his renaissance in the theater.

Max's path had been paved by one of his loyal Hungarian friends, Ilonka Vadja. He had gotten her a job as a hairdresser at the studio years ago. Now she ran a beauty parlor in Beverly Hills, which, like many of its sort, was the clearing ground of founded and unfounded Hollywood gossip.

She had given him a free and loving hair trim and filled him in. "You know, dolling, you look divine. Suffering makes character, and your gorgeous eyes are even better with your white hair. So distinguished. . . . I know what to do. It comes to me. You remember Fergus Austin's beautiful secretary. Jessica, was it Klopfinger?"

"My God, yes," said Max, remembering. "Is she still around?"

"Dolling, I'm telling you. Her name is Jessica Barstow now."

"Barstow?"

"She was married to Jeffrey Barstow."

Max clasped his hand to his cheek. He was amazed. Ilonka rushed on, inspired by the surprise that her comment had caused.

"Yes. The poor lovely woman. He died. They have a child."

"How about that old bastard, siring a child!" said Max, smiling, even more taken. Ilonka waved that away as unimportant.

"She still comes to my shop to have my operator Peter do her hair. He's the best, sweet, in town, who can give a realistic tint. Why, only last week she confided to Peter that several very important men have been begging her to return to the business. As executive or agent. But she doesn't want to get involved. She is gorgeous, dolling. And she doesn't have to work. Naturally, she knows all the story angles, having been executive secretary to Fergus Austin."

Max brooded. He remembered Fergus Austin's hatred that one long-gone night.

"Maybe, instead, an agent, someone like Goldstone or Feldman."

Ilonka held up her hands and shook her head.

"Agents are out this year, angel. Take my word. They buy your stories, they tell the studios you aren't available. They make under-table deals. *Your* talent is *their* capital gain."

"My God," said Max, "I'm glad I talked to you."

"And it just happens," said Ilonka, "she is coming here today. Leave it to Ilonka."

Max, thinking back at Jessica's position of importance, had agreed. It was all very wise Hungarian thinking.

Don't be stupid, Maximilian, he reflected. Belinda is only a child, on the brink of adolescence. That Barstow mask could fool you. . . . Look what happened to Claudia Barstow, her aunt, and her father, Jeffrey. They were beautiful actors who enchanted the world and then went to hell. It is only a coincidence that *The Oracle* is about a beautiful young virgin. . . . One step at a time, he thought, squinting at the sidewalk. And don't avoid the cracks. . . . That's psychotic. Just as psychotic as to think that beautiful young virgins are portrayed by beautiful young virgins.

◆◆◆◆◆◆◆◆

Effie Briggs unlocked the back door and came into the apartment early Friday morning. The first thing she did was to let out the dog. He lifted his leg ritually on the night-blooming jasmine and then scurried into the kitchen for his fresh dish of kibble.

Belinda came down the stairs carrying her schoolbooks and plopped down to eat.

"Morning, honey-bun," said Effie.

Belinda waved at her as she gulped down her juice like a chaser.

"You look peaked," said Effie, looking at her sharply. "Up late again?"

"Reading *The Red Room*," said Belinda. "Oh, Ef, you must read the script and see the photos. Father was so handsome, and Aunt Claudia's part was so sad. . . . And soldiers . . . soldiers . . . soldiers."

Belinda moved her hands in an arc. "They don't write scripts like that anymore. I read until one o'clock."

"You'd better not let *her* catch you," said Effie.

Belinda picked up the Los Angeles *Examiner*.

"Wowie!" she cried out.

Effie halted with a plate in her hand.

"Another crash?" asked Effie.

"Worse!" said Belinda. "Look, Martha Ralston married the richest man in the world. In Rome."

"That Greek fellow?" asked Effie.

"Yeah. Pericles Niadas."

"Well, anyway," said Effie, "she won't have to work for a living."

"Actresses like to be actresses," said Belinda. "They don't know what else to do with their time. . . . Oh, oh!" She held up her hand. "It says here she's quitting pictures. In the middle of a movie. Huh, I smell something fishy in Denmark. Probably means she's knocked up."

"Belinda!" said Effie, shocked. "Where did you pick that one up?"

"Listening to Mom on the phone."

Effie grinned.

"Well, anyway," said Belinda, "I guess that makes Titan studio pretty unhappy."

"Why?" asked Effie. "I should think they'd be glad one of their folks married such a catch. She'll get her picture in all the papers."

"They don't care," said Belinda. "Don't you read the magazines and papers? They've spent millions of dollars already on the 'supercolossal European extravaganza *Pallas Athena*, and all publicizing Martha Ralston."

She glanced at the paper and added, "'Sex symbol of the world.'"

Effie looked at the picture. A windblown young woman in sweater and slacks was shown stepping out of a tender onto the boarding ladder of the famous Niadas yacht, *Circe*. Holding her hand was a middle-aged, slim man. His dark hair was plastered to his head. He had an angled face, and jutting chin, and wore overlarge sunglasses.

"She doesn't look so glamorous to me," said Effie. "Scrawny."

"I always said she was too old to play that role," expertised Belinda. "She's a hag of thirty if she's a day."

"Obviously had it," said Effie, chuckling.

"And how about him?" said Belinda. "He's no Cary Grant. I'd have to close my eyes, and keep saying to myself, 'Think of the bankroll, think of the bankroll.'"

"Oh, lord," said Effie, "I hope you never do that."

"I'll have to do something if I don't get cracking," said Belinda.

She picked up her books and made a dash for the kitchen door.

"Chicken for dinner," said Effie as Belinda ran for the school bus.

Effie ruminated on the fact that Friday, after Thursday off, was always a bad day. She knew from what she had found downstairs what she would find upstairs.

There was a push-button buzz. She went to the hall and picked up the downstairs phone that worked as an intercom with the upstairs phone.

"Effie, for God's sake, bring me a bromo. I'm dying. And some coffee, and the paper on a tray, if you don't mind."

"Good morning; sure thing, Miss Jessie," said Effie, and hung up.

She took out the wicker-edged breakfast tray, set it up with a pink breakfast mat, flat silver, and breakfast china; put the coffee in a small Thermos, the orange juice in a bed of ice; folded the pink napkin; and looked at the prettiness with a flash of resentment.

Again, shame overcame her. Forgive me, God, she prayed, remembering. She went outside, picked a sprig of pink impatiens, and set it on the mat, then trudged upstairs and smiled as she opened the door to her lady's boudoir.

Jessica lay face-down in her Nile-green gown on the pale-green sheets. Her hand was clutched against her forehead, and her brassy bountiful hair fell in a tumble over her tanned face. The molding of her wrist, her arm, the hollow of her armpit, so carefully zipped free of hair, and the slender curve of her back, blending into the fine waist, was still in ascendancy over the face, which had lost youth quite a while ago and settled on a drawn-on beauty to hide its bitterness.

Her pose brought back to Effie a morning long ago that again caused the twin phantoms of guilt and gratitude to assail her.

That time, long ago, Effie had known that Mrs. Barstow had taken her husband to clinics and doctors all over the southern part of California, and heaven knows, there were plenty of them. She had finally settled on Dr. Wolfram, who had taken care of the studio folks for years. He had often braced Mr. Barstow with his needle so he could get to work on the set after a bout of drinking.

She recollected that last session with Dr. Wolfram, when she had heard Mr. Barstow say, "Are you certain these are vitamin shots? I have a sharp suspicion that the leftover hormones of stunt men are being pumped into my groin."

The next morning, to her surprise, as she was carrying towels into the bathroom off the projection room, where they often ran movies, she had come upon the Barstows, who lay naked and brandy-sodden, alongside Jeffrey's pet chimpanzee, Pansy. Jeffrey had heard Effie's cry of surprise, had risen up drunk and crazed, hauled her into the bathroom, and thrown her on the floor and raped her while the chittering ape watched.

Terrified and shaking, she had cried, "Oh, my God, forgive me, forgive me!"

"Get out, and forget it," Jeffrey had said, weeping.

He had never mentioned it again. After the terror of the morning had left her, she thought of quitting, but somehow she knew he was not in control of himself, and had not meant what he did. And with this strange, cold woman in his life, who never gave him a kind glance, he needed her to look after him.

In times to come, after Belinda was born, and Effie took care of the child, she had often seen Mr. Barstow look at her with affection, as if silently thanking her for the part she had taken in her care of his child, and his life.

It was meant to be, thought Effie. No matter under what circumstances this child was born to this cold lady, she was the joy of Mr. Barstow's late years, his only comfort. It was God's will. She tried to erase the incident from her mind, as she had forgotten the beatings her own drunken husband gave her before he was killed in a brawl on Central Avenue years long gone.

She remembered Mr. Barstow as a gifted and lonely man, who had thanked her a thousand times, with a glance, for everything from a rose set by his reading chair to her loving care of his Belinda. She remembered the poetry, the laughter, the rapt attention and joy he gave every living thing in his garden and his life in his better moments. And he had given her Belinda to care for, cherish, and love. That's what he would have wanted, for her to be with the little girl.

She was ashamed that she regretted the severity of Jessica, for life had not treated her as she had intended. And she longed for Belinda to have a more normal, happy childhood than was given her. So she intended to make up for it in every way she could, to expiate her sins.

4

"And how is that gorgeous daughter?" asked Peter Forch as he dabbed tint on Jessica's scalp.

"Can you believe it," said Jessica, "getting ready to graduate from junior high."

"Seems yesterday she was bringing her dolls in here," said Peter, prince of cliché. "Well, I suppose it won't be long before I'm doing her hair for her wedding!"

"Give me a break, Peter!" said Jessica. "She's only a child!"

Peter smiled, and bent forward conspiratorially. It was his favorite role.

"We were supposed to destroy this formula," he whispered. "It was made exclusively for Martha Ralston before she left for Europe to do *Pallas Athena.* But really, Mrs. Barstow, I think Greek Peach is ever so much better on you than on her."

"Why destroy it, just because Martha Ralston wants to be exclusive?" said Jessica. "She'll never come back to Hollywood, anyway. Would you, if you married billions of dollars?"

"Heavens no!" said Peter. "I'd just sail around on assorted yachts. Besides, I don't think she's very popular at the mo, around here."

This was Jessica's opening. She cast her line. Pretend to know; the old Hollywood technique, and you'll get all the facts.

"Well, she put Titan in a terrible spot."

"Terrible!" parroted Peter. "You don't know the half. Why, they're dropping options like popcorn at a double feature. Some of their greatest talent. Believe me, and I'm very close to it."

"There's always a need for talent," said Jessica. "Confidentially, Peter, I'm going back into business with a new production company."

"I heard rumors," said Peter. "You know, Ilonka does Mr. Ziska's haircuts personally. He's such a gifted man."

"We've been working night and day," said Jessica. "So tell your friend Henry not to worry."

Peter stared at her. The unsaid was now said. Henry Duval had told him not to blab, but obviously Jessica Barstow knew. Ilonka said she knew everyone in town.

"It's just a stinking shame the way Fergus Austin treated Henry, dropping his option after all that work," said Peter. "Of course, those sets cost a fortune. It's hard to build thirty-eight sets in all those out-of-the-way places. You know, you can't make palaces out of a sow's ear!"

"All that work," said Jessica sympathetically, reeling out more line.

"And that whole Greek city built on the Anzio beachhead," said Peter. "Poor Henry was just a wreck, working among all those unexploded bombs. He was terrified every time he took a step!"

Jessica remembered Henry, a production designer from the days at Titan. She could visualize immaculate, fussy little Henry, picking his way like he was walking on eggs, on the old battleground, with his balls and toupee at stake.

Peter shook his head. "Henry got blamed for those massive expenses." He looked around as if the booth had ears, but canned music and hair dryers were making a protective racket. "Now, if you say I told you this, I'll cross my heart and say it's a lie, but the production department made a *big* boo-boo. They built their enormous exteriors on leased land, and they have to pay an industrialist thousands of dollars a month. Graft, you know."

"Of course," said Jessica, "and everyone knows

Martha Ralston is pregnant. That means no production with her. Well, they'll probably recast."

"That's just what I was going to tell you," said Peter. "They won't. That Greek, Perry Niadas, who married her, doesn't want anyone else to play the *Pallas Athena* role. She's going to retire. They're scrapping everything!"

Jessica wondered if the pulse in her neck showed. It felt as if it did.

"I'd love to see those beautiful sets before they're struck," she said.

"Oh, they're just gorgeous," he said. "Imagine junking them. Henry was all set for another Academy Award."

"Has he got any stills?" asked Jessica.

"Scads," said Peter, waving his comb. "Grace Boomer in publicity at Titan gave him the whole set. They were real pals, just inseparable there in Rome, stuck away from Hollywood on preproduction for almost six months. Grace said there hadn't been anything like them since the fall of the Roman Empire. All that work!"

"Just terrible," said Jessica sympathetically.

"And poor Henry's luck, he'd made all sorts of commercial deals. A big campaign, all the slick magazines, tied up with *Pallas Athena*, you know, with the Greek key, and egg-and-dart-pattern bit, towels, rugs, toilet-seat covers, coordinated tissues and toilet paper. Just a mint in it, and now"—he gestured dramatically—"down the drain."

"Poor Henry," said Jessica. "Why don't you both come over someday and have a drink with me? I'd just love to see those pictures. You know, I might just do my new home in Greek classic for a change, get away from all this overdone French Provincial and Spanish."

"Oh," said Peter ecstatically, "that would be right up Henry's alley."

"I hate to see that talent go to waste," said Jessica. "Maybe Friday?"

"You're just darling," said Peter.

"About seven o'clock. And don't mention my plans,

you know, about those six pictures with Max Ziska, just yet. I want Clarissa to get it first."

"*Six!*" said Peter. "My *goodness!*"

His hand itched to dial Henry.

Jessica pretended to thumb through a vintage *New Yorker* with interest. But before he left the room, she held up an arresting hand.

"Oh, by the way, Peter, maybe it would be smart for Henry to bring the script of *Pallas Athena* along with the stills, so I can see what they're all about."

"Of course," said Peter happily. "And hush-hush."

"Oh, hush-hush," said Jessica.

◆◆◆◆◆◆◆◆

Hardly anyone was in the Sauna Club on Sunset Boulevard early Saturday morning. But Sonia had her regulars, who came in time-honored custom; young and old women in search of beauty and health climbed onto the bleached wood racks of the steam room, the higher the hotter.

Once one might have found Ingrid Bergman, or even Garbo, swabbing a towel in a bucket of cold water in order to bear the hot, cleansing steam.

Jessica took her place on the lower ledge, and adjusted her eyesight to the gloom. Sure enough, aside from big Sonia, who was pouring water on the aromatic hot rocks, dressed as always in a baggy, wide-strapped bathing suit, looking like a refugee from Mack Sennett days, there was a shapeless female on the top shelf, her hair in a shower cap, and a wet cloth over her face.

Sonia poured eucalyptus oil on the hot rocks and left.

It didn't take long for the recumbent form to groan uncomfortably and move to a lower shelf. She giggled apologetically for the commotion as she straightened her towel on the rack.

"Sorry," she said, "it's just too stifling up there."

"It certainly is," said Jessica casually. "How can you take it?"

"I've been doing it for twenty years," said the woman. She moved closer, and looked at Jessica's figure.

"You surely don't need it," she said.

"I just like it," said Jessica, making a point of not looking up.

The woman moved into the vapors. She was heavy, and her face was red. She peered at Jessica.

"Say," she said, "aren't you . . . ? Why, Jessica! Jessica Klopfinger . . . Barstow."

Jessica leaned on one elbow, and peered, too.

"Why, Harriet!" she said. "Harriet Foster!"

"I didn't know you came here," Harriet said.

"You introduced me when I was a kid," said Jessica. "Imagine running into you after all these years."

"I'm here every Saturday,' 'said Harriet, "That is, when Mr. Austin doesn't call me to the beach to work."

"Do you still do that?" asked Jessica. "My lord, it seems a million years ago."

Harriet sat up. "You look just the same as you did years ago. To tell the truth, I . . . I was sorry when you left. I always meant to call you, and have lunch."

"It just wasn't the wise thing to do," said Jessica pointedly.

"It wasn't that," said Harriet lamely, "it was . . . well, you can't believe it, but I've been so busy. After you left, there were other people to train. And the place seems always to be in a panic."

"I know too well," said Jessica.

"And I hear you've got a child," said Harriet, "and she's a real beauty. Well, she ought to be!"

"Thank you," said Jessica, "she is pretty. She's a big girl, fourteen. How's everything with you?"

"Well, I guess I shouldn't complain," said Harriet, "but you know how it is."

"Yes, I do indeed," said Jessica. "You know, seeing you is so strange it gives me the shivers. I was talking about you last night, and here you are."

"Talking about *me?*" said Harriet.

"Some people from Titan were over for drinks. And I said I thought it was rotten about the way they're letting the old guard go. Your name was mentioned, and

I said how helpful you'd been to me when I was starting out."

"They mentioned my name?" said Harriet nervously.

Jessica sat up. She saw that Harriet's jowls had begun to drop. A wisp of gray hair hung from under her cap. Harriet had never been anything but a motherly type, but she certainly had let herself go. And God, she looked tired.

"It really doesn't mean anything," said Jessica. "You know how rumors fly. It seems to me if Fergus Austin let you go back to the secretarial pool after all these years, you'd be the first to know."

Harriet put her hands up to her face.

"Oh . . . my goodness!" she gasped. "Who said that?"

"It doesn't matter. Nobody important," said Jessica. "I shouldn't have mentioned it. I thought you knew."

"I haven't heard a word," said Harriet. She began to breathe heavily. "Are you sure they meant me?"

"Look, Harriet, it may be for the best. Can you keep a secret?"

Harriet was so lost in her own misery that she hardly heard.

"I'm planning to go back into production," said Jessica, "and there's nobody I'd rather have run an office than you."

"I've got my mother in a rest home," said Harriet miserably, "it takes every cent. I can't afford—"

"I've got a big deal coming up," said Jessica. "Now, listen, Harriet. Max Ziska is coming back, and he has six, mind you, six magnificent properties ready to go. We'll start you in at two hundred a week."

"Two hundred!" said Harriet. She lifted up her head.

"There's only one thing you have to do," said Jessica, "to get us in business, that is, if you're in a rush. I mean, to avoid the secretarial pool. Write a memo with Fergus Austin's initials on it, to the legal department."

"Oh, I couldn't do that!" said Harriet.

"If you don't care to, I can always get hold of Bill

Baines," said Jessica. "His firm is doing our legal work. But if I find out where we stand on Max Ziska's old Titan contract, and get a release from the legal department, we can negotiate quicker with the independent company who wants to put us into business. And you could go right to work. That's all I have to know. If Max can get a legal release from his existing contract. That's not much of a breach, is it? It's harmless."

Harriet pondered.

"Fergus Austin would have my hide if I sent a strange memo through over his initials."

"Forget it," said Jessica, wringing out her wet towel in a bucket, as if she were preparing to move. "Only it looks to me like your hide is pinned without your knowledge anyway. Don't worry, Harriet, you won't stay in the pool long. Somebody will grab you. I suppose the television department is expanding, isn't it?"

"Television!" said Harriet, as if Jessica had said "Snake!"

She had visions of all the younger girls she knew, who were bowed down with long hours, and the endless pressure, week after week at television series panic stations.

"Bill Baines will handle things for us," said Jessica. "I shouldn't have bothered you. Only, seeing you out of the blue like this, and knowing about your predicament, I just thought we could expedite things, and help you out at the same time."

"I shouldn't think they could hold Max Ziska after all these years," said Harriet. Her mind was beginning to take a new tack.

"He has to be legally clean," said Jessica, "We couldn't take a risk in a production deal of this magnitude. I'm going to do what I always wanted to do. Be associated in the production side."

"That's wonderful!" said Harriet. "Gee, maybe . . ."

"I wouldn't jeopardize your situation," said Jessica, "and for all I know, Fergus Austin has no intention of letting you go. For heaven's sake, don't mention our meeting."

"Of course I wouldn't!"

Indeedy, thought Jessica, you scared, chicken sad-sack.

She stood up. So did Harriet, wrapping the towel about her torso. She seemed smaller and much dumpier than Jessica had remembered.

"Oh, Jessica, you look just wonderful. You always had a big life. Things happen to you!"

"And this is the biggest," said Jessica. "The first picture we start with is called *The Oracle*. It takes place in ancient Greece. It is a tremendous drama. Max has also written it as a novel. It will be published in the spring. Likely Literary Guild."

"In Greece!" said Harriet. "Why, isn't that a coincidence. Why, we . . ."

She halted lamely. She had almost said too much.

"Yes," said Jessica, "it's wonderful. You know, the waterfront city at Piraeus. The temple at Delphi. Beautiful palaces."

Harriet's eyes were popping.

Jessica smiled.

"Yes, Harriet. I know they're scrapping *Pallas Athena*. And our company might just move right in and buy those sets that are causing Titan's board of directors such a headache."

Harriet was thinking of her friend, nice little Henry Duval, the production designer who had stood at her desk, like so many distraught old-timers did these days. Last week he had openly cried after he came out of Fergus Austin's office.

"It was wonderful running into you," said Jessica, "and don't give my impetuous idea a thought."

"Oh, I'll call you, believe me, Jessica, you'll hear from me."

"I wouldn't want to get you into trouble, Harriet. Remember, you're very valuable."

"Oh, thank you," said Harriet fervently, "you were always so sweet to me. I'd love to work for you."

Sweet . . . thought Jessica. I took her job. And later she got most of my work fobbed off onto her, until I got my own secretary. The poor dope covered for Fergus and me for years while we got together. How do you like that! She never dug it!

♦♦♦♦♦♦♦♦

Seymour Sewell sat on the fantail lounge of his old yacht, the *Empress*. She hadn't been ten miles out of Newport harbor since 1946, when she was mustered out of Coast Guard duty.

She was seventy feet long and had a beam of sixteen feet. A cigar-shaped roller, she tossed about when even an outboard motorboat passed by the anchorage dock.

Like his obsolete boat, Seymour Sewell had been economically beached. His agency had been absorbed by a newer, bigger, smarter, and less drunk group of men.

Three wives, two bouts of hepatitis, and one potential kidney ailment later, Seymour surrendered his personality and his life to Alcoholics Anonymous. The insulting quip, the daring business acumen, the sharp wit, and the instantaneous wheeling and dealing had left him along with the stimulation of alcohol.

Having lost his world, Seymour retired to Newport Beach, where he lived, mooring charge only, rent free on his yacht, which he kept up like an old lady, with constant refurbishing, lots of paint, and rose-shaded lamps at night, to make her look better than she was.

Seymour sat in the afternoon sun, reading a copy of weekly *Variety*. His neatly crossed legs were encased in yellowed flannels. His shoes were velvet, made by Peale long ago in London, and his double-breasted jacket, blue and patched at the elbows, was gaudily decorated with flat brass buttons bearing the entwined initials J.B. This jacket, his Sunday best, pared down, was his most cherished treasure, having been left him in Jeffrey Barstow's will, for in the old days the two had balled and brawled at every seaside brothel between Monterey and Cabo San Lucas.

His Filipino steward, Angelo, served him a Shirley Temple, a concoction of Coca-Cola, phonied up with a cherry and wedge of orange.

"Well, Angelo," he said, "I see where everyone's going in for three dementia. You know, like old stereoscopes in the parlor. Seems you can reach right out and touch the tits."

"That's good," said Angelo, beaming, his gold teeth aglitter.

A young woman was clambering down the ramp to the float from the parking ground. She wore high heels, and gingerly sought her way.

"Landlubber," commented Angelo.

She passed several yachts, and moved toward the *Empress*. She stopped, peering.

"Looks like we might have company," said Seymour.

He put his reading glasses in his breast pocket and stood up. She looked like a show-business figure, overslender, and defined with a cashmere sweater, wide belt, and pleated skirt over the swinging hips.

"By God, and by Jesus, looks like we really got company. . . . Jessica," he shouted, leaning over the rail, "you looking for me?"

She waved up.

"Hi, Seymour."

What was left of his dehydrated brain clicked. Last time he saw her was at Jeffrey's wake. Claudia, who had arrived from London, had joined up with him at the Barstow house after the funeral. As the group of old-timers, business people, lawyers, and hangers-on who always dive into chicken sandwiches and coffee or liquor, according to their preferences at such events, sat around as if waiting for further news, Seymour and Claudia, feeling correctly that they were the only true mourners at the gathering, liberally doused their sorrows and their dislike of Jessica with numerous libations. Finally, at four in the morning, having outstayed the welcome which was dubious to begin with, they were escorted by Jessica and the Japanese butler to Seymour's limousine. He had been dumped, supine, on the floor. Jessica, in her black dress, was glaring down at him.

"Now, get out of here," Jessica had said, "and don't ever come back."

He peered up at her through the blear and smiled. "You're looking great, kid," he said to the new widow, as the door was slammed in his face, and the car started to move. Claudia Barstow, who was perched like a wax doll on the seat, lurched onto his face, and it was the last he had seen of the family Barstow.

But now, obviously this dame wanted something. You didn't come around this many years later to make sweet talk.

"You're looking great, kid," Seymour said, bridging the gap of years. "Welcome aboard. What would you like to drink?"

Now, what does this bitch want? What have I got that anybody would want? he pondered.

"Oh, vodka martini on the rocks," she said. "But I wanted to talk business with you."

"Well, at least you don't beat around the bush," he said. "What can I do for you?"

She sat on the fantail seat with him and leaned against the cushions, taking off her dark glasses. At least she didn't crap around, he noticed, about the sunset, or admire the harbor, or rave about the great varnish job on these solid old yachts, like most of the overpolite grabbers who came out for the bite.

"Seymour," she said, "you handled Max Ziska when I was at Titan."

"That's right."

"He's valuable property."

"Was," he said. "You know, I wrote him the best contract anybody ever got up till that time just before he left. Complete autonomy. Writing, direction, co-production, and a deal that even the papers never knew. Two and a half percent of the gross, yet. But of course he didn't have a chance to function on those terms. He's been gone from the scene over fifteen years, and everybody knows he's in a loony bin. What gives?"

"Seymour, I'm not going to kid with you; there's no

use at this late date trying to stack the deck. You know how you stood with Jeffrey and me."

"With you, lousy," said Seymour, "and at the end, Jeffrey didn't count anymore."

He leaned back. Sometimes it was good to have sold out for even small security. You could lean back on the cushions of your own yacht, and look crumbs in the eye. It was hardly possible, but she might have something up her sleeve. She never moved without calculating the ohms.

"Well, then," said Jessica, "I guess we can start all over again."

"I may not want to," he said.

"You will," she answered. She laughed. " 'The voice of the turtle will be heard throughout the land.' "

"Jeffrey taught you a thing or two," he said.

"I knew a thing or two. Who holds Max's contract today?"

"I'm his agent," said Seymour. "Now, look, Jessica, I know why Fergus threw him out of the studio. As I recollect, after you and Fergus had that big blow-up in his office, you left that Christmas party and went on to the party on Stage Five. And Fergus had you followed."

"Correct," said Jessica, "and they also found me with Max Ziska. That you know."

"Very much so," said Seymour, "and my hottest client, Mr. Ziska, poor patsy, never worked again."

"Time, tide, and a war," said Jessica. "Are you sure you didn't sell Max's contract to Star Lists with the rest of your holdings?"

"No." He thought a moment. "I didn't include his name. I hung onto his contract because we co-owned a percentage of his gross. But I consider him defunct."

"What is his position as far as the contract with Titan is concerned? Has time abrogated it?"

He thought. She has a connection with Max. It had to be carnal. And that, he had heard, was pretty good. Poor old Jeffrey had said to him once, "She has a little sailor boy inside her that grabs you, and pulls you up, up, and up, like a rope."

Jeffrey had looked wicked for a moment, and then dejected.

"But, Jupiter, Seymour, the shog that goes with it!"

"Max has got his marbles back?" asked Seymour.

"His marbles, plus six fabulous scripts," said Jessica, "and one also written fictionally, to be published this spring. All these last years while he was hospitalized, he has been turning out a product that would be a lifetime's work for some people.

"Good?" asked Seymour. "Aside from the poontang between you two, which is obviously involved, are you sure they're good?"

"They are good," said Jessica, ignoring his personal crack. He would have to be put in his place. "And the first one, which we, and I do mean *we*, just got in final shape, is *The Oracle*. It's about ancient Greece. It requires the skill of a fantastic young woman to play it. She must be a virgin—half-woman, half-child. She is the mystic oracle at Delphi. Now, Seymour, my daughter, Belinda, Jeffrey's child is fourteen. Tall for her age, too."

"A Barstow a virgin at fourteen?" he said ironically.

"She has been raised by me," said Jessica firmly.

Seymour suddenly felt chilly.

Jessica reached in her large purse and brought out a photograph.

"Max took it at Trancas beach," said Jessica, handing it to him.

Belinda was walking along the shoreline. The foam was curling over her toes, and she was bare-legged, her slim body draped in a wet towel, which she wore like a Greek woman's tunic, thrown over one shoulder. Her blond hair was blowing in the wind, and her face, with its widely spaced, black-lashed eyes half-closed, was turned toward the sun. She held her chin upward, with a faint smile on her lips.

Seymour put on his glasses. He turned the picture to the failing light and peered closer. He felt an old surge, the instinct of a finder, almost as comforting as alcohol, creeping from the back of his brain, down his arms, and into his chest and heart, making it beat faster.

He let out an involuntary whistle.

"The last of the Barstows," said Jessica. "Max calls her Jeffrey's last and greatest performance."

Angelo came from the cabin with Jessica's drink and a tray of hors d'oeuvres. She took the drink, and sipped, watching Seymour.

He looked at the picture again, paced across the deck, turned the picture, looked at it, bent over the rail, and watched the hawser rising and falling in an oil backwash, and again looked at the photograph. He sat down, saying nothing for a moment.

Jessica drained her glass and took a canapé from the grinning Angelo. She handed him the empty glass to refill.

"Fergus will never do it," said Seymour. "He'd bar me from the lot if I represented her—and you."

"You know about the *Pallas Athena* disaster?" she asked.

He nodded. "Wiped out."

Jessica smiled.

"You'd better get off Noah's ark, Seymour, and get back to the land of make-believe."

He looked at her.

"All those sets in Rome are built on leased land," she said. "The leases, by some odd fate, amount to ten thousand a month. And the industrialist who owns the land is Pericles Niadas, Martha Ralston's husband. He will be enchanted if another story fits those sets. And he is also the Bank of the West. Now, get that for a parlay. He's keeping Fergus in business. And he has complete autonomy over Titan studio. So he does quite well if this picture is made. And another thing: he can cast any role in this film as he sees fit."

"I suppose," said Seymour, "that you need me to verify the contractual situation with Max Ziska, before you get this property in motion."

"Oh, I don't think that's too necessary. You see, yesterday he fired his secretary of twenty years, Harriet Foster. It seems she put through a forged memo to legal, about releasing Max Ziska from his contract. She didn't realize that the legal department always sends out two copies of everything, one marked direct, top secret, and the other to the executive secretary. It happened to come through right at the same time there was a blind item in the *Reporter* about Max's six literary properties being readied for production. And last week Fergus found out that his production designer, Henry Duval, had queried around about selling the *Pallas Athena* sets to an independent production company."

"So Duval got flung out, too," said Seymour.

"Oh, no," said Jessica, "his option had already been dropped. It just attracted Fergus' attention to Max Ziska. He had to have him back."

"Well," said Seymour, "considering the fact that you're not exactly Fergus Austin's buddy anymore, and you seem to know all the details, I'd say that pretty soon you're going to run out of friends. Now you need enemies. So I'm supposed to rise out of the briny and get my ass in the wringer."

"For a price," said Jessica. "I think Max's situation is obviously in the clear. Apparently Max belongs to Titan films on the deal you made just before the war interfered with his career. They just sent him notice that they'll option all his properties as soon as he submits manuscripts. And one is ready to go. I just wanted to be certain that you hadn't sold his contract to anyone else. You're still his agent?"

So that's her shtick, thought Seymour; she's afraid someone will pull the old switcheroo away from her.

"You bet your sweet backside I own him."

"Then you're going to be quite well off," said Jessica. "Max Ziska Productions is still a company within the embracing arms of Titan films. And you own ten percent of it."

Seymour thought about it. This had been one of the first of the companies within a company at a major studio. It telegraphed the future power of independents, based on the luxation of talent, as control waned among the previously great film families. He knew he was partly responsible for the monster that had devoured its own body and caused disaster in the film business. The talent-owned corporation by now was sick on its own rich diet born of privilege and the saturnalia of ego, corporate advantages, and ephemeral economy.

"You might do even better," said Seymour, in spite of himself, thinking like an agent, "with a new indie deal, fifty percent ownership, tax benefits abroad, English co-production, Edy plan government financing. Max and his properties could be plasma to an independent right now."

As she smiled, he knew her answer before she said it.

"For personal reasons, I prefer Titan."

Poor Fergus, thought Seymour. God, after all he said about Max and this dame never setting foot in a studio again. What a reaming. It makes my tochas ache to think of it.

"And Max?" he asked. "I'm beginning to wonder if he has got his marbles."

"Max is just great," said Jessica. "He's a picture maker. You know that. He's a creator. He doesn't want to wheel and deal. I'll be handling those details, as his associate. He wants to see his dream children fleshed, as he says. That's the real thing in his life. And he adores Belinda. He's been working with her on the role. She's become his creation."

"Seems a little young to me," said Seymour, "but look at Liz Taylor and *National Velvet*, and after all, the kid's a Barstow. Since you have it all worked out, what's your pleasure?"

"Arrange for a film test to be made secretly, away from Titan films. This whole project has to be controlled until it's on paper. Let Titan studio test their own dogs. We could probably take space at Motion Picture Center. Max will direct. We got a great camera crew, just laid off. When it's finished, which ought to be next week, since we've already arranged for space, if you must know, I'd like a passage for Europe. I'll take the script to Niadas, to be sure it doesn't get drygulched by Fergus, and after that I'll spring Belinda's test on the home studio."

Seymour looked at her. It was getting chilly, he felt, even in the slanting rays of the late-afternoon sun.

Angelo came on deck with another martini. Jessica took it, sipped, and set it on a deck table.

"Would you like to handle Belinda as a client? You handled all the Barstows."

Seymour laughed. He shook his head.

"Jessica, since Alcoholics Anonymous has ruined my personality and my career, I don't have to crap around like I used to. And I would have to be very drunk all the time to handle a child of yours with Fergus still running Titan studio."

"You will arrange the test?" she asked coolly.

"For Max Ziska," he said, "who won a war while I got rich, and for Jeffrey Barstow, who lost a war while I got rich, I will arrange the test. And for Fergus Austin, who gave me many a bad time, and helped sell me into the camp of mine enemies, I will send you and this poor, cursed, fabulous little Barstow on your way. But after that, Mrs. Barstow, just pay me my loan for screen-test expenses at six percent, and let me rot on my yacht."

Jessica finished her drink and arose.

"You'll handle her," she said. "She'll be too hot a property for you to resist."

"And who's handling you?" he asked.

"Guess."

She left the boat without fanfare, found her way down the boarding ladder and onto the dock. Seymour, wishing her spiked heels would catch on one of the slats, watched her, but she dodged along the bowsprits that stood like sentinels with pointed lances along the way. He saw her get into her car and drive off, not looking back.

Bad cess, he thought. That broad could give you double pneumonia on the Fourth of July. She's coming on as strong as a star at a producer's funeral. . . . He shivered.

He discovered that he still had Belinda's photograph in his hand. He took it into the salon, turned on the lights, and propped it up next to the TV set.

Her terrible beauty and innocence made him, dry Seymour Sewell, want to cry.

He thought with a pang of his long-lost, enchanting friend, his boatmate, Jeffrey, who could rise from a bed in a brothel with that look of sweet beauty on his face.

And he thought of the child he had seen give Jeffrey the best moments of his life, and shuddered, thinking of what Jeffrey would have said and done if he had seen Jessica this day.

He shuddered. Oh, Jeffrey . . . oh, Claudia. Oh, Belinda—a Barstow again. Damn it, I will. I know I will.

◆◆◆◆◆◆◆◆◆

For the past few weeks Jessica had tried to be invaluable to Max. She had worked tirelessly on his script, putting it in the current, accepted form.

She had boned up like a seminar student on Greek history, mores, and manners, and had cleverly maneuvered physical aspects of his script to correspond with Henry Duval's sets already built in Italy for a defunct film that Max didn't know existed.

She was delighted to discover that in Max's script, Hermocrates, the surgeon of Athens, would be perfectly cast with Titan's veteran star Leslie Charles, who was, according to the press, holding court in Rome, recovering from the blow of not being able to play Pericles in the disastrous *Pallas Athena.*

She also recognized that the plum role of Diodynus of Thebes, the youthful soldier who falls in love with the young Pythia, sacred oracle of Delphi, would be played by John Graves, that brilliant star who had been discovered by Claudia Barstow a few years back and had been signed by Titan for an important role in Martha Ralston's picture.

It was an immense break in terms of contractual obligations and physical properties. This was something she would reveal at the proper time to the Greek financier Niadas, as soon as he read Max's script.

She had her private battles with Max, in her efforts

to bring characters and situations around to the circumstances that she alone knew existed. It taxed her imagination and her patience to invent reasons that would make this transference possible. Knowing the ego of Max's talent, she knew that he would never deliberately adjust his creation to a commercial necessity. She would just have to keep him away from the chatty studio society of department craftsmen until he was well into his film.

Fortunately, so far he had accepted her driving insistence as inner-sanctum knowledge, as long as her suggestions did not interfere with the drama and character development in his story.

Jessica had convinced Max that as soon as she read his script she knew Belinda had to play it. Alethea, the young virgin, who, because of her beauty, grand-mal seizures, and visions, was chosen to be the pythoness, oracle at the shrine of Delphi, could only be played by a virginal, rare beauty. She led Max to believe that he had conceived the idea that Belinda was meant to be an actress.

"Her beauty is of such a classic type," he said one day as they were working on the script, "she could be Alethea, stepping from the threshold of adolescence into womanhood. She could indeed have been a noble Greek. Belinda could identify with any patrician, like her father. How well I remember when he did his *Lorenzo* with me. This was an astonishing experience, for this part of him I hadn't seen. With the whole studio wardrobe at his command, he brought home a pair of tights and some cotton batting. He announced that he was going to 'think Italian'! He sat down for two days with the script, thread, and needle, and built himself, as he said, a pair of 'Italian legs.' He read and reread the lines as he stitched cotton padding into those symmetricals.

"Well, when he emerged from his solitude, announcing that he knew his own mental and muscular displacement better than anyone else, he really was a Medici. That face, and those tights, willing his flabby old legs to become handsome, made him look more noble than anyone else. He was classic to the end."

"A classic son-of-a-bitch," added Jessica, and then she sighed. "I knew Belinda would do what Barstows seem to be born to do. But not so soon. So when I read your script, Max, I'm afraid I got gooseflesh."

"You think I didn't, the day I met her?"

And so the child of flesh had begun to be written into the pen-and-ink child, as Max refined his script.

Jessica had kept Max away from Titan studio while they waited. The script was sent in by registered mail. The memos that began coming from Seymour Sewell, his legal agent, placated his vanity. He was not forgotten. After a thousand-dollar advance from Seymour, a ten-thousand-dollar optional payment was received from Titan studio, payment against a hundred thousand per original screenplay due on his old contract, with the rest to be paid in ninety days if the studio picked up its option. Jessica knew that thus, using the war as an act-of-God clause, the studio was recognizing the continuation of his contract. She also knew the next three months would decide whether or not Titan purchased *The Oracle*.

Jessica converted her small dining room into an office, set up a typewriter and an extra phone, and went to work, without discussion, as his general factotum and secretary.

Effie fed Max when he was hungry, Jessica fetched his laundry from his small apartment on Fountain, and when he got his advance, she forced him to buy some clothes, although they seemed to matter little to him, save as necessities to cover his body.

Sometimes Jessica wondered how Max could be so different from most of the men she had known. Unlike Americans, he never thought of economy. It never entered his mind to ask how she lived, and why she, widow of a great figure of the stage and screen, should be in an apartment on the wrong side of Wilshire Boulevard.

But Jessica figured that in spite of what she herself knew about her diminishing funds, Max had seen so much poverty and desolation in his years in war-torn Europe that she seemed affluent to him.

In his creative, impractical, and innocent mind, she was a woman of power and knowledge, and that was her greatest hold on him.

She discovered the one disturbance in his flowing, dedicated work. He feared that the years away from picture-making might have made him old-fashioned, even obsolete. Younger talents had copied the witty, sentimental approach to classical drama which had been his trademark. And film cutting had become swifter, sharper, moving toward the subliminal.

He also found that the idols of his yesterday, whom he had depended upon to embody his characters, had changed. A young actress he had considered for Alethea, in his mind's eye, was now a jaded woman of thirty-eight; her bitter face sprang at him on a large screen, and he sat, shocked, in the darkened theater, that her beauty had so debauched itself.

"I have lost a generation of people!" he said to Jessica as they left, stopping in the lobby to buy the endless candy bars he devoured, in his memory of hunger.

He admired and feared the burgeoning talent of the younger men who were new to him, like Rossellini, and the new Fellini, who had crossed the line, like himself, from writing to directing.

Open City and *The Bicycle Thief* left him sleepless; he wept at the beauty of Kurosawa's *Rashomon.* He recalled Renoir's brilliant *Grand Illusion,* and thrilled as he saw the master's *The River.*

Zinnemann's *The Search* shattered him.

"I remember when he was working at Alvarado, in the wilds of Mexico. He has come a long way."

He saw a new Olivier in *Henry V;* he thrilled at the color and plastic beauty of Pressberger's *Red Shoes,* and the meticulous talented direction of Willy Wyler's *Wuthering Heights,* and *The Best Years of Our Lives.*

He was delighted at the young writer, John Huston, having created two such masterpieces as *Treasure of Sierra Madre* and *African Queen.*

"It is too much. The talent has all been playing a massive game of chess; and I can never catch up with it. Perhaps I have said all I have to say."

"Don't be foolish," said Jessica. "When you left, Ford, Wyler, LeRoy, Hitchcock, Curtiz, Stevens, De Mille, Vidor, and Kazan were all top men. They still are. Partly because they get the best material. And you will be, too. How many of them are writers of your caliber? None. You have your own built-in protection. Does that answer your question?"

"In a way, but only in a way. I would never let anyone else direct what I write. I'd rather starve."

"There's a big rebound from those Italian neorealist films you admire so much," she said. "Now nations are concerned with what other countries will think of their true picture of life. And you know what that means."

"It means picture makers start trying to live and to think a lie. That is the beginning of weakness," he said.

"But it is a good time for your romantic, classic quality to be in cycle again," said Jessica. "You have nothing to fear. And don't fret about budget. Producers would rather have a few big pictures than lots of little ones. And your percentage deal involves gross, Max. That's almost unheard of today. One good reason not to go with an independent, in spite of fringe benefits. You could get only a percentage of the net, and I can assure you, that gets gobbled up in vast studio operations, or you're stuck with end money. It's a handful of nothing."

"It all seems very far from picture-making, like being a walking IBM machine."

"There is no more block booking," continued Jessica. "Theaters would rather have a Maximilian Ziska production run a few weeks at a higher rental than to have to change their programs twice weekly for some shoddy, fly-by-night production. Time and economy must not concern you. I agree, you must be what you truly are, a creator."

"There will be trouble," said Max, but he smiled. Her words soothed his inner turmoil.

"Fergus Austin thrives on trouble," she said. "I just want to be certain you do, too."

"I think we should go see him, now that he has recognized my contract."

Jessica had been waiting for this. She held up her hand quickly.

"Not yet. Trust me. You will get everything you want. You are in production with your own unit. And business is just horse-trading. We must be ready to horse-trade."

Max loathed horse-trading. He wanted to be on the set to make pictures, to hang over the moviola at night, when the actors were gone, cutting and fashioning the thousands of fragments into a mosaic that would make his thoughts and actions come alive; he wanted to live in a running stream of celluloid. If this woman wanted to be an iron woman, to compensate for some distressed area in her life, it was fine with him, as long as she kept everyone, including herself, off his back.

"And when the time comes," said Jessica, "I will take Belinda's test and your script to the backers myself, as a representative of Ziska Productions, to be certain that Fergus does not screw things up for us—for you," she added.

Max's shaggy dark eyebrows lifted.

"We are not going to test Belinda at the Titan studio?"

"Indeed we are not." She turned a smile on him and poured him a drink. "Max, my naïve dear, you know how many connections of the flesh there are in this town. Once you were up on all this folklore! You knew whose fanny you could or could not pinch at a party. But between Fergus Austin and his son, David Austin—"

"That child?" said Max, surprised.

Jessica busied herself with the cocktail shaker, and found herself answering, as if it were only another statistic.

"Again, a time lapse has caught up with you. That child is now a man of thirty-seven."

"My God," said Max, "I feel like Rip Van Winkle."

"Anyway," said Jessica, "let's not lump Belinda in with all the studio chicks, with the same makeup, and the same wardrobe, the same sets, and the same hackneyed stock player actors. Let's find a performer of substance and do the scene where the physician tries to save the girl from her seizures, realizing that if she stops having them, the oracle is finished. And when you test the other candidates, give them a lighter scene to play. While Fergus has you diddling with all these nonsensical details that keep little men busy, we'll protect our master plan."

"You sound like a Borgia." Max smiled at her.

She leaned forward, and he felt the firm flesh of her breasts pressing against him. They were alone in the apartment.

"I *am* a Borgia!" she whispered, nibbling his ear.

Many times Jessica had taken him to bed, more times, in fact, than he had taken her to bed. But his excitement these days led easily to desire.

In spite of the fact that she was eager, that she never denied him, and often seemed to stimulate him of her own accord, Max felt cheated somehow, even after the most imaginative sessions of lovemaking. For Jessica seemed to departmentalize everything, as if she thought: Now it is time for lovemaking . . . now it is time to turn it off.

She was like a very high-priced courtesan, turning her trick.

But his first instinctive feeling of excitement about Belinda continued. He found he was jealous of a dead man, Jeffrey Barstow, who had imprinted the name of Barstow on his child, along with the dolichocephalic, aristocratic head, the long-fingered hands, and the incredibly well-proportioned body that characterized his strain. She became the wellspring of his inner life; once he had cast her in his mind as the virgin priestess Alethea, he also embraced her in his heart. He thought of her when he awoke, and before he turned his light out he looked at a little snapshot of her taken in their early days at Trancas.

5

◆◆◆◆◆◆◆◆

The May afternoon was warm at Trancas beach.

Jessica sat on her beach towel and rubbed her legs with oil.

"I'll look like an Indian before you and Belinda stop talking," she said to Max as he took an orange out of the lunch hamper.

His trousers were rolled up to his knees, he wore a sweatshirt, and his white hair ruffled in the slight breeze. He was happy as he watched Belinda.

Clad in a white bathing suit, she was knee-deep in the light surf. She skipped a flat stone across the water.

Her ropes of wet hair hung over her shoulders. She spun in a full circle and deliberately lost her balance, tumbling into the water. Her dog sat trembling at the wave's edge, waiting, if need be, to plunge to her rescue.

"I'll miss these lovely days. I pray to God she's half as natural in front of the camera tomorrow," said Max. "Please, Jessica, leave her to herself as much as you can tonight. It's a time for personal growth, meditation. She must project her own being into the character of Alethea. Self-consciousness would be most harmful to her now."

He was trying to be polite about the constant masterminding that Jessica thrust at the child.

"*That* one self-conscious!" said Jessica. "Why, Max, don't forget, she's a Barstow. They were born to spill their guts out in front of an audience."

"That's a wretched concept of acting," said Max. He walked away from her.

God, she thought, he's touchy. I'll be glad when the old bastard gets on with his work and leaves me alone to run the office and the company.

Max and Belinda and the little dog walked along the beach. Sometimes Max turned to watch their random footsteps washed away by the foaming waves. Sometimes the girl—as, he reflected, only the young can do—dashed into the cold waters, with a sentence half-flung, and came back to continue as if there had been no pause.

"It must have been awful to be a priestess," she said, "to sit in a cave in the dark breathing those . . . noxious vapors."

"The Pythia had divinity," said Max. "That dark cavern was the center of her spiritual world. To be a priestess was the highest honor that could come to a woman in Greece. That in itself likely made the vapors bearable."

"The center of the earth," said Belinda, "the stone egg, the Omphalos. I looked it up. She put her hand on it. She leaned on a tripod, drank from the sacred spring, inhaled strange herb smokes, chewed laurel leaves, and went into a trance. Sometimes she had convulsions."

"Can you imagine it?" asked Max cautiously.

He feared he might open some door of panic that would make her performance static.

"Imagine . . ." said Belinda. "I know. Not only holy, but horrible."

Max glanced at her, surprised. Then he realized she had an inner vision of the character of Alethea that he had been saving as she matured into the role.

As a creator, realizing the depth of the story, for a flashing moment he panicked. What could he expect of her? What magic was he attempting to evoke?

The tendrils of golden hair against her apricot skin, the black double-lashed very blue eyes. How could this healthy child seem a sickly, convulsed oracle?

She seemed to read him.

"I can do it," she said, "but I won't until tomorrow. Because, then I will do it. And if I try now, I might lose something. Tomorrow I will be it. You know, Max, what you said."

"Empathy," said Max quietly, trying not to let her see how his eyes were seeking hers, looking into those almost transparent pale depths.

"Max, one prop I'd like. I want an ivory-and-gold bracelet with a knob, like a faun's head or something on it. And in the scene where the poets are standing waiting for my prophecy to carry the message to the king on the battlefield, then I want to pull off the bracelet, like I was in a trance, but know it's going to happen. I'll clamp it in my teeth so I won't bite my tongue, as I fall in a convulsion, over the tripod."

She turned quickly in the sand, digging in her toes. Then she rushed to him and clasped his arm, making a bracelet of her fingers.

"The bracelet will be the symbol of my tragedy. I will take it slowly off my arm, throughout the story, when I feel a spell coming on. And when you see it happen to me away from the sacred cave, you'll see that, like in your story, I am really not a prophetess, but only a sick girl being used."

Max felt gooseflesh, looking at her.

"And then," she said, "when I come out of the seizure, down in that dark cave, lighted only by oil lamps, I'll hear the cry of a jackdaw, in the blue sky up above, in the laurel trees, and the pipes of Pan. I'll take the bracelet out of my teeth, and put it on again slowly, and reach for the world up there, and the warmth of the breeze. . . ."

She moved her hands upward in a trembling grasp, her eyes rolling, the whites showing, then the pupils coming into focus again. Max stood still, the incoming tide washing the rolled cuffs of his trousers. His gooseflesh turned to a shiver.

"Someone's walking on your grave," said Belinda as she bent to pick up a seashell that had rolled against her toes. "Look at this," she said, turning it over. "You see, even without trying, it's perfect."

She tossed it away.

Max bent over and retrieved it. He wanted it as a

talisman. It was a small white murex, once home of a hermit crab. He held the convoluted chamber in his hand and pressed the ridges and swirls against his flesh.

He felt a small, nagging fear. He had always half-jokingly said actors were the most insecure people in the world. And now, this child was probing too deeply into a world that was his. He must keep control.

It is not the actress, it is the child, he thought, who is so secure. Children paint, write poetry, build great dreams before the world knocks them down. But she must be controlled; this self-assurance could crumble to pieces in a moment.

"There is one thing you must understand, Belinda," he said. "You must trust what I say, and be prepared to do what I tell you tomorrow."

She looked at him, surprised, and, he thought, for the first time, aloof. Watch out, he thought, the Barstow idioplasm is showing.

"I think we have both worked it out rather well together," she said, looking at him with eyes that seemed to have become several shades lighter and colder than he remembered.

He feared he had lost her.

"You will bring everything you know to the scene," he said, "and so will I, but if it is right, when we finish, it will be better than the both of us. Do you see?"

She moved out, step by step, on an outcropping of surf-washed rocks covered with seaweed. He followed.

"A beginner, especially, can find a subjective approach. We've been through that. But apart from your subconscious, upon which all creative people depend, you will have to rely on an objective trigger, to bring about a desired result," he said.

She was dipping into a tidepool of water, bringing up a strand of lacy seaweed. The little dog was climbing precariously over the rocks with her.

"You'll have to explain," she said reflectively.

"If I asked you to cry, right now, how would you do it?"

Belinda sat down on a rock, her feet in the tidepool. She reflected.

"Perhaps," said Max, "you would think of your mother, alone, sick, without help. . . ."

Belinda laughed.

"Mother helpless!" she said. "That'll be the day!"

Max grinned. "Very inept of me."

"I know what you mean," she said. "Someday I may not have you. So I must learn to trigger myself."

He nodded. He was getting her back.

As they pondered, the Yorkshire, sniffing at a sea anemone, toppled into the water. The tide pulled him into a whirlpool, and a wave broke over him, carrying him away from the rocks. He disappeared, and came up, coughing and spluttering, a few feet away. Belinda saw him as he was swept several yards away.

"Sarge!" she yelled.

He was pulled under by another comber. Before Max could move, Belinda plunged into the surf. She swam out after him, and dived under a breaker herself. In a second she had found the dog and grasped him by the nape of the neck as he was going under again.

Max clambered out on the rocks, holding out a hand. Belinda struck out with one hand and paddled toward him, holding the choking animal aloft. She fought her way back on another wave, grasped Max's hand, and crawled onto the wet rocks.

The small dog, coughing and retching, looked even tinier with his long hair plastered against his scrawny body. Belinda held him, and patted the shivering form until he heaved up the saltwater and began to breathe again.

"Oh, my God!" said Max. "You might have drowned!"

"He might have drowned," said Belinda, "and it would have been our selfish fault."

The tears brimmed over her wet face; her lower lip quivered, and she sniffed back a sob.

She held the little animal close, and arose; they climbed out of the rising tidepool, over the rocks, back to the sand. Belinda ran to her mother on the beach, snatching up a beach towel, and rubbed the shaking little body of the dog. She was still crying.

"Sarge almost died," she said. "Sarge almost died!"

Well, thought Max, so that's her trigger. The little dog. I'll use it.

And then he loathed himself while he made plans.

What am I starting, he thought, what wicked trigger to stir up a human soul?

And so the subject was ready for the test.

◆◆◆◆◆◆◆◆◆

Red Powell, head of Titan's publicity department, put his feet up on his desk and pushed a button on his intercom. He squinted against the afternoon sun that filtered into the room from the reaches of the street, and pushed another button, automatically closing the drapes.

"Yeah, boss," a voice answered.

"Gracie, will you close up shop and come in?" he said.

"Oh, Red," she said, "I've got all that Martha Ralston crap to get out. We have orders to bow Madame Niadas out of the *Pallas Athena* fiasco gracefully."

"That's yesterday's roses. Get here fast and bring the smelling salts," he said.

"Panic stations?" asked Grace.

"Believe you me," said Red.

He could hear her groan before she switched off the key.

Poor Grace, how many times she'd responded to his panic stations. The rest had grown old, or died, or got better jobs, or turned chicken or informer and written their cruddy memoirs that didn't half scratch the surface, and now, among twenty-five people, he and Grace were all of the original publicity department left, somehow tied down like galley slaves. They should be overmuscled on one side from tugging at the oars. Instead, they were only warped where it didn't show—the way they had learned to think.

Grace came in. She pushed a wisp of her henna-tinted hair under her hat, and the sweet smile that had marched her past the outer-office echelon fell off. Her face sagged like an old purse.

She glanced at a bottle and glasses on the sideboard.

"What's up?" she asked suspiciously.

"Grace," he said, "going back down memory lane in this rumor mill, what's the worst thing that you ever faced?"

"You know damned well, Red. That time I was just starting. Grace Boomer, girl greenhorn. That famous junket Fergus made me take with Claudia Barstow, alcoholic film star."

"Well, time marches on," he said.

He poured two drinks with a generous hand.

"What gives?" asked Grace. "We haven't had drinks like this since we celebrated Leslie Charles getting snakebit on the back lot."

"You're going to have to get the callus off your derriere again, sweetheart."

"Meaning what?" asked Grace sharply. "I haven't even unpacked from that Liebestod in Italy. Look, I handled not only the press, but Greek royalty, millionaires on yachts, Martha Ralston's hillbilly relatives, four fegelas from Dior with the trousseau, representatives from fourteen nations, and a morning-sick bride, not to mention a cast of costly hambones, like Leslie Charles. All on salary, trying to get into the act, and beginning to be very suspicious about the movie being postponed indefinitely." She laughed wryly. "Funny how actors who have been sitting on their prats on salary and expense accounts get so touchy about not having their kissers on film *right now.*"

"You got our star married, didn't you?"

"Yep, assignment completed."

"Not for me," said Red. "The Bank of the West has eight million bucks tied up in sets, contracts, overhead, and running expenses on *Pallas Athena.*"

"Sue the Greek," said Grace. "He knocked up our star."

"You don't sue the richest man in the world," he said. "Fergus thought of it. Turned out, Niadas *is* the Bank of the West."

"Down periscope," said Grace.

"Remember that campaign you did for Claudia Barstow?"

"Now you're really marching down memory lane. Stars were gods and goddesses then. People worshiped Garbo, and Clark Gable, and Gary Cooper, and Leslie Howard, and Carole Lombard, and Claudia and Jeffrey Barstow. Nobody asked them how they loaded their washing machines. It was easier, people believed."

"There may be another Garbo. A young one."

"Look, Red, don't crap your old friend."

She lit a cigarette and set down her pen and pad. She suddenly folded a little, and looked old, and tired; her mouth puckered again, so he could see the lines that went all around her lips, like a drawstring purse.

"I mentioned the worst for a reason," said Red, "because I've spent two of the most startling hours of my life talking to Fergus Austin."

"I didn't know his dialogue was that good," said Grace.

Red waved her wit aside. "Look, I'm tired. I just want to go home and chew on my nitroglycerin tablets and forget about everything."

"I'll get my hat and go with you," said Grace.

"But before that happens, Titan has to recoup the *Pallas Athena* money, and get more to add to it. You've got to take the publicity campaign and revamp it for a new star."

"I can do that sort of thing in my sleep," Grace said.

"But it isn't *Pallas Athena*. It's a new script, baby, a new property, called *The Oracle*, with new characters, a different director and producer. It seems the good Lord saw fit to hand a brilliant script with the same locale, period, sets, and general cast into the eager hands of Fergus Austin, who, businesswise, was breathing his last gasp."

"Bad timing. Drat that pony express for getting through." Grace snubbed out her cigarette. "I expected a new star, of course, but what gives?"

"It seems Mr. Niadas doesn't want anyone in the

image created for his wife and mother-to-be of his child. Your publicity campaign about Martha Ralston's goddesslike quality was too good. He believed it! This will be new, from scratch."

"I'm tired," said Grace. "Give me a leave of absence. I can't go through it all again."

He ignored her.

"It's the damnedest story you ever heard. A script approved by Niadas *before* Fergus okayed it. Then, later, four tests were made at the studio. Somehow, *five* tests got to the Greek in Europe. And Niadas picked out a test us poor chickens at Titan, including Fergus, never even knew existed. The dark horse. Ain't you curious?"

"Just another blond with a good press agent who hasn't been around the track, but will, soon. Who cares? It's too confusing. Look, I need a vacation."

The buzzer sounded. "George Ritt is here."

"Send him in."

Red swung his chair around so he could talk to the stillman and still watch Grace's face.

"George," he said, "is Hank in the lab? We have to get prints out fast."

"Sure, boss," said George. "No other press photogs?"

"Exclusive," said Red.

"I got the word. The car just came through the gate," said George.

"Then get down there. And don't forget. There's a directive from Mr. Austin. There are to be no pictures printed with Jessica Barstow in the foreground or even background. Give her the full star-husband treatment."

"Empty magazine," said George. "Make 'em happy. Lots of flash and no film."

"What did you *say?*" said Grace, sitting up straight.

Red waved at her.

"Now, take lots of pictures of the new star with Max Ziska. Since he's director-producer, it's news. The kid's too young for the sex angle, so we'll use the Svengali weenie."

"Got it," said George.

Grace was standing now. She had dropped her purse. George picked it up. She took it, mouth open. George left.

Red took Grace by the elbow and steered her like a victim of catalepsy to the door.

"Sorry you can't handle it, Gracie. The star of the new film, *The Oracle,* written and produced by Maximilian Ziska, is Belinda Barstow. You know, child of Jeffrey, niece of Claudia, daughter of Jessica Klopfinger Barstow, who, incidentally, is associate producer of the Ziska company."

"Now I know it's a gag," said Grace. "Remember, old Red, we were there when Fergus Austin told Jessica hell would freeze over before she ever got in the studio again."

"Well, let's go pick up the ice cubes," said Red. "She is about to enter the private banquet room in the commissary. And Fergus is waiting. As I said. Sorry you're not interested. Anyway, you're due for a leave of absence."

"You son-of-a-bitch," said Grace, "anybody can take a vacation anytime. You louse, you horrible man—"

"Straighten your hat," he said. "The worst thing *we* ever faced. I find myself in the ridiculous position of feeling sorry for Fergus Austin. Let's go to the party and watch them pass around the crow canapés."

◆◆◆◆◆◆◆◆

"Where in God's name have you been?" shouted Fergus over the intercontinental line.

David's voice made him cringe every time he heard it. He returned his raucousness with the usual reprimand of calmness.

Although David's voice was cool, he felt pain every time he talked to his father, for the memory of the most hateful thing a man could face came back to him, a recurrent nightmare. And he could never understand the hatred that had triggered his father.

That day so long ago had seemed so auspicious to

David. He had just turned twenty-one. On the death of his grandmother, Rebecca Moses, he had inherited the major stock of Titan studio. Jessica, Fergus' secretary, had come to Stanford to tell him of his grandmother's death, as Fergus was unavailable.

David had fallen madly and instantaneously in love with her. She was only three years his senior, and a beautiful and passionate woman. They had bedded in an unforgettable night. Then and there he had asked her to marry him, never dreaming that she was his father's mistress.

When he had told his father he was going to marry Jessica, he had wondered at the silence, the abrupt dismissal. He had blamed it at the moment on his youth and the fact that he had just become the major stockholder of Titan.

But that afternoon Fergus had planned a confrontation. He had ordered Jessica into his private dressing room and was forcing her into sexual intercourse when David was ushered in.

He saw them and fled.

The fact that he had heard of Jessica marrying Jeffrey Barstow, drunk, in Tijuana on the same day confused him even more about life.

And so David had left Hollywood, joined the war effort, and had stayed in Europe, running a growing program of studio expansion in the countries which were waking up to international postwar production.

The memory flashed on and off, and David returned to the necessary business at hand.

"Father," said David, "simmer down. You don't have to yell. The connection is fine. I can hear you. I'm at the Hassler in Rome."

"You should be here," said Fergus. "You should have stopped this mess before it began. Now I have to face this ridiculous situation alone. I should think you would have settled it by now, so we don't have to go through this farce. Did you see the Greek?"

"Just got off the Niadas yacht in Capri last night," said David. "Listen, it's the middle of the night here."

"It's the middle of hell here," said Fergus. "Well?"

"It's no use. He's sold. He's got a fetish on this Barstow child." David laughed wryly. "We saw the mysterious test. He runs it all the time. She's terrific."

"Balls to that," said Fergus. "What about the situation?"

"Well, unfortunately, Jessica Barstow had the ammunition that she was your secretary for over three years. That impressed him. What could anyone say?"

There was a brief silence. Neither had mentioned her name to the other since . . .

"You could have said that spending millions on an unknown child was folly," said Fergus sourly. "The studio's future is at stake."

"The studio's future is not at stake if Niadas goes along with us just now. Ten million more dollars. You know it'll take thirty to get it back—they don't make partners like that," said David. "Look, Dad—"

"Goddamnit, don't call me that!" said Fergus. "You're thirty-seven years old! Call me Fergus!"

There was a silence on the phone.

"Are you there?" said Fergus.

"There, Fergus . . ." said David bitterly.

His voice was more distant than the miles that separated them.

"Well," said Fergus, "I could have convinced him that you must have a star potential for a budget like that. This is no gimmick picture."

"I told you, he's gone in for ten million more," said David. "That's what he thinks of the potential."

"Deliver me from amateurs," said Fergus. "For the Greek, a write-off. For me, a disaster with the other stockholders. He's playing with lives."

"He's a man of convictions," said David. "And his holdings make this a pissant operation. Don't forget, he's a professional Greek, a Hellenist. And Max Ziska has handed him the glory of Greece between two paper covers. What can we do about it?"

"If it's this great, we can get a runner ready," said Fergus. "I'll have the New York office and Abe line up every good-looking young babe with talent in New York on and off Broadway, so when this kid stubs her toe, which she will, we can at least be ready with a substitute."

"Talked to Martha Ralston on the yacht yesterday," said David. "God, what a terrible session. She read the riot act to Niadas. She said if he used that Barstow brat, and didn't wait for her to play the role, she was through. He called her bluff, and of course she buckled. She's so angry at being pregnant. That marriage is based on a very strong bond—hate."

"Oh, God," said Fergus, "patch it up. Keep the dame off his back. Next thing we know, he'll be perching on the camera crane."

"She was advised by her husband," said David patiently, "to have her billion-dollar baby, and let us plan her future. Maybe you'd better find out if any of Ziska's properties would be right for her. That might ease things up for the future."

"Will do," said Fergus, "because from what I've heard about Greeks, if she gives birth to a girl, he'll pitch her out. He wants a son out of her, nothing else."

"Incidentally," said David, "Mother called last week. How she got to the phone and got through, who knows. She must have been in a mental state good enough to read the papers. She was babbling about Belinda and Jeffrey Barstow, and somebody took the phone away from her. How did that happen?"

"What did she say?" asked Fergus after a moment. His hand clutched the cigarette in his hand, and his heart pounded.

"Babble," said David. "Listen, I've just been to Switzerland. I got delivery on the anamorphic lenses. We've decided to go wide-screen. It's our only chance on such a big project. We've got it."

"Okay, okay. I suppose we have to follow every goddamned whim of the public. I remember when people wouldn't come in a movie house unless there was a free dish with each ticket. Send me a full report on the Niadas situation on the ticker. People are stacked up like cordwood in my office, and I have to get to the commissary for that lousy press conference half an hour from now, and meet Madame Barstow and the

Ziska group. You can be prepared to have the whole shebang dumped in your territory soon."

After he hung up, David leaned back on the chair and gazed beyond his balcony to the dark, empty Roman streets below. The theater of people had gone home for private performances.

David felt isolated, having been awakened by the phone in the middle of the night in the vacuum of impersonal surroundings of the hotel room.

As he well recollected, he was soon going to have to face Jessica. Fergus had mentioned her name to him for the first time in fifteen years. That day had ended a father's and son's relationship, and also any chance he had ever had for love.

He couldn't sleep. He stepped out onto the terrace, and looked out over the city toward the Quirinal Palace; even President Gronchi, with all his problems, was asleep somewhere, and all the government staff who milled about there during the day. Even the reviled frosty and ornate Victor Emmanuel monument, referred to by some with contempt as "the wedding cake," was silvered to beauty in the moonlight.

Two carabinieri, in their flowing capes and feathered tricorn hats, stopped on the Spanish Steps to talk to two little prostitutes who were making a last stand, hoping to catch the drunken American overflow from the late spots.

David went to the side table and poured himself a gin. He listened to the clock ticking loudly in the vacuum of the night.

Ticking for what?

◆◆◆◆◆◆◆◆

In Hollywood, after Fergus hung up the phone he sat still for a moment. He felt the cold sweat on his forehead and in the palms of his hands. Time had stopped for him, too, this moment. It was not just that he knew that David Austin was not his son, but the son of Jeffrey Barstow, that shattered him. He also knew that his behavior had been so beastly to David during the years, that if he ever found out, it would be easy for David as major stockholder, along with his powerful uncle Abe Moses, to jettison him. Certainly he wouldn't be in the studio another day.

What good had it been for him to be the cover-up for Simon Moses and Claudia Barstow? What good had it been for him to marry Esther Moses and be the heir apparent? What good had it been for him to build the studio, almost brick by brick, and fashion the whole complicated factory system, as others of the old-timers had done?

Simon Moses had always been the front man. It seemed to him that most of Titan personnel had climbed on his shoulders, and he was bent with the fatigue of trying to hold up the tumbling pyramid of acrobats.

And now David, the one the world thought was his son, if he ever knew, would understand the hatred that had triggered Fergus' every act, and then he'd become a laughingstock, the man with horns, the scapegoat who had raised insane Esther Moses' and drunken Jeffrey Barstow's son as his own.

He took his handkerchief out of his breast pocket and wiped his brow. Soon he was going to face his archenemy, Jessica. She was the one who could ring the bell on the whole sad story. And he also would have to face Belinda, the other issue of Jeffrey Barstow, and smile, and be pictured with her for the future of his studio. And of course, for his, also.

◆◆◆◆◆◆◆◆

The Titan commissary had been dressed for the occasion with spring flowers and pink cloths in honor of Belinda Barstow's youth.

The nucleus of the action was the Ziska unit. Max's large white head dominated the inner circle, as he held court, with Belinda by his side.

He was so involved discussing picture-making, trends, and his vision of his own script, that it seemed to evade his consciousness that he was at a studio party to introduce Belinda Barstow to the press. He greeted new people and old acquaintances with a brief handshake, and went on expostulating. Occasionally he beamed upon Belinda with an affectionate and abstract air, as Red Powell and Grace Boomer performed introductions.

Moving about, as opportunity prompted, was the chic Jessica Barstow, renewing the sudden friendship and enthusiasm of people who had not talked to her for fifteen years.

As associate producer of the Ziska unit, she was a woman of importance; she would undoubtedly firm up a staff, deal with casting, and select the favorites who would travel to Europe. A large number of the departmental members of higher standing, who had been invited to fill up the corners of the large room, informed her that she should have been actively engaged in production a long time ago, and it was wonderful to see Titan really come to life again, with some knowledgeable talent that realized, for a change, what it was doing. Most of these comments were judiciously made before Fergus Austin came to the party, as everyone was confused about her reappearance on the scene.

The positive protons, milling about the atomic center of the party, might be considered the executives, for without their selections, this particular flotsam and jetsam would not be present. These tycoons, distinguished by their dark suits, had flown in like a wedge of geese from the East. They were mostly members of the board. They all mingled with stars and contract players, who had been invited to the shindig to dress the set, after a careful screening of their habits and potentials.

The working press, once having listened politely to Max, tucked away an exclusive quote, met Belinda, and had their pictures snapped with her, cluttered about the bar and the elaborate buffet.

"I don't see why you have to make this picture abroad," Clarissa Pennock complained to Grace, who was signaling a waiter to bring the lady a double martini, knowing this usually brought about better comments in her syndicated column. "I think Hollywood is as good as Rome or Greece anytime."

"I agree," said Grace, "but it's a matter of all those blocked funds from our wonderful pictures abroad. And also, goodwill, Clarissa, you know, the image of Belinda Barstow, of *the* Barstows, with all that talent and fresh young beauty."

"Yes," said Miss Pennock, watching Belinda as she stood in the reception line like a good girl at a finishing school, "she is just beautiful. But I think the name Belinda is too long. I think you should call her Linda."

"Maybe so," said Grace, knowing such an ultimatum would have to come from Fergus. When it came to anything as important as changing a name, she had no authority on policy.

"You know," she said to Clarissa, "I really can't tell you how we all feel at Titan about having this precious Barstow child make this picture. Do you realize what this means? This great, great beauty, with this great, great talent, from this great, great family . . ."

Clarissa shook her head in wonder.

"I'm going to let you have the first call on her portrait sitting in London. That's the kind of sentimental slob I am. I was told you ran the first one of her Aunt Claudia Barstow."

"What a memory!" said Clarissa. "Back in 1914 . . ."

"I feel all choked up," said Grace, "and I have plans to get a shot of the same pose with the niece. You could run Claudia *and* Belinda, two great Titan stars, aunt and niece!"

"Double page," said Clarissa.

"Oh, Clarissa," said Grace, snatching a passing bourbon off a tray, "sometimes being a tired old p.a. is worth it."

"Jaysus me beads!" said little redheaded Mickey Ritchey, member of the board, "here comes old Fergus hisself, headed for Jessica."

He almost whispered the words to Red. Mickey had been at the studio Christmas party fifteen years ago, the memorable and often discussed night that Jessica Klopfinger had decamped to elope with Jeffrey Barstow, after being thrown out of Max Ziska's set, along with him.

Mickey had never known exactly what it was all about, but he had heard many rumors.

A few of them: Jessica was Fergus' mistress; she had copied his private papers; she had not informed Fergus when his son, David, inherited controlling stocks and bonds from his grandmother, Rebecca Moses. Jessica, who was then twenty-four, had then tried to seduce young David Austin into marrying her the night he turned twenty-one. And looking at the white-haired Max Ziska, Mickey also remembered the rumor that Jessica and Max, and Fergus and a studio cop, and Red Powell and Grace had had some sort of a brannigan two hours before she eloped with Jeffrey Barstow.

Mickey thought to himself: Of course, all these rumors couldn't be true. No dame could be that busy. It goes to show, a studio is a lousy rumor factory.

But as he stared at Fergus, what he couldn't know was that all these tales *were* true.

Fergus walked directly to Jessica with the elegant casualness that was his trademark. He put out his hand.

"Well, Jessica," he said quietly, "this is indeed an auspicious occasion."

Jessica held up her kid-gloved hand. She looked at Fergus through the veil of her chic hat. She stood as straight and slim, she reminded herself, as she had when as a young woman she had seen him last. His face now seemed that of a stranger. It was longer, dryer, and much more fatigued than the face she remembered. He had moved from the vigor of a young middle age to old age in these fifteen years. His body seemed sere and tidy. Jessica wondered that she had ever known it so well. Ignoring the disaster of her last meeting with him and the passion that had preceded it, she moved slowly, for she knew she must be most cautious.

"Mr. Austin, this is my daughter, Belinda. Belinda, this is Mr. Austin."

It was like a woman introducing her child to her old revered professor. Yes. Yes. *The* Mr. Austin. The vice-president in charge of production. Wheeler dealer. The man who robbed me of my chance for love. The man who humiliated me and everything I could be. The man who a thousand times could have been your father.

The man who is now going to see the object of his hatred become a great star. The man I'm going to screw another kind of way to make up for what he did.

Fergus turned his unseeing eyes on Belinda. He did not see a girl, stepping into an incandescent beauty of young womanhood, her slender body dressed in a pale-blue dress, her feet in simple slippers, her physical being dominated by the black-lashed blue Barstow eyes, and startling yellow hair falling into tendrils around her shoulders. He saw her as revenge incarnate. She was the proof that made his cry of "Lie!" untrue. She was Jessica's delayed triumph, and a vengence that had taken great doing to prove.

He prepared himself, as he did with his enemies, locked in mortal business combat, not to see her face, but what was behind her being and this meeting for himself.

This woman had cost him a son and peace in his old age. She had given him insomnia for fifteen years. Now he was faced with the competitive blockbuster era of picture-making, and he knew only too well the financial shoals that Titan films was trying to navigate. The life's blood of his career was in the thirty percent distribution this colossus of a picture would give the company. He had no choice but to accept the ultimatum of Niadas and his money, however it had come about.

The apparent calm that was his trademark stamped his masklike face. It had gotten him through many a meeting with a poise that was legendary.

Jessica, looking through her perky veil, smiled coolly at Fergus. Revenge. She remembered how he had taunted her: "That paretic old bastard couldn't have a child."

Well, look, she thought. You can see for yourself she's a Barstow, just like you have been seeing for yourself since you knew these fifteen years past when I told you that David Austin was the spitting image of Jeffrey Barstow. Maybe you denied it to yourself, maybe you thought I'd pulled a fastie, but you've certainly checked your dates a thousand times, Mr. Austin.

But now was the time to be gracious, lovely Jessica Barstow, back at the home lot once again, with a star to add luster to the Titan heavens, a star who, because of her and (oh, mills of the gods!) Max Ziska, and a Greek tycoon whose power reached halfway around the world, was pretty well protected, even from the Austin clutches.

Let Fergus blink his ice-cold blueberry-and-milk eyes, let him face the stares of the old-timers who knew he was stuck; there was nothing he could do but be nice. His ass was in a sling, and he knew it.

So Jessica smiled with dignity, made a public gesture of handing her child over to Mr. Austin, and moved slightly back, trusting to Belinda's youth and beauty and the waiting press to do the rest. What a pity, she thought, that the real truth can't be shouted aloud.

Belinda smiled at Fergus Austin. The eyes were without guile, and he found himself slightly defenseless. Usually smiles at him were predicated, and far from virginal. So this one, from eyes so transparent that he seemed to be peering right through her head, undid him.

As he looked upon her beauty, he saw a little of Aunt Claudia, beautiful Claudia, his first love.

He saw Jeffrey Barstow in her eyes.

He saw Jessica, young, and lithe, and brash, at the age of twenty-one.

Then he saw her kinship to his son, David, at that age—before he knew—and anger clouded his mind; Belinda's deep young voice broke his reverie.

"Oh, Mr. Austin, I'm so glad to meet you."

It was the Barstow voice, and it disturbed him.

Christ, next thing she's going to say: "Mommy has told me all about you." But she stopped at that, and as George Ritt stepped forward with his camera, Jessica moved in, to be in the picture. Fergus looked up into the eyes of Red Powell. The quick flicker of an eye revealed to him that everything was under control. No film in the camera.

George snapped away with a slightly overdone efficiency with one camera, then, as Fergus turned to greet Max Ziska, focused another, a live magazine, and took pictures while Grace Boomer hauled Jessica away to chat with Clarissa Pennock about Belinda.

"Max," said Fergus, shaking Ziska's hand, "I have just finished your script. It's great. Beautiful."

Max shook hands with him briefly, and combed his fingers through his white hair. Although the last time he had seen Fergus he had been thrown out on the street, never to return to Titan studio until now, the incident did not remain too strongly in his mind. So many more dreadful things had happened to him in the war-torn interval, that Fergus Austin did not really exist. He was merely an image, used to get on with picture-making.

"I am enchanted with this child," said Max, "and I am delighted she is going to begin her career with me in *The Oracle*."

Andrew Reed was a veteran newspaper columnist whose destiny had followed Titan's from its beginning. He knew where many a skeleton was hidden, and had revealed some of them to the public. His syndicated gossip column was so important that he had been flown in from New York for the bash.

He moved in to hear what the two forces were going to say to each other. Flashbulbs popped.

"You know, Andrew," said Fergus, "how auspicious it is that another Barstow is coming to Titan films."

The two men were photographed looking gravely at each other. For years they had not talked due to Andrew's revelation of Claudia Barstow's role in the death of Simon Moses at their hideaway, but time, tide, and a growing motion-picture-column syndication had given them both sudden amnesia.

"And also," said Andrew, "it is delightful to me that Leslie Charles will be in her film."

Fergus nodded and tried not to show that his soul was torn. He knew what reams of publicity would come from that situation. Everyone knew Andrew Reed had been longing for a chance to get back in Leslie's life since he had become such a great star.

Grace Boomer brought a glass for Belinda.

"Here's a Coke, dear. You've been standing here over an hour."

Belinda took it gratefully. The line broke up.

"It's a love feast," whispered Grace to the two foreign news pressmen, André Giroux and Esteban López, who stood bowing with champagne glasses in their hands.

"Regardez, Steve," said André, "caviar, Malossal caviar."

"She's going to be a big star," said López, gesturing toward the tins of caviar. "They didn't even do this for Jeffrey and Claudia."

"A love feast," insisted Grace. She peered over her shoulder a little nervously. Red Powell caught her eye and winked, as he joined Jessica chatting with Clarissa Pennock and her henchmen. After all, you had to be careful that the bitch didn't give out an interview that would get herself the banner headline as one of the few women associate producers in town.

◆◆◆◆◆◆◆◆

"These clothes will be a godsend to your cousins Deanna and Shirley in New Orleans," said Jessica. "We'll get more things in Rome that will suit your image better."

She put the last of Belinda's dresses in the box, and tucked in a shabby white fur rabbit holding a silken carrot in its mouth.

"Father gave me that!" said Belinda, snatching it back. "I want to keep it."

"Be reasonable," said Jessica. "I haven't got time to analyze all this junk. And another thing, you look very pretty in the wardrobe tests, but you're going to have to fine down a little. You could lose about five pounds without any harm. We'll put you on grapefruit and melba toast for breakfast for a while."

"But I'm not overweight, Mother."

"The camera adds a few pounds," said Jessica. "I'm sure when you get working it'll be easier. Anyway, Effie's inclined to stuff you."

"I want Effie to come with us."

"We've had that out. It would be difficult to travel with a colored person, and we wouldn't want to embarrass her, would we, now?"

The doorbell rang.

"It's Max," said Jessica. "We're taking you to the Derby for dinner. Answer the door, dear. I'll get my purse."

Belinda rushed down. Max walked in and looked at the denuded living room.

All the knickknacks had been stowed, the rug was rolled up, and the paintings had been crated for storage, including the elegant Bellows portrait of Jeffrey, in top hat and tails.

"The room looks raped," he said.

He smiled at Belinda, and saw the sadness on her face.

"What is it, my darling?"

"Oh, Max, why does it have to be like this?"

He looked into her eyes, as he had not for some time.

Recently he had seen only Alethea, pythoness of Apollo, but now he looked at Belinda Barstow.

"What is wrong?" he asked.

"Max," said Belinda, "it isn't that I don't want to go. I want to be Alethea. But it's all so fast. My school, my class will graduate without me, after we made all the plans. And I want Effie to go, too. She's taken care of me since I was born."

Max put his hand on hers.

"My dear, your mother says it would be much better to get someone in Rome."

"Better for who . . . whom?"

Jessica came downstairs. She was pulling on white wrist-length gloves, symbol of her elegance.

"Put on your new navy coat, dear."

While Belinda got her coat in the hall closet, Jessica signaled at Max, raising her eyebrows significantly.

"Belinda seems to think it's hard to pull up roots. Of course, she can't see what a wonderful life she's going to have abroad."

"I don't want to talk about it," said Belinda. "Let's just get out of here."

She gestured at the dismantled room with despair. Max was overwhelmed for the moment at how very young she was. They left.

The trees were blotting out the last vestige of twilight, and lights were turning on as they walked up toward Wilshire.

"It's a pretty street," said Belinda wistfully.

"Don't act as if we won't ever come back," said Jessica. "And when we do, dear, we'll have a house on the right side of Santa Monica Boulevard, likely with a swimming pool."

"I like it right here," said Belinda.

Jessica linked her arm into Max's.

"She's a stubborn little Barstow," she said.

◆◆◆◆◆◆◆◆

Edmund, the headwaiter of the Brown Derby, ushered them to a corner banquette, and they settled down with their menus.

Red Powell and Grace Boomer, with Clarissa Pennock in tow, stopped by their table. She beamed down from under a silk cabbage-rose hat, and Max rose from the banquette.

"Oh, now, Max," she said, "you're always such a gentleman!"

"Do join us," said Jessica, moving over.

"Oh, we can't stop a minute," said Grace. "We're going to the preview of the picture Leslie Charles made before he left for Rome. You'll love working with him."

"And we have good news," said Red, smiling at Jessica. "It's a great coincidence, running into you."

Red blinked, and Belinda saw her mother smile. Setup, put-on . . . no coincidence.

"Yes," said Miss Pennock, "and I'm so thrilled that I got to see you before I break it in my column. Banner, of course. Guess what?"

Jessica raised her eyebrows politely.

"Well, the powers that be and I had a meeting, and I have the honor of naming your darling child," said Miss Pennock.

"What do you mean?" asked Belinda. "I've got a name."

"Now, you know you can't be Belinda," said Grace.

"Of course," said Miss Pennock. "Belinda, Bedelia . . . you know. Just no good for a theater marquee, dear, and they took my suggestion."

"And there's B.B., Brigitte Bardot—the new little French sex kitten," said Grace.

"So," said Miss Pennock, "you're going to be *Linda* Barstow from now on."

Belinda half-rose from her seat.

"Linda's a crummy name. There are at least six of them in my school. Father named me Belinda, after his grandmother, Belinda Pierce, you know."

"Yes, I know," said Miss Pennock. "She played Ophelia and Juliet at Drury Lane and the Old Vic. But Linda is a lovely name. I have a grandchild named Linda."

She looked at Belinda coolly.

"I still don't like it," said Belinda.

Jessica interrupted.

"I always wanted to call her Linda. We are terribly honored that you cared so much to name her."

"But it's not my name!" said Belinda.

Miss Pennock seemed irritated. She tossed her head haughtily.

"It's a great name on a marquee," Red assured her.

Miss Pennock left, flanked by Red's and Grace's guiding hands. She'd had four martinis. They hoped she'd sleep through Leslie Charles's last Hollywood picture, (one he made before he was shipped off to Rome) that always made her give a better review.

"That child needs watching," she said loudly as they got her through the swinging doors.

"You were terribly rude," Jessica said. "We had better send her some flowers tomorrow."

"I think she is very rude," said Max. "Belinda should be part of any personal decisions."

Belinda slid out of the banquette.

"Where are you going?" asked Jessica.

"The girl's room," said Belinda.

She passed the bar, and fled into the little room behind swinging doors. A maid sat reading *Daily Variety.*

Belinda clutched her little kid handbag.

"Have you a piece of notepaper?" she asked the maid.

"They's a pad by the phone."

Belinda took an eyebrow pencil from a glass dish and scrawled her message: "You've even taken my name. I quit. Belinda."

"Take this note to Mr. Ziska's table in ten minutes. It's in the corner, next to the entrance to the bar."

She gave the maid a dime and cautiously edged her way out of the bar, through the little door on Wilshire, and crossed the street.

Belinda got on a Wilshire bus headed toward Los Angeles. She transferred, and crossed town in the unfamiliar world of darkness. She got off and walked a few blocks down South Bronson. Good thing she'd come several times to stay with Effie when her mother was in Palm Springs.

Black kids rode on bikes, and skated on sidewalks under a street lamp, and some teenagers in an old souped-up Ford roared by. Music was blatting out of some of the houses, and folks sat on front porches, talking and laughing.

She came to the neat white duplex, with its privet hedges and the geraniums growing in terra-cotta pots along the wooden porch railings.

There was the wonderful smell, as she walked onto the porch, of ham frying, and an apricot pie just out of an oven. She rang the bell.

Ottie, Effie's little granddaughter, answered it, wearing an outgrown pink dress of Belinda's.

"Why, B'linda! Come on in." She swung the door open. "Gramma, guess who's here!"

Effie came to the opening between the kitchen and the fumed-oak dining room. She peered into the darkness of the parlor, and then recognized Belinda.

"Honey-bun, what on earth are you doing here?"

Belinda put her arms about her, buried her face in her neck, and sobbed.

"Now, now," said Effie, "this won't do."

She took Belinda down a hallway, into her bedroom, and sat her down on the brass bed. Belinda noticed an assortment of snapshots, mostly of her, tucked in the mirror frame of the bureau.

"Effie, they've gone too far. I've run away. It isn't me anymore, anyway. They've even taken my name away."

"You just can't run, baby."

Belinda hung her head.

"I know it. I sat on that bus, it seemed hours. And every car that passed, I thought was following me."

"They'll figure you're here."

As if in answer, the telephone rang.

"You know who it is got to be," said Effie quickly. "I have to say you're here, or I'll be in a heap of trouble."

It's a white world, her frightened eyes seemed to say.

Ottie answered the phone.

"Gramma, it's for you."

"Coming," said Effie.

"I'll talk," said Belinda. "Let me talk. They have to listen to what I have to say."

◆◆◆◆◆◆◆◆

The house on Bronson was quiet after Belinda had been taken away.

Now was the time of day that Effie paused for a ritual, which had existed in her family since dim beginnings in a small log cabin, one of many set deep in the woods behind a Carolina plantation house.

Effie's mother had come west to be maid for a lady singer on the Barbary Coast. She had the green eyes of the portly owner of the plantation where she was born. She waited until her last hours to initiate Effie into the mystery of her secret possession.

Before she lapsed into her final sleep, the old woman reached under her pillow for a worn chamois-skin pouch. She handed it to her daughter.

"This belong to yore grandpappy, his wife wun' let 'im use it in the big house, so it comfort him in yore granny's cabin. When he pass on, nacherly it come to us. We call it Mr. MacDonald's comfort. It was all he lef' us of what he was, 'ceptin' the fine skin we come by, way of Scotlan'."

Effie opened the pouch to draw out a meerschaum pipe. Its bowl was a carved Indian head, yellowed and browned with age and use. Effie took its slender stem into her hand, and her mother clasped her brown gnarled hand over the bowl.

"No matter who own you, you jes' fine one time of day when you belongs to you. You stuff this pipe with good ole Bull, and sit back, an' no matter what happin, you thinks straight fer you, and figger yore way outta hard or soft. My mammy and me suck wisdom f'om this pipe. You fine one time of day belong to you, you kin make out. That's where white folks does it wrong. They don' seek no time they belongs to themselves."

Long after her mother was buried, Effie, facing her own tribulations, the conscience about her lapse with Jeffrey Barstow, the petulance of Jessica, and the worry about her own children, contrasted to her constant care of little Belinda, found her courage by closing her door against the outside world. She would take the pipe out of the little pouch, tamp Bull Durham into the tiny bowl, draw the string closed with her teeth, and light up, sucking the tobacco into life carefully. She would review her problems while the coal glowed, trying to seek what course the Lord wanted her to follow.

Belinda's trapped.... She can't be alone with

strangers. Jessica'll be busy. Of course, Belinda'll have Mr. Max when she works, but what about the rest? . . . Going to bed in a strange land without someone to turn the lights out, or wake her up with a voice she knows. . . . My kids are grown up. I'm just a baby-sitter to the grandchildren. . . . There's one who needs me; my honey-bun. And of course, that poor little dog. He'd get lost. . . .

The meerschaum burned down to the black lump that was only a remembrance of the glowing fragrance it had been. Effie cleaned it carefully, caressing the bowl.

She glanced at the photographs wedged around her bureau mirror. She realized what a pang the snapshots would give her if Belinda were far away and needing her.

She carefully tucked Mr. MacDonald's comfort in its chamois pouch. She knew what she must do.

If anyone had suggested to Effie that she was being traded for privilege, she would have denied it hotly. Her world was boundaried to the north, south, east, and west by her love and responsibility to Mr. Jeffrey's child. To begin with, there was the sense of guilt that she could have given birth to a child by him, the same day, conceived under the same mad circumstances, born out of a doctor's nostrums. His rape of her was not his fault; he was stimulated sexually through no choice of his own. As time had passed, she had looked upon his last years with pity for his loneliness, and pleasure at his delight in Belinda. She, too, fell in love with the child. And since she had from the beginning looked upon Jessica as a user, she knew that Belinda needed love and comfort. The fact that Belinda, never having known anything else, accepted her ministrations and care without thought, pleased her; she belonged. Perhaps it was a gut-deep cry into the past of her people. She was only grateful that the child to whom she was bound loved her and needed her.

She felt it was Belinda who had bartered. She had given up her own name, Belinda, for the privilege of having Effie come with her to Europe.

Effie grinned to herself. For Belinda would outsmart them. Just before she left, she had put her arms around Effie and whispered, "Just don't you worry. I'll go with the Linda idea just now, to get you to go, Effie. But when I'm of age and sign my own contract, it's going to be Belinda Barstow or no show!"

And now, henceforth, she must become adjusted to being Linda. It seemed so easy for everyone else.

The departure of the Ziska unit at International Airport was handled according to standard celebrity treatment.

"Red is handling the press in the VIP room," said Grace. "Those are such pretty orchids, dear."

"Miss Pennock sent them. They're not very appropriate. But she said, 'To my godchild, with my love.' " Linda scoffed, "She's *not* my godmother!"

"She is now," said Grace sharply, but she quickly corrected herself. "I mean, dear, because she named you. What had you planned to say to the press?"

"Well, I know one thing," said Linda. "I'm not going to say 'I'm thrilled to be going to Rome.' Who'd quote anything that dumb?"

"God love you," said Grace, smiling sweetly. "What did you plan to say?"

"I'll work it out," said Linda, battling for a scrap of her own identity.

Here it comes again, thought Grace. Just like the others, the great, lost cavalcade; some of them now fat salesmen and frustrated hausfraus. But remember when they were this age. Full of piss and vinegar, coming out with those embarrassing little bon mots full-blown from their pearly-gray brains. Hello, Jackie Coogan, Ben Alexander, Mickey Rooney, Jackie Cooper, Freddie Bartholomew, Judy Garland, and all. . . . Hello, Shirley Temple, Skippy Homeier, Deanna Durbin, Bonita Granville, Mitzi Green, Cora Witherspoon, Margaret O'Brien, Natalie Wood, Elizabeth Taylor, and now Linda Barstow.

"Linda, dear," said Jessica, implying that she was a fairly bright idiot, "you know we had a talk."

Here comes the mom voice, thought Grace. It always starts in strong, like a bassoon, and ends up like a woodwind lost in a swamp. Funny, the mom voice being in Jessica Klopfinger Barstow. Real offbeat casting.

Grace resented Jessica's assurance. I wonder if she thinks part of my job is to help publicize her rise to power. She'll learn.

As Frank Whitbeck used to say over at Metro: "Illusion is the only thing we have to sell." And the only illusion in this car, in spite of Max's talent, is this beautiful kernel of Barstow.

Linda turned around to see the limousine following. She waved.

Effie smiled nervously in her front seat, next to the chauffeur in the luggage car. She wore a gray suit and her church hat, trimmed with tulle. She clutched her purse, containing her passport, traveler's checks, and Mr. MacDonald's comfort in the chamois bag.

A crowd was milling about as they pulled up to the airline entrance.

"We'd better take the side entrance and get Linda out for the VIP room," said Grace.

"That's a big gang for the plane," said Linda.

"It's to see you—you might as well get used to it."

"It can't be me," said Linda. "I haven't even been in a movie yet."

Grace smiled.

"My dear child, you've had a lot of publicity already."

She neglected to say that Titan had paid fifty teenagers, and from this, a crowd of standard idlers and tourists, nursed by an announcement in the papers, had built up to a fair-size mob.

Two policemen stepped forward and held back a line of screaming girls, and the car passed through a side gate, which automatically closed behind them. They passed through corridors, and up an elevator to the VIP Club, a private reception room where drinks were being served to a group of friends and press.

The intercom announced the forthcoming flight of the DC-7 for New York.

Red, the Pied Piper, led the way down the stairs and out a gate where they could board the plane without danger of being mobbed by people who were hired by the hour to mob them.

◆◆◆◆◆◆◆◆◆

From Idlewild Airport the Titan party passed through the whirling kaleidoscope of New York. Given the VIP treatment, they were installed in luxurious suites on the *Queen Mary.*

After the confusion of passengers going ashore and the excitement of sailing, Linda watched the shoreline seem to slide away. She fell into the pattern of shipboard routine, all of it so organized and different from normal life that it seemed there had never been another existence.

Incredibly to Linda, the shorelines of the foreign land appeared. She was excited, and also, deep within herself, fearful, for she knew that it was the beginning of a new life for her, and what it was to be, she could not imagine.

Max and Jessica and Effie were busy packing, saying farewells to the bosom friends of a few days, and as Linda stood at the railing, bundled up and looking out on the swirling waters, she shivered, as if something in her was alerting her to her own shoals ahead.

II

LONDON:

1956

1

The shouting of cockney porters and longshoremen and the gold-braided elegance of the baggage porter who had been sent to Southampton from the Dorchester Hotel to expedite the handling of luggage were exciting to Linda.

She anticipated green pastoral meadows with frolicking lambs, villages with thatch roofs, thin church steeples, and quaint inns and pubs. She saw satisfactory flashes of a few of these after the boat train left the dun, commercial seaport. But most of the dreary trackway led to more squalid scenes, railroad yards, with their constant freight of scrap iron and obsolete engines, the commercial litter that signals approach to a large and ancient city.

She wasn't prepared for the grimy ugliness of the outskirts of London. The pewter-gray silhouettes of the distant city all passed. They were replaced by dreary dwellings, traffic-burdened streets, cobblestone squares rimmed with stalls and barrows, and everywhere drab crowds.

Linda was startled that there were still remnants of war wounds, pits in the city that had not yet been filled in after the blitz ten years gone.

Max sat opposite her at the dining table on the train, the crumbs of his heavy tea cake still on the plate before him.

"Why do we have to come here?" she asked, shuddering. "Why didn't we just fly to Rome?"

"That is what I have been asking myself," said Max.

Jessica adjusted the draped chiffon veil of her traveling hat.

"London is the hub of the whole English-speaking press," she said. "We will launch the publicity campaign at the press conference, and set up interviews for the future here. This is, in a sense, Linda's debut."

"I would say offhand," said Max, "that *The Oracle* is Linda's debut. I do not agree that she should be exposed to the British press. It's the sharpest and most searing group of columnists in the world."

"The Barstow name belongs to London's theatrical history," said Jessica, "and I think it is most fitting for her to meet the press here. A London dateline on a story has quality. And, of course, David Austin, who has more Titan stock than anyone, runs the whole foreign policy from his office here. In case you aren't aware of it, foreign film money has jumped from five to over seventy million annually the last few years. It is very important that David Austin meet Linda."

"Very?" asked Max.

She cast him a fast glance, and patted his hand.

The train pulled from the depressing maze of track in the railroad yard to the perpetual twilight of Victoria Station.

Effie gathered up overcoats and packages, and they stood in the press of travelers eager to get out of the limbo of the boat train.

"I hope Sarge is all right," said Linda. "I'll never make a movie in England. Imagine quarantining a nice, clean little dog."

"Don't worry, he's with his buddies at London airport kennels. You'll see him in a couple of days," said Effie.

Linda peered out at the crowd standing on the platform.

"I see Grace Boomer! Oh, look, a man's with her."

A ruddy-faced man with a bristling moustache was guiding her by the elbow. He wore tweeds, and a jaunty porkpie hat. Linda was pushed aside by her mother. An expression of disappointment crossed her face, as if she had not expected him.

"Well, who is that?" she said, straightening again.

They stepped onto the platform.

Grace bustled up, bursting with cheerfulness.

"Greetings!" she said. "You all look as if you'd had a good crossing. This is Sidney Keyes from the London office. Mrs. Barstow, Mr. Ziska, and Linda, of course."

Sidney shook hands all the way around.

"Sorry we couldn't make the boat train. Beastly hour."

He escorted them through the throngs to two Rolls-Royces awaiting outside. A third car, a Humber, was lined up for luggage. Linda halted, intrigued at the strange confusion of a foreign railroad station.

Jessica, Linda, and Max got into the rear of the first Rolls, Effie in the front.

Grace got in the second Rolls with Sidney, whom she had known in Italy. She heaved a sigh of relief.

"It's great to get away from Madame Barstow," she said. "She is programmed for complete self-interest. You can hear the wheels. And I wonder what's going to happen when she and David cross swords?

"What do you think of Linda?"

"I'm utterly puzzled," he said. "Her beauty is breathtaking. But I don't think I've ever seen a candidate for more trouble. Gad, imagine at her age being shoved into being high priestess of Titan studio, responsible for feast or famine. And with Jessica Barstow standing breathing down her neck."

"It's passed a few minds," said Grace. "That's why I brought a hogshead of bourbon with me."

"Ziska seems a decent sort. I wonder how long she'll lead him about on a leash?"

"He's been so busy; maybe he hasn't noticed," said Grace, "but looks to me like he's beginning to curl around the edges. I have one basic rule along the hard, bumpy road of life, Sid. Never worry about alcoholics or geniuses. They plot their own orbits."

In the Ziska Rolls, once Linda had become accustomed to the left-hand driving, which promised imminent destruction, she peered with interest at the green parks, where people strolled about or sat in their folding chairs enjoying the rarity of the warm summer afternoon.

"No wonder the English love their parks," said Linda, peering up at gray beehive buildings, "the places they have to live in."

"It seems to me that we could have had a much better reception," said Jessica.

"I loathe publicity," said Max.

"Necessary evil," said Jessica. "Comb your hair, Linda, there might be photographers at the hotel. And another thing, when you meet David Austin, don't pull that sad, sad tale of yours about missing graduation. Impress him with your interest in playing Alethea, and what you think of Max's script. A great deal is tied up in this production."

"Let her say what she thinks," said Max. "She is a powerful force in herself. And her youth must not be used for or against her."

Jessica smothered her annoyance. This was the first time he had crossed her. She'd be glad when he got on the set and she could run things her way.

Max reached across her and put his hand on Linda's shoulder.

"Do not be afraid to be what you are. Use it."

◆◆◆◆◆◆◆◆

The large oaken-beamed sitting room at the Dorchester was warmed by a huge fireplace. French doors opened onto a balcony overlooking Hyde Park. At each side were bedrooms with dressing rooms and baths connecting. Adjoining them, Max had a suite.

The room was filled with elaborate flowers, done in the larger-than-life elegance that characterized posh English floral arrangements.

"I didn't know we had so many friends," said Linda.

Jessica smiled wryly.

"All business-deductible; all deductible."

A waiter dressed in white tie and tails wheeled in a table laden with tea and cakes. To Linda the whole scene took on the vision of an Arabian night's magic carpet. These were the rewards of prominence, luxury far beyond anything she had dreamed at home.

She reached for a pastry. Jessica put her hand out.

"Now, we'll stop that right now," she said. "We aren't going to 'snack on' a few pounds."

Linda put her hands in her lap, and it entered her mind that perhaps all these tributes to success could be empty if you couldn't enjoy them.

Grace poured herself a free drink from a sideboard and took a list out of her bulging reticule.

"I don't like to rush you," she said, "but time is of the essence. You'd probably like a rundown on who's coming to the reception tomorrow."

She instinctively had dialed to the wavelength that was most comfortable in her relationship to Jessica.

She read off the lists of the guests, their magazines, and the type of coverage that could be expected in the run-of-the-mill power drive of the Titan publicity machine. Grace pressed its infallible importance. Even Jessica, who had long been out of action and had never been exposed to the international publicity of this new era, was astounded at the millions of eager people who paid money to devour picture propaganda.

Nothing pleased her more than the thought of airplanes full of editors, photographers, reporters, and cameramen flying from key cities all over Europe and the Near East, not only to do homage to her child, but to the importance of the Ziska unit, which would also carry the name Jessica Barstow as associate producer.

The fact that *The Oracle* production would flash on the screen "Fergus Austin presents a Max Ziska Production" also titillated her. A wave of excitement, almost sexual, engulfed her as she realized that David Austin would soon be involved in her life again. Both he and his father, in spite of how they personally felt, would have to create a working social relationship with her.

"Who is this Sidney Keyes person?" she asked. "Publicity?"

"Not exactly," said Grace.

"Exactly what?" asked Jessica.

"He's sort of liaison with David Austin. You see, David has to hop all over Europe, and while he's gone, Sidney is your contact with the home office here. He signs vouchers, approves budgets and castings, and all those details."

She waved her drink airily.

"I think I'll get a refill."

"Who said we have to have a liaison man?"

"I really don't know how the office functions. After all, I'm a stranger here myself. I suppose you'll have to ask David Austin. He ought to drop by sometime soon."

She looked at her watch.

"Oh, dear, I didn't know it was so late. You know, the sun never goes down in the summertime here. The people from *Paris-Match* are in, and I have to take them to Les Ambassadeurs for supper. I have a fierce day tomorrow, juggling planes, trains, and hotel accommodations. Titan's putting out about twenty thou on this little bash; they've taken the ballroom downstairs. Have to drop by to see what the Constance Spry staff has done about the flowers. I'll check in by phone from the office."

She escaped.

◆◆◆◆◆◆◆◆

In Max's suite, he and Sidney relaxed over drinks.

"I'm not used to traveling with women," said Max. "It's stifling."

"I'll take 'em off your back," said Sidney. "After David drops by, maybe we could take Mrs. Barstow out to dinner. There's a quiet little club, the Ward Room, around the corner on Curzon Street. People like Huston and Preminger frequent it. Then we'll drop her, and I'll take you on the town if you wish."

"Thanks," said Max. "Right now, all I'm interested in is getting down to the office on Wardour Street tomorrow. Can you get me an office and secretary? I have some notes to transcribe."

"Arranged," said Sidney.

The chap was either a loner, and would take care of himself, Sidney thought, or he had a private arrangement with Mrs. Barstow, which was convenient. A relief; most of these talented egomaniacs came off ships and planes, and because they were in a foreign place, immediately had to prove their sexual prowess. He believed his home town, London, to be the wickedest city anywhere, with all sorts of possibilities for the most exotic-minded, although usually, when the celebrities hit Paris, they all parked wives and sweethearts in their hotels, called a conference, and immediate frantic calls were made to Madame Billie or her sort to fill the bill. They had to do it at once the French way. There was something very revolting, thought Sidney, about charging a moment of supposed ecstasy to an expense account.

"When is that wretched press affair?" asked Max.

"Tomorrow, the usual resident and peripatetic freeloaders. From all the *gemütlich* nations. Due to our little stink in Suez, you can forget Egypt. Miserable market, anyway."

"I could forget it all," said Max. "It seems very far away from the days we just got talented people together and started out to tell a story. But tell me about David. What is he like?"

Sidney scowled, wrinkling his bushy red brows over his light eyes.

"Difficult to explain him," he said. "I think David's very busy riding a cock horse to Banbury Cross. He's found rings on their fingers and bells on their toes. But he's never found one who made music wherever she goes."

"I see," said Max.

He didn't.

The phone sounded its strident English bell. Sidney could hear the sharp voice of Jessica as Max answered.

"Max, please come up to my suite. David Austin has just called from the lobby. He's on his way up."

"Battle stations, I presume," said Sidney, as they walked down the corridor. They heard the muffled glide of the elevator door as it slammed shut down the hall.

Jessica was ensconced on the sofa with a teacup poised in her hand. Her pose alerted Max; she was nervous.

There was a knock. Sidney answered the door.

David Austin entered, casting Sidney a grateful glance for his presence.

Max came forward to greet him.

David as an adult was not what he had expected. He was slender, but even his Savile Row suit did not conceal a muscular tautness. His face, for a man of thirty-seven, was boyish, having no frown or laughter lines. Although Max remembered that David was only a few years Jessica's junior, he seemed quite a bit younger. He noted Jessica's white knuckles as she gripped the teacup.

David's blue eyes contrasted with his tanned skin under dark brows. His hair was blond. He wore it combed straight back and longish, in the English style. There was something about his economy of motion that seemed reminiscent to Max. He certainly, in no way, had the nervous energy about him that marked Fergus Austin. He seemed much more compact and an entity in his handsomeness. Max had heard rumors of the loveliness of his mother, Esther; he even remembered one evening with Jeffrey Barstow, sitting by the glowing logs of his fireplace in the study, when Jeffrey, the iconoclast, had mentioned women in toto, and stopped to say that in her early days, before her illness, Esther had been his ideal, the totally straightforward woman who had moved in gentleness, without malice or divided desires. He had wished he could have known her better. It was the only moment Max had ever seen him wistful.

Now, looking at David, he imagined that his qualities, and seeming aloofness, must have come from his mother. When he had seen him as a youth, he had not noticed this trait on his occasional visits to the Austin house on ceremonial Titan Sundays. But there was something about him as a man that seemed strangely familiar. His reverie was broken by David's voice.

"You look the same, Mr. Ziska, excepting for your silver hair."

His voice had the clipped quality of men who make decisions for others. He did not need to raise his voice. Others would strain to hear what he had to say.

David turned to Jessica. He seemed to look past her, and she set her cup down, put out her hand, and he took it.

"Well . . ." David started. He dropped her hand.

It reminded Max of the moment Fergus had greeted her with the same word, in the commissary at Titan studio; David approached her with the same casual elegance. That takes style, Max thought wryly.

"I congratulate you on your daughter," said David. "Her test was magnificent."

"You can thank Max Ziska for that," said Jessica. "I'll get Linda now. She's probably hanging out the window, staring out at London."

She arose quickly. As her knee knocked against the table, her teacup clattered to the floor, spilling on her skirt.

She stared at it in alarm. "Oh, my!"

"Nothing damaged," said Max, "not even the cup."

David and Jessica bent to pick it up at the same time. Their heads almost collided. Jessica nervously retrieved the cup and set it back on the saucer. She looked at it angrily.

"I . . . I'm sorry." She looked at the stain on her hem as if it were blood.

"Pardon me," she said, leaving the room.

"Out, damned spot," muttered Sidney.

"Pour me a gin, Sid," said David.

Max, ignoring the drama, got to the crux of the meeting, as nothing else really interested him.

"I hope you realize," he said, "that although Linda is still a child, it's right to introduce her now. She is on the brink of womanhood, and I feel in the next few months I can bring her into focus. We are most fortunate to have this phenomenon in this particular role. You will see. You must trust me."

"Mr. Ziska . . ." said David.

"Max," said Max.

"Don't ask me to trust you, Max," said David. "Talent such as yours is not to be trusted. It must be experienced."

Max flashed him a swift glance.

"It is either a triumph or a disaster," said David.

"You puzzle me," said Max. "I must forget the young boy playing baseball on the ocean front in Santa Monica. It is giving me a false image."

"Very false," said David. "Forget it."

The bedroom door opened. Linda entered, her mother following.

Linda's hair had been brushed into a shining, smooth fall. She wore a white dress ornamented with small pearl buttons.

David and the young girl looked at each other across the room.

"David, this is Linda," said Jessica.

"Linda," said David.

"Oh, Mr. Austin," said Linda, looking at him curiously, as she came forward and shook his hand, "I expected someone older than you."

"Linda!" said her mother.

"Is that compliment or complaint?" asked David.

"Well, I mean," said Linda, "for someone old, you look so young . . ."

She flushed and stopped.

Sidney chuckled.

"Oh, dear," Linda said, "I guess I've put my foot in it. I meant, I thought you were mother's age."

No one dared glance at Jessica.

"It's all in the point of view," said Max, breaking the terrible silence. "I knew David when he was your age. I keep discovering that a whole generation has moved into maturity while my world stood still."

Jessica went to the bar.

"Drink, Max?"

She mixed martinis in a pitcher.

"Do you think I could go to the British Museum sometime tomorrow?" asked Linda. "And I must see Drury Lane, where my family played."

"We'll see," said Max. "David likely has a schedule lined up."

"Schedule!" said Linda.

She picked up the Dorchester *London Weekly Diary* on the coffee table.

"I just glanced at this. I have to see the Old Vic, where my father, grandfather, and great-grandmother played, and the dress Belinda Pierce Barstow wore as Lady Macbeth is in a case at the Victoria and Albert Museum. And I just have to look at all those Greek friezes that Lord Elgin stole off the Acropolis. All those beautiful people. That's what this picture is all about. I have to feel the way they look!"

"You have a sitting with Orville tomorrow," said David. "He's the best portrait photographer in the world."

"And of course there's that reception," said Linda.

David walked to the French doors at the terrace, with the sounds of traffic and London auto horns punctuating the stillness in the room. They awaited his word. Max knew something was wrong. So did Jessica. She stood with the martini mixer poised in her hand.

"You're not coming to the reception," said David.

Jessica's head turned as slowly as if she were underwater.

"What do you mean, not coming to the party?"

"You may be there, and of course Max. But Linda won't appear."

"I'm afraid I don't understand," said Jessica.

"There's nothing to understand," said David. "All you need is to see those stills from that ill-fated commissary bash at Titan. It was a bobby-sox disaster. We ordered all withheld. Now, all pictures called in."

"You wouldn't—" said Jessica.

Max saw that she was taking it personally, and he held up his hand.

"Let him finish!"

Linda tossed back her hair, and her hands clenched.

"There is nothing personal in this decision," said David. "As you know, we've been aced into a situation with Pericles Niadas and the Bank of the West. The economy of Titan is at stake. And you, Max, salvaged us with this script, which was incredibly adept in using the physical facilities that were almost a total deficit when Martha Ralston dropped out of *Pallas Athena.* It was, we hope, an economic miracle for us."

Jessica twirled the stem of her glass as David continued.

"But what do we have for ammunition for our terrific investment? We have a script of great reality. A man who has not directed for fifteen years. We have Leslie Charles, our best male star, but he is aging, and he is difficult. His last picture did a terrific nosedive in spite of his talent.

"We have one of the new wave"—he turned to Linda—"thanks to your Aunt Claudia, who gave him his start a few years ago. He is a method actor, and a sexual image to many women, this John Graves, but his chemistry with this very young, untried girl will make or break our picture. And now, apologies, Linda, we have a girl who could be coming here to play *Alice in Wonderland.* We're supposed to take a very young girl, and introduce her to the tough, bitching European press as a replacement, mind you, in the public's eye, for the leading sex goddess of the industry, Martha Ralston."

"An economic miracle, you said," echoed Max, harkening back to David's comment. He scowled, and glanced at Jessica.

But Linda's sudden anger moved swiftly. She seemed to pull herself up by the wishbone, standing taller than she was. Her child's body moved under the simple dress. Her breasts stood out, her waist stretched into supple smoothness. She flung her hair back, so that it was no longer a child's waterfall resting on soft little-girl shoulders. She looked at David disdainfully.

"You think I can't do it, don't you?" said Linda. "Well, listen, Mr. Austin, for yourself, and for your father, and for all those people who wanted to hold my itty-bitty hand at the studio that day. I'm a Barstow. And I can play anything.

"That is," she amended, "anything I *want* to play. And I want to be the oracle. And I'm a woman, Mr. Austin. Yes, I menstruate. I could have a baby right now. My grandmother played Juliet at my age. And ask Max Ziska who in all the world he wants to play Alethea, even if he could have that tired old sex-pot, Martha Ralston."

"Linda!" said Jessica.

Max smiled, his spirits somewhat revived by Linda's outburst.

"Did she answer your question?"

"Not at all," said David. "Ambition is not womanliness."

"Is this womanliness?" she said.

She put her hand up and tore at the pearl buttons that fastened her dress. Before anyone could move, she had ripped the dress to the waist. She pulled it open. Her swelling breasts, with their pink nipples pointing upward, stood out in all their full firm virginity.

Max moved forward, as Jessica jumped up and ran to her.

"Linda!" she said. She clutched the dress, closed it with one hand, and slapped her with the other.

Max pulled Jessica away.

"Leave her alone!" he said, then turned to Linda. "Go in with Effie," he said gently.

Linda stalked out of the room haughtily. Her cheek was red from the slap.

David's face was flushed. Sidney looked away.

"Max," said David, "let's have a conference."

"My suite," said Max. He scowled at Jessica. "There are a few things I have just learned. I had no idea I was supplanting a Ralston film. Or fulfilling old obligations. I did not know my script and my talent were *economic* miracles!"

"I couldn't bother you with details, Max," said Jessica. "You're not stuck with costs of the other production. Seymour Sewell arranged your participation to begin with the money which starts when you do. I did a good job."

"The hell with money. My ideas have been tampered with," he said. "I have been maneuvered into adding false scenes and false sets in my script, which do not have artistic integrity. My original story has been doctored for devious reasons. I have fitted the body into another person's coffin."

"We'll talk later," said David, dismissing Jessica.

Max saw the anger in her face. He stopped briefly as they went on to his room.

"Don't blame the child," said Max, "and if you lay a hand on her, back you go to Hollywood tomorrow."

◆◆◆◆◆◆◆◆

Linda awoke to a new sound. She rushed to the window. It was drizzling, and the automobile tires made a splashing hum on the wet pavement. She heard the pulse of the busy city. It was different. It was London; London, town of her family, of great careers, of excitement.

Effie ran a tub in the ample bathroom, and Linda enjoyed the fragrance of the sharp special Atkinson hotel soap.

"It's just different abroad," she said, "even taking a bath. Oh, Effie, I love London."

Breakfast was set out in the sitting room in front of the fire. Rain splattered against the terrace French doors and dripped off the metal furniture in the cold and desolate morning.

Jessica, in cashmere sweater and skirt, sat by the phone, notes at hand. The phone rang with its sharp foreign insistence. She answered.

"Send her up." She turned to Linda. "It's going to be a terribly busy day. Grace's on her way up with lists. I have to know who most of the press is. You're going to get your hair washed downstairs in the beauty salon. Then a wardrobe woman, a makeup man, and a hairdresser will go with you to Orville's studio."

"Where's Max?"

"He's left for the office on Wardour Street. There are so many details I know he'll overlook, so I'd better pop down there as soon as I finish here and tend to them myself."

Linda suspected that her mother had not been invited, for she seemed petulant, instead of eager to roll up her sleeves and join the fray.

There was a knock at the door.

It was Grace Boomer. Her euphoric attitude meant that she was covering a hangover.

"Well, dear ones," she said, "everything is absolutely fantastic. It was a brainstorm to keep Linda away from that clambake. Important as it is," she hastily amended.

"We hardly came this far not to go to the affair," said Jessica.

"Oh, you'll be there, of course. It's terribly important for them to meet you, and Max," said Grace. "And Linda will very much be there in spirit. They are decorating a six-by-eight-foot photograph enlargement of her right now. It will be encircled with white flowers."

"Sounds like a funeral," said Linda.

"You're the limit!" said Grace, smiling too sweetly. "The photograph is in the Grecian hairdress and flowing white robe from the test. And we've corralled three duchesses, cream of the theater, the usual labor M.P.'s, a retired cabinet minister, and of course all sorts of embassy legation people, high commissioners, and visiting brass. Everyone will be there."

"Excepting me," said Linda. "I'm not invited."

Grace registered mock surprise.

"Linda, dear, this is devilishly clever. It makes you the most mysterious woman since Greta Garbo."

"It does?" said Linda, faintly intrigued.

"I didn't expect such a vendetta from certain sources," said Jessica, "and don't scuff your foot, Grace, you know what I mean."

Grace glanced quickly at Linda. No reaction.

"Wrong, wrong," she said. "David has wizard showmanship. Everyone will be awaiting Linda. You are to say she is coming. Then you will receive a message.

She will not be there. The news will spread that she has chosen to go to the British Museum to see the great Grecian sculptures from the Parthenon instead of meeting the press. And then, afterward, she will have vanished. Everyone will be looking for her. She'll have headlines: 'Star misses ten-thousand-pound party in her honor to visit Grecian antiquities!' Then, later: 'Star missing in London.' "

"Where will I be?" asked Linda.

"We'll work that out."

The romance of it appealed to Linda's imagination.

"I wish I could spend the night alone, hiding in the museum. What a gas of an experience."

"Don't get any bright ideas," said Jessica.

The phone rang. Jessica answered it.

"No . . ." she said insistently, "no. Just tell her we are not in. I do not wish to see her."

There was a pause.

"Just let her sit, then," said Jessica. "We are not in."

She hung up and looked at Grace.

"Three guesses who's trying to get into the act," she said significantly.

"If it's who I think," said Grace, "she's already called and got the brush from Sidney at the office."

"Who?" asked Linda.

"Nobody important," said Jessica.

"Lots of people try to swing on a star," said Grace. "It will happen more and more. You have to get a hide as tough as an armadillo. Anyway, Jessica, here are more press lists for you to study."

She handed her a dog-eared typed list.

"Now, to get back to the party. Every important press representative in Europe will go away intrigued, instead of just having met another budding young thing. They'll be curious. Then they can make engagements to fly to Rome or the Greek islands as we shoot, at our expense, of course, which I doubt anyone will reject. This means you will get dozens of long, personal interviews, and hundreds of items, instead of the usual blurbs that come about at a cocktail party. And Linda will be interviewed on the spot in the costume and makeup of *The Oracle,* which makes the whole picture more important. Not many stars get a chance at such promotion on their first picture. Now, isn't that wise?"

Jessica nodded.

"It's clever," she admitted.

She glanced at the press list. Her eyebrows lifted slightly, pleased. Linda suspected that this party was even more to her mother's liking without her presence. Jessica would be the one met, cosseted, and asked not only about her child, but her dear dead husband, Jeffrey Barstow, who had been a brilliant personality on stage and screen. Poor Jessica, the brave, the beautiful, the lovely widow, helping to carry on the Barstow tradition another generation.

"You're overdue in the beauty parlor downstairs," said Jessica. "You mustn't be late for Orville."

"He's a fussy old party," said Grace. "We can't get him to do a sitting anyplace but London. But he's the best portrait photographer in the world—took lots of pictures of your family. Even your grandfather, believe it or not, fifty years ago."

She looked at her watch.

"Oh, Lord, I have to get cracking. Some Dutch newspeople are coming in, and I have to take them to lunch at the Étoile. The makeup man and the wardrobe woman will be here in an hour."

The phone rang.

"This is a three-ring circus," said Jessica, "and I still have to get my hair done after I come back from the office."

She took the phone.

"Hello. . . . Oh, get in touch with the office at Wardour Street," she said. "They're taking care of invitations."

"Everybody always has an important friend when a party like this goes on," said Grace. "It's a primer for freeloaders."

The phone rang again.

"You're late at the beauty parlor," said Jessica. "I don't know why Linda can't go to the Little Orangery with her wardrobe woman and makeup man and hairdresser. Effie's standing by the phone. Do you think it would be all right?"

"Well," said Grace, "Orville's over seventy-five, and from what I've heard about him, she'd have been safe with him when he was seventeen. I'll run along. Come, Linda. I'll go down to the beauty parlor with you and sneak out the back way."

She looked conspiratorially at Jessica.

"No use running into guess-who sitting in the lobby, you know."

"Right," said Jessica.

Linda left with Grace.

"Come along," said Grace. "You must look your best for Orville. If he likes you, he may show you pictures of your family."

2

The Little Orangery was a reconstructed coach house off King's Road in Chelsea. It cornered a lane of old houses that had been overdecorated with shutters, clipped hedges, and flowerboxes set at mullioned windows.

The studio was different from its neighbors. It was painted no-nonsense white, with windows tightly shuttered against the eyes of the curious, as if great secrets lurked inside, which they did.

The entry door was Guardi green. A ferocious Georgian brass lion doorknocker, with a ring in its mouth, stood sentinel.

Linda stepped out of her Rolls-Royce with her retinue.

There was a beaming, plump wardrobe woman, who carried the robes and capes of Linda's wardrobe aloft, protecting them from the damp walk and hedges, as if she were a runner from Corinth bearing the sacred flame to the Olympic Games.

Gus, a sour, elderly makeup man, with constant indigestion and a breath like a blast furnace, scurried along with his eight-by-ten photographs under his arm, with typed directives from Titan studio regarding Linda's makeup.

Bertie, the thin, nervous young hairdresser, studied studio photographs of Linda, shaking his head with dismay. He was informed to part her hair in the middle, roll it upward from her temples at each side, and let it fall in natural tendrils at the nape of her neck. The makeup department at Titan had tried to one-up their English brethren, because they were not allowed to work in England, due to an interguild fracas. So they had dropped a snobbish note at the end of their instructions: "Make her like a caryatid from the Erechtheum, or one of Scopas' delightfully natural maidens."

Scopas, thought Bertie, one of those blokes with a plush hair salon on Audley Street, likely, that all the Americans rage about. Never heard of him.

It was an insult to his trade not to deal with wigs, false pieces, curlers, hair oil, spray, dryers, rollers, and pins.

An aesthetic young teddy boy answered the door. His glance flickered briefly over them, and rested in instant hostility on the young hairdresser.

"Come in," he said to Linda. "Orville's expecting you."

He wore snug Edwardian trousers and a Burlington Arcade sleeveless Nile-green alpaca pullover over a starched shirt, and the largest cufflinks Linda had ever seen.

They passed through an entry hall into a large studio with a lofty ceiling. The skylights lit up gleaming parquet floors. In front of a huge fire, set in a marble mantel, were Aubusson rugs, plum-colored sofas and easy chairs, mother-of-pearl-inlaid side chairs and tables, interspersed with ancient urns holding ferns, and Greek and Roman statuary on pedestals.

At the far end of the room a series of *trompe l'oeil* backdrops was hung from the ceiling beams on pulleys. The scene had already been set for Linda's sitting, a sky-blue backing, an Ionic marble column, and a chaise done in the neoclassic style, with ice-blue-satin upholstering. There were several acanthus plants, all surrounded by a maze of lights, cameras, tripods, and cables.

"Where is Mr. Orville?" asked Linda.

"Orville is here," said a reedy voice.

Linda saw a slim, elegant old man, straight as a member of the Queen's Guard, standing in the doorway. He was almost transparently slender, with an aquiline nose, pale skin, and thin pink lips. His thoughtful eyes peered through glasses with ice-blue frames. She noted that his hair was tinted the same pale blue. He wore gray trousers and a pale-gray cashmere turtleneck sweater. He glanced at his watch. The band was a bracelet of square-cut sapphires.

"Prompt," he said, looking her over. "Where is your mother?"

"Mother was terribly busy with the press party, so she can't come."

"Excellent!"

The old man studied her keenly.

"I must say," he exclaimed, "you are really one up on your Aunt Claudia. We were once great chums before the bottle robbed her of good companionship. Let's see if all of you matches up. Take off your coat."

The wardrobe woman took her coat. The old man circled her, analyzing her from every angle.

"Here, Guv," said Bertie, "these are pictures the studio sent over. Mr. Ziska told me 'e wants 'er to look like this."

Orville took the stills and walked slowly to the fire. He threw them in the flames without glancing at them.

"My dear, *I* know how a Barstow should look! Now, all of you, scat—go into the dining room and have tea." He waved them all out of existence with a limp, authoritative gesture. "That is, excepting you, my dear. I want to sum you up before the serfs move in."

They all filed off, delighted to have a snack.

"And latch the door," he called out to his young assistant.

"Now," he said in a matter-of-fact voice, "will you take off your dress?"

"Why?" said Linda, surprised. "The wardrobe woman—"

He waved off her words.

"I wish to study your bone structure; the camera is an eye, and life must be true."

"Well . . ." she said tentatively.

"If you don't wish to do what I want, go back to

your pinafores and schoolbooks. Don't take up my time. You are an actress, aren't you?"

"Of course I am."

"Then you may as well start right now. Cancel out the syndrome of the 'good child' and be an entity."

Linda thought a moment. He was an old man. And he certainly couldn't do her any harm.

"All right," she said.

She unbuttoned her dress, and it fell to the floor. She was clad in a nylon slip and a pair of briefs. She folded her hands self-consciously over her breasts.

Orville went to a Venetian commode and took out some pictures.

"I brought these from my files to show you," he said. "They have been seen only by me and the subjects. I have here photographs that will interest you very much. Since you are a Barstow, look."

He handed her a picture.

"This was your grandfather," he said. "He was in his forties when I photographed him, but still a handsome, vital man."

Chauncey Barstow, deep-chested and keen of face, could have been an emperor or a general. He leaned one arm on a column, wrist bent, and the other in front of him. His head was turned three-quarters, sharp of nose, with indented cheekbone and a squarish chin with a soft cleft in it. He was as handsome as a Greek statue. And as nude.

"*That* is a Barstow," said Orville. "The Barstows may have had assorted morals, but there was one characteristic that made them quite different from even their most gifted contemporaries. And obviously, you have inherited it."

Linda looked puzzled.

"It is their bone structure," he said.

He handed her another picture. It was Jeffrey Barstow, about the age of twenty. His back was turned to the camera, and his handsome profile knifed against the backdrop. He, too, was nude, and his torso, muscular, slim-waisted, and broad-shouldered, was as perfect as the Discobolus, sculptured five centuries before Christ by Myron.

"Your father," said Orville. "I was young when I took this one; and your grandfather. I was just beginning to be sought out by celebrities, even if I was fresh from Bermondsey. See this. Jeffrey Barstow had the elegance of an Athenian and the masculinity of a Peloponnesian. See the muscle, and tendon, and bone!"

He paused, remembering over half a century as he set down the pictures.

"It saddened me to see him play a crass Roman or a brawling Elizabethan. He belonged to the Golden Age of Pericles."

Linda's mind was whirling. It was strange to meet her forebears in their nudity, stripped of all the wing collars, cravats, and elegant theatrical costumes she had seen in books saved from her father's library. But Orville was an artist, and her own family had posed for him in the nude willingly.

He handed her another photograph.

"This was your Aunt Claudia. I took her much later. She was quite a few years younger than your father. At this sitting, I would say she was about seventeen."

Claudia, too, was nude. Black Irish and lush, she was lying on the same chaise that awaited Linda. Her slender hand was curled over her mons veneris like a Carpaccio Venus. There was a half-smile on her face, and her large, luminous eyes were half-closed. Her halo of dusky, curly hair seemed to be blowing in a zephyr across her cheek. Her breasts were full and pointed, and her waist indented, flowing into the smooth roundness of her hips, and curving in a perfect line to her legs. Her ankles and feet were slim, and her arms delicate.

"She was so beautiful," said Linda.

"She was an utter strumpet," said Orville. "Fortunately, I do not see that in you. I do not photograph people unless they are very beautiful or very famous. It's a waste of time, and I haven't much left. I was prepared to reject you."

Linda realized she was sitting at her ease on the

chaise in her undergarments. After all, she had wanted so desperately to be a woman that she had exposed her breasts last night to prove it. This man saw her as a woman.

"Now, will you please take off those wretched synthetic coverings?"

"Of course."

She dropped her undergarments and settled back naked on the chaise. She felt flattered and adult.

Orville set his camera, adjusted lights, and came forward once to smooth a strand of her hair, letting it fall between her breasts.

As he went back to his camera and put the hood over his head, Linda instinctively put one hand in front of her fleece of pale-gold pubic hair.

"No, no!" said Orville. "Put one arm in back of your head, and the other at your side. You are of a oneness, all golden. You do not have to resort to subterfuge."

She smiled. The light from the lamps warmed her, and an excitement began to pervade her, at the thought of her body being beautiful. Here she was, naked and perfect. A little pulse, forerunner of things to come, began to quiver in the secret part of her body. She was a Barstow; she was very special.

Then she remembered, with a shock, what would happen if her mother came in. At this moment, the old man snapped the shutter.

"Excellent. You have the eyes of a sinning nun," he said. "Be assured, I shall develop the plates personally, and keep them in my private files. At my death they will come to you in a sealed envelope, to do with as you please. I hope that you, in your turn, will see that they are put in the proper archives, for man to see the best of our species in our time. Beauty is a gift that is often taken lightly, because it is not earned. Treasure it, my dear, for although you do not believe it now, it is most ephemeral."

"Doesn't it come from within?" asked Linda. "Effie told me that if you lead a good life, your face will show it, even when you're old."

"Rubbish," said Orville. "Puritan propaganda. I have found madonna faces in the brothels of the world; women who smile like a Da Vinci painting while in the act of the most lascivious copulation. Or street boys who offer themselves to any buyer for any sensual service with the roguish smile of a Goya gamin. Beauty is an accident of birth and placement of flesh on bone, so do not make the mistake of considering it in any sense sacred or noble."

He sighed.

"How poets and artists have striven to make beauty divine, and how nations have fallen because of this depraved idea. And of course, since you are a Barstow, physical beauty will be a focus for human frailty. Everyone will want to possess you, one way or another."

"The same old chat," said a woman's voice.

Linda protectively put her hands over her nakedness. Orville swung about so quickly that his camera clattered over on the floor.

Standing at the foyer entrance, Linda saw a woman. She was petite, and must have been in her sixties. A feather toque was pinned on her blue-black dyed hair. She wore a black-velvet coat with a yellowed ermine collar, and peeled off overlong kid gloves as she clopped across the floor on high heels.

But in spite of her seediness and her heavy makeup, she had an aura of beauty not forgotten; loveliness remembered in the structure of her cheekbones, her arched brows, blue heavily fringed eyes, although deeply shadowed, and the heart-shaped face, which still carried a winsome smile when she chose to illuminate herself.

"My God!" said Orville, staring at her. "How did you get in?"

"Your minions forgot to latch the front door," she said. "Oh, but time doth telescope, you dirty old man. Once more I could haul you in for moral turpitude; she's a minor, you know. Just like I was, and you might have just about started to let her know how you get your kicks."

The woman moved in closer and stared at Linda. The girl peered beyond the bright lights.

"Oh!" she said. "You're my Aunt Claudia!"

Claudia smiled, her eyes taking in Linda again.

"Ah," she said, "indeed you are Jeffrey's child. In the years since I saw you, you're a young woman!"

She paused a moment, and Linda felt she might be close to tears. But she moved toward Orville.

"Fetch my niece a covering," she said with a dramatic gesture; the woman in command. Linda was fascinated.

Orville had gone to latch the front door. He came back, a bit shaken, and brought Linda a terry robe. He picked up her garments, taking them to the dressing room.

"Forty odd years ago, I was a sweetmeat like you, sitting, I think, on the same prop," said Claudia wistfully.

"I think you adequately illustrate my theory on the ephemeral nature of beauty," Orville said. "Now, Claudia, will you please leave?"

He picked his camera off the floor, and found it undamaged.

"You won't chuck me out, old cock," said Claudia. "I might ask you to hand over a few family portraits if you make a stink. I went through plenty of hell to see this child. Went on the wagon to get myself in condition. I was in fair shape a few years ago—but time and tide and the bottle. The hell with that, anyway. Then her bloody mother won't let me up to see her. Imagine, me, the last of the London Barstows, sitting on my rump in the lobby of the Dorchester like a bleeding mendicant."

"Let her stay," said Linda. "I want to hear about my family. Nobody tells me anything."

"If I hadn't read Donald Zec in the *Mirror*," Claudia said, "in that perishing lobby, I wouldn't have known where to find you. Where's the old girl? Not stupid enough to send you to this voyeur by yourself?"

"Mother?" said Linda. "She's busy getting that press party set up."

"They're a pain in the ass," said Claudia.

"But I want to see London. Drury Lane, and the British Museum."

"On with this sitting," said Orville. "Just don't hold me up with your gossip. As long as you stay out of the way . . . Claudia, it might animate my subject to listen to your prattle."

Linda felt that he was placating her aunt so that she wouldn't continue commenting on the private sitting she had walked in on.

"Let's finish up with this old lecher, and get on with it," said Claudia, chuckling. "After all, ducks, we are kith and kin. And I'll tell you a thing or two."

She turned to Orville, wagging a finger.

"Don't think I don't know the jollies you've gotten out of your little private gallery. I know a pervert when I see one."

"What's a pervert?" asked Linda.

"A pervert," said Orville, staring at Claudia hatefully, "is someone with too much imagination to satisfy himself with the obvious."

He gathered up his private collection of nudes and stashed them carefully in a drawer of the Venetian commode.

"A drop of sherry would be a pleasant little pickup," said Claudia. "I might gently step off the wagon to celebrate the debut of my niece."

Orville took a Georgian decanter and a goblet from a sideboard, set it beside Claudia.

"A word," he said to Linda, "culled from a thousand sittings. Beware of the troglodytes."

Linda looked at him in the mirror, puzzled.

"It's a word I use to alert you," he explained. "There is nothing that annoys these makeup, hairdress, and wardrobe artisans more than a firsthand encounter with natural beauty. They will try brewing Ava Gardner number five with Lana Turner number three. They will arch your natural brows, paste lashes over your own, torture your curls, electro-needle your hairline, by all means change the colors and the planes of your face if you don't take care. You either fall into the pit of their wretched lack of imagination or become known as difficult from the start and preserve your own image."

"You never talked so candidly to me," called out Claudia.

"How could I?" said Orville. "You were inside a bottle and couldn't hear me."

Orville opened the locked door, called in his cohorts, turned on wind effects, and arranged lights while the crew went to work.

"Talk to the child about the Barstow clan," he said to Claudia, "while I work. Keep her alive. She has no image to draw on yet."

Claudia savored the warm bouquet of the Spanish sherry slowly before it coursed in a trickle down her grateful throat. It took only a few sensory pleasures to bring back a long-lost feeling of well-being and expectancy. How it all brought back memories of star days years ago—when she was the darling, the pet, the loved one of Simon Moses and Titan studio. Before she had paid every cent she had gleaned from Hollywood on pictures that never paid off her investment.

How she had risen out of her own ashes, as her brother, Jeffrey, had said, like a phoenix, made a film with young John Graves, been acclaimed, then lost it again, the old Barstow pattern!

She perched her glasses on the bridge of her classic nose. There, in the bright lights, like a glorious butterfly just unfolding wings from its chrysalis, was her own flesh and blood, her own brother Jeffrey's child. She shivered, feeling that something incredibly precious had been brought into her life. A gift of the gods, an undeserved dividend.

Here indeed was someone she could help. And who could help her. Ah, to have the excitement of a new, unblemished career. The travel, the luxury, the clothes, privilege again; a place in the sun.

And she really could help her. Voice coaching. All the family things that long ago Uncle Billy Jeff and her father had taught her and Jeffrey in the salad days when Stratford and the Old Vic had been their only aim.

How they had let it all slip through their fingers. Oh, to have a chance again! But how, with that bitch Jessica running things. She remembered how Jessica had thrown her out of the house the evening after her brother's funeral. And dodged her in those last, terrible Hollywood days.

But now . . . now for a few gilded moments she would enjoy her rights as the aunt of this gorgeous girl before she was snatched away.

In this hour she might plant seeds for the future. A chance; just one chance to erase all her failures. Careers down the drain, drinking bouts. Bought escorts, lost lovers, abortions (if you had been wiser, you could have had a few dividends like Linda Barstow making the world prettier and protecting you from poverty). And after the years of tinseltown, the painful construction of a new face and body, time and liquor had again taken away all she had fought to regain.

Fighting to maintain the image, to keep the once-posh address of the Cavendish as her home, she did everything she could between bouts of despair and drinking to muddle along; bathroom laundry, handkerchiefs pressed to dry on mirrors, and brought out crooked-edged with unspoken apologies in front of shrewd, seeing agents. Refashioned ancient finery. An old hundred-quid fur collar worn on a new five-guinea coat. Gas-jet meals and a burned thumb. Kited checks, and the wretched greengages to live by earned playing witches in *Macbeth* out in the boondocks, Mother Goose in the Christmas panto in the provinces. "J. Ashley Smithers presents the distinguished English actress Claudia Barstow in her inimitable portrayal of Mother Goose." Keep sober enough to stumble on the stage, lads, and leave it to the honking trained goose under the arm to get the laughs. . . . That is, until you fell on the wretched thing and broke its bloody neck and lost your meal ticket.

Diction lessons for rich idiots, mostly American, who should have been born with what you were supposed to teach them. Entrances into hotel lobbies, chin up, veil pressed in vinegar to be stiff over your mascaraed eyelashes. Stinking eucalyptus-flavored mouthwash to hide the nip of pink gin which braced you for the ordeal. An *oblivon* tablet to hide the headache while you made pert remarks about Larry and Noël. Sharp lipstick penciled on your mouth to show what's up to date in Kansas City, even if it is Grosvenor House. Yes, yes, I was in films in America. You sometimes catch me on the late-late. Yes, yes, I heard the album of *My Fair Lady*. Rex was charming. . . . Diction is so important, isn't it?

But now she was a Barstow again, full-blooming, wise, and rare. Orville, her chum from bygone days, was asking her a favor! She suddenly scorned him for having the temerity even to question her birthright.

She clutched her handbag—in it, her talisman for this auspicious day. The little amber globule that Jeffrey had left her as a link, she felt, to connect her life with his daughter's. "She'll need you," he had said. . . . Need.

No one had ever really needed her before. Not Fergus, really—he had enough Irish drive and gall to outsit anyone. Not Simon Moses—he had a passion for her, but he still kept his own life and family to sustain him until he died in her arms. Even if he had lived, he would have left her bed to go home to his comfortable wife and mansion. He always had.

But this time, an emotion she had never felt overcame her. Fate had brought Belinda Barstow, the last of her line, into her hands. She must not lose the power that that bloodline alone gave her. They were the last of the Barstows. And how handsome and gifted Barstows had been at their peak. And this was the most beautiful of all, this young girl. Claudia forced herself not to let tears of emotion fill her eyes, and turned imperially to Orville.

"My niece and I have many family affairs to discuss," she said.

Orville turned his back on her haughtiness. Bloody bore. . . . I should have given the old harridan some lolly and sent her along to the corner rub-a-dub for a Vera Lynn.

But in spite of his irritation, he was elated. Time marches. . . . This might be his last beauty. . . . And the best. Browning's *The Lady and the Painter?* Rot! Artistry rose above common sense. Why control exuberance? This is the lodestone . . . the reason for the seeking in the wilderness. The dawn moment. Thank the gods, this young Barstow has come before this lens ere it is too late. He was suddenly ashamed of his sentimentality. 'Ave it off, 'Arry Orville, 'ave it off. Billingsgate's come a long way.

He waited patiently while the makeup men and hairdressers descended on his subject, dismissed them, then set about wiping off mat powders and lipstick and tousling the hair that had been too perfectly set in place.

"Now that we are finished with that beastly beauty-school session," he said, "I shall turn on the wind machine."

In turn he skewered her hair high in a Psyche knot, a few strands flying against her cheek; photographed her lying on her back, holding the ivory-and-gold bracelet in her teeth; pictured her slim and white in a purple cape ballooned against the pounding wind; suggested wave and storm by throwing water at her from the windscreen; and captured her half-asleep, with dewy fresh lilies of the valley and violets falling across her breast.

He was expert, artist, admirer, technician, and a bacchant with her, going about his business with the dispatch of a craftsman, and for the moment the passion of a lover.

While he changed cameras and lenses, moved props for varied compositions, he played phonograph records of *Orpheus and Eurydice, Phaedre,* and Finica Luca's pipes of Pan; flute music, he commented, Greek, by way of Romania. Linda posed in a mood of conjured magic, and listened to the counterpointed throaty tones of Claudia, who was herself in renaissance.

"How glorious," said Claudia, "to be able to talk to a Barstow. I feel it is a good heritage, at least before the animal in us takes over, which unfortunately does happen. We are sometimes a shocking lot."

"Is there a record of us?" asked Linda.

"The Barstows always had records, my dear," said Claudia, "many of them in police courts."

Linda smiled.

Claudia held up a talon hand.

"Today you may be playing a high priestess in that microcosm called *The Oracle*. A movie is a segment of capitalism, you know, not a new religion. Six more films, and some wiseacre will dream of you playing Moll Flanders selling oranges in the pit of Drury Lane Theatre, and you'll be right back where your ancestors started."

Linda laughed.

"You're funny, Aunt Claudia," she said. "Why didn't someone tell me?"

"Ah," said Claudia, "who was left to tell? Your father and I loved each other very much. Our home was the stage and the set, and our friends and lovers those who allowed us to have our dreams—in our work. The rest were our enemies."

Linda shivered, for she remembered the rich voice from the two times she had seen her, once years ago when they had fled from her elegant birthday party, to her mother's rage, and she and her father and Claudia had run along the beach with her new puppy and celebrated the joy of being Barstows. The other time was the day of her father's funeral, and her mother had kept Claudia away from her, but there had been a few moments when hand held hand and she had looked up into the face of her father's sister with love and longing to be with her. How wonderful to be able to speak with another Barstow. Claudia and she were a sort of negative and positive of each other, with their dark and fair visages.

"Enough of jackanapery," said Orville. "It's time for the serious pictures. Now, child, I want you to think like the oracle."

He gestured at Claudia to keep still, moved cautiously behind a potted palm, and watched her.

The wind machine blew at Linda's hair. She could not see the backdrop and acanthus behind her, but had to look into the circle of lights. She thought of the Greek girl, staring into the blue Delphic sky, unseeing—the terrible mystery of the sacred dark Adytum clouding the sun, the depths of blackness writhing in her memory along with the brain-coiling sacred serpent of Apollo.

She became part of the imagery which she had conjured up along with Homer, Scopas, Praxiteles, Lord Elgin, her sponsor, Pericles Niadas, her director, Max Ziska, and now Orville.

"Finished," Orville said finally.

Claudia stood by, and the memory of her own best days of inspiration and creative imagery overcame her. She felt the gooseflesh rise on her arms, and she had to choke a sudden feeling in her throat; she missed Jeffrey terribly and wished he were here by her side. He would be proud. This child was a talent, this child was the last Barstow. But it distressed her, at the same time. Oh, the pitfalls, the things she would have to learn. The terror of a career with beauty and talent, and the whole world waiting to jump at it. She knew. . . .

And the idyll was ended.

Orville looked fatigued and rather sad as the camera lights were switched off and he made order out of confusion. The troglodytes moved in to fuss, to clockwatch, to pack, and to fold away the dream.

He knew this would be his last Barstow.

3

◆◆◆◆◆◆◆◆

"*This* is Drury Lane?" said Linda.

She stood in the thronged street, looking up at the soot-gray building, disappointed.

"Young friend," said Claudia, leaning forward on the comfortable seat of the Rolls-Royce, "don't let the fact that you've come to London on Titan's magic carpet go to your head. No doubt you've heard

> " 'Hark, hark, the dogs do bark,
> The Beggars are coming to town,
> Some in rags and some in tags,
> And one in a velvet gown.' "

"Yes," said Linda, peering in at her through the open door. "Father used to recite it to me. That's a nursery rhyme."

"Wrong, wrong," said Claudia, "it's damned near the family anthem. Velvet gown or not, actors are beggars, approval means pennies. And as for this theater, aside from the immortals, Garrick, Sheridan, Kemble, your ancestors and relatives, Chauncey, William Jeffrey Barstow, Belinda Pierce Barstow, your noted great-grandmother—God, what a tyrant she was!—would have *loathed* pictures! And of course your departed father, Jeffrey Barstow, and I were weaned on a stick of greasepaint here. May I ask, if I don't presume, what the hell you expected of this theater?"

"I'm sorry," said Linda, "I just thought it might be more spectacular, and have a courtyard, you know, like Grauman's Chinese Theater on Hollywood Boulevard."

"Blimey," said Claudia, "with Siddons' and Keane's footprints in cement, I presume."

"Where now, miss?" the driver asked, cocking a disapproving glance at Claudia Barstow, who was dropping ashes liberally on his pearl-gray upholstering.

"The British Museum, I guess," said Linda.

She stepped back into the car, and they moved slowly in the afternoon traffic, arrested by the steady drizzle.

"You'd better learn proper respect for the theater," Claudia said, "of which motion pictures are a very pale, pissant bastard cousin."

Linda put her hand placatingly on her aunt's.

"Give me a break, Aunt Claudia," she said. "I really want to learn. Please tell me."

"Don't try to scuff your spiritual foot at me. Let's get one thing settled right now; if we're to have any kind of a relationship, I consider innocence is ignorance, and sweetness is stupidity. So get all that humbug out of your system. Of course, how can I blame you, with the influence of that phony southern lady-whore mother of yours, who made Jeffrey's last years so wretched. I have a few words to say on that score sometime."

"Please, tell me more about Drury Lane," said Linda. "I want to know."

"Well," said Claudia, "it hasn't got pearl toilet seats like your cinema dream palace. People didn't go there to use it as a comfort station. And anything that's been there as long as it has occasionally falls on its bum. The Theatre Royal, my dear, aside from its record of glorious actors and plays, has been closed by plagues, politics, and fires, yet it always rises, as they say about our family, like the phoenix, out of its own ashes."

Claudia lit a new cigarette on the old butt.

"The best time of my life was at Drury Lane, 1939 and on. War years, but I worked at a little desk in the basement, got together groups, and went on tour for the Entertainment National Service Association. These were hell times for most, but for me, good. That's how

I met John Graves, and I must tell you about him, ducks, before you perform with him."

"Oh, yes . . . but what did you play at Drury Lane?" asked Linda. "I bet you did everything from Juliet to Lady Macbeth."

"I never really hit the top," said Claudia. "Don't get our strain confused with the Kembles or Barrymores, my dear. Of course I butchered a few Shakespearean maidens in my extreme youth before we came to America. But your father and I messed about in that ivory rut of films, which changed our lives. And later, when we got in a brannigan with Fergus Austin, I came back to London to roost. I did fairly well in the provinces. And there was a time when anyone with an English accent could get by with murder in the colonies. And I was always, in my prime, a natural for breech parts."

"What in heaven's name was that?" asked Linda.

"Roles written for men, but played by women."

She saw that Linda was puzzled.

"You really are a morass of theatrical ignorance, aren't you?" Claudia said sharply.

"Oh, it's a good thing I met you," said Linda. "Just think of all the things I wouldn't know, if our paths hadn't crossed!"

There was a pregnant moment as Claudia reflected. The child stirred up a turmoil of family memories that had been dormant for many years. She feared caring for her, and then having her taken away, as she knew would happen. Glancing at the child's enthusiasm and terrible innocence, she felt bone-weary.

"I'm really exhausted," she said, "and dry as a herring. Look, ducks, you do that museum trash heap without Claudia. I'll just have the car drop me off at my digs, the Cavendish, on Jermyn Street. A little place, déclassé now, but once quite the thing with all of Mayfair, and there's someone I want to talk to you about. This John Graves who plays opposite you in your film. Once my protégé, bit of a cockney bastard, but I'm fond of him. Watch out. We'll have a proper chat."

"Wonderful," said Linda. "I won't be long. But I just have to see those Greek friezes."

"The driver will return," said Claudia, "and wait for you in front."

She opened up her copious wide-jawed handbag, and shook it out. Linda noticed that the soiled kid lining was hanging in strips. A shabby coin purse, a tarnished lipstick, a scratched golden compact, and a cigarette case with a jeweled decoration on it fell out. The cigarette case opened up and disgorged a couple of Player's cigarettes. The final item was an advertising match packet, on which was printed "Don't Be Vague, Ask for Haig."

"Blast that catch," said Claudia, retrieving the cigarettes. She flashed the case. "And that's a tale, a maharaja gave me that. Handsome, and rich, rich, rich. Ah, well, it's the only thing I have left to remember the last great romance of my life. Who knows, you might inherit it someday. Often pawned, my dear, but never, never sold."

Linda saw the flash of rubies as she shoved her cigarettes back in it, and then made a clucking sound.

"Damned if I haven't come away without my money. I must have a little spread of Lyons Corner House sandwiches for you, and a bottle of bubbly to celebrate, when you come back from your tussle with culture. You wouldn't have a bit of lolly on you?"

"I have this," said Linda. "Mother thought I might have to take the staff to lunch."

She reached in her purse and pulled out four white folded parchment papers. She unfolded one.

"Is this really money? It looks like a high-school diploma to me."

"Is it ever!" said Claudia, touching it reverently with her pinkie raised. "Each of these is five quid. Open sesame!"

"I was supposed to bring it back if I didn't need it."

"You need it, you need it," said Claudia. She looked out. "We seem to be approaching the Marble Halls. When you meet me at the Cavendish Hotel, I'll give you the change."

She pushed the lever that let down the glass panel to the chauffeur's front seat.

"Driver," she said grandly, "you may let my niece off at the British Museum and drop me at the Cavendish on Jermyn Street. Then return and pick her up here, and fetch her back to the Cavendish."

The driver nodded, and looked at her malevolently. Wouldn't this old has-been just keep him shuttling back and forth at these hours, bucking afternoon traffic cross town! She caught his glance and lifted her chin a trifle higher.

Claudia fished some change out of a secret compartment of her purse.

"This is more than enough for that museum," she said. "It'll just take a few sprats to buy a guidebook. All the Elgin marbles are on the ground floor. The wretched things'd fall through up above. Get that mausoleum bit over with, and meet me. God bless."

She plucked the five-pound notes out of Linda's hand as she stepped out in front of the museum.

The car pulled away. Linda saw Claudia unfold what must have been one five-pound note and hand it grandly to the chauffeur, who looked at it in some surprise and saluted briskly. They merged into the stream of traffic.

◆◆◆◆◆◆◆◆

Oh, what will I do, thought Linda as she walked down the forbidding hallway of the museum. What will I do if the Elgin marbles don't gas me? Face Max and tell him I can't play the oracle? That I'm too uneducated and too American schoolgirl to feel like I should about them? I can't lie to Max. Maybe I never should have come here. If I turn around and go, then Max will just have to conjure up the magic by himself.

No, I've come this far. The hell with Max. He and mother are having a fine old time about now, making character with a bunch of people, and me, the uninvited. Well, I'm having my own party. I have connections. I'll be sipping champagne with my own aunt. . . .

Oh!

There they are. There. *There.*

They seem to glow.

Some are just fragments of men and women.

And the horses. Look at the flaring nostrils and wild eyes. Look at the arch of their necks. They're racing in the wind.

Linda looked at the young men and women. Let's see. . . . They're bringing tribute to Athena. That hand. . . . The foot and leg. Look how the robes cling to their bodies. That's what Orville meant, the body is important. . . . And the moment, the life! They seem to stand in a warm breeze. How muscular the men are, and how freely the women move. They have dignity carrying their olive branches and offerings. They really are noble. That's why he made me stand straight for those pictures, that wise old Orville! I must do it the way that woman does.

Linda leaned against the wall and half-closed her eyes.

They move. . . . And they were carved, it says, by Phidias and his craftsmen five hundred years before Christ!

I feel cold. . . . Have they been waiting for me, Belinda Barstow, to clothe them in flesh again? Because if I can't do it, I'd better quit before I even start.

Why did that woman wave that olive branch? Why did she walk like that? She lived and moved, and what she was made an artist remember her. Centuries later she is more real than these jerks shuffling by, wondering where the rest room is, or those boys leering at me.

Now, marble woman, I am one with you . . . you with your arm raised carrying your olive branch. I stand here with you; it took several thousand years, but here we are together.

◆◆◆◆◆◆◆◆

The Cavendish Hotel on Jermyn Street seemed more a boardinghouse to Linda than a hotel.

Claudia let her into her room. In the old days it had been the sitting room of a large apartment. Now its gas-jet chandelier was converted to electricity, with bulbs and wiring visible. The ceilings were high, and the walls hung with faded but elegant wallpaper. Victorian and modern upholstered pieces mingled in a mélange of dowdy past splendor. A couch landen with silk-tasseled pillows was obviously a bed. Round tables, draped à la Cecil Beaton with Spanish shawls, supported a flock of portraits, family and friends, most in elaborate silver frames.

Claudia set up a tea table with a wrinkled and yellowed lace cloth that had been obviously dragged off a shelf. A Sèvres plate held a combination of Lyons Corner House sandwiches that had begun to curl at the edges.

At the side of the table, a chrome stand held a jeroboam of champagne set in ice. It had already been opened, and puddles on a tray holding two champagne glasses betrayed Claudia's impatience.

"Well, did you get your belly full?" asked Claudia.

Linda noticed that her curls had slid to one side; the ebony cluster was alien, pinned on like a flower.

"No," said Linda, "I didn't get my belly full."

She stared at her aunt. Claudia was tipsy.

"You see," said Linda, pressing her advantage, "it took those Elgin marbles to make me realize they were only people, just like you and me. I can be one of them. I just have to think the way they did, and be real, and I can make them come alive again."

She picked up a sandwich and gobbled it.

"I haven't served tea yet," said Claudia.

Linda looked at the champagne.

"I think you have," she said. "Pour me some."

"Well, by God!" Claudia cackled, poured her a drink, and then filled her own glass.

"Here's to Barstows!" she said.

Linda sipped it. Not good, but necessary. She looked out the window at the traffic moving along the street below.

"Cocktail time," she said, "and about four hundred

people are at the Dorchester waiting to meet me, and they aren't going to."

"Come again?" said Claudia.

"The party," said Linda. "They think I'm too young. I'm not the image Mr. David Austin and Titan films want me to be yet. So my dear mother, and Max, and David Austin and everyone are all taking bows for me. Here's to us Barstows, Aunt Claudia."

She drank the champagne down.

Claudia drained hers, set the goblet down sharply, and sat on a little gilt chair at the table.

"Sit," she said, "and tell me that again."

"I was canceled out," said Linda. "Wiped. Not the sex image to meet the press. Everybody from Europe is flying in. And where's the new pride of the Barstows? In a large picture hanging on the wall. To be seen only in makeup, not the flesh."

"You've still got your makeup on," said Claudia. "Where's your costume?"

"In the car," said Linda. "The wardrobe woman left the costumes on the hangers in the trunk; they're supposed to go back to Wardour Street tomorrow."

Claudia picked up the phone.

"Get me the Dorchester, Albert," she said, "and while you're doing it, have the porter bring up the hangers of costumes in that Rolls-Royce waiting outside. . . . And have room service send another cherrybum of champagne. . . ."

There was a pause.

"Well, then, send her up," she said. "She'll hear from me personally."

She hung up angrily.

"If I choose to give my niece her debut, I'll give my niece her debut."

Claudia opened her purse and fished through it and took something out. There was a knock on the door. Claudia answered it, to talk to a small gray-haired woman.

"Rose, I am giving my niece, Linda Barstow, a debut," said Claudia imperiously. "Some of the most important newspaper people in Europe will be here. I want the Elinor Glyn room, champagne, and some decent hors d'oeuvres—none of your pig-liver pâté, but the works, and I want it ready in half an hour, and no argument. Just long enough for them to get over here from the Dorchester. And in case there's any argument, here's your security."

She handed the woman the maharaja's ruby-studded cigarette case. Linda saw the flash of the jewels as it exchanged hands.

"Miss Claudia," said the manageress in a gentle voice, "you know you'll be sorry—"

"You've pawned it before," said Claudia with a regal gesture, "and you can do it again. I shall redeem it, you may be sure, and give you a proper bonus. I have a very fine engagement coming up in Newcastle on Tyne. *Devil's Disciple*. Tyrone Power. Meanwhile, get the dust out of that miserable parlor. Air it, spray it with Tantivy, and get some flowers in. Make it worthy of Barstows."

The woman gave her a querulous look, glanced down at the cigarette case, and nodded.

"As you say," she said, "since you've paid your rent. And, by the way, thank you . . . for the rent money."

"Let us not go into these vulgar details," said Claudia quickly.

She closed the door and looked at her niece.

"Now, let's put your hair up and do a little more lip rouge on your mouth. My bath's in there, ducks. We must launch you right." She looked at her. "You look fine. No problem. Off with the bra."

The phone rang.

"Yes . . . yes. Dorchester? May I have the banquet room where the Titan party is being held. It is very important that I speak to Mr. Fred Christy. Yes, the *Variety* editor. Thank you. Barstow is the name. And page the editor of *Paris-Match*. This is an emergency."

While she was waiting, she turned to wink at Linda.

"I have a few friends, sweetie, and I know a lot of the press bloody well better than that boring Jessica Klopfinger God-'elp-us Barstow. We can't have any auslanders taking the bows for you in our very own London, now, can we?"

Linda looked at her aunt in admiration, as she poured herself another glass of champagne. She nodded in agreement.

"I don't mind you being a little tiddly," said Claudia, "but it's going to be a long night, and I rather imagine you'll want to say a few things to the gentlemen of the press, so easy on it, love."

◆◆◆◆◆◆◆◆

"Something very fishy is going on," said Sidney to Grace Boomer. "This is the fifth time I've seen a newsman go to the phone, and then make apologies and vanish."

"You know, I noticed that," said Grace. "I can't imagine why anyone can walk out on this; it's a swinging party."

The room was decorated with masses of Constance Spry flower arrangements, one of the best name bands in London was blatting away, and a bevy of beautifully garbed women and important-looking men was chatting. It looked like something spawned out of the *Tatler* by way of *Vogue*.

"But only the freeloaders are staying," said Sidney. "The most important editors, the old guard, are peeling out."

"Do they know Linda isn't coming?" asked Grace.

Sidney shook his head.

"Nobody knows that," he said. "Incidentally, is she tucked away upstairs?"

"I suppose so," said Grace. "What is the competition around town?"

"Nothing much today," said Sidney. "Duke of Edinburgh leaving the London airport, several exhibits of paintings; and the racing crowd at Newmarket isn't here anyway."

"I think I'll mill over to Jessica and Max and see if they've heard anything," said Grace.

She moved into the group who were paying their

grinning, courteous obeisances to the charming Mrs. Jessica Barstow, while an equal number of waiters pressed trays of hors d'oeuvres, which would more than make a meal, and a glistening assembly belt of delicious drinks.

Jessica was bedazzled by the questions about her child, herself (who should indeed, all agreed, be in front of the camera), and her departed husband, Jeffrey Barstow, who had enchanted so many of them when they had been students at Oxford or young diplomats in London and New York.

What utterly charming people. What an intelligent world!

Max was knee-deep in old cronies from varied banks of the Danube. He had fallen on the necks of some he had thought dead, of some who were relatives of those he had known, and of a few new Hungarian beauties who were doing well in the marts of the world.

A bellboy brought Jessica a note. Politely she turned with an apology to peer at it.

Grace, holding her drink in front of her farsighted eyes, beamed at her.

"Everything all right?" she asked. "It's a smash of a bash!"

"Pardon me," said Jessica.

She took Grace by the elbow.

"It's a note from Effie. Linda isn't back from Orville's yet. She wanted to know if she was down here. Isn't it a little late?"

Grace looked shaken.

"My God, she really *is* missing." She recollected the publicity ploy they had arranged for Linda not to appear at the party.

"We checked out the time cards of the makeup people at Wardour Street before I left to change my clothes, and that was at four. What time is it?"

Jessica looked at her wristwatch.

"It's almost seven o'clock."

"I'd better tell Sidney," said Grace.

"Maybe David," suggested Jessica.

David was talking to the photographer from *Life*

magazine. They were reminiscing about the time they had both parachuted into a brothel outside Rome on a very private mission during the war.

"Maybe not either one," said Grace. "This might be handled between us chickens. Let's just check a few things."

"What do you mean?" asked Jessica somewhat haughtily.

"Look," said Grace, having had enough liquor after a hard day to be tougher than usual, "we've had a little trouble already with Linda, and this picture hasn't even started yet. I mean, like, there's no film on her. There could be a replacement."

"You shut your goddamned mouth," said Jessica. "I won't tolerate such talk!"

Sidney, seeing their two angry faces, smelled trouble. He broke in.

"What's wrong?"

"Well," said Grace quickly, "Linda isn't home yet. She's probably lurking around the British Museum."

"Hardly," said Sidney, looking at his watch. "It closes at five o'clock. I think we'd best make a phone call or two."

"You stay," said Grace to Jessica, "and hold the fort. I'll do some checking with Sidney and let you know if anything develops."

The first call Sidney made was to Orville. It took a moment to discover that not only had Linda finished at three-thirty, she had left with her aunt.

"Her aunt!" exploded Sidney.

"Oh, God!" said Grace. "Not Claudia Barstow again!"

Sidney turned to her, pulling on his ginger moustache.

"Gad, what I suspect!"

The doorman confirmed his alarm.

"Mr. Percy of the *News* left something in the checkroom," he said. "Do you recollect where you directed his cabbie?"

"Why, yes, sir," said the doorman. "Most of the last

batch have been going down to Jermyn Street. The Cavendish."

◆◆◆◆◆◆◆◆

Flashbulbs popped like summer lightning in the Elinor Glyn room of the Cavendish. A small band commandeered hastily in a cab from Earl's Court Road ground away on "trad" jazz, the English version of Dixieland.

It was easy for Sidney to find the center of population, for a mob carrying drinks and laughing focused to a screaming voice that trumpeted the front-stage-center presence of Claudia.

She had removed her civilian clothes and was garbed in one of Linda's Grecian robes, a lilac one, belted in purple tassels, which hung down in loops almost to her ankles. She was crowned with a wreath of violets and pearls. While she did not exactly look like Aphrodite, she managed the assimilation of the costume as part of her entity, which was a Barstow characteristic. She danced to the music, and flashed her little feet in front of old swains.

"Get the twigs," she said, pointing one leg like a ballet dancer. "Who says the old girl hasn't got it yet! Remember, Alec?"

An elderly man with an autumnal fuzz of blond hair and flourishing a thick ex-RAF moustache received a slap on the back from her to which he reacted by returning a collop on her rear.

"Best gams in Mayfair," he said.

"Still up to your old tricks!" said Claudia.

"There hasn't been a winger like this since you and the chums cut it up in the Elinor Glyn room in the old days," he said. "I say, you've certainly got a winner in that beautiful filly!"

He peered into the room, craning his neck.

A cluster of newspapermen gathered about Linda. She wore her short Grecian peplos. Her hair was pinned on top of her head with two large jeweled hatpins, filched from her aunt's treasury of junk jewelry. Her face was flushed with the excitement of conquest, flattery, the querying interest of the press.

She was not disturbed by the pads and pencils that flashed to jot down the measure of her words, and she preened with young animal pleasure as cameras clicked at her reclining figure. She postured on the immense sofa known well to the third-estaters as the battleground for some of the most noted amorous struggles of the early twentieth century.

"Of course, I know the Barstows all suffer from a contagious wave of emotional instability," she said, as a flashbulb popped, "but I enjoy being one."

She was grateful for the photographic memory that gave her scraps of information to pass on, with all the right terms and nuances of wiser, older persons. It made it so easy to startle people. For the first time she saw the manic delight of devoted gossip mongers. She interpreted it as a particular ecstasy engendered by her person.

"How do you feel about inheriting the famous Barstow beauty?" asked one. "Do you think it is a handicap?"

"Orville, who gave me a portrait sitting today, said the Barstows are supposed to have exceptional bone structure. As a matter of fact, today I saw some magnificent nude pictures of my father and grandfather . . . and Aunt Claudia."

There was almost a gasp at this.

"I posed nude myself," said Linda. "Why not, it's one of the family assets, isn't it, Aunt Claudia?"

"That's been discussed pro and con," said Claudia, winking at one of her old cronies.

Someone laughed.

"You really posed in the buff?" a reporter asked Linda.

She cast a quick glance at her aunt. Had she gone too far?

"I guess the only thing we have to be careful of is not to brutalize ourselves. As Aunt Claudia says, fierce living and loving sometimes disturbed our performances. I guess you know, many of you must have been there."

There was a titter of laughter at this.

"I presume you are being personal," said Claudia.

There was laughter at this. Then sudden silence.

Claudia's glance sought the sudden arc of eyes.

Sidney pushed his way through the crowd, trailed by Grace Boomer.

"Oh, God!" said Claudia. "I knew it would happen."

She picked up a bottle from a passing waiter and stopped in front of Sidney, barring his path.

"This is a private party. Get out and go back to your own clambake."

"I think I'd better speak to you, Claudia," said Sidney. "You know, Linda is a minor—"

"She's my blood relative," said Claudia, waving the bottle, "and you can tell your chum David, that bastard, to give her a break or I'll—"

"Break it up," said Grace. She reached with amazing dexterity and took the bottle away from Claudia. As it lowered, a spout of champagne poured down the front of Claudia's tunic.

"My God, are you still alive?" said Claudia, staring at Grace.

"The party's over, gentlemen," said Sidney.

The band stopped playing quickly. The leader occasionally worked for the music department at Titan films out in Elstree.

Linda glanced up as heads turned, and arose from the sofa.

"Well," she said, "what's the matter? Did David send the nanny to get me?"

Sidney flushed but took her wrist.

"We'd better get home," he said. "Your mother's quite worried about you."

Linda laughed.

"Worried! Afraid the meal ticket's going to run out! Not a chance. You know, I'm going to be the best of all. The best goddamn Barstow."

"Bravo!" said Claudia.

She came to her niece and hugged her, just as Sidney got a better grasp on the child's arm. She was weaving a bit. At that moment the cameras popped again.

"You'll be in court for contributing to the delinquency of a minor unless she goes now," said Sidney quietly as he moved Linda toward the door. "Come on, Linda, you wouldn't want to get your aunt in trouble."

She turned to look back.

Claudia stood in the wreckage of the party.

"Go on, ducks," she said. "We'll catch up again. There are still a few things I have to tell you. How I wish I could teach you what I didn't teach myself. Don't muck it up as I did! Oh, I could show you the way. . . . I could . . . I could."

She saw Sidney glaring at her.

"I want you to teach me," said Linda, crying. "I need you. I need help."

The words tore out of her. She was afraid. She knew suddenly that she was alone, in a strange country, and everyone was bearing down on her.

"It's no use," said Claudia, sobered by the turn of events. "They might get the fuzz after me. They just would, you know. Don't let me get you in a worse mess than you're in now."

She stood with two streaks of mascara falling from her teary eyes. Grace and Sidney propelled Linda through the crowd.

As she disappeared through the door, Grace stared back at Claudia, distressed at the role she was forced to play. After all, there had been good times at Titan and memories of the old days in Hollywood when they were both young.

"Troglodyte!" spat Claudia after her.

She, too, had a memory.

She turned to the press.

"Well, chaps, you see how it is. But it was a proper debut for her, wasn't it?"

The group began to break up. Many of them were touched by the defenselessness of Linda and the valiant stand of Claudia. But most of all, they were newspapermen, and they had immediate and important dates with typewriters and photographic development laboratories.

Claudia sat down on the sofa. An elderly waiter began to clear away the debris.

She peered at the confusion of the room.

"Was it really a proper debut, Angus?" she asked wistfully.

"True-blue tradition," he said.

She smiled, without seeing him, and pulled down her crooked tunic, because, as she had insisted with Linda, she was sure real Greeks didn't wear undergarments beneath their clothes.

So Linda was gone. . . . Gone, as she knew would happen. She had only really known her niece eight hours, and she missed her this moment more than she had ever missed anyone in her whole life.

◆◆◆◆◆◆◆◆

Linda sat on the bed in her flower-sprigged flannelette nightgown and robe, sipping cold milk, while Effie sponged her bedraggled Greek tunic.

"I'll never forgive that old Miss Claudia for givin' you a sour stomach," she said.

How like Effie. The least thing Aunt Claudia had ever been blamed for was an upset stomach.

Her mother had accused Linda of being a Barstow, in other words, of being drunk, debauched, and deceitful.

While Linda mutely listened to the abuse that spewed out of Jessica's mouth, she realized how her mother loathed the Barstow name. Her father had cost her mother an important executive career and left her plunged in debt, living like the poorest secretary instead of a woman of importance. There had been many men who had wanted to marry her. Instead, she had chosen a senile sot because of her pity and respect for his misused talent. She had been put through indignities that could never be told, and now all her payment for suffering was a child just like him.

Once she had friends, savings, privileges. They had all melted away, she held forth to her daughter. And now that she had a chance to take her rightful place in the world, Linda had proved that she was tainted with her father's blood and was going to ruin the whole thing.

"You either do as I say, and behave the way an aristocratic southern girl should behave, the way I taught you, or you'll go home."

Linda's insides churned with a strange, defensive ecstasy. She had cut the Jessica Klopfinger bonds; she had joined up with her Aunt Claudia and family memories. There was nothing her mother could do about it. Linda knew it as she saw her mother walk away from her in anger, for she had not been defeated, only lectured. Mom was scared.

She hated her mother's pretenses. In several trips to New Orleans she had stayed at the phony pink-plaster French Quarter Mississippi Belle motel, which her tired Grandma Klopfinger managed. She reasoned, now, that since this social background was a lie, it was also possible that her mother had not been an executive whose services were vainly sought. Jeffrey Barstow, she kept mentioning, was an old man when she married him. There must have been a damned good reason she did.

The bedroom door squeaked. She glanced up suddenly, and there he was. Trim, elegant David Austin. He took a cigarette from his pigskin case, tapped it, and snapped his lighter, while he walked into her room with a casual air.

Effie responded to a tilt of his head. She left the room and settled on a luggage bench in the private hall.

That's his way. . . . Order people around. Well, not me! Linda tossed her hair back.

"I'm about to go to sleep," she said.

"Your mother said you were still up. We've got to have an understanding."

She looked at his long-fingered hands, the peaked hairline, the dark brows that shaded his blue eyes. Handsome. . . . Only he's not going to trap me.

He walked to the window. She noticed the crisp way his hair grew. Even the back of his neck had style. That you couldn't make up. It just happened. Like the Barstow bones. Wonder if Orville would like to photograph him nude? . . . She flushed at the thought.

"We couldn't have an understanding, Mr. Austin," she said.

He sat on the slipper chair by the window and tapped his cigarette into a stand ashtray.

"You don't seem to realize what this career is all about. It isn't entirely your fault. Your mother maneuvered cleverly to get you a contract. Max Ziska, a brilliant talent, entered the scene at the right time, with the right property for you. And now your Aunt Claudia has used you for her place in the sun. So far, Linda, you've been a pawn."

"Everyone seems to have some angle," said Linda. "What kind of pawn do you want me to be?"

"We're all pawns," he said. "To become a star, you have entered a corporate marriage with Titan films. You may not love, but your contract says you will honor and obey."

"Do you think I'm old enough for a corporate marriage?" she asked sarcastically.

"Possibly not," said David, "but your test made Titan think so. And personally you have all the wrong things that blend, God forbid, to make a star. A genius for disturbing behavior and for publicity."

"I have to be what I am," said Linda. She was frightened, so her voice was shrill.

"Your private behavior is not completely your choice from now on, Linda," he said. "An individual must live up to the written agreement of a corporation. Titan takes a risk with you. It based its investment on your potential performance, your beauty, and your name."

Linda's eyes flickered.

"And because Mr. Purse Strings Niadas insisted. I'm not so dumb. You tried to get rid of me after our first meeting. You just can't."

"Nonsense," he said. "Niadas chose you on the basis of your test. Titan's board of directors agreed, even though you're really several years too young."

Linda tossed her hair back with one hand.

"I'd very happily give up my virginity, to be more

mature for Titan," she said. "Maybe you could help me out. Nothing personal; for good old Titan, of course."

She watched to see if he was shocked. He didn't seem to be.

"Instant maturity is seldom achieved by rupture of a membrane."

She tried to hide her embarrassment by turning her head away and flipping her hair back, a trick she was finding convenient.

"I know you don't care much for me personally," she said, "so what's your message?"

"Linda," said David, looking at her sharply, "let's keep our relationship impersonal. That way we will not have the luxury of hostility or the blinders of affection. You need someone who is a fair judge of your value in your professional life. Analyze what the papers say about you tomorrow. Some of it will flatter your ego. Some will embarrass you very much. You will no doubt begin to think about what you want your public image to be. But, more important, you still have to sustain a characterization all through a picture."

"Max says acting is a constant search for the truth," said Linda.

She had forgotten her personal vendetta with David, and was thinking about acting.

"Then," said David, "if you seek truth, watch out for that natural pitfall, the unfortunate vulgarity of showing off, before or behind the camera. That is what happened to some of your really talented family."

Linda frowned.

"Everybody criticizes Barstows, but everybody seems to need what they have!"

He put his hand up.

"Yes," he said, "if you live with Titan Corporation, as I do, you know it is a cold, calculating machine, based only on financial morality."

He gave her a fragment of a smile. Maybe he was on her side.

"Do you want me to quit?" she said.

He shook his head. This child could not know that the fate of Titan studio lay in this film. In her slender body was the vision that kept the current Midas, Pericles Niadas, pouring his gold into the coffers. Still David felt sorry that he had to deal with the life and future of an untried young human being. He wished he had the courage to tell her to quit, to run as fast as she could in the other direction. But at least he could alert her to the problems she was facing, and help her as much as he could.

"Those who suddenly find themselves in a situation of power can be clobbered so quickly they never quite know what happened to them. People drag all the failures of past lives in a heavy, invisible burden. What has happened to them before will trigger what they ask of you. If you become a star, you will assume power beyond your control, you will become a touchstone for all they have missed in the past. Your person will become the magic that they pray will salvage them. They will bleed you white; no woman of flesh can live on a pedestal as a goddess. If you knew now what people would seek from you, you'd run."

"I don't want to run," she said. "I'm going to be a star."

He looked at her, saying nothing.

"But there's one thing I need," she said. "I'm alone. I must have help. And there's only one person in this world who can help me."

He waited.

"I want my Aunt Claudia to go with me. I want her to be my coach, to teach me not only the right things to do, but to keep me from doing the wrong things."

"Claudia!" said David. "Claudia help you!"

"Yes," said Linda. "Coach me, give me the Barstow voice. Show me what I can be. Look, nobody can play Alethea but me. But I can't do it unless Aunt Claudia works with me."

David thought a moment, walked to the window, and looked out reflectively. Finally he spoke.

"It will take some doing. You realize of course that the moment she starts a turmoil, she'll have to be jettisoned."

"I'll take that risk with her," said Linda.

David took a notebook out of his pocket and scribbled on it.

"I'll see what can be done," he said. "You'll have to trust me, and go on to Rome as planned. If you get cornered, here is my private number. And meanwhile, we won't discuss our conversation with anyone. Understand?"

She knew he was the only one who could help her. She nodded as he handed her the slip of paper. As she looked at it, he left.

He paused to talk to Effie, who sat near the open door.

"Good-bye, Effie."

"Bye, Mr. David, and thank you."

She had been listening.

"Thank you for what, Effie?"

He glanced, surprised, at her face, and was taken aback at the warm gratitude that shone on it. Such expressions did not often come his way. He was embarrassed.

The door to the hall closed. Linda sat still for a moment; then she opened the window to the sharp cold air and looked out on the blackness of Hyde Park, its gates locked for the night against teddy boys, mugging, and lovers.

The gentle drizzle halated the car lights along Park Lane. Double-decker buses, with their lighted cargo of doll-like people, counterpointed the sounds of horns, claxons, and the steady sloughing of tires in the wet.

From the distance came the mysterious clop-clop of the horse guard. In the staccato beat Linda thought she heard old voices from her family calling.

She climbed into the high, comfortable Dorchester bed. As she often did, Linda embraced her pillow and pressed her face against its laundry-sweet softness, to drown out the smells and sounds and sights of everything save her own self.

She heard Effie in her sanctuary, the large white bathroom, where she couldn't disturb Linda's rest with a light on in the bedroom; she could hear her close the toilet-seat cover as she settled down to read the cast-off morning paper. She soon smelled the fragrance of the sweet tobacco from Effie's pipe, which, of course, was no secret to her, although she pretended she didn't know about it.

With the security of this familiar scent, she fought the faint pressures of a headache, composed of the memories of the day and her first champagne.

Oh, that Aunt Claudia. She was on her side, ready to battle and to protect the Barstow image. Claudia had to be in her life. Linda wondered if Claudia was thinking of her too. How terrible it was, the way they had parted.

◆◆◆◆◆◆◆◆

Effie sucked on Mr. MacDonald's comfort. It was strange to look at the yellowed Indian-head meerschaum in the antiseptic elegance of a large London hotel bathroom. The old sachem seemed mighty far from home. She took one fond look at the hatchet face, smoothed the bowl against her nostril, and gave him a faint smile.

Thank God honey-bun's got me. . . . The Lord was good to make people take me for nothing, so's I can sit and hear their problems. That poor David Austin. He was such a good-looking little kid. I recollect that Mr. Jeffrey used to take pictures of him out of newspapers and magazines and prop them up on his desk for days at a time. He really must have liked him, and found him special. Mr. Jeffrey didn't fool around with sentimental things much. But somehow . . .

Notice how that poor David never says "I." He looks in the mirror, and he sees nothing. . . . Well, one thing, sure enough, he pushed Belinda right over the edge to go her way. Nobody's gonna stop Jeffrey Barstow's kid, nobody. . . . And he'll get Claudia to come. She needs her, no matter what they say. She's got to have kin!

She tamped out the pipe, put Mr. MacDonald's comfort back in the chamois pouch, and tiptoed in to see that Linda was asleep. A piece of paper was clutched in the hand that folded over the pillow.

4

◆◆◆◆◆◆◆◆

In the next few hours Linda Barstow became news all over the world. The great publicity machines of the modern age, all manner of communication media, swiftly changed her from an obscure American teenager to a hot front-page sex image.

Aided and abetted by the Barstow myth, her Aunt Claudia, and the eager, scandal-mongering London press, she had done more to engender publicity than Titan's forces from Red Powell to Grace Boomer could ever have done with all their massive budgets and well-organized propaganda machine.

Wire-photo impulses were sending pictures of her to every country in the civilized and uncivilized world. News services had picked up the juiciest quotes from her London interviews; hawkers were already selling eight-by-ten glossies of her on the streets of London, and they would soon be available throughout the world. The endless savagery of despoiling shrines would begin again. Pictures of Jane Russell, Marilyn Monroe, Elizabeth Taylor, Anita Ekberg, Gina Lollobrigida, and Sophia Loren, and even the new French sex kitten, Brigitte Bardot, would be tossed out for this newest image of the star syndrome.

As her half-nude body and voluptuous face stared out from the corners and kiosks of London, Linda Barstow became the new desired commodity. She was categorized between the virgin and the femme fatale; the young victim of fate who would be "la divine." She was still pure, and she was destined to suffer; she had a wicked background and a perverse innocence.

Like long-gone on the screen, but remembered Garbo, she gazed with heavy-lidded fatality on an inexplicable world that would use her. Like the Greek image of tragedy, she was the victim of fate over which she had no control, and like Brigitte Bardot, she had a body that made every man who looked at her picture consider fornication under various ecstatic conditions, heretofore undreamed of by him.

In other words, the public wanting to consume her, she was ready to be a specific motion-picture star.

◆◆◆◆◆◆◆◆

With no time to waste. David faced the necessity of immediate action. This time he could not have Sidney Keyes be his henchman while he fled to a distant assignment in his empire.

First on his agenda, of course, was Claudia.

He called on her at her digs at the Cavendish. She had ensconced herself protectively behind a silver tea service, puzzled at his call. Scanning the room, which was overdressed with framed pictures of the Barstow clan and various celebrities, his eyes glanced quickly away from one, twenty years before, with a young and vivacious Claudia and his smiling, handsome grandfather, Simon Moses. Noting the absence of valuable furnishings and paintings of a past wealth, he knew how to approach her. She was obviously nourishing herself on memories, and little else.

"Claudia," he said, "let us ignore social amenities and get down to what I have to discuss. You likely think I have come to speak to you about the uproar you and Linda raised with the press."

Claudia, elegantly pouring tea, glanced up at him. He was impressed, considering all things, with the stylishness that clung to her, along with the remnants of her beauty.

"Yes, I did," she said. "No doubt you'd like me to arrange with Grace Boomer to have an added interview, laced with apologies."

"Wrong," said David.

As he took a teacup from her, he glanced in the direction of a table draped with a Spanish shawl. Linda as a child with her father, a few stills from various pictures with Jeffrey, all stunning and rich, remnants of the golden days of Titan. One, smiling with Fergus and Simon Moses at an Academy banquet.

"You have inherited a responsibility," he said. "Linda is the last Barstow. And you know as well as I that it is a strange trick of fate which has put her in the position of beginning her career in this massive production. She is too young and too untrained for *The Oracle*. Look what happened with the press at your well-meaning party. Imagine what is to come. . . ."

"I wanted to help her be herself," said Claudia. "You know she is stifled by the people around her, all so much older than she. And all *raddled* with ambition. What will happen to her?"

"If anyone ever had a blueprint of imminent disaster, it would be you," said David.

"I know," said Claudia. "You know, as everyone does, that I'm on my uppers. I had so many chances, and I mucked them all up."

"I've studied all your films," said David. "I know how talented you are. And every error you made could be a warning signal to help your niece."

"So? She won't be near me. She'll have that iceberg Jessica telling her how to behave. And Max is too soft. Oh, Jeffrey would be so disturbed!" Her eyes filled with tears, and she angrily wiped them away with her tea napkin. "Sorry, I don't usually fall apart like this."

"Do you think she has talent?"

Claudia arose. Her face was transformed with a radiant smile. She moved across the room and leaned against the marble mantel, every bit the star taking stage center.

My God, thought David, watch that timing. What a teacher she could be. . . .

"Talent!" She laughed. "You should have seen her at Orville's sitting. She gave me gooseflesh!"

"Claudia, I want to put her in your hands. She needs

so many things you could give her. Only you could see what she might be."

Claudia stared at him, astonished.

"Me!"

"She needs voice training, and she must know the rudiments of acting when she goes up against those pros."

"I can't believe it," said Claudia. She glanced quickly at the nearby picture of herself and Simon. "You know about your grandfather and me. How he died in my arms. I thought of putting his pictures away when you came, but decided against it. We loved each other a long time, and our work together was wonderful, now that I look back on it. But mostly, you know about the bottle, and my whims . . . and all. How can you dare take the risk?"

"We are not dealing with the past," said David. "We are thinking objectively of the future. Your whims must be forgotten if you care about the child. I know what you did for John Graves; you took a cockney kid and molded him into the man who became a fine actor. I know what a teacher you are. If you think you can do it, I want you to settle your affairs here, and get to Rome immediately. I am certain you can use a good salary. I know we need a good dialogue director. You can help John Graves with his scenes. You have worked through the years with Leslie Charles. And Max made good pictures with you. I run them from time to time."

"But . . . what about Jessica?" asked Claudia.

"I shall handle that," said David. "And Max, and of course, Fergus Austin."

He knew he had won. She was already plotting her course.

"My God," said Claudia, smiling, "if that isn't ever a round robin!"

"Can you handle it?" he asked.

She put her hands to her lips a moment, looked up at him with her startlingly blue eyes, and smiled instead of crying.

"I think I can," she said.

"You understand," he said, "that if there are any major problems of your doing, you will have to leave. And if you do, after you have established a platform on which Linda feels secure professionally, you would most likely pull the whole edifice down with you. Can you realize thc enormity of this?"

Claudia nodded.

"If I could do it for a cockney kid like John Graves, I could certainly do it for my own flesh and blood."

◆◆◆◆◆◆◆◆

To Max, over a drink at the Ward Room, David presented a different face.

"Max," he said, "you have stewardship over this miracle. She is magnificent. You helped to make her so in the test. But you and I know it was only a fraction of what she has to do. You are going to be involved with massive production problems. You are working with an enormous cast. You have innumerable scenes with Chloë Metaxa, Niadas' long-time protégée, who, God knows, even if she is the best in Greece, is far from an easy actress, no matter how great her talent. And the fact that she *is* Greek, and so close in emotional kinship with Niadas, will raise problems there. You have scenes with John Graves and Leslie Charles that exclude Linda. All of these people are dynamic individuals on their own. Linda needs someone to work with aside from you, to understand her, and to help her to live up to her potential. You can't stop the rhythm of production to work with her beforehand on every scene."

"I know," said Max, twirling his glass thoughtfully. "I have been thinking about it."

"I have a plan," said David. "I want to fight fire with fire."

Max glanced at him, waiting.

"She needs a continuum of interest in the work she is going to tackle. You know what this means to the studio, and of course to you. I don't want you to be shocked at what I am going to suggest. You yourself and your past work long ago at Titan are partly responsible for my decision. I want Linda's coach to be Claudia Barstow."

Max silently sipped his drink, set it down, and his eyebrows met in a frown.

"It's an audacious idea. But I think I understand what you mean. I will be away from Linda a great deal during production. She needs an emotional involvement in her work. How do we approach it?"

"Claudia becomes dialogue director for the whole production," said David, "so Linda will not be self-conscious about being the only one needing help. If Claudia could discover and coach Graves, as she said, she certainly can do the same thing for her own flesh and blood."

He heaved a sigh of relief as Max nodded agreement. But he put his hand up quickly.

"Under one condition," said Max, "that *you* tell Jessica."

◆◆◆◆◆◆◆◆

Sidney Keyes was astounded at his friend David Austin. He had never seen him involved with production problems in such a personal way. And when David told him he was going to face Jessica himself, Sidney was only able to smother his surprise by hiding his face in a pink gin as he sat with his friend in the Dorchester bar.

◆◆◆◆◆◆◆◆

"This is the way it will be," said David, concluding the painful meeting. Jessica sat on the sofa in front of the fire, looking at him white-faced.

"I know you have plans on how you intend to run *The Oracle*. You can scrap them. My decision is that Linda needs every bit of help she can get, and the skills of her Aunt Claudia are essential. Both of them have agreed that if there is any problem, we will face it head-on. But the girl needs the best of what the Barstows have to give, which is considerable."

"But after all that newspaper scandal!" said Jessica.

"That scandal was based on an eccentric but true family pride. Claudia will come to the Niadas villa as soon as possible. And any interference from you will be known to me immediately."

And that ended the session, with Jessica hating him as he walked away.

It was a different thing when he called Fergus Austin in Hollywood. After hearing the turmoil of publicity, Fergus was starting the new day sitting in his pajamas, taking antacid tablets to battle his ulcer.

"How in God's name could you be aced into thinking of bringing a woman like Claudia into this child's life?" he screamed over the phone.

"Because she's a Barstow. There's no other way," said David. "She needs great expertise. Look, how short a memory do you have? I've run her old films. Some are classics. She was the backbone of Titan at her peak. And she's had her hard knocks. Look what she did for John Graves!"

"It's on your head," said Fergus. "I want to be on record with the stockholders. I have nothing to do with this folly."

"I am the major stockholder," said David, "in case you have forgotten. Like it or not, the fate of Titan is wrapped up in *The Oracle*. If Linda Barstow can't cut the mustard, I would say that the whole of our empire falls with her. I expect your cooperation, your goodwill, and for once in your starchy life, a little gratitude for what is being done here."

He hung up. Fergus was astounded. This was the first time David had ever stood up to him.

Then he broke into a sweat, realizing what dynamite it was to have Jessica, Claudia, and Linda under the roof of the Niadas villa. If Jessica ever blurted out the secret of Jeffrey Barstow being David's natural father, with Claudia his aunt and Linda his half-sister, the powder keg would explode. And if that day ever came, Fergus could pack his briefcase and walk out of Titan studio forever. What could he do? He realized it was the only life he had ever known since he was a kid of eighteen and had brought Claudia to Hollywood to found Titan for Simon Moses.

Because she's a Barstow, David had said.
Fergus shuddered.

◆◆◆◆◆◆◆◆

In New York, Andrew Reed, in his apartment at the Dakota, stared unseeingly from his desk across the room to a midmorning movie, scheduled at this dead hour to feed the voracious maw of the soporific dragon, television.

The events of the last few hours had made Reed the dean in charge of information regarding Linda Barstow. Since he had published the only known New York-oriented newspaper interview on her, his own phone had been tingle-tangling all morning. He was more valuable than ever as a newsmonger, for he had the inner track on a new celebrity.

After all these years, and his brush with the Barstow family, and Fergus Austin, as movies had grown, he was amused. One of the images bobbing about on the television screen caught his eye. He moved over to the sofa to watch.

And then *he* came on, Leslie Charles, and Andrew's heart beat in his throat again with memory. It was the picture *The Darkening House*. How well he remembered that day—the ill-fated set where Mr. Moses had an attack, after the disgraceful set-to with the drunken Claudia. At least, good had come out of it for himself, and most of all for his dear Leslie. What a heavenly week together they'd had. How young, how very young the world had been.

He looked at Leslie on the screen, unbelieving. He seemed all eyes and Adam's apple, he hadn't filled out yet, and his amateurish gestures, youth-green and eager, were endearing. How different he was from the elegant, polished actor waiting now in Rome to support this little Barstow, this niece, of all things, of the fury, the disaster called Claudia.

He switched the television off, put a sheet of notepaper in his typewriter, and clacked away.

Dear Leslie,

Linda Barstow will be blowing into your bailiwick any mo, and I wanted you to know that it brought back a bubbling caldron of memories. Yours truly is stirring up the old witches' brew on a new Barstow career. She is a moppet who is also undoubtedly going to stir up a great deal of excitement.

I read in *Variety* that your box office on the last prod did a bit of a nose dive. I gave you the best review I could, boysie, and blamed it, of course, on the overdone script written by eight eager beavers, under the influence of that old pep pill Fergus Austin. But this magnum opus you are about to launch has that old black magic of Maximilian Ziska in it. He remains a pillar of taste in the middle of this current muddle. I am going to go all out for this Barstow brat, and I will three-star any info you can give me from Rome, Greece, or wherever, on her antics. Try to get yourself tied up with her in publicity, you old twat, and I will be the font that pours this golden legendry into the world.

How's the star, John Graves? Of all things, Claudia's protégé. Having come full-blown (to coin a phrase) from the London scratch-ass ateliers of Muloch and De Kayser, is he Stanislavsky by injection through Lee Strasberg, or did the Royal Academy and the Bristol Old Vic rub a slightly more Olympian bloom on his posturing?

I just saw you on the idiot tube in that old flick *The Darkening House*. What memories that antique film brought back—oh, so many springs ago, Leslie, ere you learned your calling. Of course, then films were as young as we were.

I expect that Titan will be sending me over on one of those junkets like they usually do, to lounge about your amphitheater. Remember how long ago I introduced you to Rome's glories! We must continue where we left off. Be warned, dear boy, and don't get tied up with anything that can't be interrupted.

Yours enmeshed in memory,
Andy

Leslie Charles, as Andrew well knew, had set himself up as the super motion-picture star, the *amico ameri-*

cano, when he had arrived months ago in his favorite city, Rome, for *Pallas Athena*. But when Martha Ralston's pregnancy had closed down the film, Leslie felt that a new campaign for his image would have to be created.

For *The Oracle*, especially since Jeffrey Barstow's daughter was going to be the focus of publicity, it would have to take a new tack, have a new angle. It was indeed disturbing to have to play his scenes with such a young girl, and he suddenly felt a generation older, and realized that if he didn't watch out, he could well be relegated to being a character actor.

For his peace of mind it was necessary for him to be *au courant*. He desperately feared being déclassé. He recalled with a nagging horror the life of an elderly director who had been very close to him at one time. Now the gray-haired old man, still of considerable wealth, lived in a penthouse on top of a building he owned off the Sunset Strip; the area was known locally as the Swish Alps. The old fellow could now be seen late afternoons cruising the adjacent streets at hungry time, looking for young boys who accepted food, drink, and shelter, along with petty-cash handouts, in return for their company.

Leslie stepped out on his balcony with a jaundiced eye. Rome was really changing too, too much. But neon lights, jukeboxes, Vespas spawning like blowflies on spoiled meat, new concrete blocks of tenementlike apartment houses, and the constant hiss of espresso machines filled him with dismay. He grimaced, something he hardly ever allowed himself to do, for his fine-boned face and ironed-out eyelids were without a crease.

Rome isn't what it used to be! he thought sadly, echoing a comment Nero had made a few blocks away, a few hundred centuries before, as the Christians began to outnumber the lions.

That led him to reflections about Andrew Reed's letter. His visit was one load he would rather forestall. Like Maeterlinck, he knew that two queen bees in one hive were trouble.

It seemed incredible that he had once cared so much

for him, and trusted his advice and taste. Now he had gone far beyond his mentor, and dreaded his florid presence in Rome as an "I-knew-you-when" companion, just when he was trying so hard to make an elegant and more youthful image for himself. Yes, the only key to this puzzle was an important and publicized camaraderie with Jeffrey Barstow's child. He wished her good landings and a pleasant disposition.

◆◆◆◆◆◆◆◆◆

As the plane flew high over the cloud-borne road to Rome, Linda, Max, Jessica, Grace, and Sidney shuffled through the complete press-clipping portfolio which had been assembled by the Titan publicity staff in London.

Sidney leaned close to Grace, who was occupied with a bundle of the clippings.

"How can one young girl, and one old girl, blab so much in such a short time?"

He read a few of the choice headlines.

"CLAUDIA DISHES THE DIRT . . . BARSTOWS IN THE BUFF . . . BODS ARE BETTER THAN CROWNS . . . BEAUTY FOR BIRDS, SAYS BARSTOW . . . CLAUDIA RERIDES AGAIN . . . I'LL NEVER WEAR A BRA . . . and, oh, God," he said, "VIRGINITY IS A BORE."

"If she keeps on at this rate, she won't be bored long," said Grace.

She unfolded a three-column picture of Linda, long-legged and coltish in her short Greek peplos, her hair skewered up on her head. Her face, made up artfully by Claudia Barstow, one of the best makeup artists in the world, was a study of a very young and beautiful wanton.

"She certainly takes a great picture." Grace sighed.

"She certainly bridged that age gap you were all so worried about, without a sex potential," said Sidney, tugging at his red moustache.

The next picture was a two-shot. Linda, smiling and pert, holding a goblet in her hand, and next to her, rigged in a scanty Grecian costume, was Claudia, lifting up a jeroboam of champagne. Her air of reckless abandon and joy in the grape looked more like the decline and potential fall of the Roman Empire than a niece's introduction in a film that was part of a Grecian idyll.

"I think," said Grace, "maybe I ought to try to get some new, higher-class type of work, say like playing the piano in a whorehouse."

"They wouldn't have you," said Sidney, waving a clipping at her.

"Or," said Grace, "I could always write a dirty novel!"

"Dull," said Sidney. "Truth is so much madder than fiction."

The warning placard began to flash: FASTEN SEAT BELTS.

Max put his hand on Jessica's. She was leaning back, her eyes half-closed.

"Soon Rome," he said, "Rome, the eternal city with the modern air."

Jessica peered below. A shroud of cotton clouds swathed it from view. Only a few rifts revealed beautiful apricot-hued Rome with its gleaming domes and shimmering Tiber.

Jessica clutched at his hand. He was surprised. She rarely moved in an unrehearsed way.

"Oh, Max," she said, "I don't want to be stuck out in that villa outside Rome, while you're at the Hassler. I've a terrible feeling about handling this . . . this situation."

"Now, now, Jessie," said Max, "I must have a suite in Rome for business reasons. There is plenty of room for me at the villa. Once we have settled these silly amenities of me being in Rome, I shall haunt the guest wing. We must think first of the picture, and of Linda, and then, my dear, we have ourselves."

Jessica saw the need in his eyes, and she reacted to it. She turned her hand, and caressed his, with a sudden, soft touch. She needed all the power and support she could get.

"I see no reason why I couldn't stop off with you this evening and settle you comfortably. Linda can get bedded down by Effie tonight. I'll go back to the villa later."

She leaned forward, and touched his face.

"I'll bed you down," she said.

III

ROME:

1956

I

After the well-greased obsequience of customs and passport control at Ciampino Airport were finished, Lancia limousines met them, with attendant luggage cars. Linda, in a car with Effie and Grace, drove along the dreary road toward Rome, staring out the window.

She thought the long-marching ruins of an aqueduct veered like a frozen serpent into their horizon. They passed the outer suburbs of Rome, concrete and colorless in the humid air.

"I can't wait to see Rome!" said Linda.

"Well, you won't tonight," said Grace. "We're going to pass along the Aurelian wall, and get out to the Villa Madonna della Rosa. You know, it's just off the Appian Way."

"You mean we aren't going to live in Rome!" said Linda.

She cast an I-told-you-so look at Effie, who was peering out at a shining espresso machine sending out a screaming spray of steam in the window of a neon-lit trattoria.

"Oh, we're in a suburb of Rome, dear heart," said Grace. "It's a beautiful villa, owned by Mr. Niadas himself and lent to you. It has marble halls, and gorgeous gardens, and wonderful statues in the most dramatic places. It's only a short distance from Cinecittà, and you'll be very glad for that when you're shooting. Why, my goodness, the people who live in the new apartments out at Parioli have to go lots farther to work!"

"Sounds like Forest Lawn," said Linda.

The sun came out in a giant burst, gilding the dark-red and mustard facades of the distant city. The car moved away from life, it seemed to Linda, along the Appian Way. The ancient walls along the road pressed in on each side of her, a smothering presence.

Chunks of marble, umbrella-shaped stone pines, sections of ruined aqueduct, accented the melancholy *campagna.* Occasionally a crumbling and forlorn tomb rose up in sad permanence, older than the memory of the highborn person who had been buried in it.

In silence they passed the round tomb of Cecilia Metella, moved along a cypress-lined walled lane, and then into a driveway, where a gateman opened enormous squeaking gates and bowed low as they entered the drive of the Villa Madonna della Rosa.

The garden in the late afternoon was perfumed by the *ponentino,* the little west-wind sea breeze which cooled the oven of Rome. Out here in the *campagna* it released a fragrance composed of stone pine, cypress, new-mown lawn, ilex, magnolia, wisteria, lilies, orange trees, and innumerable roses.

An enormous villa sprawled in the center of the greenery, its balustrades, loggias, and terraces of marble gleaming a rosy gold in the slanting sun.

The car halted in the circular drive. In front of the massive wrought-iron-and-glass entry-hall doors stood a man as if he had been awaiting this moment throughout eternity.

Linda stepped out of the car. The man, impeccably dressed, bowed, his head shining in the sunlight, for he did not have a hair on his head.

As he stared at Linda from an ivory mask of a face, neither young nor old, he seemed astonished.

Linda stared back. She had never seen a man before who had no hair on his head, no eyelashes, no brows, or even a beard. His bone structure, aristocratic and refined, made him look like a piece of sculpture, betrayed into life by his dark, liquid almond eyes.

"Nice to see you, Ubaldo," said Grace, breaking the moment. "Linda, this is Ubaldo, the majordomo of the villa."

Ubaldo inclined his head slightly.

"Welcome to the Villa Madonna della Rosa, signorina," he said formally.

His voice was rich and warm.

"Oh, honey-bun," said Effie, her head thrown back, eyes closed, inhaling the delicate warm scent of the afternoon. "Remember?" said Effie, "remember. . . . Honeysuckle time."

There was suddenly a long-remembered stirring in her, which choked up her throat, as if tears were sprouting from some forgotten source.

Ubaldo was forgotten.

"Yes," said Linda, "I remember honeysuckle time."

"Long, long ago," said Effie. "With your father in the house in the valley. It was like this, at the end of day, after a hot Santa Ana had made all those flowers give out that stuff they grew for. Then a breeze would come over the pass from Malibu way, and everything would just set in its own sweet juices, and send out signals. Your daddy called it 'honeysuckle time.' "

Linda almost saw him. The blue eyes and the secret smile, the joyous fleeting escape the two of them shared, a little girl carried high in his arms as they fled Mom and the large restricting house.

"Honeysuckle time," Jeffrey would say, sniffing.

Her father would pretend to hunt for the sweet flowers with her, and then turn with a wonderful mock surprise and nuzzle her cheek as she clung to him, giggling.

"There it is!" he'd cry. "My honeysuckle vine!"

And he'd kiss her and inhale for a moment, and pause as if he knew there wasn't much time left, his eyes closed against the velvet of her cheek. . . .

The elegant, hairless man moved again.

"May you have as happy memories here," he said, as he saw the smile on her face. "May I show you the villa?"

Linda nodded, fascinated by his shining white teeth as he forced a smile. He stood very erect, and gestured with a long-fingered hand. She noticed the shine of gold coins on his French cuffs and found herself wondering if he had hair anyplace on his body.

The servants lined up in the gallery were introduced to her by Ubaldo. There were maids, footmen, four white-clad men from the kitchen staff, including Mario, a tall-capped small man with a wiry moustache, a gifted chef from Abruzzi, where, Ubaldo explained, the great chefs are born.

They all bowed as she faced them. She caught several of them glancing at her surreptitiously, the women puzzled and disappointed by her youth, some of the men gazing with open-eyed admiration at her hair and young face.

She was as imperious as she could manage as he led her through the large rooms. . . . You'll see . . . you'll see, she thought, I'm not really what I look like in these baby clothes.

They passed through the small salon and another long gallery laden with Greek and Italian marble statues, most of them with broken noses.

"Looks like a shooting gallery," said Linda.

"Those are true antiquities," said Ubaldo, "most of them excavated here on the grounds. Only the spurious ones for sale in the Via Veneto shops for tourists have noses. These rooms are the *sale di ricevimento,* where have been entertained the famous people of the world."

Marble floors were scattered with Aubusson rugs. Large French and Venetian mirrors echoed the stately gold furnishings and brocade-draped walls. Olivewood and marble-topped tables, polished and grand, held art objects, Roman and Greek marbles, Chinese jades, Ming horses, and Etruscan statues, little carved treasures taken from churches, and occasional tanagra figurines standing on alabaster bases.

Linda peered into the *gran salone.* It had furnishings to accommodate fifty.

"Not exactly cozy."

Her voice echoed.

Ubaldo led her to the end of the lofty gallery. A stairway, curving gently, with shallow renaissance steps divided into two staircases, led to an upper hall of vast proportions with baroque painted ceilings.

Her attention was arrested by a figure on the landing that divided the two stairways. It had been designed as the focal point of the palazzo.

In gently lighted radiance stood the nude statue of a young maiden, revealed in its almost flesh-pink youth. She gazed straight ahead of her, as if she were trying to see beyond her horizon. One arm was curled slightly, the hand at her slender waist, and the other arm held her discarded robe casually, as if she were about to bathe. Her hair was in curls at the nape of her neck, with a roll twisted high on her head. Linda, as she moved up the stairs, noticed that wavelets lapped at her feet, and a little fish lifted its head out of the sculptured water by her toes.

Linda felt she could have posed for her.

Effie saw it too. Her eyes widened.

Ubaldo halted, his face impassive.

"Praxiteles," he said, in such a low voice she could hardly hear him, "would be delighted to see that you have found her."

An expression of awe crossed his face as he looked from her to the statue; then he gestured, leading them up the grand staircase.

"She is so real!" Linda said.

When she turned, the man had already opened the double doors to a suite. The sitting room was shaded by an outside gallery from the afternoon sun. It was elegant, with brocaded upholstered furniture. The high walls were hung with paintings. Masses of white roses and lilies in crystal bowls perfumed the air.

"Where are the Niadases now?" asked Linda, feeling she was intruding in their private lives.

"Traveling on the yacht. Or in Greece, or Paris, or London. Wherever life takes them. It is rather uncomfortable now for the signora here in the heat of Rome.

"I shall leave you to your privacy," said Ubaldo. His white teeth flashed both at Effie and at Linda. "Mr. Niadas insisted you use his suite. May you find it to your liking, and may I be able to supply any demand your heart desires."

He bowed formally, and left.

"Glory be!" Effie called out from the next room. "This is fit for a queen!"

Linda followed, and saw that she stood speechless at the elegance before her. The enormous bedroom was done in tones of pale blue and silver, toning down the rich sensuality of its furnishings.

The bed stood on a dais. The headboard was a cluster of carved baroque seashells. The twisting headposts of silver led up to a canopy supported by silver cherubs. They held back blue-damask drapes that could be let down for privacy.

As a temple of Venus, the splendid bed dominated the room.

Linda dived headlong onto it, sliding the lace-and-satin covering aside, scattering the pillows. She lay back and looked up at the brocade dome with the cupids smirking down at her.

"Look at this, Effie," she said, throwing her arms wide. "It's mine—the famous place where Martha Ralston put it on the line!"

She sat up, laughing, her skirts pulled high. She kicked off her shoes and pulled off her bobbysocks, wiggling her toes into the lace.

"Now B'linda," said the reproving voice of Effie, "I didn't bring you up like that!"

"Don't you know I'm a movie star!" said Linda.

She wandered into the adjoining dressing room. It was enormous. Scented closets were lined with satin. She thought how silly her small wardrobe was going to look, lost among the ruffled sachets and quilted hangers.

She sat down at a large Venetian dressing table, with professional makeup lights rimming the mirror.

The bathroom was made of pink marble. An enormous antique Roman head snorted forth bathwater from the nostrils, when she turned the gold taps. That amused her. The sinks, the shower, the cabinets and mirrors, and a wonderful contraption that almost got her face wet when she turned it on, a bidet, fascinated her, and also the fact that the tub was recessed in a window, one could bathe in privacy, with all the distant beauty of tall cypress-laden gardens and Roman sky for a background.

She whistled. This was really living. Why, the kids at home wouldn't believe it. The apartment south of Wilshire was a million miles away.

She was interrupted by Effie. Her mother was on the phone. She picked up the gold-and-crystal phone on a porphyry table. "Hello, dear, are you comfortable?"

Linda knew the sweetness meant that Mom was somewhere with Max, and very comfortable herself.

"It's just super, Mom," she said. "Wait till you see it!"

"Well, I'll be back very late. I'm at the Hassler now. They dine very late here, it seems. I hope you don't mind."

"Okay by me," said Linda. "Just let me see there's a guide to get you to your room. Believe me, Cleopatra never had it so good."

"That's nice," said Jessica. "So have a good dinner, and get a good rest."

"Okay, Mom."

She hung up and peered out at the dark garden.

The vastness of the place, and the silence of the *campagna,* now that the twittering birds had nested, hit her. There was a soughing of evergreen needles sifting the wind. The sun was down, and the drowsy scent of night-blooming flowers drifted through the open windows. The marble floors seemed chill. She was sitting in the dark when Effie came in.

"Do you want to eat downstairs, or send it up here?" she asked, turning on lights. "That Ubaldo just asked. Imagine, a dining room just for the servants. They have so many here that they have a special cook for the help!"

She grinned at the marvel of it. Linda knew Effie would be a favorite, with her good looks and her warm smile.

"They asked me to eat with them, but I'll stay with you if you're lonesome," said Effie. "What shall I tell that . . . that Ubaldo?"

"You eat downstairs, but tell him I'll eat up here," said Linda. "I'm going to study for my part. And tell him Mom will be in late from the city."

After an elaborate dinner on a tray, Linda took a perfumed bath in the sunken tub, anointed herself with various oils, and got into her nightclothes.

If she had not been promised by David that Claudia would join her soon, it would have been a lonely evening. But she looked at the splendor around her, and thought it was only befitting that Barstows live in a palace. She must get used to it, and be a princess.

But now for her characterization. Max had told her how to go about it. She gathered together several large picture books on Greece, and thumbed through, looking up Praxiteles in the index. The photographs were magnificent color plates from museums and archaeological sites throughout the world. Praxiteles, it seemed, lived in the fourth century B.C. and was a sculptor who excelled at depicting emotion with grace and relaxed strength. She marveled that here, under her own roof, was this statue, with a romantic linkage that brought her together in an eerie kinship.

She left her bed and tiptoed out of her suite into the upper hall. The palazzo was still, but the lights were aglow for her mother's return.

Linda went down the great staircase to the landing, studied the flesh-toned statue so much like herself. She attempted the same stance. It was not quite right. She dropped the shoulder straps so her own breasts were bare. There, that was it. She struck the pose, and lifted her chin, dreaming of a distant shore on the Aegean Sea, and of the most beautiful woman of her time performing the magical ceremony. Ah, that was it; as the books said, the peak of perfection, the worship of godhead by beauty.

Below, in the hall, Ubaldo sat in an alcove reading a book, awaiting Jessica's late arrival. He sensed a movement and glanced up. He stared in disbelief at the young girl, her breasts bared, a replica of the statue. She did not see him, and he did not move, but sat, with a chill prickling his scalp.

For a moment she stood, breathless, and then she lifted the straps of her gown over her shoulder and put her hand on the foot of the statue.

"Good night," she said.

She walked slowly up the stairs and entered her suite.

Ubaldo set the book down and took a handkerchief out of his pocket. He mopped the back of his neck, for he was sweating; a cold, unexpected glaze of excitement quickened his pulse. He settled back and closed his eyes. He heard the door shut upstairs. He sat still, trying to quiet his pulse.

The blood about his heart congealed, and for a moment it seemed as if a forgotten fever and longing had snakestoned back into his brain.

Oh, no . . . there must be no more emotion. No yearning. Ubaldo had lived on the dead craters of the moon too long to look at the light of living stars. His marble Phryne with her cool thighs of white Paros marble was woman enough for what he had become. He had lived among memories long enough to know the life to which he had been born was ended.

No more was he a Roman prince with curling black hair and glittering wealth to match his handsome youth.

Since the Villa Madonna della Rosa had become his and he had excavated the statue with other objects of Roman conquest in the treasury he found in this earth, he had always bade good night to his Phryne. And now a girl of pulsing flesh had disturbed his idyll.

He left his book and walked up the steps to the statue. He touched her marble foot with the little fish nibbling at her toes, just as Linda had. But for the first time in years it was not the beauty of the statue that possessed his thoughts.

He had functioned as the Greek Niadas majordomo incognito, to be near his treasures when he could no longer afford them, rather than have the new state of which he was no part confiscate them. There was no other place for him to hide them.

Now he thought of a flesh-and-blood girl, who had gone upstairs to sleep in the bed that had once been his when he was the master of this house. All was lost to him in the convoluted paths of war and postwar taxes.

He rang for the night butler to attend the Signora Barstow when she came in from Rome. He passed through the servants' wing and went to his own small room up the back stairs. He undid double-bolted locks and closed the door quietly.

A Napoleonic campaign bed, a Venetian painted chest, a Spanish olivewood vargueno, with the lid open, revealing ivory-inlaid drawers, a Savonarola chair, and a threadbare silken Isfahan rug were the furnishings in the room. A small vigil light cast a flickering gleam on a golden object at his bedside table.

Ubaldo went to it, picked it up, cupping his hands about it. He held it to eye level reverently and then caressed it, his eyes devouring its beauty. It was a goblet, small and battered, having the form of a woman's breasts. The large nipples were formed of a green stone, zinnebar.

And even now, as he held the treasure, and moved into memories almost forgotten, he would have been astounded had he known that the future of this young girl, Linda Barstow, was bound with the treasures that he had amassed in those perilous years, it seemed a lifetime ago.

He was transported twenty-one years back, just half his lifetime away, to the moment the goblet was put in his fevered hands. He was lying almost unconscious on the square couch in a native hut outside Jamjam in Ethiopia, the ancient land of Abyssinia. Thc Waizaro, witch-priestess's gentle hand lifted up his head, as she helped him hold the golden cup.

"Drink from the cup of Makeda," she said.

At the word Makeda, the onion-thick layers of memory pricked his brain, and death lost him. Surely this Makeda was the one known as the Queen of Sheba. In this wild land on her return from the court of Solomon she had paused in her crude goatskin tent and given birth to her son by the great king.

The thought that the Queen of Sheba and Solomon had pledged from this chalice had sent an awakening shock through his body.

"The gibril bird has cast his shadow upon you," said the Waizaro, "but drink from the true goblet and you shall live."

After he drank, he slept, but he was awakened as the earth burst with an attack by Italian bombers. He found the Waizaro dead under the smoldering beams, the sacred cup in the dust, where it had fallen. Ubaldo picked it up, dressed in a native chamma, and hid it in its folds.

No matter how hungry, cold, or sick he was, he never parted with the golden goblet. Using his knowledge of Arabic and Ge'ez, beginning his trek he followed the black marked paths along the Blue Nile, making his way as a trader, using native silver crosses tipped with earspoons for his barter.

All those wandering months finally along the yellow, arid sand of the *quolla* he had puzzled that no one questioned him as a fereghi. His proud Italian visage was so classically what it was.

But when he entered the city streets at Assab Bay, he wondered no longer.

He wandered through the graystone customs building on the water. The windows were still intact.

And there he saw a black man, stone bald. Hollow-eyed.

He paused. So did the man.

He moved an arm. The man did.

He was reflected in the window. He was the man.

◆◆◆◆◆◆◆◆

He returned to Italy, working with a part-Lashkar crew on a Panamanian registered rust-bucket freighter, part of the Niadas Greek fleet, fiercely protecting his golden goblet. His body was still infected with fever and chills, but he was purged clean of any germ of fascism.

There was no place for his fever-shattered body in the hordes marching in uniform, to the glory of their land along with their Nazi brethren. Unashamed, he was grateful.

Ubaldo returned to find that the family palazzo in Rome had been confiscated.

The Fascists were now after the rich. The old aristocrats, who had tried to be part of Mussolini's regime, following his father's friend, the Duke of Cesaro, had long since resigned from office.

Back from battle, a broken civilian, he dressed in a fine silk prewar Via Condotti suit, mingled with the crowds on the Corso, in Piazza Navona, on the Pincio and the Gianicolo. He saw old school chums, and young Roman sweethearts who were holding the hands of others. He cautiously held back. No one recognized him. There was no gesture of his hand, no manner of his flung-out right foot, once famously broken in the ginco del calcio game, no warm smile that had once been kissed in adoration, no wicked glance of his eyes, now lashless, which brought back a flash of memory to them.

His essence, he realized, had been, not that he was himself unique, but that he was a thick-eyelashed, curling-haired, wealthy aristocrat.

Some looked at him, abashed at the hairless, browless wonder, beardless skin. He saw poorly concealed relief in their eyes, that such a disaster had not happened to them. He might as well have been their grandfather.

He was twenty-two years old.

He revealed himself to no friends.

He retired to the Villa Madonna della Rosa, the family country estate. His sister, a hopeless religious fanatic with the family female weak heart, wept for two days, and then asked if he would mind remaining in seclusion while she entertained princes of the church. It was her war effort, and she wanted to bring them pleasure, not distress. Did he mind if she said he was still away?

His mother had died of thrombosis the winter he was gone. His father was long in the *camposanto* family vault, having been murdered by Croats on the cruiser *Puglie* sabotage, when Ubaldo was a child.

Without telling his recluse sister, it amused him to select a marker and have it engraved with his birthdate. He set the stone in the empty tomb next to his father's. Other noble Romans had done the same for beloved ones who had not returned home. So he laid himself to rest, and set about to see what he might do with what was left of the body that had once been Principe Govanni Ubaldo Albini. Only the soul, he thought, amused at the obsolete idea, was trapped in his framework.

There were meager remains of the family fortune. He set to work mapping the grounds of the villa, slowly excavating them. Since student days, when he had found shards and fragments of marbles, and coins from the time of Hadrian. he had been suspicious of the fact that a powerful Roman official or general had shipped vast stores of Grecian plunder to this country place for the glory of his conquest and the future embellishment of his tomb, as was the custom. The treasures of Delphi, he knew at the time he dated his findings, were alone plundered of more than five hundred pieces of statuary.

No one cared to bother with what seemed to be a bald, sun-scorched *vecchio signore* digging in his rundown estate, planting vegetables and living off the land, with other old gardeners carrying earth about, and enriching the markets of the city; which needed food.

Ubaldo sorted the treasures he discovered, hiding the best in long-forgotten catacombs sealed off under his villa, and taking archaeological fragments into the city, cautious that no one traced him, or knew from whence he came.

With these treasures, and his vegetable produce, he maintained the small staff, until the Germans began overrunning the Roman streets. Then, after he was followed several times from his visit to the antiquity shops, he knew that someone was on his trail. He was terrified that Goering would hear of his bounty, and arrange to confiscate the villa.

From then on he sent his oldest, most threadbare gardener into town to sell vegetables, and subsisted on this meager living.

The day he discovered the marble Phryne, he and the gardener and three old tenant farmers blanketed her and carefully transported her inside the house on a wheelbarrow. They hid her in a downstairs cloak closet, padded with blankets and down quilts from the ancestral beds, against possible air raids.

The war was ended. Taxes and civil affairs were burgeoning. Ubaldo realized that if the Villa Madonna della Rosa were confiscated and put on the block for back taxes, his statue of Phryne would be discovered. She and all his treasures would leave him for a cold home in a museum.

There was only one thing to do. Sell his villa to

someone who would not only respect the contents, but keep them *in situ.*

Ubaldo analyzed the millionaire market.

Americans were out. They would want to ship the treasures to Cleveland, or Dallas, or any hometown to present their gilded image to their fellow citizens.

There were few great Continental fortunes left of vast buying power. Even such social bulwarks as the Rothschild family had ransomed members of their vast dynasty by signing away many of their properties to the Nazis, and the English were taxed and double-death-taxed to the point of poverty; and their economy was frozen.

Latin or South-American fortunes were unthinkable in terms of preserving his treasures; a sudden revolution could bring his collection to a distant auction block piece by piece. The thought of such a possibility awoke him in the midst of the deepest sleep, sweating with horror.

For years his delight had been the arrangement and rearrangement of his precious objects, which in time became more alive and real to him than the shadowy images of the humans who so rarely crossed his path in any meaningful manner.

The best security for his collection was among the golden Greeks, the new society of tradespeople and shipping tycoons springing up in the circles of international tax-free machinations. Admittedly their ships flew the flags of Panama, Honduras, and Liberia, nations that had degraded themselves with their dummy corporations, and paid homage only to their four freedoms: freedom from taxes, freedom from inspection, freedom from collective bargaining, and freedom from legal responsibility. And Liberia had added a fifth: freedom from war risks.

The whole ploy had been summed up rather neatly in the words of Aristotle Onassis, one of the new argonauts, who had said to the press, "As a Greek I belong to the West. As a shipowner, I belong to capitalism. . . . My favorite country is the one that grants maximum immunity from taxes, trade restrictions, and unrestricted regulations."

This Greek society, with its yachts, personally owned islands, private airplanes, villas on the Riviera, apartments in Paris, London, and New York, palazzos in Rome, and numbered bank accounts in Switzerland, was fattening on its merchant shipping, oil monopolies, and Middle East trade franchises.

One man among them was his choice. He was the one they called the Platinum Greek, Pericles Niadas. Not only had he boundless wealth, but a great reverence for Greek antiquities.

Another reason Ubaldo selected Niadas was that he had once met him by an unusual chance; the events of his life seemed predestined to connect with this man again.

It was many years ago. He had just turned twenty, and full of the glory of his nation, the rousing speeches of Il Duce, and the manifest destiny of Italy, he had driven southwest from Genoa, on leave, in his gleaming new Alfa Romeo roadster.

After a gay holiday in Monte Carlo, seeking a breath of fresh air, he drove out of the principality of Monaco to Roquebrun, and followed the Grande Corniche road, along the track of the Old Roman Via Aurelia, doubling back to Le Turbie.

Here, standing on the top of the Tête de Chien, was a whisper of a ruin, but as a Roman he stood admiring it, leaning against a toppled pillar drum. Before Christ was born, the Emperor Augustus had erected these marble columns. The monument was called the Trophy of the Alps. It celebrated the conquest of the Ligurian mountain men who had blocked the Romans from Gaul.

He looked fifteen hundred feet below, into the harbor, and to the shimmering Mediterranean. The ruin was a natural resting place in time, perched, a forgotten sentinel, above the yachts of Monaco.

He pulled off his tunic and shirt, folded them to make a pillow, and settled back, relishing the dusty warmth of the afternoon. He closed his eyes, inhaling the cool breeze that washed off the stale fumes of women and wine. The wind against his curly black hair felt like clean fingers combing away his debauched nights.

A shadow robbed the red warmth from his closed eyelids. He glanced up, to see a young man looking at him. His head was a shining cap of straight black hair. He wore American sun goggles, a yachting jacket, and white flannels, and he stood, his neatly shod feet apart, his tanned face split with a shining, white-toothed smile.

Ubaldo shook the sleep out of his eyes and pushed back his hair.

"You startled me," he said in English.

"I am most sorry," said the young man. "You looked so like a Roman sculpture, with your nude torso against the marble."

Ubaldo grinned and pulled on his shirt.

This was not an American, he realized. The sudden gush of his conversation, the British accent overlay of another accent, with an occasional syneresis, and dieresis revealed him as a Greek, a well-born Greek, reared in the Kolonia, schooled perhaps in Switzerland and England as well as Athens.

"I am a Roman," said Ubaldo, "just as you are Greek."

"Correct," said the young man.

Ubaldo figured him as about twenty-two.

The young man picked up a chip of marble, examined it to see if it had any outstanding archaeological significance, and then shagged it down toward the little funicular cable that led to the principality below.

"Now," said Ubaldo, smiling, "you have disturbed another archaeological potential of this site, by throwing away a fragment of its past. That was a broken bit of pediment."

"No more than other vandals did to the Greek temple below on the Rock. It's destroyed completely."

He gestured far below.

"Which you Greeks, in turn, placed on Phoenician ruins," said Ubaldo.

"You are an archaeologist?" asked the Greek.

"My hobby," said Ubaldo proudly. "To you, this place is Moenikis, and the temple dedicated to

Heracles is Greek. And to me, it is Porta Herculis, the old Roman fortification. And of course, up here, the Trophy of the Alps is, to a Frenchman, the place where Napoleon rested and later caused the Grande Corniche road to be built. I wonder if a conqueror is ever satisfied with the feats of those great men before him, or if he always has to eradicate their memory, to prove he is greater?"

The Greek sat down on the drum, pulled out a gold cigarette case, and proffered Ubaldo a Papostratos number one. They lit up together.

"To a man who stops to rest," he said, "it is a shrine on a headland, looking out on an incredibly blue sea. No matter what we are, I feel our denominator is the beauty we leave to show we have passed this way. I do not want to have the mystery of the temple revealed to me. I only wish to worship in it."

"You differ from me," said Ubaldo. "I want to know why we worship."

"You need not know the reason when you see a magnificent statue," said the Greek. "Man has done what God has not. He has suspended beauty in its full flower in art. To possess this beauty is the highest attainment. All else is ephemeral, and can only eventually fail the human soul. I know it is a dream, but I expect to find a statue by Praxiteles every time I set foot in a temple. Well, perhaps someday I shall. . . ."

He stood up and stretched. Ubaldo rose too.

The man was taller than he had thought. He remembered one holiday he had spent at Knossos in Crete, and the fierce islanders with their thick boots, their baggy trousers, and the chibouk pipes clamped to their strong teeth. This was such a man. He, like most, seemed dual in nature, Greek and Oriental at once.

As if he had been induced by the thought, the man took his gold (obviously Cartier or Asprey) cigarette case, snapped it shut, put it in his jacket pocket, and without being aware of it, took a smooth circle of komboloi, amber worry beads, out of his pocket, and began to finger them like a Turk.

"Perhaps we shall meet again," said the Greek.

"Since I intruded on your reverie, I should introduce myself: Pericles Niadas."

He said the name looking under his eyelids slyly. The young man would know, as did everyone, that this well-favored heir of a shipping family was concluding his first highly publicized spaghetti pipeline deal in the Near East, to go on to London, which was the triumphant hegira of all would-be important Greeks this season, for the Greek Princess Marina was marrying the Duke of Kent.

It gave Ubaldo a slight tingle of pleasure to bow from the waist and introduce himself.

"Giovanni Ubaldo Albini," he said.

Niadas topped him, clacking his beads.

"Prince Albini, of course," he said. "I had the pleasure of looking through the galleries of the Villa Madonna della Rosa with your mother and sister, I believe. But I fear you were away at the time. Your charming sister . . ."

"Ah, yes," said Ubaldo, "I recollect your name on the guest register. I was excavating with my old professor, Dr. Fratelli, in Addis Ababa."

Niadas wagged a finger at him.

"And making a few notes for Il Duce?" he said. "You will no doubt be there again . . . soon."

Ubaldo could have been angry. But it was true.

Niadas smiled and put out his hand.

Ubaldo remembered that the man was reputed to have a way of slicing at the heart of things, and then disarming people. In this way, the Greek discovered what he wanted to know, by exposing a nerve, and then backing away after his suspicions had been verified by the quickest flicker of a glance or unbidden reflex.

"Perhaps you would dine on my yacht tonight?"

"I must get back to Genoa," said Ubaldo, putting on his military tunic.

"I hope next time we meet," said Niadas, "that we shall worship at the same temple, and that you will find me my Praxiteles."

They both walked to the roadside together.

A sleek black limousine awaited with one door open.

After amenities Ubaldo drove back toward Italy in his roadster. He resented Niadas because he had made the error of intimating that if an Albini found a Praxiteles, Greek money could purchase it. Well, Rome had absorbed Greece before, and it might just do the same thing, with Il Duce's dreams of empire. But for a moment they had met and communicated through the glory of beauty and the past.

However, as the years passed, Niadas' good fortune seemed to have counterpointed Ubaldo's own unfortunate fate, along with that of his nation. The wrong time for an Albini to be born, the right time for Niadas.

Out of the pain and agony of the war had come the mighty new argonauts, masters of the burgeoning lanes of independent shipping. Labyrinthian corporations cleared the way with the machinations of their banking, diplomatic, military, and legal connections. Straw services of American citizens in purchasing the orphan "war babies," Liberty dry cargo, Victory ships, and T-2 oil tankers made way for fortunes. The world was avid for oil, machinery, steel, coal, pipelines, building materials, wheat, and varied foodstuffs.

The new breed of supertankers that could carry oil from the Persian Gulf to the East Coast of the United States at three cents a gallon were built in the shipyards of the German and Japanese nations, which had sunk their predecessors during the world war. Construction money, which brought a wave of prosperity to Kure and Hamburg, was often obtained on insurance from war-sunk ships. Economy flourished, while the men who had gone down with the ships were forgotten.

And so, recollected Ubaldo, the Delphic fleet of Niadas had multiplied one man's pleasures, and like many rich, he now turned as his shadow lengthened, and sought his beginnings. The new Prime Minister Karamanlis was working within the framework of constitutional monarchy to put Greece back on her feet after the ruinous World War and civil war, which had pitted brother against brother and destroyed the old village way of Greek life.

Ubaldo remembered the voyage he had made from Abyssinia on one of the Delphic fleet. He recollected the sick and sweating days on the death ship, Panamanian-registered, beating its way back from Assab Bay, the drinking water unpotable, living conditions as stinking as on an ancient Greek trireme. The fever-infested untended dead were slipped silently into the boiling Red Sea under the sticky cover of the night.

How bitter, that out of these ways of profit, a man came to be custodian of the taste and treasures of the world.

Now, to keep his Phryne from being debauched by the groping hands of tourists, who could know her for a few small coins and make vulgar remarks in their native vernacular about her teats, Ubaldo would turn her into the keeping of this one man, who at least worshiped beauty for itself alone.

He had his trusted *procuratore legale* contact the Greek. He suggested that the pearl of the collection, Phryne, be examined by any staff of experts. Marble from known fragments of Praxiteles' statues, and marble from Paros, in the known areas of the quarries selected by Praxiteles and other sculptors around 400 B.C. could be analyzed to authenticate the statue, which would be sold, unlisted, with the villa.

Without revealing his identity, he negotiated. The only stipulation to the deal was that a conservator of the family was to remain for his lifetime as manager of the estate and curator of the treasures, which were to remain intact.

Ubaldo knew that Niadas had a dossier on every scientist who examined the Phryne. After they had authenticated the statue, they were informed that any mention of its verity would result in dire distress to themselves and their families.

Each expert was ordered to prepare two reports. One, a certificate of verification of the authenticity of the statue. The records were taken out of Rome and put in the private files of Niadas. The other paper was a certificate claiming that the alleged statue of Phryne by Praxiteles was a modern copy of a privately owned Greek statue, which had been destroyed at an Albini villa outside Cassino during the past war. This would allay repercussions of any rumor of the discovery of the statue, and prevent seizure as a Roman national treasure.

Unknowingly, Niadas paid off the massive family debts by puchasing the villa. One Ubaldo Vivaldi became the steward of the treasures within it. Countless young cousins were sent to schools and colleges, without having to be beholden to a freakish relative.

Elderly relatives and retainers of the family were restored to decent housing and medical care. None of them bothered to remember the handsome young prince who had vanished like so many others in the misbegotten war. They had all lost so much; one more was just a legend in a glittering parade of another day.

Who was to say, thought Ubaldo, who was the master and who the servant? The master toiled in the marts of the world, and the servant was curator of all the collected treasures that were dear to his heart.

Ubaldo believed Niadas had expected an octogenarian who would sit among his musty books and scrawl down crabbed-fingered inventories. He was surprised, it seemed, and not quite comfortable with the elegant hawkeyed perfectionist who managed every function of the villa with an aristocratic taste.

The Greek, Ubaldo reflected, had even wanted to promote him as overlord of all his residential staffs, but he had refused, saying he had no wish to travel; he had connections that kept him in the vicinity.

Niadas had given him the courtesy of not smiling at this remark. But Ubaldo saw a look of slight contempt pass his dark face, at the idea of a linkage of the flesh keeping a man from a more important destiny.

Like all Greeks, thought Ubaldo, he really despises Romans. Ah, if he knew it was a marble woman kept me here!

◆◆◆◆◆◆◆◆◆

Ubaldo felt a personal excitement, which had been dormant in him these years, at the thought of the girl who lay on his bed upstairs.

Of course, he had often satisfied his flesh, but a yearning of the spirit had been long gone. He would have given, not quite, but almost, this Phryne to be what he once was, handsome and proud, stepping by excited invitation into the bed of that sweet, perfect flesh.

For a second he considered alleviating himself in the welcoming arms of the parlormaid Rosina, whose door would be unlocked for him, or for the new linen maid from Siena, she with the delicate seamstress hands which had fondled him gently in the dark, consoling him, since he could not see the wide peasant face, and could dream for the moment of the hands of a lady. But he rejected them both.

This was different. This was not merely a turmoil of the flesh, the blood and veins and tumescences of a man, involved in the age-old outcry.

He disrobed and put on his silk pajamas. Ah, the soft Parian breasts of the statue he knew so well, which had been exposed from the dark earth by the soft camel's-hair brush of his meticulous archaeological care, and the softer breasts of the young girl, with their exposed pink virgin nipples. He moved uncomfortably in the confines of his hard campaign bed.

His emotions mounted with the images he conjured up out of the stimulation of his mind and hands. In his secret way, he possessed the marble statue and the flesh Linda in his lonely room.

He finally lay back spent, but he did not sleep. Confusion had entered his soul. It was easy to find a climax in the adoration of one of the greatest beauties the world had ever known. She was preserved in marble, her corporeal being gone to dust over these two thousand and more years.

But it was disturbing to know that a young virgin with all her divine attributes was sleeping in the bed that once had been his.

He tried to smother his niggling resentment of Pericles Niadas, who owned everything he held dear, and who had conceived an heir in the very bed in the master suite that should have held the ecstasy and the promise of his own seed.

It distressed him that this young girl, Linda Barstow, was in the bed that the Greek had vulgarized with

Martha Ralston. The sudden instinctive feeling that Niadas owned this virgin one way or another annoyed him. He would have to make himself her confidant. It was necessary. Most necessary. She seemed to have an eager mind. How much he could tell her! Rare thoughts no one knew, for he had locked them in his heart these years. Perhaps now he could get out his old archaeological journals. Start on his book. Put his footsteps back in the path that was intended.

He arose, washed, arranged himself for sleep, rubbed apiserum from Paris on his hairless head carefully, rinsed his mouth at the alabaster Roman basin on his Venetian bureau, splashed Cuir de Russie on his hands and wrists, and picked up a copy of Wyndham Lewis' *Time and Western Man.*

Unfortunately he thumbed to the chapter on the child cult.

Was he a victim of the spirit of the *recherche du temps?*

Or was he demented, inverting his onanistic sex drive into the imagined body of the child who slept upstairs?

He slammed the book shut with disgust, switched off his light, and turned his face to the wall, to outwait the night.

2

◆◆◆◆◆◆◆◆

Effie tucked Linda in in the massive angel-crested bed.

"Don't get lost," she said, looking up at the cupids and curtains.

"I've got Sarge," said Linda. "I'll be fine."

"I'm downstairs," said Effie. "There's a nice maid's room and bath for me. This is a mighty big place. Call me if you want. There's a buzzer on that phone that connects us."

Linda was already thumbing through the Greek books again. This one was a color-plate edition of the treasures in the villa collection. It said the statue was a fine copy of the original, destroyed in a bombardment in World War II.

"You know who the model was for that statue on the stairs?" she said.

"I don't know," said Effie, "but it could have been you."

Linda was pleased.

"Her name was Phryne, it says here. One of the hetaerae of Athens. That means paid companions. Very high-class, though. Sometimes she got a thousand dollars a night."

"Land sakes!" said Effie. "Whatever for?"

"I wondered myself," said Linda. "Of course, they were all very sexy. They seemed to go in a lot for that. A sort of body cult. But can you imagine! Now, if it were today, aside from *that*, boy, for the money, I'd Simonize their car, press their suit, fill their fountain pen." She giggled. "I guess you'd even have to block their hat and give them advice on the stock market."

Effie smiled.

"I guess, in their way, that's just about what they did. With entertainment and a ten-course dinner thrown in."

"And dancing girls," said Linda. "Anyway, this Phryne was also the sweetheart of Praxiteles, the sculptor, in her spare time. She was so beautiful that she was the talk of fourth-century Athens—B.C., that was."

Effie nodded.

"She appeared in public completely veiled"—Linda flipped to a page of the text—"and once a year at the festival of Pos . . . Poseidon, she disrobed, and went to bathe in the sea, naked. Of course, everybody looked. You know, I think that's what the statue is. . . ."

She stood up in the middle of the enormous bed and took the stance of the statue.

"Phryne, stepping into the sea," she said dramatically.

"You sure know a lot about Greece," said Effie, admiring her. "You're a born student."

"Well, I'm going to know what I'm playing," said Linda.

"Looks to me that this what's-her-name . . ." said Effie.

"Phryne," said Linda.

"This Phryne was pretty smart. She sort of mixed up her good looks with religion," said Effie.

"Yeah," said Linda, "that's pretty irresistible, isn't it?"

Effie agreed, and kissed her good night.

"I'll take Sarge for a walk, and have a cup of coffee with the help downstairs. They're real nice to me. They have a sitting room all by themselves bigger than ours at home."

"Watch out for that Ubaldo," said Linda, smiling.

"He don't tangle with the backstairs folks," said Effie. "He's the boss. He's got a sort of office like a library. They serve him there on a silver tray."

Linda settled into the lace pillows. She did not dwell

on the baroque beauties of the room. She thought of Greece, and then of modern people like Martha Ralston and Pericles Niadas.

That Pericles Niadas must be real gone on ancient Greece, with these statues and art books around.

◆◆◆◆◆◆◆◆

It was a scented, bee-struck Roman day.

Linda, in her white bathing suit, entered her upstairs sitting room from the terrace steps that led down to the swimming pool. Her mother and Max had gone to the studio, and Effie was somewhere doing Linda's laundry and pressing.

She felt adrift, wondering when she would be allowed to go to the studio, and be involved one way or another with the picture.

Her Yorkshire, following her, began to yip. She looked across the room, and there, standing by the fireplace, was Claudia. She wore a tweed traveling suit, and she was just pulling off her hat and shaking free her black curly hair.

"Aunt Claudia!" said Linda. "Oh, you're here! You're here!"

She rushed to embrace her.

"Don't get me wet!" said Claudia. "I need a drink, and I've sworn off. . . ."

She lifted her arms expressively.

"Do you realize the magnificence of this place? I've been around a bit—even to a maharaja's palace in India—but I've never seen treasures like this!"

"It's awfully big and lonesome at night," said Linda, "but now you're here, things will be different!"

Claudia took off her jacket.

"Now, first things first. We must get tape recordings of your voice. Get the Western twang out of you. Teach you to enter a room, not gallop."

Linda was crestfallen.

"Aren't you glad to see me? You're so businesslike."

Claudia laughed.

"That's a compliment I rarely get. Do you think we

can make it for two Barstows to be efficient together? . . . Well, I guess we can. Your father and I did pretty well. On film, that is. I wouldn't vouch for our extracurricular activities. Anyway, I've brought a crate of books from London."

"Where are your rooms," asked Linda, "and did you meet Ubaldo?"

"I have indeed," said Claudia. "Now, there is someone extraordinary! I'm not onto his wavelength yet, but give me time. I'm settled way down yonder in the guest wing, a neat little suite all gold and red."

"Not near me?" said Linda, disappointed.

"Good lord, no," said Claudia. "I have to be on my own some of the time. I am a dialogue director, not a nanny on twenty-four-hour call."

Linda smiled. Already she suspected Claudia was battling an inner tenderness.

"Can I help you unpack?"

"No, Agnesina, that sallow-faced maid, is doing it, and naturally Effie has already told her she'd like to do it. A small battle is going on downstairs."

"One-upmanship." Linda grinned.

Claudia sat down and picked up an art book.

"Well, I see you've started your homework. We'll make a schedule, and we'll keep it. Now, your job is to keep me busy so I won't get in trouble. Agreed?"

Linda laughed and kissed her.

"Pads, pencils, papers, tape machines, and all that crap. We'll show 'em how Barstows function. Right?"

Linda nodded, enthralled. Her eyes followed Claudia's every move. Oh, to move like that . . . speak like that!

◆◆◆◆◆◆◆◆

In the days that followed, Max and Jessica worked at Cinecittà, preparing the production crossplot and coordinating the American and Italian staffs, which merged, it seemed, amicably in the fraternity of picture-making.

Such films as *Roman Holiday, Summertime, Three*

Coins in the Fountain, and *War and Peace* had already established an international liaison among the workers. Max had a choice of proven craftsmen, whom he selected and interviewed with the aid of Sidney Keyes, who had final approval as David Austin's representative.

Jessica knew that Sidney kept in constant touch with David wherever he was—London, New York, the new Titan studio stages building in India, a location in Kenya, or even Niadas' yacht, *Circe,* moored at various ports in the Mediterranean, Ionic, or Aegean seas. She watched Sidney's reactions to her suggestions carefully.

She knew also, because in her secretarial days she had developed a skill for reading papers upside down on a desk, that Sidney had a memorandum on preproduction expenses which involved a crew of expert technicians sent from Rome to install a projection room complete with wide screen and stereophonic sound, on the yacht. This meant Niadas could look at the rushes whenever he wanted.

Some days, when conferences did not take them to the studios, it was satisfactory to use the elaborate facilities of the Villa Madonna della Rosa, which was run in the Niadas tradition like an exclusive small hotel. Staffs of day and night butlers, chefs, servants on duty at all hours, and endless corridors of lavishly equipped rooms made the estate a cosmos of elegance that pampered any need.

Jessica installed two secretaries, a multilingual girl for the telephone, and a typist. A constant stream of social figures, the usual rabble of agents and actors, visiting studio executives, and top professional men connected with the staff flowed in and out of the villa.

Twelve to twenty lunched daily on the terraces by the pool, mostly in the informal attire of studio craftsmen.

Ubaldo supervised the household staff, impervious and slightly contemptuous of this raffish, sport-shirt world. However, he watched the expert organization take form. The meticulous coordination of Max and the staff with Ralph Lloyd, a down-to-earth unit manager from Titan studio, intrigued him. It was as precisely planned as a military maneuver. He was exposed to the production designer's detailed sketches of sets and camera setups. He saw the painstaking research of the costumes, the reproduction of artifacts, the wigs, the plastic noses to be worn by some actors whose own equipment was something less than Greek. Experts gave infinite care to each detail, even to the imitation of the ancient patrician garments from the island of Cos, which were woven like those of the National Theater of Greece with weft of silk and warp of cotton. Ubaldo respected the scholarly re-creation of ancient Greece.

As a young man he had seen the films of Max Ziska. He admired him as a talent. He observed with admiration as Max guided the production. He managed to obtain a script, and respected the manner in which Ziska had found the true form for his modern play, recreating the proud spirit of the ancient world without losing the realism of modern drama.

But his interest in Linda's training was something quite different. He watched the dramatic education Claudia was giving the girl with a grudging admiration. The woman was a dedicated teacher. He knew from the wardrobe sketches that Linda would be dressed in a more worldly and carnal sense than her years should allow. He read the scene, beautiful as it was, where she bathed in the sacred waters of the Castalian spring, nude and lovely in the Greek dawn, while the young soldier watched her, unobserved. He felt personally affronted that this beauty should be duplicated and expanded on thousands of screens, to be seen and lusted for by a public avid for a new sex symbol.

Why was such a rare person fated to become a film star? He would have liked to carry her away and give her such a life of devotion, adventure, and elegance that she never would have dreamed of as a public figure.

He had seen some of Claudia's films, and remembering her capers, which had been magnified in the scandalous Italian movie magazines, was impressed with her dedication to her niece. Admiring women of beauty and spirit, he respected her far more than Jessica, for to him Claudia had style and Jessica was an opportunistic poseur. Claudia didn't have to put on side for him; she spoke to him as person to person, and he found himself explaining the history and beauty of some of the rarest objects in the villa.

As for Claudia, she watched Ubaldo's expressive eyes as he revealed his knowledge and love for the treasures in the villa, and she recognized that he was no mere majordomo to this Greek's fabulous collection. But she bided her time, not even mentioning it to Linda, as the two came closer and closer together in their studies.

David's warning had alerted her that any emotional disturbance of anyone she was involved with could be laid at her feet, and Jessica would jettison her.

It was the first time in her life that she had trod softly. One look at the eager face of Linda, and the joy she had in their work was enough to stifle her remarks and turn her face in only one direction.

Max was engrossed in his work, and his life began and ended at the studio, or meetings with his staff in Rome or the villa.

Jessica tolerated Claudia with the detachment of a busy executive who must be polite to the staff. Dinners together at a vast candlelit table were shared with enough people so they were rarely intimate. Once or twice Jessica complimented her on the tonal quality and diction that were finding their way into Linda's voice, and once on the fact that at last Linda had entered the room like a lady.

These comments were met by quick eye-to-eye flashes between Linda and Claudia, and an unspoken agreement that she did not bother them; they had more important things to do than listen to her lip service.

Both of them found their days full, and settled into work, seeking a pace Claudia never would have believed possible.

She accepted a solitude she had never known before. Her sitting room and bedroom were decorated with her favorite photographs: Jeffrey and her, Simon and Fergus—souvenirs of her days as a reigning star. It was difficult for her to forsake the comfort of her bottle, but a picture of Linda, young and joyous, running on the beach at Trancas, was her inspiration.

Now that she had achieved sobriety, she was able to review the errors that her family, especially Jeffrey and herself, had made, and then chart a better course for Linda.

Even the name bugged her. They both had a pact that as soon as possible it would revert to "Belinda," but they would not stir up trouble at the moment.

She was grateful that she had John Graves and his success as an actor in her background. It had been the beginning of her realization that she was a good teacher. And since Graves was starring in this epic, and would play opposite Linda, she felt it was a very good omen she was here.

She was puzzled by David, and by memories of a few chance remarks of her brother, Jeffrey, about his interest in him; she marveled that he had come into the picture as a sort of catalyst, to save her when she needed spiritual help, as well as financial.

Is this a true renaissance of me? she wondered in her solitary evenings. Or is it possible that age has crept up on me, and I'm converting my sexual drive to other things? Good God, I hope not; there surely has to be another man in my life! But she studied and planned, and was even slightly annoyed with herself for occasionally reverting to prayer. Wasn't it a little late for a copout aimed at heaven?

The two Barstows doing their exercises on the outdoor terraces or empty tennis courts avoided the clustered conferences. They paid little heed to the stream of gardeners moving cartloads of soil in basketchains from a distant area of the garden. But one day Ubaldo came to them.

"You're working diligently, in spite of the people milling in and out. I think you will be surprised. Please follow me."

He led them along winding paths of flowerbeds and a formal lane of hedges punctuated with white-marble statues and benches. At the far end of the garden they turned into a field backed by a hillock that had been used for growing cut flowers and vegetables. They rounded a row of dark sentinel cypress trees and halted.

Beyond them, freshly washed down and gleaming in the sunshine, was a small Roman amphitheater, its stage nestled against the gentle hillside, which had been planted with flowering shrubs. Most of the semicircular seat rows were in ruins, but the stage floor had been restored, and massive pots of flowering plants had been placed dramatically at each side of it.

"Of course," said Ubaldo, "the *skene* is long gone. The whole theater area was overgrown with weeds, not having been used for many years. But now it is yours. May the Barstow theater bloom!"

He gestured elegantly and smiled, handing it to them as if it were a hand-carved gift of his own making. And so, in a way, it was. He had ordered the gardeners to arrange an umbrella table, a few folding chairs, and cushions to one side of the stage.

"It has been used from the *phylakes* to *commedia dell'arte,*" he said. "Now, when Mr. Ziska holds those interminable staff meetings, you will have a place of your own."

Claudia was visibly stirred.

She looked at Ubaldo with a sudden curiosity. He seemed aware of her scrutiny, and retreated into a mask of aloof dignity.

"Your lunch will be served here when you wish," he said stiffly.

He bowed and left.

"This is a most unusual man," said Claudia.

"Our own theater!" echoed Linda, touching the rough stone of a seat. She moved toward the stage.

"Now," said Claudia, "never step on a stage unless you know what you are going to do. I shall tell you when you're ready."

For several days she made Linda walk up and down the steep stone steps of the amphitheater, controlling her breathing, reciting without a pause, the beckoning stage as her goal. She taught her never to allow her physical efforts to interfere with the resonant tones of her voice.

"We will start on our stage with the quotation from Euripides," she said. "Now, remember, it must be all of one piece, one string of pearls."

She climbed up on the last row of seats, and Linda, in a white dress, stepped onto the stage and spoke her lines.

> Then streams the earth with milk,
> Yea, streams with wine and nectar of the bee,
> And o'er the earth soft perfume streams
> Of Syrian frankincense. . . .

Claudia stood far atop the ledge of stone against the blue sky and threw the speech back to Linda. Linda's words had poured out. Hers were sonorous.

"You see," she said, "the words must have a sound and scent. Look at the stage—you are standing on a legacy."

"What do you mean?" asked Linda, puzzled.

"All the Barstows, terminating with you. You must be the best, or our line has lived in vain. This is your moment in time and space to bring these words to life. We should be very glad they're busy with preproduction so you have time to learn your skills."

Claudia folded her arms and stood back waiting.

Linda pushed her hair back from her cheeks and lifted her head higher, closing her eyes and then opening them in the wonder of the poet's message.

As she listened, Claudia tried to hide her emotion. In teaching this child, she would have to smother her excitement. Was it too early and easy, this Barstow gift? A twinge of envy tore at the part of her that was actress. Her own years of training and growth had been so laced with success and flattery, combined with a madcap personal life, that it was difficult to separate one memory from another. And it had been a hard and dreary road being a fallen angel.

But now, as she observed Linda, she washed away

the past in her mind and saw that Linda also was deeply involved in her Greek world of mysticism. The girl did not even seek or need approbation. She was on a plateau beyond it.

"Well," she said softly, the part that was teacher taking over, "that is what it is all about."

"You know," said Linda, "you're a director at heart."

"I'm an actress, and I'm a teacher," said Claudia, "but if by any chance I saw that Max was leading you the wrong way, I'd have to interfere. I don't care, Linda, it's you I care about."

"Well, how could you interfere?"

"We could have an arrangement, for example, if I were on the set . . ."

She moved her expressive hands.

"A handkerchief," said Linda. "I think I could see you wave it, out of the side of my eye."

"We'll see."

She hoped Linda would be smart enough to be controlled without revealing it. It would take careful work and cautious planning.

"You are talking to the expert in breaking up movie scenes," she said, "if you're not happy with what's happening—and believe me, you'll have an instinct if you're worth your salt as an actress. You can go dry on your lines, or cough, or step off your marks, or look the wrong way. I've even deliberately used a mannerism that infuriated my director in order to get out of finishing a scene if I wasn't happy about a situation. And then, of course, you can give the director-writer, which Max is, the double whammy and say you don't understand the scene, the words don't seem right."

"I should think people would hate you if you did those things," said Linda.

"A successful career is not a popularity contest," said Claudia. "And you're coming up against a bunch of old pros. It won't be as easy as working here by yourself in our Barstow theater. Leslie Charles is a shrewd, successful man. I know, I've been through his whole bag of tricks, and take my word, he's good. And as for John Graves, you know I picked him up as a cockney kid and took him to see *Pygmalion,* so he'd know what diction was all about. And later we made a very good movie. He's successful and sexual, which is a rough combination to put a young kid like you up against. Have you . . . uh . . . any interest or any experience with the opposite sex?"

Linda looked at her with surprise.

"I kissed the football captain behind the bleachers, at school," she said, "and a couple of kids pinched me at dances, and I think my algebra teacher brushed my breasts a couple of times when we were working at the blackboard."

Claudia tried to stifle the thought that this girl seemed a little retarded to be a Barstow, but of course she had that watchdog Jessica behind her every day, and also, had not experienced the freewheeling backstage life that Claudia herself had been exposed to at the same age.

"Well," she said, "that's not exactly a preparation for love scenes with Graves, but thank God I'm here. And also, we must realize the competition you'll get in your scenes with Chloë Metaxa, from her highly stylized and dramatic National Theater training. That will be a challenge."

Linda was alarmed.

"Don't be afraid," said Claudia. "We'll conquer all."

Linda had her first premonition that it wasn't going to be so easy.

◆◆◆◆◆◆◆◆

Max had finished his after-dinner coffee. He picked up a tiny Venetian liqueur glass, twirled it absently, and glanced across the candlelit, flower-laden table at Linda.

"It's time you got to work. You're losing touch with reality in this steamy elegance. How far actors have come! In my youth in Germany they used to say *Kinder hängt die Wäsche weg, die Schauspieler kommen.* 'Children, put away the wash, the actors are coming.' I wonder if it's wise for you to be a princess, so isolated."

"She isn't," said Claudia. "We've gone through Rome from the Campo di' Fiori flower market to the Catacombe di San Callisto."

"From jukeboxes and Marlon Brando haircuts to skeletons in monks' robes," said Linda. She imitated an Italianate Brando strut, scratching and slouching.

"Really, Linda!" Jessica said.

"It's just an improvisation," said Linda. "We do them all the time."

Max's chair scraped the marble floor. "I don't want any more of these vulgar improvisations. This child is not playing an Italian clown. She is playing a Greek priestess."

"You're wrong," said Linda. "I'm playing a girl who becomes a woman. I am not a puppet!"

Claudia bit her lip to keep out of it.

"You are very rude," said Jessica. "You may go upstairs."

Linda walked out of the dining room and along the marble gallery to the glass-and-iron entrance doors. She had no intention of going upstairs like a punished child. She pulled one of the doors open and slammed it loudly behind her, wandering into the darkness of the night.

She followed the gravel paths past trimmed hedges, pink azaleas, ranks of heavily scented roses, loggias supporting nodding purple bougainvillea, along corridors of ghost-white statues that seemed to turn to watch her as she moved faster away from the villa.

She was confused. A war was being fought over everything she did. She felt like a horse, traded from one rider to another, with no real direction of its own.

She passed the sentinel cypresses, dividing the living world from the dead, and moved onto the stage, facing the empty stone semicircles of the amphitheater, peopled, she felt, with toga-draped transparent spirits.

She moved her arms, watching the slender companion shadow the moon gave her. She waited for someone to come find her. There was no crunch of feet on gravel paths. The bright-lit villa seemed miles away; she was a pagan outside a Christian citadel.

No one cared. Max had mocked her. Her Aunt Claudia hadn't defended her. Mom really showed only the emotion of irritation with her; the rest was sham.

She felt akin only to the actors, long gone, who had once strutted and postured on this stage and had been part of the joy of being a vessel for words and movement, bringing self-forgetfulness to those who had listened.

She thought of the lines of Keats she had just memorized. She planted her feet firmly apart, lifted her pale head to the moon, and spoke slowly, finding satisfaction that in the night every syllable seemed crystal-clear.

> Come then sorrow,
> Sweetest sorrow!
> Like an own babe I nurse thee on my breast;
> I thought to leave thee,
> But now of all the world I love thee best.
>
> There is not one,
> No, not one
> But thee to comfort a poor lonely maid;
> Thou art her mother,
> And her brother,
> Her playmate and her wooer in the shade.

She pitied herself.

Something moved down the stone rows silently. But it was only one of the kitchen cats. And then, from the side of her eye she saw someone moving slowly toward her.

"Max!" she whispered.

She rushed to embrace him, to be forgiven and forgive. Before she could put her head on his shoulder, she halted. It was not Max. The scent of Cuir de Russie prickled her nostrils.

She pulled back.

"Ah, that was beautiful."

The calm hands of Ubaldo moved gently to capture her own, cautiously, and then released them.

"Oh," she said, "you scared me!"

She felt awkward, standing on the amphitheater stage with him, as if they were doing an act. Their words seemed to strike back at them. He motioned to a stone bench behind a wall.

His profile looked classically Roman in the dark, she thought, not baldly freakish as it did in the bright daylight. He asked permission by a gesture, and lit a cigarette. The glow accented the bright eyes and the highly bridged nose.

"Should you not go back?" he said.

"If they want me, they'll come," she said.

She started to wipe her tears away with the back of her hand. He proffered his handkerchief.

"They all want you. You see, you are a prize. Your beauty and promise ignite the imagination. You give one a chance at something that has been missed in life. . . . To each person it is different."

He escorted her to the brightly lighted entrance of the villa. As he held her elbow she felt the touch of his fingers pressing her flesh; it was very personal.

He said nothing more.

When he opened the door, Max was standing inside. He had been peering out.

"Thank you, Ubaldo," said Max formally.

Ubaldo bowed and vanished down the hall.

"You didn't need to send someone for me," she said. "I am not a child."

"I am sorry," said Max. "One becomes nervous."

His brown eyes looked into hers with warmth and compassion.

"There is so much to do, my darling. You, too, have been wandering in the maze. Forgive me."

"There's nothing to forgive," she said. "I don't want to be a clown, Max. I want to be Phryne."

She led Max to the statue on the landing.

"Does she look like me?"

"My God, she does!" said Max.

He put his arm about her shoulder and kissed her cheek. She nestled her head on his familiar shoulder.

"Isn't she wonderful, Max?"

"You are the wonder."

She saw that the statue didn't mean as much to Max as it did to her. Phryne was an inanimate object. To him it might resemble his living actress; that was all the marvel that was in it. Max moved in rooms, among furnishings, ate food, wore clothes, and traveled in limbo. He didn't care most of the time where he was. He was enveloped in the moving drama of his own making. That was why he loved her; right now she was his creation. And she loved him.

"Oh, Max! Max!"

She shook her head, forgetting her tears, to smile.

"We shall be working soon," he said. "Get your rest. We are going to begin a wonderful world, together."

He kissed her brow. Already, she could tell, his mind was on the script that would be on his bedside table.

As Effie brushed her hair in her dressing room, she looked at the handkerchief. A crest was embroidered on one corner.

"Look at this, Ef."

"Looks mighty high-class, also looks like a gentleman's handkerchief. Where did you get it?"

"My secret. Wash it and give it back to me."

"Got a beau?"

" 'A wooer in the shade'?"

She saw the suspicious, guarded look on Effie's face.

"Heaven forbid," said Linda. "And you know, I think fun's done. Now on, work. You'd better pack my bag for the studio. We leave early."

"Praise the Lord!" said Effie.

Linda glanced in the mirror at Effie's familiar, gentle brown face, realizing how lonely she must be in this strange land. Even Effie depends on me to keep her busy. They all want to give, but they have their price.

She looked down at her feet. The little Yorkshire had a squatter's claim, sitting on the edge of her dressing gown. She couldn't move without disturbing him.

"You, too, Sarge."

"What was that?" asked Effie.

"Just talking to him."

She reached down and patted the little dog, who looked at her with adoring sad eyes.

"You go too."

He pricked up his ears at the word "go," which meant inclusion.

Even the dog . . . even the little dog.

3

It was not fated for Pericles Niadas to arrive in Rome for the first day's shooting of *The Oracle*. The morning of July 9, the Greek world was stunned by a tremendous earthquake in the Cyclades.

Santorini, the mysterious volcanic island where Niadas had his villa, in the town of Thera, was shattered. It lay atop the crescent-shaped dark mass of land, along beetling black crags. Little sugar-cube houses tumbled into the blue-black waters of the great bay, following into the volcanic crater tomb of the ancient city, Kalliste—the Very Beautiful—the rumored secret sunken citadels of lost Atlantis.

Six hundred and eighty steps leading in hairpin curves down to the slim jetty on the bay folded and crumbled into a gigantic slide. Masses of pink and purple and green pumice boiled up from the scalding sea depths, floating like vagrant jewels in the roiling waters.

Niadas' luxurious villa was named Kalliste after the town of ancient glory. Its white garden walls with antique statuary placed against the heaven-domed view, its terraces, and blue vaulted drawing room were thrown like a pack of cards into the sea a thousand feet below. The gatekeeper, his wife, and child fell to their doom entombed in their tiny cellhouse.

Pericles Niadas and Martha Ralston fled on foot with their household staff toward their vineyards and gardens in the lower countryside, away from the beetling cliffs.

The *Circe,* at her mooring on a large buoy below Oia, three miles away, hauled anchor and moved out to sea away from the deadly twelve-foot tidal waves that were dashing caïques against the small jetty at the cliff-fringed Skala.

Captain Petroulis stared up from the yacht at the arsenic-green cliffs, and the bobbling floats of pumice, red, purple, and cobalt that were vomiting up from the steaming waters, and wondered if even the eighteen-hundred-ton yacht would survive volcanic eruption long enough to establish ship-to-shore touch with Niadas. As he moved out to sea, *Circe*'s hull grating against the floating tufa chunks, he made contact by transceiver, to send the Grumman widgeon perched on the raised afterdeck to land. It was launched on its crane with difficulty.

Wheels uncranked, the plane landed on a roadway among the newly shattered ruins near the lacy white tower at Pyrgos. Martha Ralston Niadas babbled in terror as she and her husband and an old midwife, Phoebe, carrying her gear in a ragged bundle, boarded the amphibian.

They were quickly flown over the devastated area, passing the Niadas cement and pumice works, where a veil of fine dust rose like sacrificial smoke, powdering the adjacent landscape in a smothering scarf.

They flew from the rim of the island, Niadas peering down at the new-tumbled rocks and cliffs; guts of exposed black, red, and yellow strata were splitting into the sea. The crater and scoriae of Nea Kaumene, Burnt Island, was disgorging boiling bubbles, sulfuric fumes, and steam. It was strange up in the sky to hear no sound, as tons of boulders and earth plunged into the foaming surf.

They circled the natural seacoast. As they gained altitude, Niadas almost expected to see the volcano explode and throw them into a million bits, its power a thousand times greater than any atomic bomb.

Even the *Circe,* its three hundred sleek feet afloat outside the eighteen-mile rimmed bay, looked like a white cigarette butt flung in a flecked sea; Niadas realized the flecks were fluffy floats of pumice, bobbing like twinkling sequins on the waves.

He made a mental note to have his caïques collect the valuable harvest.

The Grumman widgeon flew over the spiny mass of the island of Pholegandros. A strong northerly squall sweeping in downdrafts rocketed the aircraft. Martha began to whimper.

"Shut up," said Niadas.

"We're going to crash!" shrieked Martha. "Oh, my god, Perry!"

She threw her head back, opened her mouth, and began to scream. He turned in his seat and hit her strongly across the mouth. "Shut up! Must I strike you again? Where is your pride? These people have lost everything."

She drew in her breath and stared at him in fear, reduced to sobbing.

"I am sorry," he said, "but you must control yourself. You are my wife."

He put his hand out to touch her arm. She drew away.

"Don't touch me!" she cried out.

He turned, his lips thin, his dark eyes glistening.

Touch! How long since he had wanted to touch her. How long since he had. If it hadn't been for the burden she carried in her belly, he would gladly have wished her fallen down into the sea of Santorini.

The plane gained altitude; he could almost see tidal currents from the quake floating toward the distant blue mountains of Crete. It could be more than an antique rumor that the great explosion that had made a crescent out of the ancient round of Santorini had destroyed the civilization of Knossos in 1500 B.C. with its drowning sixty-foot tidal waves and smothering blanket of ashes.

The island of Melos hove into view. Its enormous bay was also a sickle rind; reminder of another ancient volcanic disaster. The great deep-blue bay sparkled below, with the Plaka snuggling against Mount Elias, the chapels, shrines, buildings, and windmills glittering clean white against the rock-spined dark earth.

Niadas could see his shipyards and docks coming

into view, the silver tracks of commerce, the warehouses, drydocks, storehouses, the experimental gear, as the plane lowered. After this, a quick panorama of wooden landing frames, forklift trucks, high-pressure hoses with their hoisting magnets, gantry cranes, and his experimental conveyor belts, shunting produce from a hold to a dockside plant.

They passed his sprawl of Delphic shipyards, with their familiar roof insignia of the laurel wreath of Apollo, and lowered to the little runway off Adamas Bay, where another of his villas nestled, looking out to sea.

Here was his business retreat and guesthouse when he visited the German technicians who ran his experimental work.

A pier stretched spidery legs into the bay, large enough for the *Circe* and visiting yachts to disembark their cargo by launch in front of the house.

They circled slowly, settling like an insect on tender feet, pulling up at a ramp, where a servant was rushing to tie up.

Martha was cautiously helped out of the craft, waddling on her edematous legs. A doctor and nurse had been summoned by radio to attend her and check the fetal condition of the Niadas heir, who so far had survived the holocaust.

In the hours that followed, newspapers and radios throughout the world broadcast tales of their dramatic rescue. Foremost was the bulletin that his personal publicity representative, Nikolas Kykkotis, released.

The Greek shipper was performing valiant work in rescue. His planes and ships already had orders to shuttle to and fro among the islands, rescuing the wounded and aiding in evacuating inaccessible danger zones.

It was reported that the vaulted blue-and-white drawing room of Villa Kalliste, so recently pictured in *Art and Architecture*, had crumbled into rubble. Niadas had barely escaped with his lovely wife, the American film star Martha Ralston, who was enceinte.

It was not reported that he had knocked her out, as

she was too hysterical to be controlled, and that she would not allow her husband to come near her and had sworn that she would not bear her child in this ridiculous hell called Greece.

Once the fear of miscarriage had been overcome, she was placed in nurses' care in the villa at Melos, and sat in the garden, her swollen limbs propped on pillows, staring at the windmills that whirled in the wind like mad daisies. She refused to look out at the sea.

"I want to go home," said Martha.

"Home is where I am," said Niadas. "Certainly not in Hollywood, where you slept with everyone. Yes, my dear, I have the dossier now, and my son will be Greek."

Her reddened eyes were bereft of the thick lashes and mascara that had entranced him in his more amorous days. She put her hands across her mouth and whimpered again.

"You wanted to marry me," she said.

"I wanted a child," he said, "and I had been beautifully set up, my dear. Only a stupid woman could do it so well. You were very good at fornicating when you wanted something, and your theatrical facade was excellent. But you did not pay your doctor as well as I did to discover how you plotted."

He left her and went to his office.

He called Ubaldo to inform him that all was well; it was all over now, his heart was heavy for the dead, but he would do what he could for the living. At least, rebuilding was always an improvement. Madame was fine.

He looked forward to coming to Rome. Thank God many of his treasures were safe there, where there was no quake to topple a Phryne off her pedestal. She was safe, was she not? There was no temblor in Rome? Ubaldo assured him the villa was undisturbed.

Good. . . . He was sending a private plane flying a little gift to Linda Barstow, and please inform her she must not concern herself about his welfare; he would meet her in due time. He regretted the fact that the gods had postponed their meeting.

Ubaldo was puzzled as he hung up. The world was startled at the Greek quake, headlines conjectured about Niadas and Martha Ralston's safety, hundreds of injured and dead were being attended, and this man in his country, where millions of drachmas of his own investments were involved, only wanted a young actress he had never seen not to be worried about his welfare, and receive some little gift.

He realized that Linda was graven in the Greek's mind as a live and pulsating force. Niadas was striving for some strange sort of immortality in this picture. Knowing no modern Praxiteles, and wishing to honor his land and its past, he would seek his dream in the temple of film, the fluid art of the moving flesh. It seemed more important than his brush with death.

Phryne! What would have happened if the statue had been at Villa Kallistc!

At the thought of this, Ubaldo examined the statue, and studied it, with the possibility of sinking a small spike at her back, with a chain on the wall holding her, so that if there were a tremor, she would not topple down the stairs from the landing.

But he winced at the thought that she would have a spike marring her tender Parian flesh. It would be like wounding a woman. He decided against it. If she fell, so would the halls fall about her, and if that should be, he would as soon go with them.

◆◆◆◆◆◆◆◆

Cinecittà was several miles away. Max drove out early in the morning with Linda.

"I want your fellow players to be introduced to you in your costume," he said. "We will rehearse on the set, and learn to be a living part of the world we have created. I will not go as far as the Japanese director Akira Kurosawa, with his precise Jidai-Geki style, and expect to have you sleep in the beds on the set, but I feel it will at least be better for you to meet Charles and Graves on equal grounds."

"Shall we have a dinner party?" asked Linda. "I wondered why I hadn't met them."

"As Alethea, in costume," said Max, "as the oracle."

"You mean, not as a child," said Linda. "Oh, Max, I see through you!"

"Good, then I won't have to invent any lies, will I, my love?"

He thumbed through his script, and Linda, the little dog in her lap, looked out upon the countryside. The poppies and wheat in the fields across from the mustard-arched entrance of the studio still glistened with dew as they drove in.

"It's big!" said Linda. "It looks like Hollywood."

The chauffeur, Vittorio, pulled up in front of a sound stage. Max, with his briefcase bulging under his arm, turned to Linda. "It will seem utter confusion at first, but you will learn to find your own self in the center of it. Don't be afraid."

He patted her cheek with a sudden warm affection.

They walked by two carpenters who were singing an aria from *Tosca* as they hammered. Linda entered the enormous sound stage, where the hillside with the reconstructed Temple of Apollo at Delphi lay, the Italian sun slanting on it through open stage doors. It was painted in vivid reds and purples.

She whistled.

"It's beautiful, but it's so . . . so colorful!"

"Of course," said Max, "Greek buildings were colored when they were new."

In her mind she had envisioned a bone-white framework of romantic ruins and figures.

There were indeed statues on the set, famous ones like Pythagoras of Rhethiumas' great charioteer of Delphi, and copies of the work of Greek sculptors, statues of Apollo, Athena Pronoea, and famed athletes. But they were all brilliantly painted in a lifelike manner, some with golden curls. They looked like magnificent actors, waiting for their cues.

"They're all painted!" she said.

"I feel bewildered, too," Max said. "It will be a challenge to make actors compete with these beautiful vivid forms. But it is a directive from our fussy Mr. Niadas. He insists we be true to the classic ideal. Statues were painted in ancient Greece. He sent a corps of artists and archaeologists to do them correctly."

Linda touched the charioteer.

"We will have to be very beautiful to compete."

Linda's dressing room was decorated in Aegean blue and white. A bouquet of violets was set in a delicate and ancient urn on a table. She bent down to smell the fragrance of the flowers. There was a card. She picked it up and read: "For Alethea the beautiful, my Oracle. These were picked by moonlight near the waters of Lethe, for the forgetfulness of all sadness, and remembrance of all joys. And the urn was excavated in the shadow of the Adytum at Delphi. Until we meet. Pericles Niadas."

"Well!" she said. "He seems to be all right, after the earthquake."

"He had them flown in for you from Greece," said Max.

He shook his head.

"I received a directive from him. It too came by plane this morning. Not as felicitous as yours. But he would not let anything spoil this day."

He lifted up the fragile urn. A nymph ran, pursued by a satyr, their feet in a flowery field.

"It must be priceless. I hope this isn't symbolic." Max set it down cautiously.

Linda inhaled the scent of the flowers.

"He's running our pre-production set tests constantly. The latest is, there are to be no approvals on anything until he sees film. Everything must be authentic. By the time he gets through, we may have to post a guard on the props alone. I wouldn't be surprised if he sacked the Athens museums."

"Does it bother you?" asked Linda, shucking off her woolen pullover.

"Nothing in props bothers me," he said. "Only live problems like actors. If anyone focuses on props, then I'm not very good at my job, am I? Or you at yours?"

She nodded, agreeing.

"Of course," said Max, "we will not go into what various departments think of their importance. You must always respect them for what they contribute, but watch them, too. Like a preview I attended before we left. A film of your friend Marlon Brando."

Linda pretended to clutch her bosom.

"The green man came out of the auditorium after it was finished. Fans were lined up nine deep writing out those 'they-were-great' cards. The green man shook his head sadly and turned to the assistant director standing with me. 'Did you see that big hambone at the end of the picture?' he asked angrily. 'He read his whole damned speech in front of *my* plants!' So you see, no matter what you do, someone suffers."

There was a knock at the door. Giuseppe, a pudgy little makeup man, introduced himself. He was armed with boxes of cosmetics and glossy eight-by-ten portraits of Linda's makeup, which had been directed by Max in Hollywood.

"Look," said Max, "follow these exactly. I have to go on the set and get the camera crew in order."

Giuseppe was followed by a stream of voluble hairdressers, a body-makeup woman, and a wardrobe woman.

Linda was glad that her chiton was a simple two squares of material, pinned at the shoulders with large golden spikelike pins, and girdled in the style of the peplos of Athena, to nip in over a bloused tunic with a golden cord.

Again her attention was drawn to Niadas' gift. She smelled the violets, then touched her tongue to them before the moisture on them had all evaporated. She would taste the waters of Lethe, so that she, too, would know the magic of forgetting all sorrows and remembering all pleasures. What a romantic man Mr. Niadas must be. Pity he had to be tied up to that creep Martha Ralston. And yet—she smiled—if it hadn't been for Miss Ralston getting knocked up, she wouldn't be here.

◆◆◆◆◆◆◆◆

As the makeup man finished shading his cheeks and his jowls, Leslie Charles looked at the simple knee-length chiton he would wear, and the purple palmette-embroidered linen cloak. It would suit him, and so would the character he would portray.

His first concern, he thought, was to make an alliance with Linda Barstow before John Graves turned on his vulgar low-class sex appeal. Linda, of course, was too young to be an actual love target, but girls will be girls. While the makeup man went to fetch him coffee, he had a little work to do, fast, without an audience.

He opened a briefcase and took out a stack of eight-by-ten glossies. Good old Grace had brought them from Hollywood for him. He rummaged through them and finally selected one. On the back was pasted a strip of typewritten paper, prepared some thirty years ago by Grace, when she was a junior publicist at Titan. It read: "Credit Titan Films: Jeffrey Barstow, the great stage and screen actor, in his forthcoming role as Augustus Caesar in the Titan superproduction *Mountain of the Gods*."

Leslie carefully ripped off the strip of paper, took out his fountain pen, and scribbled on the photograph, "To Leslie, man among men, always, Jeff."

Leslie slipped the picture into a thin silver frame, pressed down the brads securely at the velvet-faced backpiece, and propped it up on his table. It looked pretty good. Of course, a tunic was not a peplos, and a Roman looked different somehow in his hairdress than a Greek, but the image was close enough.

His makeup man brought him a cup of coffee.

"There," said Leslie, implanting the gossip, "is my ideal."

"Accipicchia!" said Alberto, thrilled at the confidence, "but it is the great Jeffrey Barstow!"

"Taught me a great deal," said Leslie, "helped me when I was a stringbean youth in my first classic role at Titan. He showed me how even the cleverest wardrobe department couldn't give me muscles like he could stitch in tights; he called them symmetricals, learned it on the stage, he said."

Leslie smiled fondly. "So when I put on those cotton legs, I thought I was the noblest Roman of them all."

"You look not unalike," said Alberto.

"Accent it. Do my eyebrows up a little sardonically, like his."

When he was dressed, he drew on his embroidered cloak and strolled to the set. He would make his introduction in a romantic way.

He was pleased to see that his set trailer was placed near Linda Barstow's.

He turned his chair toward the open door. Beyond him, the phaedriades, "shining rocks" of Delphi, arose above the temple of Apollo. The olive tree and spring flowers seemed to have sprung from seed in this earth. Well done, he thought. He studied the painted figures. How well they would work with some of his monologues, the scenes where he stood in reverie, as the priest had descended into the adytum to hear the priestess declaim. He was amused at the idea that statues at least could not upstage him.

Linda entered the open stage doors. The sun shone on her blond hair and her chiton, making it seem transparent. His eyebrows lifted. Beauty! He felt a prickle, as he had when he worked with the greatest of the exciting women of film and theater. In a way, this girl reminded him of the great beauty Claudia had at her peak, when he had become sophisticated enough to recognize it. But where Claudia had been all beauty of the flesh, this young girl suggested the spirit as well.

He walked out to greet her.

He planted himself in front of the Doric temple. Linda's mouth opened slightly, her eyes wide.

He walked forward, the robe aristocratically draped across his shoulder, and took her hand.

"Alethea."

"Mr. Charles!"

"Hermocrates," he corrected. "You couldn't look more lovely. We're early birds, my dear. I must see you privately a moment. I have something . . . special for you."

He took her hand and guided her to his dressing room.

He gestured for Linda to proceed, and he closed the door.

"Please sit down."

She sat on the couch in the small trailer. He looked at Linda gravely, put his hands out, and held hers.

"My dear, I had to see you alone. In some instances, introductions in a group can be very painful. At least . . ." He hesitated briefly, and she almost believed there was a tear in his voice. ". . . at least, with you. I almost didn't have the nerve, but when I saw you, I knew it was right. You see, I have something for you. You are a Barstow. You are beginning the big adventure. We all pursue the dream, but sometimes, maybe once or twice in a lifetime, the dream crystallizes. And this is what makes memories."

She looked at him, puzzled.

"Wait," he said. "I am saying this for a reason. Once, someone helped me very much. And I pray with all I learned that I may help you. . . ."

His eyes seemed full of memories. He reached to the table and took the picture of Jeffrey in its silver frame. He looked upon it as if it were an icon. He handed it to Linda.

She took it. It seemed incredible, but as she compared the picture, she felt that Leslie Charles could have been her father.

"Oh, Mr. Charles . . . it's my father! You . . . you look so much alike."

"No, my dear. Not alike, akin. This has been my treasure. Gone everywhere with me. Always on my dressing table. But now, I want you to have it."

She held it tenderly. She didn't feel like crying. She just felt exultant, as if her father had suddenly stepped out of the past, and was here in blood and flesh to help her.

"How can I accept it?"

"Because we'll make more memories. Now, forgive me for being a sentimental old slob, dear child, and run along before I change my mind."

He smiled, and at that she was close to tears.

"How can I thank you?"

"Just don't upstage me, dear." He had resurrected her from the brink of tears, and she arose, full of joy, clasping the picture to her bosom. He had indeed created empathy.

"Tell me about him sometime, will you?"

"We were good pals."

"Tell me everything."

"Everything."

He made a gesture that was the promise of a future, of endless fealty and magic things to come.

How handsome he was, and how . . . how noble.

"Where is John Graves?" she asked him.

"He is not in this sequence, thank God. You and I are starting the picture together, I am glad to say. However, let me give you your first lesson in set etiquette. Never ask one actor where another actor is." Leslie smiled brightly. "As far as I am concerned, there is only one actor. Me."

Linda giggled.

As if by magic, Claudia appeared. She had stood in the background and spotted Leslie's ploys.

"Well, Leslie," she said, "if you haven't got yourself up as a roadshow Jeffrey Barstow!"

Max joined, for he had given Claudia the go-ahead to break up the overblown entente he had seen aborning.

Leslie decided to ignore the dig.

"Claudia," he said, embracing her, "how enchanting you look! I was utterly delighted when Max told me you were going to work with us on the dialogue. Just like old times. And about that niece! Need I tell you how lovely she is, or should I tell you later, to keep her from getting vain? How auspicious to be starting her career!"

Max circled him, looking on with a sudden cold eye. "It seems to me that some adjustment has been made since your makeup and wardrobe tests. I'm glad it was brought to my attention before we got film on you. Now, we wouldn't want a roadshow Jeffrey Barstow, would we? We want the real Leslie Charles."

He turned to his assistant. "Dave, have the makeup department get the test stills, and adjust Mr. Charles's makeup. Meanwhile, we'll get the background action going, and do some establishing shots."

He took Leslie's arm. "I know you are always looking for perfection, Leslie, and I do think you look patrician. But I don't care for the sardonic eyebrows in your characterization. Let's get back to the original."

Leslie smiled. "If you say."

There was nothing else he could do. He gave Claudia a flashing glance of annoyance, nodded to Linda, and walked to his dressing room, head held high.

"Linda," said Max, "all these myriad details may seem very confusing to you. Believe me, it all comes together. Meanwhile, I think it would be wise of you to go to your dressing room and run through the scene with Claudia. Then we will block the action. I want you to know the set as if you were raised here. Remember, Delphi is now, so to speak, your backyard."

As Claudia and Linda walked toward the set, Claudia peered toward Leslie's dressing room. Several makeup men, a hairdresser, and a wardrobe man were rushing toward the brightly lighted interior.

"Blimey," said Claudia, "I really did it, didn't I?"

Linda was looking at the framed picture of her father.

"Where did you get that?" asked Claudia.

"Oh, Mr. Charles gave it to me. Said he'd always carried it everywhere he went. But that he wanted me to have it."

"Well," said Claudia as they entered the set dressing

room, "that seems odd. I never knew Leslie and Jeffrey were such chums. Don't tell me there was something about my brother's private life I didn't know!"

"What?" said Linda, eyes wide.

"Nothing," said Claudia. "I must learn to button my lip. Now, let's get on with the dialogue. Leslie is really a nice man. You need all the friendship and support you can get. And the fact that he tried to look like my brother was only a compliment. Let's not go into it again. Okay?"

Linda nodded and set the frame on her dressing table. And it didn't look like Jeffrey's handwriting to Claudia. But whatever she discovered, she must keep her mouth shut. She certainly could do without the enmity of Leslie Charles and his old buddy, that newshorn Andrew Reed. She'd had enough trouble with them in years past.

"Okay," said Linda.

"However," said Claudia, "that doesn't mean I won't protect you with the waving-handkerchief bit if I see things going wrong. I guess I know more about camera angles and the angles that happen in front of a camera than anyone alive. But for God's sake, don't let anyone see you peering at me, in case I have to use it. Do you think you're capable of seeing me out of the side of your eye?"

Linda laughed. "For you, I can do it!" she said. "Oh, Aunt Claudia, what would I do without you?"

"Possibly better," said Claudia uneasily.

Leslie's makeup had been adjusted, and everyone found it provident not to mention it. Once he got into the lights, and assumed his character, he became a different person to Linda. The amicable image of her father was gone. He glanced at her with the authority of a physician, studying the symptoms of a girl he knew was not well. He examined the teeth marks on her bracelet, asking her why she bit into it in the sacred cave. She admitted that she had seizures when the holy vapors hit her face.

After many meticulous rehearsals, Linda felt the flutter of Claudia's handkerchief. She coughed, breaking up the scene, and rubbed her nose. She apologized and went to her dressing room.

"Leslie was upstaging you right into the scenery. And most apparently, Max didn't notice. Even if he did, it's no good to start out that way."

Claudia wheeled her about, showing her how the camera would work on her face.

"The minute you feel that keylight on your back, you're in trouble," she said. "Hardly anybody ever got to be a star on an unplanned angle."

"What do I do?" asked Linda.

"If you feel it happening, just break up the scene and say you're off your marks. Then stare at him. He'll know what you mean. But feel that lens. And learn exactly where you should be in the rehearsal."

Linda adjusted her curls and went back to the set. They played the scene again. This time Linda moved cautiously from her marks as Leslie began to move her around again.

"Cut," said Max.

He came close to Linda and spoke very quietly.

"I don't know what's wrong," he said in a confidential voice, his eyes flashing, "but don't ever let me see you try to maneuver another actor around."

He took her hand and led her out of Leslie's earshot.

"I know Leslie tried to upstage you. But this is your first day, and I didn't want you to feel awkward. I'm giving you a closeup later, naturally. But if anyone interferes with my direction, Linda, there's going to be trouble." He glanced in Claudia's direction.

Linda noticed that she moved quietly away. There wouldn't be any more handkerchiefs flashing behind the camera.

She resented the fact she was put in such a position with Max. Not only that, he was disappointingly much less personal with other people around than he had been when she made the tests. She realized that she was working in a jungle, a jungle of human beings, each of them selfishly intent on making a deep impression for his own good. Perhaps there was no friendship, no loyalty, and no surcease, once the bright lights and camera eye were on them.

It was strange, those in front of the camera making ordered sounds, and those in back signaling and treading on velvet feet. She also noticed the rising irritation of Max, who never rested on the set, he had so many things to coordinate.

They did the scene over and over. Linda realized that she had barely been initiated into picture-making in her tests.

The prop man must stir the waters offstage to make the reflections of the little rill that seemed to be flowing from the sacred Castalian spring. Birds had been trained to fly into the trees. Even an eagle dipped down, apparently from the "shining rocks," and back out of scene onto the gloved hands of his trainer.

Extras walked by carrying snowy lambs, leading bearded goats, riding donkeys. Others carried amphorae of wine, oil, and honey, or sheaves of grain, sacks of wheat, baskets of bread and grapes.

A horse, bearing a bearded soldier garbed in armor, passed by. An old woman tugged at a recalcitrant beast laden with panniers of olives.

There was the sound of footsoldiers as they clanked by with their swords and shields rattling. Actresses who played priestesses, wearing their holy white garments and their wreaths of laurel leaves, stood placidly in the background by the shrine.

Each of these moved on cue; several assistant directors signaled silently so that all would mesh. If all was not according to Max's ordered rhythm, he would stop the action short, even if he seemed to be concentrating upon the lines and action of his two principals, Leslie and Linda.

While the lights were set up, Claudia closed the dressing-room door and sat down.

"Now," she said, "Leslie's trying to do it to you with his voice."

"I didn't notice anything," said Linda. "What did he do?"

"His voice has gone down a couple of decibels in the

last readings," she said. "Make your dialogue as crisp as his, but not more so. He's pulling the old gag of undertoning. He's forcing you, and everyone else, to listen to his words. Well, you make him listen, too, if he's going to play it cozy. You know, you can play that bit until both of your voices fade from the scene. If anyone can whisper, it can be you, because you're sacred. *Feel* sacred."

Linda nodded.

Claudia watched as she returned to the set. Her shoulders were squared, her face impassive. The laurel-wreath crown and the expression of her eyes made her seem the pythoness at the shrine of her god, her beloved Apollo.

Linda did the scene, listening to Hermocrates' lines, growing fearful of his warnings and his medical diagnosis of her illness. The sanctity melted as the young priestess was bowed down by the knowledge the physician imparted.

As the scene ended, Claudia noticed the imperceptible pause before Leslie Charles left his marks. Linda had impressed him and held her ground.

Linda herself for the first time felt that she had forgotten herself. What happened with extras, pigeons, animals, and even the warmth of Max's approving brown eyes, as he stood entrenched beside the camera, were all aside from her personal experience.

"Cut," said Max.

"Save the light," yelled Hank.

Linda stood for a moment in the sudden turnoff of fever brightness. Leslie had walked off, without a word, to his own dressing room.

"Auguri, auguri!" said an Italian workman, giving the characteristic cry for success as he carried a lamp in his gloved hands.

"I wish they wouldn't say that," said Max, shaking his head. "Personally, I like the affectionate *'Hals und Beinbruch'*—'break your neck and legs'—we say in Germany, or the more down-to-facts French *'merde'* that always initiates a plunge into the arts. This politeness makes me nervous."

Linda started for her dressing room. Max put a hand out to stop Claudia.

"May I have a word with you?"

He led her aside.

"I know your main interest is Linda. That is why you are here. But, Claudia, you have obviously interfered with my production. You have signaled to Linda during a take; you have antagonized Leslie Charles. I shall have to ask you to work with Linda at the villa or in her dressing room. If I did not know how much you care for her, I would relieve you of your job. I know it is difficult, you have been a big star. I have directed you in many memorable scenes. Leslie has worked with you through the years. But you must understand, I cannot have my authority on the set undermined."

Claudia felt her hands getting clammy. Her first instinct was to rail at Max, but she knew she had no clout; those days were gone. She must divorce herself from the gall that rose in her throat, and think of Linda. Otherwise she wouldn't be here.

"I'm sorry, Max," she said. "I knew there would be trouble when I confronted Leslie on the set. I could have bitten my tongue. It was stupid. I have been too protective of Linda. Please, understand. It won't happen again."

To her surprise, Max took her hand.

"I know how it is," he said. "I find myself wanting to give the scenes to her. It is perhaps once in a lifetime that one finds a perfect creature, untouched so far with the wrong things. And I know you can give her a training that is out of my orbit. Help me, Claudia."

In the old days she would have been furious to be exiled. But now she was touched. How long it had been since anyone had told her she was needed! Linda, of course, but that was family, and accepted as a natural gift, as often happens with the very young.

"I'll do what you say," she said.

He was still annoyed; she saw it in his glance. She swallowed back tears. What's the matter? she thought—getting soft when I should be fighting for my place in the sun!

"I heard the scene in the sound truck," said Max, "and I want you to get the tape machine, and have her hear how she matches with Leslie. Could you work that out? And also, I don't want her to get involved with the hurly-burly of the social lunch hour just yet."

"I'll work with her, and we'll have lunch sent into the dressing room," said Claudia.

⬥⬥⬥⬥⬥⬥⬥⬥

Linda slipped on a silk wrapper. Claudia came in, followed by Vittorio, the chauffeur, carrying a tape recorder. She ordered it plugged in.

"What is this?" asked Linda.

"Just a little scene insurance," said Claudia, as she opened up the script. Linda thought she seemed flustered. "It's our machine from the villa. If you'll excuse me, I have to get some more tapes. I'll be right back."

As if on cue, Max came in as she left. Linda suspected collusion.

"Max, are you going to take me to lunch?"

"No, my darling," he said, "I am going to ask you to have your bite here. You know things do not always go smoothly the first day. And I want to tell you right now so you will understand that I have had a few words with Claudia. I made it plain to her that I need her to help you, but not when I am directing. We've settled our misunderstanding, and there won't be any more wig-wagging behind my camera. You may think that I am a dreamy old fool, but my honey can turn to gall, my dear, when it comes to work. And on the set I have eyes in the back of my head."

Linda saw a flash of anger, which fired his eyes. They were suddenly not akin to the soft brown orbs of the poet who had worked with her so gently.

"I'm sorry," she said. "We just wanted to be better."

"I shall decide what's better," Max said ."So now, as I said to your aunt, let's forget it. She is a brilliant coach. She will block out the scene with you. But there is one little problem."

"What's wrong?" asked Linda.

"It is not your fault," said Max. "Pictures are teamwork, and adjustments must always be made. As a matter of fact, it is the way I prefer to work. Long shots first."

He noted her startled look.

"You must not be concerned. Chemistry with another actor is hard to come by. It is possible to correct things now. Just a little study. Phonetics is a precise science, and your aunt is the best teacher. I will see you later."

As he left, Claudia returned with a fixed smile on her face.

"Your smile is too bright," said Linda. "What's up? Max was just here."

"Never mind, it's settled. Let's get down to business. The problem is only corrective," she said, "and it comes from a sound-booth taping. Linda, we have to adjust the slightly western edge of your consonants, and make your vowels less butter-soft. We'll work a little longer on this sequence."

"You make me feel like Eliza Doolittle!" said Linda.

"Nonsense," said Claudia. "Leslie Charles's diction is so good that even an actor like John Graves, fresh out of London, can't make him sound colonial. And we have to lower your pitch a bit. That's all."

"All!" said Linda.

Claudia ran a tape of the scene that had just been shot.

Linda heard her voice, immature and high, balanced against the sonorous tones of Leslie Charles. She put her hands to her face.

"It's terrible! Do I sound like that!"

"You won't." She put her hand on Linda's diaphragm. "Now, say that line from your gut, not your nose."

They practiced voice-placement exercises until Linda's tonal quality fell into place along with the replayed words of Leslie. Linda forgot it was corrective; in a few moments she found a harmony of pitch.

"You see," explained Claudia, "in a perfect scene, actors must emerge as a harmonic whole. Only comedy and frailty are revealed by dissonance, and that has to be carefully studied. It's like an artist gathering paints for a picture. Max knows what he wants, and I am only preparing the palette. And I'll stay in the background."

Linda saw respect rather than irritation on Claudia's face as she spoke of him. And she herself was in awe of the change; the creative man, it seemed, was quite different from the sort who was a teacher and just drummed lessons into your head. This was a new Max, and she'd have to be on her toes.

After lunch hour the company moved as lethargically as honey from the mild sunlit outdoors onto the set. The odor of sour wine and garlic sausage mingled with the scents of watered-down earth, plant spray, paint, and animal dung, which was swept out of the incubator of the hot lights by men with brooms and shovels, referred to by Hank Waters, the second American assistant, as "the turd team."

But when they got into their scenes, Leslie noted the change in her voice and performance. He cocked an eye in Claudia's direction, then decided it was wise to say nothing, but join up.

As Max led them into the labyrinth of movement and sound, life seemed to stir again at the imaginary shrine of the Delphian Apollo in an imaginary Greece, surprisingly fleshed with real people.

When Max called cut and the hubbub of Italian chatter swirled about them, Linda clutched at her head.

"How can this mess seem so real!" she said.

Leslie grimaced at her across the harsh arc lights.

"This is where the magic enters, my dear," he said. "You would never be a star, nor I, if we couldn't bridge the gap between this chaos and convincing reality on film. You know, I have come to believe that illusion is life, not life the illusion."

"All this commotion for a few seconds of film," said Linda.

"Filmmaking still seems a series of interrupted disasters to me," said Leslie. "It takes a genius like Max to put the whole mosaic together."

"It's the waiting between setups that bothers me," said Linda. "You aren't on, and you aren't off. You're in limbo. Claudia has warned me, also, that I have to carry over the same pitch and pace, even if I do the rest of the scene three weeks later."

"Claudia's obviously a gifted teacher," said Leslie. "Now, don't get buck fever. And you've got Ziska. My heart hardly bleeds for you, beginning your career here. You go home to a fabulous villa on the Appian Way. Why, my dear, we will have many days off. And I shall be delighted to chuckle with you at *la società del materasso.*"

He smiled knowingly.

"Whatever is that?" she asked.

"The society of the mattress," he said, "the joking name for the *aristocrazia.*"

As Linda and Leslie left the set, a young bit player, a handsome Italian boy about sixteen, with long curling lashes, jumped forward, offered her an orange, and stood grinning. He could have been a kid from school at home.

"Grazie, grazie, bene," said Linda, accepting the fruit.

She was the recipient of a flowing torrent of staccato Italian. Blessings were rained on her from all the saints in the heavens for her beauty and her noble nature.

Leslie grasped Linda's hand, bowed to the boy stiffly, and marched her into his trailer dressing room. He closed the door firmly.

"Keep far away from that nonsense," he said.

His dresser had brewed tea and set out fragile Crown Derby china from an elaborate teacase. Leslie poured, passed a plate of tea biscuits, and settled back. Linda started to peel the gift orange.

"My god, no!" he said, taking it from her and dropping it in the wastebasket. "Lord knows where it's been, likely wandering about during takes under some Italian armpit."

"Ugh!" said Linda.

"First thing you must realize," said Leslie, "is that such gestures from these creatures are rarely from the heart. You will have to pay with endless civility and priceless wasted time for that wretched orange. That young man will be sidling up to you in scenes, and if the assistant doesn't pick him up for tomorrow's work, he'll scream that you're an ingrate. And if he returns, he'll insinuate a personal relationship, and try to get in a still with you that he can carry around as proof. Then somehow his impoverished grandmother, pregnant sister, and all the grubby family children will be brought around to meet you personally. That's only a starter. You will then be informed that the next infant will be named after you. You will be expected to hand out cash and costly gifts. You will be invited to the christening at some rabbit warren in the slums of Rome, with all the neighbors hanging like laundry over the balcony railings, will suffer through an interminable pasta dinner, and a blood relationship from then on will be expected of you, which will be sheer horror."

Linda looked at him, laughing.

"It is no laughing matter," said Leslie. "These bastards will know when you arrive at any railroad station or boat terminal before the publicity department; they explode on the scene loaded with sticky wilted flowers and fly-blown pastries."

"Thank you for telling me," said Linda. "I guess I was foolish. I don't know anyone my own age. I thought it was a charming Italian gesture."

"Fame and prestige put you in a position of being a patsy," said Leslie. "They all think you can offer them some magic, a potion, a heady draft, moonstruck from your own success. Don't forget, the ordinary people of the world hardly ever approach luck, and think you can become their touchstone. They all have grabs for anything. Ask me my philosophy? I can give it to you in two words: *En garde!*"

He smiled, but sadly.

"Thank you," said Linda. "Everyone tells me how to act, how to use my voice, how to move, but nobody ever tells me about life. People leave me in a sort of quarantine, as if childhood were some sort of loathsome disease. You will take me into Rome with you?"

He nodded, smiling.

"What can I ever do to repay you?" she said.

Leslie looked at her in the mirror as he patted his chin.

"I know one thing you can do," he said. "You could arrange for me to get my closeups before the sun goes over the yardarm. I'm beginning to look like an old shoe, and you're as fresh as a daisy."

Later Linda thought about what he had said. Of course, he had delivered the message in a humorous vein, but she felt that she had heard this same warning before.

Then she remembered her conversation with David Austin in London. "If you knew how empty their lives are when they come running to you, you'd turn and run the other way."

It was all part of the same thing. The touchstone of magic that everyone thought a person of importance could bestow to fill an unknown emptiness.

◆◆◆◆◆◆◆◆

As time passed, the staff of *The Oracle* seemed so intent on its own errands that Linda felt very much alone. Claudia seemed powerless, afraid to step out of her own orbit, and Max was more and more preoccupied with so many people and details that had to be solved with an immediacy as the momentum and obvious massive expenses of each day's work progressed.

And worst of all, to Linda, when the daily rushes finally came in, it was decided that since she had no professional experience, she was not to see them; it might affect her performance. Max, Sidney, Lloyd, the unit manager, the cameramen, and the assistants all went to the projection room and returned, all of them discussing the production but not talking about the quality of her scene. Obviously Claudia was outlawed.

Finally Linda burst into tears one afternoon, returning to the villa in the car with Max.

"You might as well tell me," she said. "I'm a flop. Just a flop. You won't let me see the rushes. I know! I know!"

Max took her hand.

"You must not decide, Linda," he said. "You photograph beautifully. We knew it would be difficult at first. Your voice is improving. You have much to learn, and must do it step by step. Trust me, my darling, and it will work out."

"Work out!" she echoed. "That isn't what you expected. Work out!"

"You did it in the test," said Max. "You will do it again."

"You mean I haven't yet?"

"I am not concerned," said Max. "You are fine."

"Fine," said Linda. "That's not good enough. Nobody who's a star is just *fine!*"

"Just for practice," said Max, "we are going to let you do some dubbing. We have that new French system, instant playback. Now, we'll loop your speeches with Leslie Charles before we move in for the real work. Claudia will be a great help."

"You mean I'm going to get to see the rushes!" said Linda.

"Just loops . . . chopped up rushes," said Max.

He chose a night when Jessica had invited some of her newfound Roman social friends to dine. Max, Claudia, and Linda left almost as relieved not to have to go to the party in the salons of the villa as Jessica was to get rid of them. Her relationship with Max had faded as aristocracy found her fair.

Claudia tucked the thumbed script under her arm, and they set off in high spirits. She was delighted to be going out with Max; they could talk shop without confrontation on the set, and not having Jessica in tow was like a holiday in itself. Many a time she had gritted her teeth, and marveled at how she could sit out the untenable situation. How incredible to have been a motion-picture star, and yet feel she was *de trop* on a set. The most difficult thing in the world to her was to take a back seat to the importance of Linda's career. And yet she knew that if she had any sort of a set-to after her lapse with Leslie and Max, she'd be out, and Linda would be in limbo.

"It's just as well to get used to lip synchronization," said Claudia, "before we go on location, where you usually have to do the soundtrack all over anyway."

"Those workmen's squeaky shoes," said Max, "are still in the soundtrack."

They dined on the terrace of San Callisto, on *pollo alla Nerone,* aflame in brandy-drenched laurel leaves, and sat under the stars, feeding the scraps of chicken to the prowling cats.

They drove through the scented evening to the studio, which seemed a world of their own, with only a few night workers going about their tasks, and settled down in the dubbing room.

It took Linda a few runs to adjust to the film. The loops were processed in black and white. The raw print made her seem quite different from the studied colored test she had seen in Hollywood.

It took her a few moments to get back into the dialogue and mood of a scene that had been worked on days before.

Claudia watched the film loop on and off endlessly, with its cue marks for speeches to start. After a while Max asked her to join in on the readings, and she showed Linda how to breathe properly into the microphone, to make the words seem natural in action.

The sound was played back instantly. If Linda was too off sync, Max said "Cut," and it was run again.

When the final "Go again" was ended, with Max's "That's it" and a nod from the sound technician in his glass booth, a new loop was played a few times, until Linda felt at home with the movement, and began to repeat her line with her own previous dialogue on earphones to guide her.

After a session, she turned to Max.

"Now, next time you roar at that set for those clowns to quiet down, I won't think you're too severe. Aren't they awful!"

"They are dreadful," said Max. "The pranks of the

empty-minded cost thousands and thousands of dollars. There's not much you can do about it with so many people. And even a well-meaning grip with a slight bronchial cough can cost more than if we replaced him ten times. Now you know why I'm such an ogre."

He made a gargoyle face and clawed at her. This was his world, and he was so happy in his own métier. Linda felt a burst of love for him; she belonged because of him.

"Oh, Max, I love you!" she said.

"If you do," said Claudia, "then get your voice down, dearie. You sound like you're about to cheerlead for your high school."

She turned back to the looping, and when the voice of the Pythia spoke again on the screen, it was warmer, soft and deep, charged with the mystery of the fissured vapors and incense at the shrine of Delphi.

"Beautiful," said Max.

They drove home happily tired, and sneaked up the back terrace steps. They could see the flittering shapes of some of Jessica's gay group as they danced and laughed on the terrace.

"What a *fritto misto* of society," said Max.

Linda yawned.

"Good night all, and thanks. Are you satisfied with the looping?"

"You are going to be very good at it," said Max. "I'm not in the least worried about having to dub on location, now. Good work, Claudia."

"Thank you," she said. "Thank you for a lovely evening—my best in Rome."

Linda left.

Max took her hand.

"Claudia, thank you for what you have done for Linda. She improved her performance tonight. I must tell you, I am relieved. We can go on now. You know, I was afraid of you when we began."

"Afraid of me?" she said.

"Yes," said Max, "afraid of the powerful star ego image, which I had feared in years gone by. Afraid of the talent you had, which could have caused so much disturbance today in a young ego, if so you had chosen."

"How could you fear me," said Claudia, "when you knew what this child's career as a Barstow would mean to me?"

"I was afraid, because I knew Linda needed help to get the raw west out of her diction. She also needed not to rush her phrasing the way young people do in the first quick gush of their growing life and vitality. You must remember, English is not my language; you know it better than I, and I feared that you might give her a rich, false voice-building, which would saddle her talent."

"I would not do that," she said. "I have seen talent smothered by too rich a voice. And too rich many things, I may add."

She sat on the ledge of the terrace. The garden light silvered her back and neck and cast a dark shadow on her beautiful face. Max could see her wide, sad eyes staring up at him in the night. He lit one of his black cigarettes, offering her one, which she took. He lit her cigarette, and the flame glowed against her face.

"How soft your eyes are," he said.

She looked at him a moment.

"Maybe you're reflecting your own. You always remind me of Rabindranath Tagore when you look a certain way."

"I thank you," he said. "I guess I never knew you."

"You aren't afraid of me," she said, "you are afraid for her."

"Not altogether. I also feared that you, being an actress of importance, might open up a world of thought which would conflict with my dream of Alethea. But you are letting her find herself at the same time that you are helping her to mature."

"Mature at her age! God help her," said Claudia quietly.

"The old lament," asked Max, "about being an actress and leading a false life? Let us instead pray she makes it. My dear Claudia, of all people, you know better than that. . . . But do you think the acting life could possibly be worse than the life of anyone down there?"

He made a gesture that embraced Jessica's party below.

"They're all selling their wares with desperate futility in a much smaller and less satisfying stage. You saw Linda's pleasure tonight as she attacked the difficult problem of dubbing. You know some people can't dub well at all. I was halfway prepared to have you pinch-hit, if she couldn't do it. It isn't necessary, because I see you have taught her to carry her own tuning fork."

"Thank you for noticing."

Rumba music struck up below them.

They went inside. It was all sound and light and echoing confusion below, as they peered down into the gaiety.

They could see over the head of Phryne, who stood forgotten, like a painting at an art gallery vernissage when café society holds its free cocktails in hand and turns to stare only at each other.

"Well, it's what Jessica wanted," said Max. "Good night, Claudia, and thank you again."

He wandered down the great staircase, staying close to the wall so that he could not easily be seen, and she saw him turn into the labyrinth that would take him to his guestroom. No one noticed. They were all too busy selling themselves.

She went to her own sitting room and settled down for a moment to finish his cigarette. A black cigarette with a gold tip, strong, made especially for Maximilian Ziska, the whim of a man who needed no whims, undoubtedly some forgotten symbol of a past time and place, which was forever fresh in his mind.

She found herself secretly rejoicing in the fact that Max was so apart from Jessica this night. It was not his life, she was not his woman, whatever had happened. She had suspected that the bond was Linda, and now she knew it.

On the way to her bedroom she paused and saw her face, soft and defenseless, no longer young, in the mirror.

"Don't be a silly fool," she said severely to herself.

She went into her bedroom, lowered the lights, and began to undress.

She was disturbed about the rushes. Max was playing a fighting game and would not admit it. There had been too many calls from David Austin, and even several from Fergus Austin lately in Hollywood. The mystic pythoness was not on film yet—only a beautiful young girl, and a smart aging actor who was wheeling and gesturing too much. More of this, she thought, and this picture's going to follow the fate of *Pallas Athena*. Pageantry and beauty were not enough at this price. What could she do? What could Max do?

She adjusted her night light and opened the script. Then she set it aside. She'd better clear her mind of it or she wouldn't sleep.

Ghosts from the past that had always haunted her were replaced by concern about the future—and a young girl whose fate was in her hands. Hers—a woman who had lost the game, but might win it again.

With a start she thought that, incredibly, her life was also in the keeping of another person—her niece.

4

Fergus Austin, in Hollywood, wondered how long Abe Moses would bug and insult him on his increasingly frequent trips to the coast. Abe, just turned seventy, held control of the theater chain. His bald, sunburned head, heavily spotted with liver marks, his sleek, well-cared-for jowls, his trim figure and London clothes spoke of a plethora of worldly care. Fergus knew there were always hotel suites, private planes, clubs, resorts, and starlets of various types at hand for his consumption. It all disgusted him.

Having elected to stay with the theater holdings of Titan when the Supreme Court ordered a division between studio and theaters, Abe had jettisoned his Titan holdings in exchange for theater stock. Now he was literally in an expanding real-estate business, as small theaters connected with suburban development were coming into their own. Even the land that housed the monstrous theaters, now becoming obsolete in the cities, was valuable for the gigantic structures being erected throughout the land.

As Fergus awaited his visit, he paced to and fro, realizing he was wearing a path in the carpeting in his office. Nervously he crushed out one cigarette after another.

Now that he had no large studio roster to call upon, and stars were receiving hundreds of thousands of dollars and joint ownership for their services, since they had all turned independent, he was in a bind. Sometimes, even when a new script was ready, it took a year or two to get an actor who was suitable star material to sell to backers. He had great hopes for the promised scripts from the master hands of Max Ziska, but at the rate the film starring Linda Barstow was moving in Rome, God knows how long it would be before he could start shopping around with the next one.

This was a time when agents, stars, and bankers all dealt the cards with their package deals, and studio overhead still went on, no matter how much he cut back. And every time he did, the rumor was out, loud and clear, that at any moment the Titan water tank with its famous old logo of the clenched fist sprouting lightning might topple for progress.

Thinking back on the years he had worried about Jeffrey and Claudia Barstow, their problems and pyramiding expenses, which had been such a problem to him in their reigning years as stars, he smiled bitterly. At least they had garnered millions for the studio. But now the studio's future might depend upon the whims of the last Barstow. He cursed the day Linda was born, disturbing his peace of mind. She had been a hex to him from her beginning. Now she might even topple the financial structure of his wobbly empire.

He had listened to magnified gossip over the intercontinental lines from Rome. Niadas was madly extravagant about her; the great expenses of the villa in Rome would be tacked onto the budget. Most of all, this young star, cosseted and admired, was likely to be a worthy successor of her Aunt Claudia, in being the spoiled brat of all time.

When he had heard that somehow or other Claudia had gotten into the act, after the scandalous publicity in London, and was now working with Linda as so-called dialogue director, he had been so angry that he had to call the studio doctor to give him a sedative.

In vain he attempted to reach David. Why in God's name didn't he take care of this supercolossal olympiad? And then he had to recollect that David had as little desire to cope with Jessica as he did. After all, he had wanted to marry her, had seen her copulating with him, and then had been chagrined at her sudden marriage to that old sot Jeffrey. So now, no doubt, by plan he was deep into Kenya supervising a picture company on safari, and unreachable.

Sidney Keyes was his surrogate, and very unsatisfactory he was! After all, he was only a staff member. Although he was the recipient of Fergus' wrath by phone, he knew that Sidney listened politely, agreed, and rang off as soon as possible.

So when Abe came into his office, breathing affluence, and lit up his Upmann cigar, settling back, with one leg up over a leather chair arm, Fergus tried to keep from clenching his teeth and settled back to look comfortable and prepare to lie.

"Well," said Abe, "I hear they've got you by the kishkas in Rome. And that ain't nothing to what's going to happen on location in Greece."

"Is that so?" said Fergus, leaning back in his desk swivel chair and clasping his hands behind his head. "I'd like to know who your informant is. Did you know that Niadas is absorbing a great many of the expenses privately? You're just pissed off because I got Mr. Niadas on my side, before your group could con him into building an Athens International Theater chain. For your information, he is mad about Linda Barstow, is pouring funds into her promotion, and has upped our budget millions. Why, the artifacts and furnishings alone that he is pouring into our production would enrich ten museums."

"Props and furniture ain't box office," said Abe, smiling, "and if you don't watch out, the stockholders are going to be on your neck. All I can say, old pal, is that picture and that Barstow kid ought to be goddamn good, or your butt is in a sling."

"Of course," said Fergus, "but I've seen the rushes. So just stand in line if you want *The Oracle* in your houses."

"I'm loaded with plenty of fine independents," said Abe. "Don't know as I want to roadshow such a biggie."

He looked around the room.

"Ain't it about time for you to do this office over? It still looks like it did when my brother Simon had it.

You know, we've moved our offices into a new complex on Park Avenue. All steel and plate glass. How about that!"

"Congratulations," said Fergus. "I kind of like this shabby genteel look. It has class. I'm not trying to compete with bankers and agents. Titan stands for quality."

"It did when my brother ran it," said Abe.

The new secretary buzzed him. Fergus missed comfortable old fat Harriet Foster, but he had sacked her when the fracas with Jessica forced him to let her go. And one young thing after another annoyed him and was replaced. Harriet would never have put a call through when Abe Moses was in conference.

"Call from Rome, Mr. Austin," said the secretary, unfortunately over the intercom.

If there was one thing Fergus did not want, it was a call in front of Abe about some dire happening.

"Tell them I'll call back," he said testily, "and no more calls."

He turned to Abe with a smile he hoped didn't look false.

"And now," he said, "let me just give you a rundown on the plans we have for the next year. You won't believe it."

And Abe didn't. Only they all had to play one-upmanship in this giant intercontinental chess game. He wanted *The Oracle* in his theater chain. It smelled of excitement, he thought.

◆◆◆◆◆◆◆◆

Max finished with Linda and Leslie's opening sequence.

As the camera crew took up the tracks, he turned to Sidney Keyes, who as usual was watching over David's interests. Front offices always had someone who made a detailed report, and Max was relieved to know it was Sidney, for they understood each other.

"I'm glad this is over," continued Max. "Leslie's an old pro, but he was pussyfooting into the character himself, finding his own depth and breadth. But we need some vitality. We've worked out Linda's voice placement, thanks to Claudia. I was fearful of that more than anything. And of course, the camera has established her beauty. Now I must find some stimulus for her reactions. God knows, Fergus Austin will be on my neck."

"David won't be," said Sidney. "Last letter from Kenya on location, he's pleased with the production report."

"Good," said Max, waving it aside. "Linda's got to be a woman. Let's take a chance on that obvious sexual flamboyancy of Graves. It may trigger her."

Sidney watched him flip through the script pages, playing the scenes in his mind with relish. He marveled at the businesslike way Ziska had disassociated his personal relationship with Linda. He apparently was planning to sacrifice his darling, come what may, for his picture. It was as if he hoped an adult sexual stimulus would come about from the meeting of the girl and John Graves. Most directors wanted the leading female for themselves, he thought, but this father image was passing the kid off on the young male star.

"All the other women go for him," said Sidney wryly. "I'm sure you'll have no problem."

Max ignored his comment.

"And let's get rid of that cackling gaggle of extras."

He looked at the mob with disgust. They were all well off after a spate of work, plunging into a saturnalia of gambling, eating, playing of portable radios, and euphoric horseplay.

"Good," said Sidney, "out with the infernals."

"Give Graves his call," Max said to Hank, his assistant.

"Easy," said Hank. "He's in for his last wardrobe fitting."

He knocked on Graves's dressing-room door, and then walked in.

Graves, overdressed in his jockstrap, was reclining on his cot. His current inamorata was in the adjoining bathroom, the shower turned on full force.

"You're on tomorrow," said Hank.

"Have a beer," said Graves. "It's about time. I'm tired of sitting about waiting for nursery school to let out."

Hank took a beer out of the refrigerator, uncapped it, and took a swig.

"It's none of my business, Jack," he said. "We've been good drinking buddies along Hollywood on the Tiber on *Pallas Athena* and on this. But the Barstow kid is no Martha Ralston."

"Thank God for favors," said Graves. "I couldn't go through another spell with Niadas' detectives trailing me."

"Well, this one's jailbait," said Hank. "They'd be looking for a misstep."

Graves stretched wearily. "Looking for a misstep. My dear Hank, my whole life is one fortunate misstep. I've skirted along the edge of disaster so long, I couldn't have it any other way. I can assure you I won't stub my toe on this little sprat."

He smiled, reminiscing.

"I can't imagine any niece of Claudia's being jailbait. By the way, I haven't heard a word from her. Is she on a binge or something? I thought she'd be on my trail."

"Far from a binge," said Hank. "She's been on the wagon, working with the white hope of the Barstows, and doing a good job. By the way, wait until you see that kid. Believe me, you'd like to be around when she isn't green fruit anymore."

"Listen," said Graves, "I've got my hands full with this tootsie from Soho." He nodded toward the shower. "Well, I'm glad Claudia's on the wagon. I would like to see the old girl."

"You will. There's some directive, I think, to keep her out of your hair for the moment."

"I can handle her," said John, remembering. "My God, she picked me up when I was a cockney string bean. We did a picture due to her guts and know-how. Later on, as I moved along, our companionship deteriorated, but never the way I feel for her. She is all woman, all inventive in her craft, and all weakness, but I love her."

Hank had never seen this side of Graves. It intrigued him.

How could he know, or why should he be told? thought Graves. After their fortunate independent film, *Quest for a Key,* he was offered a magnificent play, *A Majority of Devils.*

Fortunately for him, Claudia had again been in residence in England, and she taught him how to cope with his character. She wisely alerted him to the fact that he had played himself in the film.

"There are several dangers in the film world, the stellar personality who forever plays himself and the egotist who is only natural and goes no further. But now you have a chance to get away from yourself and truly act."

She felt he had not been able to imagine himself on the stage, save in terms of himself. But she had told him to get inside the character he was playing, thinking of himself as an outside entity. Thus he could move and speak and behave in a different manner from his personal attitudes. In doing this, John had won his spurs as an actor, and liberated himself.

The night the play opened, he had two seats, front row center, for Claudia. She had promised to bring Orville, the famous photographer. "He'll love your face, and your sensuality, I know," she prophesied, "but I don't know if your body is up to the aristocratic elegance he prefers. Anyway, he's good for you to know."

But as John got into the play, and the audience was his, he had a chance to gaze out and see two empty seats. Claudia had been so excited about the debut of her protégé that an early snack at the Savoy had been her undoing. After a quart of champagne, Orville had taken her home to her digs with a crying jag (because of her lost fame, she said) and had sat by her while John was winning the affection of London. John, hurt at her defection, ceased seeking her out.

A Majority of Devils moved from the Royal Court on Sloane Square to the Cambridge Theater. John found himself one of the darlings of the West End, and fresh meat for the lionesses of Mayfair.

As for Claudia, she was in and out of failures, trouble, and economic disaster. He respected the fact that as his success accelerated, she would not accept a penny from him, as a loan, or under the guise of occasionally helping him with his character analysis.

In the years between, he lost her, but often thought of the wise things she had taught him, and wondered whatever would happen to her. She was beyond his help.

Eventually, Titan, representing the Platinum Greek, Pericles Niadas, signed him for *Pallas Athena.* Martha Ralston only bored him, and Leslie Charles looked at him with disdain from his lofty platform of long success. And the rushes of the film bothered him. Still he could not adjust to the bifurcation of himself on the screen. He became aware of how he looked in everything he did, and it was not pleasant. He felt that was all there was to life; he was his own self-conscious voyeur.

And now, of all strange chambered-nautilus convolutions of life, here they were, he and Claudia, with Linda Barstow their annealing agent.

When the script of *The Oracle* was handed to him, and he knew that Max Ziska was going to be the genius to guide him, he was elated. It was the difference between a big, flossy film and a potential epic. And then, he began to have qualms about himself.

The thought of Linda Barstow had bugged him, the few days he was in London, before he came back to begin the new film. She was too young to be indoctrinated by the common leveler, sex. . . . And remembering how Claudia had been so important to him in his youth and career, and how Linda's father's image had been so impressive to him in growing years, he deliberately sought out an antidote to any small disturbance that might interfere with his performance.

Susie Grimmitt, a showgirl, had been a casual nocturnal companion in London. She was slender of body and brain, traveled with little concern for the place or time, and was suitable for his living pattern, taking all the trouble and waste of time out of pursuit and conquest. Avoiding the social elegancies of an important picture company, he avoided his former quarters at the Hassler. He found a studio in the rundown artists' quarters in Via Margutta, bought a Vespa, and he and Susie lived like gypsies, ate in cheap pizzerias, and occasionally stepped out into the permissive Roman nightlife. An actor as important as he was could afford to be eccentric.

Now that the new picture was starting, he knew he would have to get the bloat off his belly and the fumes out of his head and have just one more fling. Well, this was the night. Tomorrow he'd meet the new Barstow.

On a whim, he tired of Susie Grimmitt's jeans and fuzzy green Italian sweater. He took her to Fontana, where he caused a furor with staff and patrons. He selected a model's beaded and satin gown, and they took it along in a box. That night, breaking patterns, they dined at the elegant Hosteria dell'Orso, and caused quite a stir on their arrival by Vespa in proper dinner clothes.

The press was alerted by the time they left, again on the Vespa, and in a nimbus of flashbulbs they exited.

The next morning he set off for work, feeling seedy, and irritated that Susie was along, clinging to him, complaining of a hangover. He was more concerned about Linda. How could he tell her that her Aunt Claudia played such an important role in his life, without looking as if he were striving for a point?

He had seen the press, was amused at the way Claudia had managed to get back on the front page, and then amazed that she had been selected to be Linda's companion. Yet, knowing how skillful a teacher she was, he realized she must be needed. But how would they cope with her follies?

The Barstow girl certainly could be a sitting duck in this society, undoubtedly, from her pictures, ripe, ripe beyond her years, ready for picking, and somebody was going to do it.

He hoped he would have the opportunity of a talk

with her. Christ, he was thinking like Leslie Charles, as set rumor had come to him, reaching for grabs!

He motored into the studio ill-at-ease. He was annoyed suddenly at Susie behind him in her dirty jeans and poison-green sweater. Her unkempt hair and sour breath were disgusting.

He was aware of the ogle-eyed observations of the workingmen who stood gaping as he got off the Vespa. She got off too, and stretched and yawned.

"Why don't you bug off and get cleaned up," he said. "Christ, what kind of woman are you? Take the Vespa, I shan't need it."

He gestured angrily: get lost!

Standing behind a group of workmen, a little man took a camera out of his lunchbox and caught a picture of the gesture, as Graves dismissed her. No one saw him.

Susie looked at him sleepily and shrugged.

"Give 'em what they want," she said, "and you get it in the bum."

She turned the machine about, looking at Graves with a swift expression of hatred. She, too, was caught on film. She revved the motor and careened off toward Rome. The camera that recorded this scene was stashed away from confiscation in a heroic poor-boy sandwich.

Angrily John went into the studio. He was irritated at himself; his own personal criticism was closing in on him, and he didn't like it; he had always made such a point of being a free soul.

◆◆◆◆◆◆◆◆

Linda peered out of the portable-dressing-room door. On the set John Graves was slouching on his canvas chair. In a few moments the set would be lighted, and they would go into their first rehearsal. She had gone over the scene with Claudia endlessly the night before. But Claudia had awakened with a cold and was staying at the villa. Linda wondered if it was true or if there was some hidden reason for her absence. She felt bereft and alone.

She was almost fearful of appraising John Graves, for she would have to face him alone, a man-to-woman confrontation for the first time in her life.

But she watched him, as he sat slouching on his canvas chair. He wore a hoplite's short tunic, with the greaves and shoulder strappings of leather. She saw his feet, clad lightly in leathers and buckles, and his muscular legs and strong thighs. He was not as rangy as she had expected, but solidly framed, with wide shoulders, and arms that were muscled.

When her eyes sought out his face as he turned to glance in her direction (thank God, without seeing her and her vantage point), she saw a flash of blue eyes, and the strong-chinned, wide-eyed handsome face that Claudia had told her about.

"Somehow that little cockney bastard turned into one of the sexiest men I've ever seen. That cleft chin, and those arrogant glances of his, just seem to send women off into a hissy-fit."

Linda had smiled at this at the time, not realizing that her aunt was trying to ease the meeting with humor, but now that she looked at him for the first time, she felt a stirring and an unease in his presence which she had never felt before.

Even looking at him made her feel as if she were about to take a step onto the shores of an unknown land. She closed her dressing-room door cautiously. She must compose herself. Nobody could help her now. She was *on*, and as Claudia had told her, that's what her family did best.

There was a rap at the door.

"Ready," said Hank.

She swallowed. It was up to her. She at least must look like a pro.

The scene was the first for Linda with any physical contact in the picture. Graves, as the soldier, confronts Alethea, the oracle, recognizing her as the unknown woman he met on the stormy seashore the night before. He accuses her of being a fraud in her prophetic advice on what Athens should do in the current political situation. The young oracle lashes out at him for his distrust. Disturbed at what has happened the night before, she caresses the sacred egglike stone Omphalos, ornamented with its ribbons from the various states, and wonders in her heart if she is false and has betrayed her trust. She finds a spell coming over her, and she falls into his arms. He mistakes it for her surrender, holds her to him, and kisses her. Although she responds, she pushes away and faints, as the vapors rise up from the sacred shrine.

Max led them into the protection of the mood. The bit players who sat about were hushed.

The stage door slammed. Linda suddenly froze in the arms of Graves. Max turned, to see Jessica approaching him officiously, carrying a sheaf of papers.

"My dear Jessica," said Max, "this is her first love scene. Do you mind?"

Jessica looked annoyed. "I just got a directive from Hollywood about the press lists. It's rather important."

Max's eyes closed down.

"I'm making a film," he said, "and I don't give a damn about the press. It's difficult enough to make a fourteen-year-old girl seem to be in the pangs of her first love, without having her mother watching."

His voice was louder than he intended.

Linda caught the echo of his remark, as Jessica flounced out angrily. She looked in sudden panic at John Graves. He gazed back at her with amusement.

"Don't be afraid of me," he said quietly. "Just feel as sexy as you looked in those London pictures with your Aunt Claudia at the Cavendish. How clever of her to drag you into her digs."

Linda lifted her chin.

"Of course she did," she answered hotly, "and showed me all my family pictures. If she 'dragged' you, you're lucky too. I think she's wonderful."

John felt ashamed. Christ, what was happening to him? He had done just the thing he had warned himself he would not do.

"She's quite a valiant old girl," he said.

He confused Linda with the sudden warmth of his voice. It seemed a sort of apology.

"Now," said Max.

He turned for a signal to the cameraman.

"And *you* needn't be afraid," said Linda haughtily. "I know what I'm doing."

Graves looked at her. Even makeup could not disturb the porcelain beauty of her face. His eyes moved to her breasts and to the pulsebeat in the hollow of her slender throat.

"Places," said Max softly. "Let's run through."

Linda tried not to reveal her naïveté by falling too much into the mood. She also remembered that Claudia had warned her she must not play the rehearsals with the full impact of the final take. The scene must be fresh and new, and not go stale.

They did the scene; Max halted them just before she was to crumple into John's arms and be kissed. She was not surprised. She knew he believed that too much familiarity took the excitement away. She knew Max had analyzed them both and improved on their performance, leading them to a moment which they themselves had not yet realized.

"Children," he said, "we are going to experiment. We will be daring. You are two beautiful young people, a sensitive virginal priestess and a valiant warrior. Your lips have never met. When they do, you are both breaking a tradition, and sacrificing something of what you have both been trained to believe. But you cannot help it. You are destined to love. I am going to photograph you the first time you come together. Go on with the scene naturally."

He turned to the cameraman, busy adjusting the lighting. Max drew back into the dark shadow of anonymity.

"Don't tell me you've never been kissed?" Graves asked quietly during the interim.

"Of course I have," said Linda. "What do you think I am, a square!"

"I think you haven't been kissed properly," he said. "Now, don't stick your neck forward, like most of the dear little ingenues, and be kissed from the chin up. When I kiss a woman, I kiss. I will hold you with your breasts against me, with your stomach flattened against mine, and with our bodies meeting, as if we meant to merge. That's what a kiss means. It means I would like to kiss your beautiful body all over."

Linda looked at his sensual lips. She should have been angry at him, but felt weak, ready to be conquered in a way she didn't know.

"That is," he said, "if you're capable of imagining, infant."

The mike boom twitched.

Linda glanced at the sound man wearing earphones. He was a member of the American sound crew. She flushed, realizing that there was no privacy on a set; even the most intimate conversations could be heard by mechanics, as if they were in a theater.

"All right, now," said Max.

The set again gathered into silence, focusing on the nimbus; the two, with the vivid light playing on their bodies, became the reality that was encompassed in a frozen moment.

"Quiet!" said Hank.

"Action," said Max very quietly.

They did the scene. It was quite different from the rehearsal. Linda felt the people around her and the camera melt away. When John Graves looked at her, she saw the world-weary fatigue of the footsoldier Diodynus of Thebes, reflecting his disgust that a sacred woman had been naked in his arms the night before, when he had rescued her from a storm-tossed sea.

She found herself flinch at his mistrust of her as the Pythia, who should be holy enough to perform an act of perfect surrender only to her god, Apollo.

She saw his doubt, although from her lips came the oracle's voice of intolerable sweetness, from the truth of the Delphic shrine that bore the legend "Know Thyself."

As Alethea, she fought her own overpowering emotion in responding to him; the human voice took the place of the words of the divine creature, reality undraped her, the miracle of love cleansed her of the pomp and incense of the artificial world.

When she fell forward, he embraced her with one arm, and held her face upward with his free hand, lifting up her chin so she could not move. He kissed her. His lips found hers, forced them slightly open, and sealed them both together. She felt a giddiness, and pressed closer in his arms. As he had promised, they seemed to merge, their bodies glued against each other.

Linda pulled away, twisting her head, dismayed at the idea that he misunderstood her; looked at his lips, which had ravished hers, and back into his eyes.

Then her eyes turned upward, and she fell limply against him as he held her cradled in his arms to keep her from slumping onto the earth.

High up in the catwalk above their heads, sitting crouched in the terrible rising heat, a little man pretended to be adjusting one of the brute lights. He pulled a small camera out of the back pocket of his trousers where it had been tucked under the protecting bulk of his work gloves.

He maneuvered his position, to shoot down as the two actors merged. He could see the valley between her young breasts, and he could see the hardening of his masculine strength, as Graves pressed his body into hers, groin-to-groin.

He was sweating when he finished, not only from apprehension that he would be caught, but at the animal force that the two seemed to release as they joined in this kiss.

He clicked his camera again, stuck it away, and wiped off his sweating face with his glove.

As he climbed down the steep ladder bolted to the side wall, he was exultant. He would get his pictures right into his darkroom, and slip out of the studio before anyone recognized that he was a ringer and had been on the set only this one day.

Somewhere, Max's voice said, "Cut and print."

There was a rare moment's silence, which revealed a mass hypnotism on the set. Each individual had been carried away, in spite of a world of false glaring lights and papier-mâché.

"Bravo," someone said.

"You can stand up now," said Graves, sotto voce. "The fun's done."

Linda pulled herself away from him, embarrassed that she had been like a rag doll in his arms after Max had said "Cut."

Two little men let out a whistle, threw their electrician's gloves into the air, and called out, *"Bis! Bis!"* as if they were at La Scala.

John Graves walked away from her into the back-set confusion.

"Madonna mia!" said a carpenter. "He must be on fire!"

Linda moved slowly out of the light. She was afraid she would cry. He'd just left her flat. She wanted to tell him to go to hell. Why should she care! She must do something to protect her dignity.

Max wandered toward her. His eyes were bright with excitement.

She swallowed and smiled at him.

"You know, Max," she said, in a loud voice so everyone near could hear, "I wonder how he shaves the hair in that dimple in his chin."

The men started to laugh. Those who were bilingual interpreted for their Italian friends. A ripple passed into dark corners.

Linda walked gaily to her portable dressing room. She sat down, and stared at her face in the mirror. Her lips seemed swollen by his kiss, and her lip rouge was smeared. She began to cry.

Max came in, pushing the hat back from his white curling hair. Linda noticed that his hand trembled slightly.

"Now, now," he said, "you won your spurs."

"I don't know why I'm so upset," she said, blotting tears from her cheek.

"Don't let Graves bother you. I was forced to do this scene now for dramatic reasons. It was necessary you be exciting together. And you are."

"It had better be good," said Linda.

She took a piece of tissue and blotted the mascara from her lower eyelid.

"I'll send in makeup," said Max. "I'm going to take a chance on the master scene as it was, spontaneous and breathless. We'll do cross-shots of the dialogue and closeups later. Don't hurry, my darling, we have to re-light."

He thought for a moment, and put his hand on her head.

"Do not let that young man disturb you. Do not take it personally. You are an actress now, and he is an actor. You are good chemistry."

"I guess that's all that matters," said Linda.

"Strange thing for a director to say to an actress," said Max, "but you couldn't possibly live all these emotions that various roles will give you. You'd be burnt out if you did. You know, there will be lots of John Graveses in your life."

The makeup man came in, and Max left.

When he was finished, Linda opened the door to the dressing room. The heat seemed oppressive to her. Several workmen turned their backs elaborately and self-consciously. She felt she would stifle.

"I think I'll take a breather," she said.

The large stage door slid open for air. Linda walked out with dignity. It was a warm day with a faint breeze. She walked around the corner and stood in the street looking at the barnlike buildings, and the racks of Vespas.

The street was suddenly alive with a group of tourists who stepped out of a sightseeing bus. They stared at her. The slight cooling *ponentino,* a relief from the heat, and the sense of needing freedom stopped her.

"Well," said a voice, "I trust you have recovered from my dreadful embrace."

Graves was holding a bottle of chilled beer in his hand, and smiling, she thought, in a self-satisfied way.

Linda turned on him angrily. This was too much, in front of people.

"Get lost, you damned teddy boy!" she said.

She gave him a push as he turned to walk away from her. He hadn't expected to be attacked, and he fell off-balance. His bottle of beer spouted up in a gusher of foam as he toppled on the pavement, in an instinctive gesture to save it from spilling at all costs. He sat, staring at her, looking foolish in his hoplite's short tunic costume, with his greaves and his shoulder strappings of leather.

He looked up at her, his mouth agape, still holding the foaming beer bottle like a holy grail.

There were several flashes.

Linda looked up to see that a young man was snapping a series of pictures from an open window on the tour bus.

"Va bene!" he shouted with glee. He jumped out of the vehicle and ran toward the studio gate. He clasped his hands over his head as if he had won a prizefight.

Linda went back to the set, her hands shaking with anger. She tried to compose herself. She'd better not mention it. No use to stir up a fuss and upset Max. What an annoying thing to have some wretched tourist take pictures!

5

Max became so engrossed with the production of *The Oracle* that most casually, several times, he had rejected Jessica's attentions.

She was relieved to break the sexual bond without difficulties. Her executive position no longer had to be secured, she had a contract for her services, the picture was in production with a well-organized staff. For once, Claudia was a welcome addition, for she took the responsibility of Linda off her shoulders.

Now that the glittering society of Rome had opened some of its doors to her, due to the glamour of the picture company, she dreamed of a life much more chic and exciting than any she had ever known. Fergus had hidden her as his mistress, and Jeffrey had been old and alcoholic during their marriage.

This evening she left for Rome in her limousine. She settled back, enjoying her elegant Fontana ball gown. She had packed an overnight bag with her necessities and a suit she would wear to the studio the next day.

Tonight she would stay in a beautiful hideaway, a penthouse built on a roof terrace overlooking the enormous Piazza Santi Apostoli and the elegant palace of the Colonnas.

She was slightly piqued but inwardly amused that her escort of the evening, a handsome and titled young man, was quite a few years younger than she. Usually this sort of an arrangement was not to her liking; she preferred the dignity and gratitude of older men.

But this young man was so intrigued with her that his excitement and eternal, almost apologetic caressing and lovemaking had quite overcome any social obstacles. There were advantages to being loved by youth, particularly when she still looked so young herself.

She had left Linda, Max, and Claudia bent over their bible, the script, the light from a chandelier sifting down upon them.

They barely seemed aware that she was leaving, although their mouths politely said good-bye. Before the door to the drive was opened, Max's voice had droned on.

My God, what a small world he lived in.

In Rome the young marchese, his elegant evening cape flung over his shoulder, looked like a fine coin, his handsome Roman profile pale and stark against the curled profusion of his black hair, his eyes liquid as he admired her.

He escorted her out of the car to the glittering staircase of the palazzo, where the ball was in full swing, carrying her light fur wrap, touching it fondly, she noticed, as if it were her skin.

A little man popped up and shot a picture of her.

"Oh, Giorgio," she said, "stop him!"

Giorgio stepped forward, cursing him out with Italian bravura. But the man was already away.

"Let's go," he whispered. "We are fools to go through this interminable evening, when we could be sitting enjoying the *vita spensierata,* drinking cool wine in our cool skins on my terrace."

"You're wicked, Giorgio," she said.

No one was going to interfere with her entrance as she walked down the courtly marble staircase at this glittering party.

That part came later; when she daringly stayed with him, amused at the comparison between the polite manners of high Roman society and the abandoned services of young love, in the swan bed of his baroque apartment.

The next morning, as prearranged, she arose from his embrace, stepped into her working clothes, leaving her wonderful chrysalis of gown, satin and froth, by the side of his bed for him to pick up after she had left.

He had promised he would return it surreptitiously to the villa, up the back stairs, with his own adoring hands, the next evening. She could not very well take it to the studio! And then he would see her again.

She slipped out of the building, and passed a news kiosk on her way to catch a taxi. There on the front page of the *Giornale del Mattino*, like a map for the whole public to read, was a spread which led off with her in her lovely ball gown, stepping proud as a princess into the ball that evening with Giorgio. Next to it was the identical gown, worn by someone called Susie, and that incredible John Graves, of all people, dismounting from a Vespa, right in front of the Hosteria dell'Orso. This Susie person's dress was up above her thighs, and she revealed all of her length of long tan legs.

The next picture was a snap, obviously snatched at the studio gate, of John Graves, gesturing to his seedy girlfriend, Susie, to get the hell out on the motorcycle. She was casting him a look of great hatred.

The adjoining picture was of Linda lying in John's arms. His hand was curved around her breast; one could sense her surrender.

The final snapshot, which the others merely framed, was of Linda in action in her Greek costume. Her hand was moving in an arc, her curls flying. She had landed a haymaker on John Graves. He had fallen to the pavement, and was looking up at Linda in total surprise, a large gusher of foam leaping up into the air out of his beer bottle, which was held below his waist, while his other hand propped him up solidly to keep him from lying on the pavement. It was an accidental shot, but the pornographic suggestiveness was clear.

The caption, which Jessica scanned quickly, in Italian, while her heart froze, was only half-decipherable to her. But the inference was that she, Linda's mother, and Susie, this stripper, had something in common. They shared the same Fontana ball gown. Linda and

Susie also had something in common; they shared the affections of the same man, John Graves. The little Barstow was in the clutches of the great love, and the English showgirl had been sent packing back to London.

Jessica gasped, and turned back into the building. She found her way up the stairs, to the foyer, took the elevator, and stepped off at Giorgio's door. Thank God she had not quite closed it in her careful tiptoe out of the apartment.

She would have to wake him, have him brew her a cup of coffee, steady her nerves, and have him translate the article and the captions completely before the whole town fell on her neck.

The apartment was very quiet as she came in.

She opened the door to the bedroom.

The swan bed was empty. But the room was not. In front of an enormous pier glass, Giorgio stood preening. He wore her ball gown and gloves, and he was blowing a kiss to his reflection when he saw her like a shadow in the mirror.

He let out a slight squeak, and put his kid-gloved hands to his flaming cheeks.

Jessica stood a moment, staring, and then turned as if she were a ghost, and left.

It seemed the longest trip she had ever taken, as she drove in the taxi through the streets of Rome and out to Cinecittà.

◆◆◆◆◆◆◆◆

The news spread through the little espresso bars, trattorias, and rosticcerias where men ate standing, moved like a tide along byroads, the fountains, Trastevere, in rooms in beehive tenements, and flowed down the Spanish Steps.

It would move with Americans to the arty studio apartments in Via Margutta, where part of it started, to the new balconied buildings in the Parioli district. It would travel along with two gossiping monks carrying briefcases, from the obelisk in front of St. Peter's to the gelaterias, jukeboxes, and espresso bars on Via Flaminia.

Two guards would stop to talk at the Regina Coeli prison, and a trusty would snatch a dropped paper, take the picture of Linda Barstow, and hide it under his mattress.

Wire services would flash the picture of Linda's first kiss with John Graves, reaching such varied groups as the 380,000-plus readers of the *Neue Illustrierte Wochenschau* in Vienna, the *Goed Nieuws* of Antwerp, the 750,000 subscribers of the *Journal Dimanche* in France, the six million readers of the London *News of the World,* the *Ilkones* illustrated feature magazine in Greece, and even the *Kobieta i Zycie* behind the Iron Curtain in Poland, whose 550,000 captive readers' tongues would be hanging out.

People who had never heard of Linda Barstow or John Graves, but who had heard of sex, looked at the picture of the two in their first breathless embrace, imagined the rest, and cut out the picture, to refresh themselves, and join the cult.

Authorities such as drunks in all-night bars, minor American actors who made a living dubbing the Italian spectaculars, taxi drivers in Piazza del Popolo, American expatriates playing gin rummy in restaurants, and children playing soccer in the piazzas along the Tiber revealed their secret sources; Linda Barstow, in the true Barstow tradition at the age of fourteen had seduced the star John Graves and taken him away from a woman of twenty-two.

A man shoveling up elephant dung at the Borghese Garden zoo had a niece who worked on the set, and although he and others knew she lied for attention, she claimed to anyone who would listen that she had seen the two actually fornicating in back of the Treasury of Athens on the set.

Two gypsy extras from the Porta Furba colony announced that John Graves liked men, and got in a fight with two prostitutes on the Spanish Steps who said

Graves was living with an English girl, and was no queer, they had all had him at the same time.

Two black musicians carrying a harp up the steps stopped to watch the fracas, and got in a fistfight over the scandal with three southerners from an Elks convention cruise ship moored in Naples.

By afternoon a knot of people stood at the studio gate at Cinecittà. Several wanted to be blessed by the lovers, two wanted to have their babies touched, three barren women wanted Graves to lay his hand (or whatever) on them, four wanted money to educate relatives, six wanted to pinch the Barstow behind, for either good luck or just high spirits, three coveted a lock of her hair, five tourists wanted to have their picture taken with her to show the folks back home, and five were newspapermen in very thin disguise who wanted to get more pictures to add to the burgeoning set that was becoming an interesting collection.

◆◆◆◆◆◆◆◆

Linda sat in her dressing room.

"Now you've really done it," said Jessica. "The first time in London with Claudia could have been a mistake. We blamed it on the bad influence of your dreadful Barstow relative. But this one is your fault. And you even got me involved in your vulgar mess, and I was only attending a social event. And about your behavior on the set! Just what are you trying to do? Hitting a man in public like that. What ever made you think of *doing* such a thing?"

"He made me mad," said Linda, "and I'm sick of people treating me like an idiot just because I'm young. After all, you all expect me to be a woman in this picture. Treat me like one, or I'll quit."

She enjoyed seeing her mother pull at her handkerchief. That meant she was disturbed. Any mention of quitting always did this to her. Linda pursued the subject, using her advantage.

"I wish I'd never heard of the picture. Why should I be blamed?"

"Because you're a cheap, vulgar, dreadful child," said Jessica, "Barstow to the bone."

As an aftermath to the discussion, Jessica went on, "And speaking of Barstows, since you insisted on having Claudia come along, why wasn't *she* around, so that such unfortunate meetings with John Graves could have at least been supervised? Maybe someday these people who are making such a spoiled pet of you will understand that you are not capable of being left to your own devices."

There was a knock at the door.

Leslie Charles, very elegant in his slacks and sport shirt with a soft silk ascot at his throat, stood with his best professional smile. Today he was not working; he was a visitor.

"Oh, do come in," said Linda.

She was delighted to see him, especially since he had broken up a scene with her mother that could only have ended in lengthy castigation.

"Well," said Leslie too heartily, "looks like you're getting all the publicity. With that teddy boy."

"Believe me," said Jessica, "it won't happen again, Leslie. I'm dreadfully upset."

"Really, my dear, you should allow the child a little more latitude with the proper people. For example, for one, I would be delighted to squire her about to fun summer things, like the open-air ballet at the Villa Giulia, and the Greek outdoor theater at Ostia. With your permission, of course."

He bowed, with a kindly smile toward Jessica.

You old SOB. You know we've got a hot publicity rock here, and you're going to get in on it. You're jealous of the furor John Graves started. But God knows, you're chic . . . and safe.

"Linda's off bounds for a while," she said, "and I'm very much concerned about the reaction to this dreadful publicity. But after the press gets straightened out, I'm sure Linda would be most appreciative. Wouldn't you, dear? Do you realize how fortunate you are to have a gentleman like Mr. Charles ask you?"

"Thank you," said Linda.

All of a sudden Leslie Charles had lost his glamour. He certainly was not in a class with John Graves, who was young, handsome, exciting, and a real man. It was obvious Mom was beginning to run John down; the way she had said "gentleman" in itself was just enough of a nudge for her to know that she was eliminating John Graves from this category.

"All promises, promises," said Linda. "I'll never get out of jail. You won't even let me eat in the commissary."

"Now, Linda, mind your manners. You know there are photographers all over the place."

"They're even in the rafters," said Linda. "Could I help it? If a director asks you to kiss, you kiss. If you don't, someone else gets the job."

Leslie chuckled.

"The child has a point. I remember when I was a young splinter, and had to make up to your Aunt Claudia—oh, my!"

He realized too late he had touched a sensitive family nerve. Linda smiled. Jessica frowned.

Linda met her eye-to-eye. What was there to say?

"I must get to my desk," said Jessica nervously.

While she talked to Linda, her mind darted about. There'd be hell to pay about this cheap publicity at the home office. Out of context, she thought of the young Roman *ammiratore* who had touched the fabric of her garment the night before and said to her escort, "You have really hit the jackpot, Giorgio."

It became clear to her. It was not a personal compliment. It was the dress he was admiring. She flushed; that meant she had become involved in a society of transvestites. Everyone in Rome knew more about them than she did. And there was her picture in the paper for all to see. But this was a private concern that could be straightened out as she found her way around a correct Roman society. The main problem was Linda, who, unfortunately, was in the driver's seat. As a minor she could not be held to blame for breaching a contract. It would take a great deal of diplomacy to keep her in line. Jessica certainly would see that she was kept away from John Graves. Maybe Leslie Charles was the proper social takeout. Time would tell.

Like it or not, it was probably necessary to have Claudia at the studio. She could stay in the dressing room, and at least protect Linda from further association with John Graves. She'd talk to Max—that is, if she could ever get his attention. When he directed, it was like watching a man under water. She could see him, but he couldn't hear her.

◆◆◆◆◆◆◆◆

Max studied the scandalous layout in the morning paper. He sat in his trailer office, elbow-deep in scribbled script notes, office memos, daily worksheets, and stacks of casting photographs for minor roles in his next sequence.

He rejected calls from the front office, urgent messages from Grace for comment to the press, and again stared at the paper while the crew set up the lights.

A security guard had flushed two press photographers, literally out of the lavatories, another off the catwalk, one out of the prop Treasury of Athens, and one out of the commissary, where he was posing as a *parmigiano* cheese grater in the scullery.

The set would now have to be watched as if an enemy were trying to infiltrate a strategic military objective.

Like most men working against time in the fulfillment of his craft, Max was only irritated at set scandals and had no desire to hack away at any personal Gordian knot. That was for less creative people. If he were about to shoot a scene, and a dead elephant was on the doorstep, he would walk around it, go on with his business, and expect the prop man to remove it before the stench offended his nostrils.

Max glanced at the pictures of Linda in the paper. He knew that time and talent would obliterate the memory of this fracas. It would titillate the public for a day or two. But the loveliness of the child was still captured inviolate.

She was beautiful in the arms of John Graves, as Max had wanted her to be when he directed them. Ready for love, and glowing in the first awakened awareness of passion. It was indeed a picture of springtime.

He paused to glance at John Graves. Even he revealed a tenderness which was never seen on his face in life. The strength of a warrior, whose mouth had slacked in an almost sad, silent cry for love and beauty; the longing eyes of a lost boy, the sexual power of a hungry mouth. It was what Max had longed for, what he had sought in his mind as he had fashioned his scenes, and to see his dreams brought to life with such an intense and personal effulgence shook him deeply. It he could carry this auspicious scene on, he was blessed; his actors had superseded his imagination. Let Fergus Austin see *those* rushes.

Although he resented it, he was intrigued at the picture of John Graves and Linda as she had just shoved him to the pavement outside the set. Her anger was heroic. It became her, along with the style of her tunic and the gold-banded curls. This was a Fury, classic in anger, a Hecuba aroused, and this in tandem with her young beauty was the making of his film.

He looked at Graves, with the astounded expression on his face and the geyser of beer which sprang up, it almost seemed, from between his legs; a freak and wretched photograph.

He saw on his face what he wanted to see, an aroused man, a surprised man, and he wondered if it was more than the incident of a quick exposure of film.

After a conference with Jessica, who discreetly said Linda would be better off with more supervision, he called Claudia at the villa.

"You'd better come to the studio and be with Linda. Stay close to her. Get her ready to enter the scene without being too nervous. I know it's asking a lot, but you must play hide-and-seek and stay away from Graves until this confrontation today is ended."

"Well, at least I'm not to blame this time," said Claudia. "You certainly have to admit Linda is publicity-prone."

"Get right over," said Max. "I'm going to shoot some background material to fill in until you get here. Talk to her about transforming the realities of life into a truth in performance. That may help."

"I'll drag along the old Stanislavsky primer," said Claudia, smiling to herself.

"Claudia, I need you," said Max.

Again the word "need." As Claudia hung up, she looked at the welter of clippings spread over her desk and on the floor. All over again, the insatiable beast of publicity, titillation to those unseen hordes in thousands of homes, who thrilled to the stimuli of other lives. This was what sold tickets, this was what built tremendous empires, as Titan once had been. At what personal price? She knew . . . she knew. . . . This desire for attention, this whirling road to madcap behavior, had put her where she was. And she shuddered as she knew that Linda, her own bloodline, was starting along the same erratic path. What could she do?

"Need," Max had said. That was no pasteboard slogan. For once it was truth. She was needed.

◆◆◆◆◆◆◆◆

"Ready, Mr. Ziska," said Hank, sticking his head in the door.

Max set up the camera for the old woman with the donkey bearing panniers of olives; the donkey should be exercised first so it wouldn't dump on the set. He had the animal trainers alerted to release the hungry eagle that would fly over the shining rocks for his reward, a chunk of putrid horsemeat, and ordered the two lambs sedated. They were to look as if slaughtered, lying limp on the sacrificial altar with catsup for bloody slit throats. He ordered fresh spring flowers for the white-clad children to carry and had their mothers send them off to the toilets, and hold up their tunics, before they got powdered and combed for their angelic scene; this was all par for Max, the day's planning as a director. These meticulous little ploys were part of the pattern which made Max Ziska known as the genius who could bring the true bucolic nature of his scene to life as no other man since Borzage.

Claudia, entering the sound stage, watched Max, impressed with his precise organization, but slightly disappointed with him. He seemed to have shucked off Linda's problems so easily that she felt he was callous.

She settled down in a canvas chair, close to Linda's trailer, where she could retreat if she saw John Graves. All about her, people were crackling their newspapers, bearing the gossip of the night like a wind that had blown dry whispering leaves all about. She'd like to have had a few sharp words with John, damn his arrogant sexuality; he'd always had it, since he was a kid. But there was little she could do; that ultimatum from Max remained: hide-and-seek. One more ruckus, and she'd be sent packing. Then what would happen to Linda?

She closed her ears to the liquid chatter that slowly gathered force as the idle extras and crew members became used to her presence. As always, the work was slow, preparing the scene, rehearsing the actors, who suddenly seemed more stupid than the beasts they were supposed to own, and alerting the staff for the unexpected action of animals that found themselves inexplicably thrust into a world of false smells, tastes, lights, and human behavior.

◆◆◆◆◆◆◆◆

John Graves sat in his dressing room. The morning newspaper was folded discreetly on his table. Contrary to his usual habit, his door was not only closed, but bolted. The lights were low, and he was alone.

There was no uncapped bottle or emptied glass at his elbow. There were not even cigarette butts crushed out on the floor, or a litter of garments that he usually dropped off, for someone else to pick up.

He sat with his arms propped on the table, staring at

the paper. The newsprint seemed to throb up at him, despite the fact there was no new liquor in his system.

He felt rotten.

He was stunned at himself for having let this girl upset him. He had really lost himself in the moment he caressed her. And as he had walked away, and caught a glimpse of her, deserted, standing in the bright overhead lights, her lips almost quivering, he had fled from her distress.

It was sometimes entertaining to be a brute among sophisticated people, who could lash back, but to do it to such a young creature was another thing.

And then, when he had confronted her on the street, with that therapeutic beer in his hand, he had pretended to leer at her, just to feel at ease. Her sudden attack, and her savage childish fury, literally and figuratively knocked him off his feet. She surprised him.

Later he felt that her act of violence, her naked anger, reaching out at him, had satisfied him somehow. It was not a performance, it was real.

He had gone home to his apartment, relieved to find that Susie had decamped. He had fallen into a thoughtful, drinkless night, unique for him, and amused himself by watching the cockroaches crawl in and out of the cracks in the walls.

As morning came, he went to the window and saw the gold and scarlet hot light of Roman dawn, which threw molten shafts of light on the familiar buildings and rooftops, making them strangers to him. He bathed in his clawfoot tub, dressed, and went down Via Margutta to an espresso bar, inhaling the morning air. At this hour the rush of Vespas and motorbuses had not yet commenced their pollution of the air.

You bleeding boy scout. . . . He grinned at himself as he ate a peach dripping with juice, had a *panino* and coffee.

As he ate, he was aware of three giggling young girls who were peering at him, their eyes wide over their coffeecups. Several early birds, white-collar men, folded their morning papers and stared at him with their hound-dog brown eyes, resenting his fame, wondering about his sexual activities.

What a bore to lose one's anonymity, he thought idly.

When he reached the corner to signal a taxi, he came face-to-face with himself in the *Giornale del Mattino* being stacked by an old man on kiosk racks.

On the road to Cinecittà he tried to decipher the text and studied the pictures. He examined himself kissing Linda, himself sitting like a fool on the pavement in his leather soldier's costume, and the absurd figure he cut on the Vespa with Susie. You had to be well-tanked to think such an escapade was amusing.

He was revolted.

The studio, of course, was the natural refuge against the probing eyes and ears of the world. The real and the unreal were used to merging. He sat in his dressing room in limbo, awaiting a call to the set, staring at the paper. Then he unlatched his door and shouted at his dresser.

Luigi, as usual, sat on a chair in the hallway, relishing the newspaper that he hastily hid when Signore Graves called.

The signore amazed him more than the scandal in the paper. First, there was no more Susie; she must have really been jettisoned. And there were no drinks or drinkers. John ordered Luigi to take a taxi, round up every white lily he could find, and fetch them as fast as possible, even if he had to strip the Piazza Esquilino flower market.

The note to Linda was difficult for him to write. He wrote and rewrote, and was annoyed at himself while he did it; he was split two ways; first, he was starting on the most important role of his life with this young girl, and had likely sabotaged his relationship with his overt rudeness. Secondly, he was deeply indebted to Claudia. . . . She'll eat my ass out for what I did, he mused.

Finally he made the simple note: "I deserve a black eye as well as a sore rump. As John Graves, I apologize. As Diodynus, soldier of Athena, have pity on me."

He was not surprised when Grace Boomer and Sidney dropped by. Sidney was tugging at his red moustache, and Grace as usual was fluttering a sheaf of papers.

"David will be sizzling," said Sidney, "since the main manifesto hereabouts was to keep Linda under wraps. He's back in London, and I'll have to tell him she has obviously been launched . . . again."

"I'm afraid our young star is slated for scandal," said Grace. "Ah, well, that's the sort of thing brings in the shekels."

"There will be no more problems from me. I have had my frolic. Up to here." John crossed his throat with his forefinger.

"God help what happens when you get over the hangover," said Sidney.

"I wish Chloë Metaxa would get here," said Grace, "so we can have our press party. The latest is she's supposed to be Greece's official hostess at the Athens festival. You know how Niadas is about his Greek festivals."

"Speaking of Greek festivals," said Graves, "when is Martha going to whelp?"

"Well, I figure," said Grace, "that Martha Ralston Niadas is going to have an eight-pound premature baby somewhere around October.

"And now I have to call Fergus Austin in Hollywood and tell him the bad news," said Grace. "That is, unless he's heard about the Rome papers and is on a plane. I may be the one gets the sack."

"Over my dead body," said Sidney. "I will swear you were at your faithful station at the bar in the Grand Hotel while all this was going on."

Hank came in.

"We're doing a pickup shot next," he said, "with animals, thank God, no hambones."

Hank took a beer, opened it, and sat, one leg hooked over a chair, and stared at John balefully.

"Max's very jittery," he said, "biting on his hand,

and scratching his hair. He has the morning papers folded into his director's chair pocket. Congratulations, old buddy. You really did it."

"No fruity epithets," said John. "Look, I'm fed up with myself. Nothing moral, mind you, just basic animal revulsion. I looked a proper horse's derriere in that spread on the Vespa. Susie's gone, along with it. I'm moving out of Via Margutta, into some decent digs. I am going to get drunk only with intelligent people, under auspicious circumstances."

"Well, it's been fun knowing you," said Hank, grinning.

◆◆◆◆◆◆◆◆

On the set, Hank talked to Max.

"Boss, I think everything's quiet on the western front. That is, with Graves. The girl from Soho jettisoned, and he's moving into decent digs. He really has pulled himself together."

"For today, Hank?" said Max.

"Well," he said, "I wouldn't expect miracles. I just meant, today he isn't loaded, and he was polite."

"That's good," said Max, "because today he has to kiss Linda again."

He walked back and forth, and snapped his fingers.

"That's it! That's it!" he said. "I'm going to throw them together."

He looked at Hank.

"Meaning?" said Hank.

"Look," said Max, "I know what's happening. I'm not stupid. Linda's excited by Graves. I don't blame her. He's handsome and animal. And her beauty has shattered him more than he knows. Why not? She shatters me. I must get them together, so she doesn't fall apart every time they touch."

"Ain't that loading the pistol?" said Hank.

"It isn't a pistol," said Max, "it's a cannon, and it is loaded. Do you know that the possible future of Titan films is tied up in this picture? This is a situation, I now find out, where I am carrying the burden of millions of dollars in a previous disaster, and more millions to finish this. It is going to be in production a very long time. We cannot sit out puppy love. So if this is going to trigger Linda, let's make it volatile."

"How do you handle that?" said Hank.

"I shall take care of it," said Max.

"You aren't sizzled at Graves?" asked Hank. "*You* don't want to replace him?"

"For God's sake, whatever for?" said Max, his eyebrows lifting. "For some pedestrian gentleman! Look, my dear young man, I worked with the best, her father. This young man reminds me somewhat of him. He is a vital, gifted force. And as I said, he'd better imbue Linda with an excitement. She's young, but she's female, and I need romantic impact desperately for the good of the picture. We mustn't lose those gonads."

Fat chance, thought Hank. He'd spent a great deal of time with John Graves this past year. But as he went about his tasks, he could not help glancing at Ziska, fussing about his script and uncapping his pen with a slightly unsteady hand. Hank realized that his fatherlike devotion to Linda was not as protective as it seemed. Apparently performance came first in his book.

◆◆◆◆◆◆◆◆

Linda stood in the pool of key light, her eyes cast down; she seemed frozen.

Max was apprehensive. With the instinct of a man who had made many pictures, he knew that the film they had shot yesterday was the first thrillingly exciting footage in the picture. Now he feared that the unfortunate publicity in the gossip-seeking Roman press would inhibit Linda's performance. And being actor-wise, he also observed the overpoliteness of John Graves. He, too, was disturbed, and that took doing.

After the stand-ins had posed patiently while the lighting was set up, he called his two principals. He would approach the situation with an extreme closeup of Linda, so her rankled spirits would work for him, rather than against him. Later he could block and refine in the longer shots. He would have to gamble on the use of raw emotions. After all, Linda was not a veteran. And he could not tell which way Graves would jump in his attitude toward a girl he could not control with his usual easily unleashed sexuality.

Max linked them by holding an arm of each, and pulling them toward him, their three heads bent together in a verbal conspiracy that was so soft-spoken that no one standing near could hear.

Claudia, in limbo, stood nervously peering out of the set dressing room, longing to help Linda, but knowing that this private analysis was the nucleus, the form that picture-making must take. She prayed that the discipline and control she had tried to imbue in her would now come to her aid. If she turned self-conscious at this important moment, they might just as well fold up like the *Pallas Athena* company and write the whole production off.

"Now," said Max, "we must obliterate ourselves, and assume the problems of these two lovers who lived so long ago. We must give them breath again, or we are merely doing an ornate pageant instead of a pulsing human drama. It's difficult to erase the scribble of our modern lives, but it must not show on our faces in any way. What you ate for breakfast or what stupid thing disturbed you before you got to this moment must be cast aside. You are Alethea, a Greek girl, an oracle at the sacred shrine. . . . And you are Diodynus, a footsoldier of Athens. That is all I am interested in. You are about to break the vows of your society. Realize that, above all, what is exposed on this strip of film is here forever. If only one-tenth of what you are registers, that is all of you that will remain, long after you are old and far away."

The three assistants gestured for quiet on the set. For once every man jack responded, not from courtesy, but out of curiosity.

Max noted that Linda was still withdrawn.

"Forgive me a moment," he said.

He took her aside, and they whispered. John cautiously glanced over, and once saw her lift her hand and wipe a tear away from her eye. Max patted her, and he busied himself with a cigarette as they came back to the camera. He signaled to John.

"We're ready," said Max. He looked at Linda quizzically. She nodded her head, her eyes lowered.

They went back into the scene, and faced each other.

"I'm sorry," whispered John. "I'm really dreadfully sorry. . . ."

She still seemed adrift.

"It happened so quickly," he said, "I hadn't intended rudeness."

"Please let's not talk about it," she said through tight lips.

He felt like a blundering schoolboy. She was so young. Her porcelain complexion, without a pore, the overlong lashes and heavy-lidded eyes, and the soft, unmarred lips even in the bright lights seemed unreal in their perfection; tantalizingly, not quite ripe.

"Did you get my flowers?"

He was surprised at himself for asking.

She nodded mutely, her eyes almost tearful, as if she were forcing herself to hold back her weeping. It made them shine like agate. The flowers obviously were not enough. He had thought they would be overwhelming in their profusion.

Max returned. He put his hand gently on her shoulder.

"Now we will shoot," he said. "When you see Diodynus, you must awake from your distant dreams." He moved closer to her and whispered, "When you see him, he must be only Diodynus to you."

He turned to Graves.

"You, Diodynus—you have a longing to possess this virgin woman. You are illuminated by the sort of shattering passion that has crumbled dynasties."

He paused for a moment.

Linda turned her gaze from him to John Graves. Max hardly breathed. Her reaction, her return to a manufactured reality, was the fulcrum upon which his career and twenty million dollars of invested money balanced.

Linda looked into John Graves's face, and she seemed to find Diodynus. Standing close, he encompassed her, without touching her. The cleft in his chin, the strong sculptured lips that once had pressed against hers, the eyes that searched into the depths of hers, the puzzlement of brows as if he wanted to discover her secrets. The muscle-corded neck, wide shoulders, and breadth of his body. He was a man; strong.

Max's voice came over.

"Wipe the sound, boys, we'll do it silent. . . . Action."

The camera slowly moved in on the track to an extreme closeup. Graves stood, with his shoulder in the shot, and as he watched, he was ashamed of the inner functioning of his method technique, for he felt he was facing naked reality.

"And now," said Max, "the sorrow in your heart makes you know that though you desire this man, this is not a time for love. Something near and very dear to you is in peril."

Max paused, hardly breathing. Could she sublimate? Would the sense memory work for her now at this crucial moment?

"Great peril, for something you love," he said.

Again the silence. Something beyond herself clouded her brow.

"Perhaps never again will you see . . ."

He was silent again. Her face changed to a mask of fear, terror barely controlled.

John stared at her. She seemed to have total involvement with the young Grecian priestess. Her glance raked him with a last tenderness, then appraised him with a shocked incredulity as Max spoke to her. With a gasp, her lips parted, tears filled her eyes, and she pulled away, rejecting him. But in those moments of the silent scene, John Graves knew he had seen an infinity of emotion in a woman's life.

"Cut," said Max. "Now, John, we turn to you."

As the attention changed, Linda fled. It was not rudely abrupt, like Graves's march away from the scene the day before. It was sudden and terrifying as she ran to her set trailer.

"Oh, Christ," said Graves quietly to Max, "she'll never forgive my rudeness yesterday."

"Forgive you?" Max lifted his dark eyebrows. "My boy, don't you realize what I just did? I gave her an 'emotional memory,' as Stanislavsky would say. I discovered it at Trancas last summer in California. This trigger was the motive force I used in her test. It worked again."

"What in God's name was it?" asked John.

"I'm not certain I should tell you," said Max.

"I wish you would. It might help," said John.

"Well, since you asked. I asked her what was the most shattering experience that could happen in her life. She answered that if anything happened to her dog, she'd just die. You see, Jeffrey Barstow gave her that dog when she was just six years old. She had transferred her love of her father to her dog, and that is therefore the emotional trigger."

John tried to disguise his disappointment. He had thought her response was the awakening of a growing passion. While he saw it, he wondered how he would handle it, but now that he knew it was not so, he was humiliated.

Somehow his virility had been betrayed. He had been shaken by the beauty of this young enchantress.

He plucked his package of Gauloises out of his tunic, lit one, and opened the script, following the paper trail of Max's words, seeking the dimension of character that would take him from himself, and give Diodynus life. But each scene he read led him back to the seeress, and the heart-shaped virginal face of Linda.

Max watched him, and was pleased. And since he was master of his craft, he knew exactly how the scene would be. His ploy worked.

◆◆◆◆◆◆◆◆

In the many long waits while camera setups were changed, Max often talked to his actors. It was a time to have them study the script, analyze their characterizations, and in a sense, warm them up on the sidelines for the game to be played that must bring reality to film.

He was not surprised when he went to Linda's trailer to see her petting her little Yorkshire terrier. To him this meant she was still relating to the emotional mechanism they had discussed.

"What would I do if anything happened to him!" she said.

"Don't get carried away," said Max. "He's very healthy. Now, I must have a word with you. Why do you think I perform this very difficult task? Why don't I just sit back and quit?"

Linda shook her head.

"I believe in releasing man to fancy we have unbound him from his tensions. . . . Away from the arid plain, the dreadful acceptance of our time. The artist can perform a temporary lobotomy on reality."

"All right," said Linda, smiling, "being the smart little student, I've been doing my homework: just leave it to me—on to the phaedriades, the shining rocks of the Delphi."

Max frowned.

"No lip service, Linda. Don't let anything interfere with what I expect of you. Nothing—love, friendship, can interfere with my work. I can be a severe taskmaster if necessary."

He left abruptly, his brows drawn together in a frown.

She was afraid. This Max she had not seen before. He was considering closing her out of his world and his affection. She no longer was his pet who could do no wrong. She was on trial.

However, in spite of Max, she was going to be involved with John Graves, because she was an actress. It was the only way she could know him.

She opened the drawer of her dressing table and took out the newspaper layout of the scandal that had disturbed everyone. Alfredo, the makeup man, had sneaked it to her. She looked at the picture of John Graves kissing her. She shivered with anticipation.

◆◆◆◆◆◆◆◆

"Now, how long do you think you're going to hide out from me?"

Claudia, script in hand, was sitting in Linda's set dressing room, alone. John Graves came to her and put his arms about her. For a moment she enjoyed the luxury of his familiar, warm masculinity.

"You bastard," she said.

She pulled away and looked him over from head to foot. How right he was in his hoplite's costume, how put-together, and as always, so damned attractive.

"Sit down." She breathed a sigh of relief. "Well, there's nothing I can do about it now. I tried to stay away from you until you made a relationship with my niece. You certainly surpassed any expectations."

He sat down, frowning.

"What's to be done?" he asked.

Once more they were two people working together. The bridge between the years closed. There was a moment of silence as they both chased a trail of memories mingled with concern.

"You know," said Claudia, "I remember you about Linda's age, trying desperately to get into my life, those topsy-turvy war years. Remember that night we faced a bombing in that tube station in London, and clung to each other? I know now, that you, as they say, were trembling on the threshold of maturity. You wanted to belong to my world, and you wanted me. Didn't you?"

Graves smiled at her.

"I did, Claudia. You know damn well."

"I was too old for you, but I represented an unknown, sophisticated world. Now, don't you think there is a similarity to what is happening to Linda?"

"It never entered my mind," he said.

She reached in her purse, and handed him a cigarette, took one, flipped her lighter to him. He lit them up, and they settled back.

"Is she liable to come in?" he asked.

"Max sent her home with Effie," said Claudia.

"Why are you avoiding me?" asked John.

"Both you and Leslie Charles. First by my own bleeding girl-scout tactics of not hogging the limelight. Later, everyone agreed Linda should make contact on her own." She laughed. "Shows how stupid you can be. With the attributes of this child, fat chance of me taking over her spotlight. I'm afraid for her that she'll be more tortured by attention than inattention. But good god, John, everyone around her is ages older, successful, charismatic, and you, of course, oozing with sex, as I said to you six years ago when we made our picture and you got launched. How do you think a schoolgirl from Beverly Hills is going to adjust to this?"

"A cockney from Notting Hill Gate still has his lumps too." He grinned. "Life is far from serene with me. Work is my only continuity."

"Join the crowd," said Claudia. "If this child weren't the last Barstow, I'd be at the bottom of a hogshead of booze sitting it out someplace until they gave me an obituary in *Variety*."

"Never! As your brother used to say in the fan magazines I devoured as a kid, you come from a long line of phoenixes who rise up out of their own ashes. But how do we handle this delicate situation?" He shook his head in an afterthought. "She is enchanting."

"I'm glad you said that." Claudia smiled. "From my point of view, I love her, cherish her for Jeffrey, and also I pity her."

John nodded reflectively.

"What do you think?"

"We have to consider the picture," said Claudia, "or all hell will break loose for everyone. That's the one element that makes it difficult to control a girl trying to get into the adult world too fast. The picture focuses on her sexuality—innocent or not. How do we give her a feeling of security? My suggestion is, do not be the mysterious presence she rarely sees, save for torrid scenes in front of the camera. You did a lovely thing with all these flowers."

She gestured at the profusion of white blossoms that filled every spare space in the small room.

"I felt like a proper horse's ass," he said. "You know, Claudia, you still gesture like a queen. I hope she learns from you. I can attest to the fact that you're the best teacher. I thank you every day of my life."

"Stop the bullshit," said Claudia, trying to hide her pleasure at the compliment. "There are rough curves ahead, young friend. Now, my suggestion is that you occasionally drop your eccentric life in Rome, come out to the villa, do normal things like swimming, visiting, eating, and even make a pose of working on the script with Max and me. It seems I have the phony title of dialogue director to throw Linda off the track of realizing I'm her duenna. Fancy me, Claudia Barstow, the nanny. I bet Jeffrey is up there . . . or down below, with his friends, laughing. So if I can take it, so can you. You say you thank me every day. I'm glad, John, because I love you. You often remind me of my brother. This situation ain't easy. And if you see me reaching for a bottle, will you be a buddy and break my arm?"

"It's a promise," he said.

"We'll try to establish some nucleus of life for her with you, away from the set. All I can say is, be prepared. Expect the unexpected."

◆◆◆◆◆◆◆◆

Linda rushed up the marble stairs. She stopped briefly, as usual, to touch the fish wriggling at Phryne's curved toe. The statue had come to be her touchstone. She smiled at her as a friend.

Later, as she sat soaking in the pink-marble tub, she looked up from the mound of bubblebath. Jessica stood in the doorway. She was pared down to somber black linen, with pearls as her only ornament. She looked angry.

"Well," she said, "I'm exhausted."

"I haven't seen you all day," said Linda.

She wanted to say "as usual," but she didn't.

"I've been hanging on the overseas phone," said Jessica. "You certainly created a hullabaloo with your antics, having a vulgar brawl on the street. They had a meeting about you in New York. We have to report your schedule and activities and create a complete publicity campaign on your personality, and a spotlight is on the activities of all of us. I hope you're satisfied."

"Where are you going?" asked Linda, ignoring her criticism.

"To Rome, to the theater," said Jessica, "with some friends."

"Why can't I go?" said Linda.

"Are you out of your mind! Of course not. You have a big scene to study for tomorrow. I should think you'd have enough sense to stay home and attend to your own career."

"Why can't I ever go anyplace?" said Linda angrily. "I've got to have a little freedom, and not be tied down all the time!"

"When the picture's over," said Jessica firmly, "we'll see that you have a real vacation. I don't know what you expect. You're living like a princess. You have a role every young actress in the world would give her eyeteeth to get. You got to have Effie come with you to look after you. You even got your Aunt Claudia, against my will, to coach you. Max spends every waking moment training you for a great life. You're deeply ungrateful."

Effie brought in a fluffy robe.

Jessica walked out, slamming the door.

"She hates me," said Linda.

"Don't you ever say that," said Effie. "She just needs a little more love than she got in life. You mustn't be cross with her. Maybe she's just afraid that you might not love her back."

"I tell you, Effie, she just can't stand me. And I return the compliment." She put her hands to her head. "I'm getting nowhere personally. Up at five-thirty—makeup, hair, wardrobe. Dramatic scenes with thirty people staring down my throat. Coaching between scenes. Home. Dinner on a tray. Study script for next day. I'm bored!"

Effie sat down, awaiting her.

"What are we going to do?" said Linda.

"We ought to have somebody who understands, and who knows how to help you get your own life organized. How about Max?"

"He's too busy with his picture," said Linda. "He thinks I'm Alethea. He gets a little put out at me when I am being myself. And Aunt Claudia can't help, because she's afraid of interfering with Max on the set, and of course she can't stand up to Mom, or she'd get lost mighty fast."

Linda vanished completely and bubbled up again, her hair clinging like seaweed to her cheek.

"You're the limit!" said Effie, grinning.

Linda sprang up out of the water like Aphrodite rising full from the sea.

"Aren't you going to soak?"

"Get me a pencil and paper," said Linda. "There's work to be done."

She dried herself, nestled into the robe, and sat at her mirrored dressing table writing a list. After she had pondered, she turned to Effie.

"Take Sarge out, Ef," she said. "I'm going to take care of something my own way, and I don't want you involved."

"Now, honey . . ." started Effie.

Linda put up her hand.

"Scram, take Sarge out."

This was not the tractable child who had cracked her schoolbooks open on order on South Palm Drive. So Effie nodded mutely and picked up the dog.

She walked down the stone steps to the garden, with the mimosa and roses filtering their fragrance into the darkening sky, where a pale crescent moon ushered in the evening.

Here where Effie stood, the garden was too beautiful; an elegant stone statue stood as white and stricken as Lot's wife. Effie had an aching nostalgia for her street, for all the plain familiar things, the milk bottles on the back porch, the round laundry rack on its pole in the cracked cement, the bicycles left sprawled on the front lawn.

The little dog sniffed about her feet. She touched a nodding cabbage rose, which rested in her hand like a small white animal nuzzling to be petted.

Ah, this was a good moment. She reached into her pocket and brought out the limp leather pouch. Out of it came the old pipe, Mr. MacDonald's comfort, and her tobacco bag. She tamped the tobacco in, struck a match, and sat down on a worn marble bench. For a moment the tobacco seemed to glow, and she breathed deeply of a mother comfort from another world, drawing in the moment that belonged to Effie—Effie Briggs alone, be it Hollywood or Rome.

She smiled at the hawk face, brown, proud, of the Indian chieftain, and rubbed the bowl along her nostril, wondering what the wise thing would be for her B'linda.

◆◆◆◆◆◆◆◆

Linda picked up the phone and buzzed.

"Ubaldo," she said, "I want to put in a call to London. You know, hush-hush, away from everyone. Could you do it for me, old buddy?"

She opened the drawer of her dressing table and pulled a folded piece of paper out from under her talc box.

"I have to talk to Mr. David Austin in London. I think he's at this number."

For a moment Ubaldo sat in his office. The coffee on the silver tray cooled while he sat back and smiled at the strange trick of fate that had made this incredible young *donna fatale* call him "old buddy." It tortured him and delighted him at once. He had only contempt for her mother, and was pleased to be part of a plot. He put the call through, sitting it out with the operators.

"Hello . . . hello . . . Oh, David, I'm so glad you

were in. This is Linda Barstow. You did give me your private number. I didn't bother you before, but now I must."

"The Roman papers got here on the company plane," said David, "and of course the wire services picked up everything. Hollywood and New York have been calling all day."

His voice could not have been more impersonal. She was glad of it.

"I'm sorry," she said. "It's not what it seems. You remember our talk in London."

"Of course," he said dryly, "especially that your whims would be allowed as long as they did not interfere with the welfare of the picture. Remember that?"

"So maybe I shouldn't have gotten angry," said Linda, "but I'm only human, and everyone's squashing me. Look, David, you said I was chosen on the basis of my test."

"You still have to live up to it," said David. "What do you want?"

"You said there was nothing personal between us," said Linda, "not the luxury of hostility, nor the blinders of affection. You hurt my feelings when you said it, but right now, I need someone who is fair. Too many people pretend to love me and don't do anything. I need help."

She heard a little click. She could visualize him, the widow's peak of his blond hair against his tanned skin, and the dark, frowning eyebrows. That click would be his long-fingered hands lighting a cigarette with his gold lighter. She congratulated her memory when she heard him breathe. He was exhaling. That meant he was settling down to listen.

"This is what I want," she said, holding the list. "You said I was the replacement for the sex goddess Martha Ralston. And you also told me to think about what I wanted my image to be. And to go from there."

"Your public image," he corrected.

"So far, that's the only image I have. I'm getting all the pressures without any of the benefits," she said. "Max wants the divine fire. He thinks I'm a baby

Garbo, Duse, and Bernhardt all mixed up in one. Aunt Claudia helps me all she can, but her hands are tied. Mom wants me to be a sexy actress during the day, and get into my rompers at home when I'm not in front of the camera. But *she's* never around."

That figures, thought David. From the pictures in the papers, he knew the life Jessica was living in Rome. It disturbed him, for he had surrendered completely only once in his life, and the memory had never left. This child who was spilling out her despair could almost have been his own child with Jessica; she was conceived, in fact, three months from the physical possibility.

Then the old sickness gripped him, for with his own eyes he had seen that his father, Fergus Austin, could almost have been the father of this child, too.

"Get to the point," he said.

Linda had never heard such a severe voice. She returned it sharply.

"If Mr. Niadas is satisfied, then I deserve a little satisfaction too. First, I want my own car and driver at my service in my spare time to use as I choose."

David listened grimly. Ignoring the silence, she plunged on.

"I want a wardrobe suitable for my public image. And I want to be identified as a public figure, not hidden in a nursery. Most of all, I want to get out of this mausoleum once in a while, and join the human race."

David heard echoes of all the female stars he had placated in the years since the war, when he had run the affairs of Titan films abroad. It was as if the bitches were tuned in on a shortwave that told them their rushes were going to be spectacular. It never failed. Here was another monster being born.

"How do you expect all this to be done without revealing the fact you telephoned London?" he asked.

"You just *tell* them," said Linda. "What do I care?"

"Remember," said David, "you were warned you'd never be a private citizen again. Are you ready for the emotional and physical problems you will have to face? You're asking to be set free of your childhood. It will be gone from you forever. Do you know what that means?"

"I welcome it," said Linda. "Who wants to be a child, pushed around by grown-ups? And one more thing."

Even as she spoke, her voice became more charming, less waspish. He knew what the question would be. They all ended this way, after they saw how their demands were answered. And if they found they had no power, their voices crumpled like a paper flower in the rain.

"How does *he* like the rushes?" asked Linda.

The two of them had cut across the ribbons of social conversation and come to the core of discussion between management and star. Now that she had tried out her muscle, the ego had to be sated. "He" had to be Niadas.

"He is satisfied. He calls after he sees them on his yacht. Then they are shipped back to Rome."

"I see," said Linda. "I would like to hear from him myself. I'd feel much more secure."

Of course, thought David. Another ultimatum, until you think of something else. The little ego is getting inflated, but it needs support.

When she hung up, she was astonished at her own audacity. She threw herself back on the bed, looking up at the fat bottoms and legs of the silvery baroque cupids suspended above her in the ornate folds of the canopy.

She wondered if she had shaken David a little, even if his voice was so severe. He seemed to have given in. She was a Someone. She had to be. Niadas saw those rushes first. No one was allowed to run them unless Max gave his approval, although he often let the company personnel view them with him. So if the Greek was seeing them first, it meant Max didn't know it. She tucked the information away. She'd confront her mother with it sometime, and see how she reacted.

Effie came in discreetly.

"I did it, Ef. I talked to David Austin in London. He's going to fix everything. No teenage crap. Big star."

She rolled on the bed, hugging a lace pillow ecstatically.

Effie looked at her worriedly, her brows pulled together.

"Did you hear, Ef—I talked to David Austin himself. And he listened to me. Every word."

"The man who never says 'I,' " said Effie softly.

As she switched out the lights, Linda thought about it. It was true. Somehow, what David said was different. He was so impersonal. She recollected what she herself had said, and flushed remembering the I's that had peppered her conversation. It was something to watch.

Her thoughts drifted to the day with John Graves, how he had warmed to her, after his erratic behavior. Why, by the time the picture was ending, she would be going on sixteen, and who knows? . . .

She felt deliciously warm, and tingling, as she thought of him, and of the kisses that she would have before the many pages of Max's script were finished.

She switched on the light by her bed and thumbed through the pages of *The Oracle*. And as she came to a love scene yet to be shot, and thought of him embracing her, she found an excitement rising in her, and a little throb, like a promise of a storm to come, possessed her in her secret place, and she knew, for the first time, what it was going to be like to be a woman.

◆◆◆◆◆◆◆◆

And then the shadow of man's law fell on Linda all the way from California.

She was sitting in her dressing trailer one morning, when she heard her mother's voice. It usually presaged a demand for sittings in the new wardrobe to be shot for publicity or a request to appear someplace for some high-toned charity affair, naturally, to aid her mother's image. She would be snatched in and out like a materialized ghost for thirty minutes, and then whisked away in her car, while her mother stayed on, taking bows at the elegant, boring festivities.

But this time, as she heard her mother's oversweet tone, she was alerted.

"Linda," said Jessica one lovely September day, closing the thin door as if it would shut out the world, "summer is finished. The vacation period is over."

"What vacation?" asked Linda. "I've been working."

"As you know very well," said Jessica, "we are bound by the Beverly Hills Board of Education laws wherever we are. You have to continue your schooling until you get your high-school diploma. It's part of your Titan contract. We will have to adjust the shooting schedule to your studies."

"Oh, Mom!" said Linda. "I can't! I just can't!"

The happy summer times of larking, of watching the others do their scenes, off hours with Claudia, swimming, lounging, and looking at movies with guests at the villa were all being rolled up in a golden ball and snatched away from her.

"We have no choice," said Jessica. "I know you're very bright. If you're lucky, you can get through high school early, and be done with it. Maybe by the time you're seventeen."

"Seventeen!" said Linda, clutching her hair in distress. "I'll be an old hag by then."

She had been so absorbed in this new Roman Linda that she had forgotten there was another Linda who was just a schoolgirl in the eyes of the Board of Education in a place called Beverly Hills.

Of all people, Leslie Charles came to her rescue.

"I know a very nice young man, by a fortunate coincidence, a teacher from Beverly Hills. He camc over on a sabbatical to do research on a book he hopes to publish about the history of roses. He got in touch with me while we were working on *Pallas Athena,* wanted to know if we were aware of the fact that roses were the sacred flower of Athena, goddess, it seems, in charge of marriage and the family.

"Well, this young chap found that there was so much material, he's staying on, and he's broke. He does have the right credentials, and if it could be arranged through the studio, I'm sure he would be delighted to go easy on you, and pursue his rosaceae."

"Oh, Leslie, you know everybody!"

"Well, don't expect this one to be an Adonis."

Linda met him. His name was Andrew Webster, and he was neither a Merry Andrew nor a Daniel Webster. He was a thin pallid fellow who drifted like a soft breeze through the lush gardens of Rome.

He was ideal for the job. He helped Linda make out her own grades, while he sat in a corner reading in a soricine way. Even Jessica was fooled into thinking he was a professorial type, and a thorough scholar.

Actually he was a sort of opium eater without addiction, living his gentle life among the rose petals. Somewhere in his middle distance he saw a young girl who had to study those awful things which didn't matter. He helped her out of her dilemma, as she helped him.

He was well-nourished by browses in the lush flowerbeds of the Villa Madonna della Rosa. He made friends with a few effete young gardeners, and settled into a happy niche, notepad in hand, protected by everyone who wanted to get on with the picture and not have any trouble.

Even Leslie Charles's group looked upon him with amusement, as an oddball, referred to him as "the flower-fucker."

So it was that Andrew Webster took care of Linda's education, to everyone's best possible satisfaction. He ended up giving Claudia signed reports to ship to California which solved all problems henceforth.

6

Linda glanced once more in the mirror, and her own sad face told her that she could not just sit there admiring herself as an image on or off screen. All the fuss David Austin had made after her phone call had altered her life only to a degree. She was still not where she had wanted to be, and she was lonesome.

Effie had gone to her room to write the dozens of messages on picture postcards to all the members of her Baptist church in Los Angeles.

Mom, of course, was at a party in Rome, but that was a bonus.

Claudia and Max had gone into town, and from the remarks she overheard from Hank on the set, Grace would be at her usual stand at the Hassler bar.

Several fashion sittings with top photographers, and many more to come, and raves from the visiting fashion editors of French *Vogue*, American *Vogue*, *Harper's Bazaar*, *Bellezza*, *Marie Claire*, and *Town and Country* had already assured her she was starting a new trend in fashions. So what?

She sat down at her dressing table, pulled the curls away from her face, and studied it in the mirror. It was flawless, but what difference did that make? There was no one to see it; it might as well not exist.

She wondered what John Graves was doing. Of course, it was a midweek night, and she had an early call; she couldn't have gone to town anyway, even with Claudia and Max. They were likely talking about her—her characterization, the picture—the same routine, day after day.

Contact with John had been made, but the terms were not like her dreams. Together with Claudia, or Max, and sometimes Leslie Charles, on several weekends they had savored the rich brew of Rome.

They had laughed at the *pappagalli*, who dropped their clichés like plastic flowers at the feet of pretty American tourists. They had watched the outdoor operas, complete with live horses and camels, bought trinkets at the Sunday-morning stalls at the Porta Portese fleamarket, eaten *zuppa di pesce* at Ostia, devoured waffles in her spurt of homesickness at the Madison House, and gone to English-language movies at the Fiammetta cinema.

But they socialized as a group. And even a little carefully chosen word dropped to John at unguarded moments always seemed to be overheard by begging nuns and boys, men selling sunglasses, ties, or walking dolls, or even her loving friends, who would break into a moment of what she hoped might have grown to tenderness to share some moment or comment.

She felt bilked, as if the family had decided to give a young girl a big dose of her first unsuitable romance by having her beau around until the novelty wore off. Even the moral climate of Italy seemed to have settled into an acceptance of the *gruppo Oracolo* as it moved about together. Romans were used to the affectionate, incestuous clannishness of the foreign motion-picture companies, glued together in groups as they sat out their spare time awaiting their real lives on the set.

The very fact that they were all seen banded together was a letdown to the Latin imagination, which would have relished illicit segregations. They were sometimes followed about by the pesty photographers who would in a few years be nicknamed *paparazzi*, but they clung to the privacy of their various retreats, and often meandered in places like the Borghese gardens, which were not chic enough for the news hawks. After a flurry of pictures, they were let alone.

Linda slowly lost the excitement of the public fuss she and John had stirred up in their first clash.

The hopelessness of her crush had come to a head

the previous Sunday, when they were swimming in the pool at the villa. They had both plunged under the water, and come up, face-to-face, laughing together. For a moment, the larger-than-life image of wet face, teeth, and clustered lashes confronted them. John had drawn her close to him playfully by her wrists, and then let her go.

"What's the matter," she said, gasping, "don't you like me?"

"No, I don't *like* you, Linda. That's not the word for it. Unfortunately, the whole bloody situation is premature. I never was one for raping little virgin girls. So I'll keep my distance. When things change a few years hence, let me know."

He swam out of the pool and went to the dressing pavilion.

She padded out, bereft, and walked up the marble steps. Max was standing under a cypress, watching. She picked up a towel and walked up to him, drying her arms.

"Oh, Max!" she said sadly, wondering if she was really crying, or if her face was just still wet.

Water and all, he put his arms about her.

"My darling," he said, "love comes hard, and sometimes, at the wrong time. I know . . . I know."

"What do you do about it?" she whispered, putting her wet head against his shoulder.

"It somehow takes care of itself," said Max. "Just be grateful for what you feel. It's much worse not to feel anything. That, also, happens to some."

Jessica walked out on the terrace, as if she were illustrating his point.

"What's the matter?" she said. "You look like a drowned sparrow."

"Linda is tired," said Max.

He patted her head.

John came from the bathhouse. He carried his bathing suit in his hand, and Linda looked at him in surprise.

"Aren't you staying for dinner?"

"Sorry," he said, "some old chums from Earl's

Court days are here, and you know how they are. We have to find a trad-jazz spot."

He smiled at her and turned to Max.

"You know how these damned tourists get, away from home. They think they have to swing about on chandeliers."

Before she could say good-bye, John took her hand, pecked her on the forehead, and was gone, his Lancia and chauffeur awaiting him in the curved drive.

And that was the way it had been that Sunday.

So now she picked up the phone and called him at the Villa Victoria, his new digs. There was no answer. A torrent of Italianized English, once she had left her name, informed her he was out. She hung up and sat pitying herself. Who knew how many pretty Susies were with him? Not one of them was as pretty, or as clever, or as wild as she was about him. She would do anything for him, anything, but society wouldn't let her.

She had to figure some way to impress him. Then she thought about Chloë Metaxa. She would soon be arriving, to take her place in the cast as co-star. Linda knew that when she appeared she would be competing with a woman, and a fascinating one. Having trained with the greatest teachers in Greece and abroad, Metaxa was now carrying the honors for her country. There was only one thing to do. Why hadn't she thought of it before!

Leslie Charles was the answer. She knew he was an opportunist, that was obvious, but he took her to the most sophisticated places, had even surreptitiously allowed her to sip a bit of golden Frascati or a glass of champagne. He always made a fanfare of their entrances and exists.

She called him. Fortunately, he was in.

"Dreamboat!" he said. "How charming of you to call. I've been sitting here dishing the dirt with an old buddy, who, by the way, knows you."

"Knows me!" said Linda. "Who?"

She couldn't imagine an intimate of Leslie Charles having known her.

"Andrew Reed—seems he did about the first interview you had when you made your debut in Hollywood."

"Oh, dear!" said Linda.

"Anything wrong?"

"I was such a . . . such a child!" she said.

"He remarked on the fact that there was quite a gap between his first impressions and your ah . . . debut in the London press."

"I should think so! Why don't you bring him out to the villa for a cup of coffee and liqueur, and he can see for himself."

She had visions of herself in a pale-green-and-silver Fortuny teagown, her hair held up with a filet of silver laurel leaves, serving them golden Strega in tiny Venetian glass goblets. It made a pretty scene.

"Oh, my dear," said Leslie, dispelling her dreams, "I wish we could, but we're up to our *ears* in plans. You understand, boys' night out in Rome."

He winked at Andrew, who was sitting with two long-haired *finocchi*. They were lighting cigarettes in unison with two shiny new American cigarette lighters. Andrew grinned.

"Oh, that's nice. Of course, I'm actually rather busy myself."

"Naturally," said Leslie, getting off the hook. "Anyway, we shall let Andrew announce our betrothal, come the day."

"Oh, Leslie," said Linda, seizing the opening, "the lady always announces it first. Maybe at the party for Chloë Metaxa."

"Pardon my impetuousness," Leslie said gaily. "Anyway, I do want you to be the first to know this. I'm planning the big 'do' for Chloë Metaxa when she arrives week after next. I thought I'd introduce her. After all, she's the leading light of the Greek theater. She ought to have a significant sendoff. I'll likely take over a charming place, you know, like the Borgia Room at the Hosteria dell'Orso, and we'll give her a Baccarat-crystal-and-gold-service bash, with all the women wearing golden gowns and diamonds. And, of course, you'll stay up for it!"

He sounded as if she were a favorite niece given a special treat for being a good child. There was the grown-up mind again, chopping her off where she lived, handing her a taste of the other world like a gratuitous lollipop.

Her mind stabbed out to counteract the ploy, and she answered in a deep, full voice, as if she were playing Alethea in her sacred role, for that was all she had to offer to combat this other world. "It sounds marvelous," she said. "We must have your party, but you should have let me know. You see, *I* am giving her the welcoming party."

There was a slight pause, which gave her a chance to move more firmly on the path she had just taken. She had the terrible feeling of being a sort of Theseus who had entered the labyrinth without a ball of twine with which to backtrack. But she had to battle for survival; there was no other way.

"You," said Leslie.

His voice revealed a world of previously hidden values, relegating her to some obscure shadow while he stood on an Olympian pinnacle of power. She smothered her anger before it revealed itself in her voice. She spoke quietly, being cautious not to rush but to keep that deep, authoritative voice.

"You see, Perry Niadas asked *me* to introduce her to the society of Rome."

"He did? You hear from *him?"*

"Constantly," said Linda, crossing her fingers.

Since the telephone call to David, she had received excerpts from the interoffice memoranda that Niadas sent to the London office. Notated were fragments that discussed anything to do with her scenes. They were signed with his elegant signature, and were mostly a carefully conjured commentary on his Hellenic fantasies; Claudia had scoffingly referred to one as the crystallization of a dilettante's dreams, which had ended her seeing them.

"Well," said Leslie after a beat of silence, "it's most

strange *I* didn't hear of this. Grace Boomer and I have been working on the lists for some time."

"Grace knows very little about Niadas' plans," said Linda.

She was annoyed that this publicity chess game had gone so far without anyone bothering to checkmate it, and realized that her mother had slipped a cog, spending so much time with Roman society. She should have been better protected.

"Are you certain about this?" asked Leslie.

His voice was waspish. She wondered how she could ever have nourished the idea he was anything like her father.

"Of course, as a matter of fact I'm busy with Ubaldo making plans. He'll fly to Greece to make the final arrangements. It will be at the Niadas villa, naturally."

She attempted to make it sound as if Leslie had been extremely gauche to consider another place for the party.

"And," she continued, "it's going to be very Greek. Dress, food, and all."

"Greek!" said Leslie. "But, my dear, the *haut monde* cuisine is French. . . . Greek!"

He rolled the *r* in "Greek," casting it away as if she had pulled a faux pas by suggesting it.

"Well, that's not the way Pericles Niadas feels."

That ought to put him in his place.

"Oh, naturally," said Leslie, "considering his background. Brilliant man, really."

She could hear the little birdfeet of his retraction.

"We'll discuss it tomorrow," she said. "I don't want to keep you, and Ubaldo and I are up to our necks with invitations."

She hung up, both piqued with Leslie and frightened with what she had done.

Who could help her? Naturally, the person she had subconsciously mentioned. Ubaldo, of course. And she had her reasons for knowing he would be the one.

There was no possibility of any other action. Chloë Metaxa had to be introduced only by her. Last week

Claudia had dropped a copy of *Current Biography* on her desk for Linda to read.

"You'd better bone up on your co-star," Claudia had said. "It's always good to know what they're all about before they start to upstage you. And this one is something."

But now the bare facts had better be studied.... She shuffled through some magazines and found the article. If she was going to protect herself, she'd better analyze what these facts were.

Let's see. . . . "Metaxa, Chloë Athena . . . Born April 10, 1930."

She's eleven years older than I am. She's not so young. Been around a lot. I just bet . . .

"Actress, singer, dancer."

Too much . . .

> She was reported to have worked as a child as a commandeered *Dienstmädchen* in a German club in Crete, during World War II, acting as liaison, carrying messages to Greek and British naval intelligence.
>
> During the Civil War she worked with ELAS forces, combating Communist guerrilla bands, who were laying waste to the village populations. Here she met Pericles Niadas, which led to her later association with the Institute for Hellenic women which aids the young women of Greece who have no family to protect their personal needs.
>
> After the perils of the Greek Civil War she appeared publicly for the first time, dancing with the Dora Stratou dance group. She was admitted to the Athens National Theater, where she won a following in revues, light comedy, and heroic costume pieces.
>
> In Greece she worked with Paxinou, Verghi, Sinodinou, and was brought to the attention of the producers Minotis and Rondiris. She appeared in the ancient Greek drama at the Athens Festival, and the following year worked in the amphitheater at Epidaurus.
>
> Later that year she created a scandal picketing the Hiera Hodos, the sacred way between Athens and Eleusis, Syntagma Square, and even the Kyfissia area, from the Old Palace to the exclusive villas; sleeping in the open, singing, performing and dancing, passing the *defi* like a street dancer to collect coins, in an

open protest for money to train the talented young women of Greece.

She has appeared in five Greek films: *Death of the Village, Megas the Vigilante, The Rape, Pride of Athena,* and *Rousfeti.*

"It is my desire to bring Greek theater to the world, and to bring the world to Greek theater."

Miss Metaxa has not been married; believes in traveling light. She lives in hotels, says that sets and stages are her real home, where she truly lives.

She works in her spare time on charities at the Institute for Hellenic Women headquarters out of the offices of her long-time sponsor, Pericles Niadas.

Linda set down the magazine.

It was Chloë Metaxa's privilege to belong to a country small, ambitious, jealous, and proud, where everything you did was talked about in the marketplace.

She opened a silver-gilt jewel box and lifted up the velvet pad. Underneath was an envelope. It had been studied from time to time for several weeks. With it was Ubaldo's crested handkerchief.

No one knew about it, save the research department and herself. She had thought about it quite a bit, and wondered how she would use this secret. And she knew, now, why it was here. She shivered, thinking of the convolutions of fate. Now she needed it.

Now was the preordained time.

Linda smoothed the fine texture of the handkerchief linen and studied the embroidered crest. Now, that name that they researched from the crest, it's got to be Ubaldo's. . . . How about that! A prince in disguise. Something terrible happened to him. I bet it was in Ethiopia; this document said he was there. That's how he lost his hair. A fever . . . terrible . . . and Mussolini failed. And he went broke. He wanted to be near his things. That's why he's here. He's in love with Phryne. I don't care what the reports say—that she's a copy. He said, "Praxiteles would be glad you found each other . . ." or something like that. And I do look like her. . . . Now, what else do you need when you want help? And I do. She recollected how Ubaldo had confessed he had seen her breasts as she stood next to the statue of Phryne. He had said, "You are the Phryne who brings magic."

Linda had wondered if she could compete with the grown-up world. She knew she could compete with a statue of the adored Phryne, who had not only inspired Praxiteles and Apelles, but who, when she was called into court for asking too much money for her favors, had been defended by Hyperides, the orator, another of her lovers. She had won her case, not by her lawyer's golden-tongued oratory, but merely by unpinning her tunic and exposing her flawless breasts to the judge and court.

Ubaldo was right. Beauty was magic. Perhaps that was why she wanted to be an actress. If what she had inherited was a lodestone of magic for the hungry world, then it was all right for them to see her. It was a sort of gift. . . . As it was to Ubaldo. Lonesome princeling. Lonesome as she was. Imprisoned.

She called the Yorkshire terrier and walked down the terrace steps, across the mimosa-laden drifts of hot Roman darkness, feeling her way along the clumps of night-black cypress and ghostly statues to the amphitheater. She adjusted her eyes in the moonless sky to see Ubaldo's black shadow against the faint sky-glow of Roman night lights in the distance. As he drew in smoke from his cigarette, his profile knifed against the dark in its sharp handsomeness. She was startled when he glanced up and saw her standing there.

"I didn't mean to intrude," she said, "but I was walking my dog."

"Signorina," he said, "you could never intrude."

He bowed formally.

"You know," she said, "I didn't get a chance to thank you for the night you lent me your handkerchief. I still have it."

"It is honored," he said.

He perched on the lip of the stage.

She sat, slightly away from him.

"You know, Mr. Ubaldo—"

"Ubaldo," he said.

"Would you please call me Linda?" she said.

"It would not be fitting," he said.

"Aren't we friends?" she asked.

She held up her hand.

"Now, don't say you would be honored. That's too formal. And if we had met, say, at another time, we would have been first-name friends. That is, if *you* would have allowed me."

He moved his head swiftly, looking at her.

"I know, you're the prince who owned this whole countryside."

He stared at her a moment; she could not see him well, but she could almost feel his surprise.

"I heard rumors about how this estate was sold," she said. "And I saw your love for it. I know who you are. I had you traced by your crest on the handkerchief."

He looked at her, and as he puffed on his cigarette, she could see his liquid eyes gleam.

"How simple . . ." he said. "Please, I beg of you . . ."

"You needn't beg. I cross my heart." She moved her hand in an X over her breast. "That's the American way of saying I promise not to tell."

"It was so easy for you," said Ubaldo, "and yet the bloodhounds of Niadas never found me out."

"They did not live with you," she said.

"And they were not Phryne," he said.

"She means very much to you," she said.

"She is my reason for being here. I could not bear to lose her once I found her. She lay in this earth until, as a young man, I excavated her. Ah, I wish I had known you then. When I was young, handsome they said, and had the treasures of my world to offer."

"I wasn't even born," said Linda.

"I mean," he said, "that I wish we had been of an age in such a golden time as my youth. How much I could have given you!"

There was a long pause. The kinship of loneliness reached across the void more easily than social amenities could have done.

"Signorina . . ." he said, in apology.

"Linda, please," she answered. "You know, I need a friend, too."

"Linda." It sounded like a caress as he said it in his soft Italian voice. "My identity, what is left of it, is in your keeping. I have been stupid. I shall burn all my crested handkerchiefs at once. I must tell you, it was the Phryne that made me stay, because I could not bear that anyone should move her from my villa. That is why I am caretaker for this Greek tycoon. To be near her. And when you came . . ."

He shook his head, and paused for a moment, too disturbed to speak.

"You are the magic," he whispered.

"You are the magician," she said. "You found her. Without you, she wouldn't be seen. Just as I'm trying to find Alethea, the priestess of Delphi. I will bring her to life. That's what acting is. It fleshes the dream, Max says, just as you brought Phryne out of the earth to life."

"I did not think of acting in such terms," he said.

"I intend to make something exist that was only a legend," she said.

He was silent.

"What's wrong?" she asked. "I hope I didn't disturb you terribly. But I knew, and I had to tell you."

"It is disturbing," he said, "because now you've made me alive again. For a long time I was dead. Now I must adjust my thinking."

"We all do," said Linda. "It's difficult for me, too. Don't you know that?"

"I have seen you changing," he said, "and it had distressed me. Is it wrong for such beauty and quality as you possess to be sold by the ticket? Of course, in my world, as a young man, you would have been carried away, to be loved by a . . . by a . . ."

"By a prince," she said.

"Yes," he said, "and be adored for a lifetime."

"Well," said Linda, "Martha Ralston got her prince."

He almost snorted. She was surprised.

"What's the matter?" she said.

"Prince! A fortunate merchant who parlayed old Liberty ships into an empire. An entrapment," he said, "an entrapment on both sides. It is the old, tragic pattern. For Niadas, conquest of the sex symbol, well-sold. For her, marriage to one of the most important pirates in the world."

"What is he like?" she asked.

"Do not ask me to explain him," he said. "I presume I have the inborn resentment Greeks and Romans have for each other. And this robber baron is all Greek, a rich, modern one, which means he is driven by a largely avaricious drive, attempting to live up to an ancestry that is false. Like all of his kind, he is closer to Persia than to Athens. He fumbles with his worry beads, and enjoys smoking his amber-stemmed chibouk. He controls an enormous empire through every mechanical device known to man, and yet whiles away his sybaritic leisure hours leading a semi-intellectual rich peasant's life; one might say he is a superstitious packrat, gathering treasures for the afterworld, to convince himself that a man of quality passed this way."

She heard a faint whistle, as Effie, standing on the balcony, was giving Sarge his signal. He barked back.

"Oh, dear," said Linda, "Effie's looking for me. She's probably worried about me wandering about in the dark."

She whistled back.

"Indeed she should worry," said Ubaldo.

Sarge wandered, sniffing, on the amphitheater stage, the only performer on it.

"You must go," said Ubaldo. "I would not wish them to find you here with me. They might misunderstand."

Linda glanced at him fleetingly. He steered her delicately with his arm.

"I guess we can't talk very easily, can we?" she said.

"I am afraid it is most difficult," he said.

"But I need your help," she said. "They are all trying to put me down. Chloë Metaxa is coming to Rome in two weeks, and Leslie Charles wants to introduce her with a party. I said on account of the picture I wanted to give a Grecian banquet. Leslie thinks it should be French, you know. . . ."

"Ah, yes," said Ubaldo, "hams from Luxeuil, Brittany fish, peaches from Gironde—all that elegance—his taste."

"Linda," called Effie. "Honey-*bun.*"

"Coming, Effie," she called out. "I'm finding my way."

Effie was shading her eyes, trying to peer into the darkness.

"Could we possibly," said Linda in a lowered voice, "get Mr. Niadas to let me give a party here? You know, a real Greek feast, a marvelous banquet that would go well with the picture. I know you and I could work out the details. Chloë Metaxa should be introduced properly."

"It would be fitting," said Ubaldo. "She will stay here; the gold-and-green suite is always at her disposal."

"What did Martha . . . Mrs. Niadas think of that?" asked Linda.

Ubaldo looked at her. Now she could see his face in the light from the villa. His eyes seemed to have closed in a little, not seeking hers.

"Madame was told what to think," he said quietly. "But about your party. If you wrote him in your own way, saying that you wished to entertain the leading actress of Greece, and that you feel to do it in the Greek manner would be most fitting, it seems to me you would receive approval. I shall see that it goes right to the yacht instead of being lost in some secretary's desk. That's communication headquarters wherever he is, while Kalliste is rebuilding, after the earthquake.

She felt his fingers touching the soft skin on the inside of her arm.

"You do not come to see Phryne anymore," he whispered.

"How do you know?" she asked.

"I read every night in the hall, hoping," he said.

She knew what he meant. He was exacting the price. His grasp on her arm was softer, moving upward.

"I must go in," she said.

"Tomorrow, before you go to Cinecittà, if you will have your letter, I shall send it to Niadas," he said.

"Thank you," she said, hurrying away.

She rushed up the stone steps. The little dog followed after her.

"Linda," said Effie, "you shouldn't go out in the yard alone."

"It isn't a yard," said Linda, "it's a garden. And *you* go out alone."

"Well, it's different with me," said Effie, giving her a toothy grin. "Besides, don't forget, honey, with my complexion I can just sit there and hide in the dark!"

As she entered her sitting-room doors, Linda caught a glimpse of Ubaldo below as he looked upward at her.

Several hours later the villa was silent.

Ubaldo sat in the large hall reading his paper. He felt a movement on the balcony. He hardly dared to look. His pulse was throbbing. He lowered his paper as carefully as a man does when he is spying on an animal in the forest and does not wish to disturb it.

She moved on slim, pale feet to the curve of the great staircase. This time she was completely naked.

He saw the triangular fine golden fleece on her mons veneris, the curve of her supple waist, her flat silken belly, and the firm rounds of her breast as she slowly drew herself into the classic pose of the rosy statue. The two women stood, one above the other, so living, and yet so still in the silent night, that it would not have surprised him if the marble woman had moved and the flesh one had remained frozen.

Although he knew she was performing in a way for him, paying a debt, there seemed to be something ritualistic about the act.

For the moment she stood; he was tempted to run up the stairs to her, to take that sweet human flesh in his arms, but she was gone as suddenly as she had appeared.

He folded his paper carefully with trembling hands, and sat, composing himself, staring at the marble woman.

Was it an invitation? Did this young creature want to pass the threshold of youth into maturity, and had she chosen him for the age-old ritual? Or was she rewarding him for a favor?

A saint would have been aroused by this tender offering of beauty, and God knows, he was no saint. But he looked down at his hairless hands, and remembered.

He knew well what would have happened if in his youth he had seen this proffered beauty standing in her naked splendor in his villa. He knew too well. He would have hurtled up the stairs, and he would have carried her into the very bedroom where tonight she would sleep.

He moved toward the stair. Could it be possible? Would he be trapped by his desire and her youth? Would she cry out in terror, not realizing what passions she had unleashed? It was possible. She was not a wanton, but she had shown him all the secret mystique of her beauty—almost all. The thought of probing into the pulsating secret of her womanhood led him farther up the stairs.

He paused at the landing.

There was a flash of car lights in the drive.

There was not time to come down the stairs. He stood by the statue of Phryne, adjusting it slightly on the pedestal and arranging the vases of waxen white roses which surrounded it.

Staccato footsteps on the marble floors caused him to turn. He took a last look at the gentle, aloof expression of his Phryne to give him courage.

Claudia was coming toward him, to enter the corridor where she lived. She had a handkerchief in her hand; she had been crying.

"Ah," he said, "good evening, Signorina Barstow."

She looked up at him with tearful eyes.

"Good evening, Ubaldo," she said.

Her voice was thick with unshed tears.

"May I assist you?" he said.

"Oh, no," she said. "I'm . . . sorry. It's just a stupid, emotional thing."

"Nothing emotional is stupid."

Her disturbance had helped him over the erotic impact of the moment before.

She looked up at the statue.

"You love her, don't you?"

He nodded, unable to speak. He had the terrible feeling that his love for Phryne and for Linda was fusing, and that if he did not watch himself, one might reveal the other.

"Well, perhaps you are fortunate," she said, "that you love a marble woman. Sometimes it is very difficult to be in love with a mortal."

He felt somehow unsexed that this woman, in essence so worldly, who seemed at the moment as naïve as a young girl, had chosen to confide in him. He bowed politely.

"Love is always difficult," he said, "for it is ever changing. We fear change, yet we embrace it."

He saw that he had diverted her from an inner trauma by his words.

"You are a wise man," she said.

He wanted to blurt out how unwise he was, for he was beginning to realize the horror of his position. If it had been Jessica Barstow who had come in, it would never have entered her mind that he was adjusting the flowers around Phryne; she would have immediately known he had some motive in coming up the stairs. And if she had found her daughter still nude, in her room, she might have suspected more than the truth.

He had visions of exile from this villa under conditions of intolerable humiliation.

"None are wise in love, signorina," he said, "and you are rather pale. I shall send some cognac to your room?"

"Thank you." She turned to walk along the corridor.

It was the first time she had considered accepting a drink since she had been in the villa.

Claudia got to her room and sat down.

Then she began to laugh. Her rich voice pealed out

in the deep silence of the vaulted room. She looked at the golden bed with its drapes of Venetian red velvet, and she began to laugh again.

She had to stifle it when there was a knock at the door.

"Come in," she said, as Gabriele, the night butler, brought in the silver salver with a slim decanter, and one glass. He poured a drink, and bowed politely as he left.

The hell with the wagon. Maybe it was a good idea, get smashed, let it spin.

She laughed again but it turned to hysteria, and tears coursed down her cheeks. What was wrong with her? Could it be that Claudia Barstow was in love with an old Hungarian she hadn't even looked at in the days when he was top director at Titan! All these years, time lying on her too. God forbid, the word "love."

Max had been adrift in Rome, not living in the villa, because life was too complicated there, only house-guesting occasionally. And Claudia, asked by him to literally hide out from the people she should have been with, stars like herself, Leslie Charles, and her own protégé, John Graves, how foolish. And how ridiculous that she was a duenna—*duenna!*—to Jeffrey's child. What kind of a cocked-up world.

Instead of the life that should have been hers, she had sat endlessly with Max listening to his favorite anecdotes, his chosen music, and to the Hungarian chatter at the Piccolo Budapest, so rapid and so vociferous that one person could not hear the other—not that it mattered—and listening to his plaints about production problems, and his plans for future staging as they wandered from one spot to another.

Where was her head? This was not her life! But strangely, gradually his hands found hers, his warm brown eyes had looked into her own. He had been nervous and quick-moving these days, but still he sought her company.

She had never listened like this before. She had never been the secondary one. But somehow she was. And then, he had kissed her.

And she had given his emotion back, with a clinging, and a thrill that she had thought long gone. She ached for more. Imagine, Claudia Barstow, without a drink in her system, longing for another kiss, just a kiss, from white-haired Maximilian Ziska.

But this night, after a late supper, still drunk from the violins playing Moli's *Tzigane,* they had strolled through the heady anonymity of the Roman night. Max had pulled her aside in a secret enclave of wildly flowering bougainvillea, thrust his hand into the lace-filled décolletage of her dress, and lifted her white breast into the moonlight. He bent and kissed her nipple, as she gasped. He rose, his eyes glowing pools in the moonlight.

"Love, tonight you must come with me. You will?"

He put his fingers on her lips.

"There is nothing to say," he said, "that your eyes and your sweet breast have not told me."

"It's insane, Max," she said. "It's me—Claudia."

He put his arm in hers.

"I will love you," he said, "and you will love me. What else is there?"

They had walked into the forbidding formality of his hotel.

Max had latched his sitting-room door and opened up the bedroom curtains, looking out over a small balcony onto the magnificence of the Spanish Steps.

He came to her in the soft darkness and embraced her.

"Go into the bathroom," he whispered, nuzzling her hair, "and leave your clothes."

How ridiculous, she thought, anyone telling *me* to go to the bathroom to undress, when I usually dropped my clothes right on the floor then and there! But she acquiesced like a timid young woman. As she undressed, she looked in the mirror. Not bad for her age, but the sensuous, lithe young body was not there. She switched off the light.

She came into the darkened room. Max fell before her naked, clasping her waist with his arms. Then he arose, kissed her, and took her to bed.

"My beautiful Claudia!"

She caressed him. Oh, how long, how very long it had been since she had been able to love someone, to blend. He responded, but soon she realized that the moment that should have sealed them had passed. She caressed him shyly, afraid to be the dominant partner in this first encounter. Soon they both knew there would be no passion for them this night. It had not come to his body.

He pulled away.

"I . . . I am sorry," he whispered.

He walked to the balcony. The French doors were open. Rome, that promising city glimmering below. He hung his head, humiliated.

She came to him, put her cheek against his back, and her hands gently on his shoulders.

"It doesn't matter Max. . . . I love you."

She went to the bathroom and dressed. As she arranged herself, powdered her face, put lipstick on her pale lips, and blotted her eyes, to her annoyance, she heard the overrich Italian voice of a nightclub singer in the distance singing "Love Is a Many-Splendored Thing."

She switched off the brightness of the bathroom, and came into the dim bedroom. Max was sitting naked on a chair, his head in his hands.

He arose. "I'll call a car and take you back to the villa."

"No, Max, it would look odd. The doorman will get me a car. I'd rather you didn't."

Before he could protest, she walked out the door and closed it quietly.

On the Appian Way she wept. Oh, it had been so close, and so dear. Was it too late for Max? Or was it her own humiliation? No longer was she Claudia, the symbol of sex, who could and did excite a man. Much less a man who professed love for her. She smiled bitterly with scorn at herself, at this time in her life dreaming love could be hers.

And now, in her room, the evening gone, what would tomorrow bring?

Poor Max, how difficult it would be for him to face her on the set.

How lonely this villa would be. She thought about Linda. No one realized her own brand of loneliness, a Rapunzel in her tower. She walked out in the hall, glanced up at glorious Phryne, a strange feeling assailing her. She had been pursuing her own life and emotions, as had all the selfish people in this luxurious fantasy of a life. How dare she think of a love affair gone wrong with such distraction when Linda had been put into her keeping?

She knocked at Linda's suite. There was light under the sitting-room door. She turned the knob cautiously. The door was ajar in the bedroom. She moved in. There, in front of a pier glass, stood Linda, nude, admiring herself. Her pose was like the statue in the hallway. For a moment Claudia stared at her, mouth agape. Then she spoke.

"Now, just what do you think you're doing, miss?" she said.

Linda jumped, startled. Then, seeing it was Claudia, she smiled.

"Oh, you scared me!" she said. "For a minute I thought you were Mom."

"God forbid," said Claudia. "*What* are you up to?"

"I'm practicing being Phryne," said Linda lightly. "Don't I look like her?"

Claudia nodded.

"Too, too much. Just be careful who sees your impersonation. Good night, love. Get to bed. You're up late. Tomorrow, unfortunately, is a working day."

Linda threw her arms around her and kissed her.

"What about you? You just got in."

"I'm too old for it to matter," said Claudia.

As she walked back to her room, she thought: Isn't that the truth! Once in her room, she picked up the glass ambered with cognac. She unstoppered the decanter, poured it back in, and as she undressed, reasoned with herself. It was time for Linda to take stage center. Forget affairs of the heart. . . . And a little shadow crossed her mind. What if Ubaldo had seen

Linda posing as Phryne? What was he doing on the landing? It was just a thought. A vagrant thought. She turned out the lights and tried to compose herself.

◆◆◆◆◆◆◆◆◆

The wound of remembering what was gone forever was the hardest and most mortal pain to bear, thought Ubaldo.

He could not hide in self-life-death again.

He could not conjure up the woman in his arms in the darkness of his onanism.

He was, the devil take him, alive again. Death was not possible now. He would have to find his footsteps among the living once more. It was painful to be a Lazarus.

He sat at his desk thinking of the evening.

He was incredibly grateful to Claudia. The sad and lonely woman had unwittingly saved him from momentary madness.

He was able to visualize himself, as he was now, through the eyes of a young creature like Linda Barstow. She would have been horrified if he, with his bald head and his hairless body, and no longer the flamboyant handsomeness of youth, had entered her room and even, under the most romantic conditions, tried to press his own flesh against her.

It was time for him to cast off the dream of the youth who had once passed his passionate, flower-strewn path in and out of some of the most select boudoirs of Rome.

That man was dead. Dead. Done, and forgotten, as if his bones were really whitening in Albini's *camposanto*. The curtain was down on that.

From the bottom drawer of his desk he took out a small oval picture of himself. The thick curling hair, the rain eyelashes, the determined curve of lips, and the arrogance of his youth and beauty disturbed him almost as much as seeing Linda naked.

A fantasy began to form.

That young man walked up the stairs. It was his

house. His bride was getting into that princely bed. The angels were hovering over the silks and linens, blessing him, as his own mother had once said his bride would be blessed.

The youth was taking the rewards of his nuptial night. The house of Albini was alive again, pregnant with promise, living and voluptuous with its new blossoming.

But here, in his private room, surrounded with equal treasures, but of the intellect, lived Ubaldo. He had many years before him, time and comfort in which to use the facilities that he had gathered, to take out the notes that only his eyes had seen, to create the reputation that he, now the elder of the house of Albini, would leave to the world of letters and science.

From his vargueno he took out first the sacred golden goblet of Sheba, then a yellowed manuscript. He opened it and turned on the reading light. He pushed the picture of the young man away. Let him take care of himself. While those imaginary young lovers were up there spending passion in the careless rapture of youth, he, the forgotten scholar, the head of a great house, would work on his manuscripts and see that the name of the family would be recorded in unforgettable pages.

"The Lion of Judah . . ." he read. "The legend of Makeda, known as Queen of Sheba, and her son, Menyelek . . ."

He turned the pages, frowned at a word, and reached into another drawer, pulling out an ancient, treasured scroll.

The Kebra Nagast. The Glory of Kings. The yellowed pages were written in Arabic, and he translated, reading of the 409th year of Mercy, when Lâlîbâlâ's scribes told of the pearl which traveled from the body of each holy man, from Adam until the appointed time when Christ would be born, the final product of the precious seed.

He corrected a phrase in his own manuscript, and turned another page. He became lost in the peregrinations of the fabled Queen Makeda, as she settled with her wild tribesmen in her high mountains to give birth to Solomon's son on the way back from her holy pilgrimage to the wisest of kings.

He smiled. What convoluted sentences belong to youth. It would take editing, and analysis, but he had been a good student, and he had amassed material that would enrich history; some of it was so rare, and secret, considering his long-lost sources, that no scholar but himself in the world could do this task.

The excitement in his loins abated. He felt filled with a life force that was flowing from his brain, through his fingers, into his pen. Let the young scatter their seed. In his maturity he would gather harvest from his brain.

He smiled with warm affection at the young princeling, Ubaldo, with his shock of curls, and his rampaging sex, who was fecundating the beautiful young woman in the Albini bed; how little he knew of the true fruitfulness of life, the controlled and extended arc of creativity; the true ecstasy, the poetic trance.

Throughout the night there was no time, only the scratching of his pen. He was astounded when the chef called him on his private phone to receive morning orders. Only then did he stretch his arms, to find them cramped.

He wondered how she was, beautiful Linda, with the angels spreading their arms over her upstairs, and if the dream host, the young Ubaldo, would have been sleeping his heedless, glutted sleep, if he had in fact been there.

◆◆◆◆◆◆◆◆

For several days Claudia avoided Max on the set. But finally he came to her.

"I want to drive up into the Sabine Hills and dine in some little inn," he said. "I think we could use the mountain road as the sacred Hiera Hodos leading from Athens to Ephesus. Would you care to go?"

"Thank you," she said, "but Linda has to work on the scene of the sibyl breathing in the vapors and giving the oracular speech. I think I'd better work with her."

"Don't be afraid, Claudia," said Max.

"Next thing you're going to say is, we can still be friends," she said, managing a smile. "I think I must realize Linda takes center stage now."

"You are right," said Max. "Sometimes we forget why we are here. She needs you. We shall take our drive another time. And while you're working on it, remember, research suggested that although there was an unearthly beauty about Delphi, with its olive, laurel, red poppies, daisies, asphodel, and the scent of wild thyme and mint, the rock of the sibyl under the Pelasgian wall contained a fissure. It likely belched noxious gases out of the earth, causing the oracle to have convulsions when she went into her trance. There should be a feeling of horror underlying the mystic beauty of the scene."

"I understand." She should be angry at him, he was so casual about their aborted affair. Why did she feel like an idiotic schoolgirl around him?

That night, after a lone dinner on a tray, she called Linda's room by interhouse phone. Disturbed at her constant thoughts of Max, she decided to busy herself.

"I'd like to run lines if you'd like it," she said. "Those fashion sittings have taken so much of your time, and we ought to go over tomorrow's scene."

"I'm rather involved," said Linda. "Ubaldo's here, but come up."

Again a little chill hit the back of Claudia's neck. She was remembering Ubaldo standing at the landing by the Greek statue the night she had come in from being with Max. It would be just as well to see what was happening in that increasingly private world Linda inhabited.

She found Linda seated on the sofa, surrounded by sheaves of lists and brilliant picture books.

Ubaldo smiled, bowing courteously. Was there a new unctuousness in his impersonal, courteous manner, almost as if he admitted a stranger into an enchanted circle, or was she imagining it?

Effie sat knitting in her usual, I'm-not-included-so-

I'm-not-here attitude, with the little dog sitting on top of her feet.

"What on earth is all this?" Claudia asked.

"I'll tell you what," said Linda, stretching her arms fetchingly, her pale-blue robe falling away from her slender arms. "You are going to see a way-out banquet, the likes of which hasn't been seen since Cleopatra and Mark Antony lived it up in Egypt."

Ubaldo nodded his head in agreement. Claudia realized that he was enchanted, and the child knew it, and was using him.

"The renowned queen did not have the facilities we will enjoy," he said, "for the wealth of kings could not provide the fast transportation that Niadas will employ. He is outdoing himself for the glory of Greece, Chloë Metaxa, and, of course, Miss Linda."

"You'll be surprised," said Linda.

"I love surprises," said Claudia, "what is it?"

"You'll see, and Chloë Metaxa will see. . . ."

"Is it for her?" asked Claudia as Linda swung up theatrically and moved across the room, posing with one hand on the mantel.

God, she thought, she's imitating me; got me down pat, or was I that good?

"Chloë Metaxa," said Linda, "is only a guest. She may be the most celebrated actress in Greece, but it has a small theater population. After all, she started as a Bouzouki singer in the streets. Now, Aunt Claudia, she can see how a *Barstow* does things."

"I shall leave the lists for your selection," said Ubaldo.

He handed her some typewritten pages in a thick vellum envelope. Claudia quickly noted the embossed circlet of laurel leaves on one cover, a famous logo, which meant it had come from the private desk of Niadas. So, Ubaldo was the go-between. For what?

He bowed and left.

Linda opened the letter. She waved it, and smiled.

"He's coming!" she said. "He'll be here for my party. He not only wants me to introduce Chloë

Metaxa to Rome, he is going to be here to do it with me!"

She grasped her aunt's hands and scoffed. "Isn't it just a crying shame that Martha Ralston can't come?"

"I heard that Leslie Charles was giving the welcoming party," said Claudia. "How did this all come about?"

So, thought Linda, even you heard about it too, and didn't tell me.

"Well, I decided that if I was going to be a star, it wasn't good enough to be permitted to come to someone else's party as if I'd been let out for good behavior. Everyone can damned well come to *my* party. And since I've been corresponding with Mr. Niadas, it all worked out. You know, this sort of publicity can't be bought, and it's going to help make me a star."

She looked triumphantly at Claudia.

"You did not come to Rome to play Cleopatra to Mr. Niadas' aging Caesar, my girl. That bit has already been played, badly, I may add. And since you're also aiming at being a star, don't try to pull anything on me. I wrote the book, and look where I am. One thing I'd like to mention. As lovely as it is to have Mr. Midas give you a party, the camera isn't interested. Remember why you are here."

Linda wavered. This was not what she had expected from her aunt. She hadn't faced hostility from her before. Perhaps she should follow her own course. Everyone was trying to pull her in a different direction.

"I don't think I'll work tonight," she said. "I have to get up at five-thirty. Maybe you could run over the lines with me when we get to the studio."

"Maybe," said Claudia haughtily. She left.

As they parted, both felt bereft.

Claudia was hurt. One complication she hadn't considered was Linda moving away from her sheltering protection.

Linda realized how close she had come to being pushed aside again when the adults had their social celebration. She had to do everything possible to ensure the admiration of John Graves. That, and the personal sponsorship of Niadas, would help overwhelm the child image she loathed more each day.

The next day Claudia sat on the sidelines and watched Linda. She noticed how the crew had begun to fawn over her. It had come about little by little, as she had been allowed to circulate more freely in an adult world. A few more quips and a few more pranks were allowed to vulgarize the young star.

Linda was beginning to preen and act the pretty clown, trying desperately to cover her youth.

Now, how do you suppose she could do anything else? Claudia thought. Look what happened to me. How can I blame a child? She must talk to someone who had a vision beyond her own problems on the set. And, of course, for personal reasons it was impossible to contact Max.

Jessica was scheduling the forthcoming location in Greece with Sidney, two assistants, cameramen, the unit manager, and a location expert who had just flown in on one of the Delphic Airline DC-7's.

Besides, Jessica was the last person Claudia would consult on the tender subject of Linda's getting out of hand.

She thought of Grace Boomer's publicity factory. Good old Grace. She knew what went on.

She wandered down unfamiliar corridors to a long glass-lined office, where the clack of a dozen typewriters suggested a fury of material being digested.

She paused long enough to observe a pool of secretaries with flags of their languages stuck up over their desks. One of the girls was even typing in Arabic.

Grace peered out of an open door with her glasses hanging low on her nose.

"Welcome to hodgepodge lodge," said Grace. *"Entrez."*

Tacked up on the wall was a large cork board. On it was a schedule of magazine interviews and release dates. It seemed as complicated as a studio production board.

"Take a gander," said Grace, tugging at her limp hair, some of the white roots showing. "In no time

Chloë Metaxa arrives, and we have to get some of these things out ahead of schedule to attack her problems. Leslie and John are in line. But the requests are coming in like crazy for the material on Linda."

Claudia studied the board.

"It's more complicated than it was in my day."

"So's life," said Grace. "It takes a lot of imagination and sweat to create a multimillion-dollar image of somebody who last year at this time was told by her mother not to roller-skate north of Wilshire Boulevard. And if she doesn't make out with this epic, you know damn well there's no career."

"And if she's a success, she's stuck with the image you invent for the rest of her life." Claudia sighed.

"Listen," said Grace, "she's having a ball. You know they always do, the first time they're a star! Remember?"

"That's just what I mean," said Claudia. "I'm beginning to see the makings of a shrewd, too clever egomaniac."

"Well," said Grace, "as we used to say, iris in, came the dawn. Just what did you expect of a beautiful young kid in never-never land. After all, I cut my teeth as a young press agent, dragging *you* around the country. Shall we flash back into some of the things you did?"

"Let's *not* go into it!" said Claudia, smiling. "Once I'd have had you sacked for saying it. But times have changed. The trouble is, I think she can do anything as an actress she wants to do."

Grace stared at her.

"What's the matter?" asked Claudia.

"I have goosebumps," said Grace, rubbing her arm. "That's what they said about you when you were a star."

"Well," said Claudia, "in those days you could lean against a flat, bat your eyes, and get by with it. But this one has voice, beauty, a flexible body, and a great name."

"So did you," said Grace.

The phone rang. She smiled and winked at Claudia as she answered it.

Claudia, realizing she was no help, thumbed her nose at her and left.

7

Rome lay gasping under the pressing fingers of the heavy autumnal heat that followed a sirocco. The actors sweated in smothering body makeup, wigs, curls, toupees, and the false beards and lashes. Everyone was irritable and nervous.

Linda's damp peplos glued itself to her body, and she was aware of the eyes that followed her, the revelation of her contours perhaps more sharply accented by the clinging drapes than they would have been in the briefest bikini.

Linda and John Graves faced each other under the hot lights while a final adjustment was made to eliminate the shadow of the light boom.

"Oh, if I could just take a shower," she said.

"I'd like to be in the sea at Ostia with you right now," he said.

His eyes could not help but seek the shape of her breasts.

"Camera," said Max.

They did the scene. The footsoldier flees into a cave, hiding the young girl who is sought by soldiers and priests of the oracle. Diodynus hides her under his cloak, and she clings to him, terrified, as he speaks to soldiers, who peer into the darkness. At the end of the scene, he picks her up and carries her across a pool of water to a hidden altar.

She felt a trickle of perspiration fall from her arm to his hand. He looked at it as it glistened. For a brief moment he forgot his newfound reticence with her, and she was held in his embrace with a tenderness and strength new to her. She felt his body harden against hers, and she knew he was affected as deeply as she.

As the scene ended, he pulled his robes about him and called out to Max.

"I don't give a damn what you say," he said, "I'm going to cool off. The heat, plus this love scene, is too much of a snash."

There was laughter as he left the set.

"You go, too, Linda," said Max. "It must be a hundred and ten degrees under the lights."

He walked with his arm holding her thick braid of hair up in the air; she knew he was saving her dignity, by going with her.

"Shower, love," he said. "Just keep your face out of it, and we'll patch up the body later."

"Save the lights!" yelled Hank.

He and the cameraman dived for the sound truck in the alley, where a case of beer was stashed.

"Why don't we all go to the villa after work?" said Linda. "We can swim in the pool, and have supper on the terrace. You, and Aunt Claudia, and John, and Leslie, and me. Mom's got a date."

She said it conspiratorially, so he'd know they were free of Jessica.

"Good," said Max. "I'll get a movie, and we'll run it outdoors. How about *High Society?*"

"Oh, I love Grace Kelly and Frank Sinatra," said Linda. "You ask John and Leslie. I'll call home and order the table set outdoors."

Leslie had bowed out, as Linda had known he would. She had overheard a phone call to Andrew and elaborate plans for an evening at George's bar. But suggesting his name had made the evening seem like a gathering.

"Glorious," said Claudia. "Did you ever see *Philadelphia Story* with Katharine Hepburn, Cary Grant, and Jimmy Stewart?"

"That was before my time," said Linda.

"After mine, unfortunately," said Claudia.

Linda was not thinking of Kelly versus Hepburn, or Sinatra versus Stewart. She was thinking of John

Graves and how he had said he would like to be swimming with her at Ostia.

She thought about posing nude for Ubaldo and flushed, because she had used her body as a bribe. Of course, he hadn't come near her, but he wanted to see her, and she had pleasured him. How easy it had been to slip him the note to Niadas. Within a week Ubaldo had been summoned to Greece and had come back with plans that would giddy the imagination of any hostess in the world. All because she had given him, in a way, the gift of seeing her naked body. If she could arrange the same thing with John Graves, she knew it would give her power again. He would be astounded by her beauty, and he would make love to her. It was time. She ached for it.

Since the evening she had started making elaborate plans for the party, there had been a coolness between herself and her aunt. Now, for her own reasons, she wanted to correct the situation. She needed her help, and she also wanted to have her out of the way.

"I have to talk to you," she said, having arranged for Claudia to drive back from the studio with her in the limousine, with the glass partition closed to the driver's compartment.

"What now?" said Claudia.

Linda put her hand on her aunt's.

"You'll have to help me, Aunt Claudia," she said. "It's that I'm confused in my characterization. Maybe it's because I'm . . . well, growing up. I have to tell you that I want to make love."

Claudia tried to keep her hand limp, and not reveal her concern.

"Go on," she said after a moment of silence.

"I don't know if it's the image of John Graves as Diodynus in the film, or it's John Graves himself. You know, Max has drummed empathy into my head. Is it the image in the script and on the stage?"

Claudia was touched. She squeezed her hand.

"John Graves is a very attractive man. As you know, I've known him since he was a boy. And you're not alone, thinking he is a very desirable man. Also, perhaps Max has written more romance and fidelity into him than he really has. You know, his track record with women is not unassailable. Listen, kiddie, I fell in love with a great many of my leading men. It usually ends with the film, so it's more than possible you're really in love with Diodynus, the noble Greek soldier, and would find life with a wandering minstrel like John not so much fun."

Linda watched with cat's eyes as Claudia related to the problem. She had won her back, enlisted her aid.

"I know what *you* would say," she said sagely, "for you and I think alike. But I want you to talk to Max. I just couldn't tell him myself. Because what Max taught me might influence my performance, I'd be embarrassed. But through you we could work it out. Maybe you could talk to him this evening. Do you mind?"

"Not at all." She put her hand impulsively in Linda's.

⬥⬥⬥⬥⬥⬥⬥⬥

Claudia, swimming in the cool water, watched Max's patch of white hair against his dark face as the shadows of the evening blotted them all into lonely entities, refreshing themselves in their seclusion. Oh, if life could be so sweet, falling into a pool together, yet not touching, with this man she loved, dreaming dreams in a rhythm of movement and suspended responsibilities.

It came to her as a sudden surprise that perhaps one reason she was in love with Max was because for the first time in her life she had not been sought out as a stellar attraction, or a mad sex object. She was earning a relationship within a normal framework of knowing someone she admired, and finding an infinity of interests aside from a passionate encounter. Over them, the wondrous distillation of the night loosed songs of a nightingale and a scent of jasmine that pierced the lowering darkness.

Dinner was pleasant on the terrace, a chilled consommé with grapes and sour cream; a fine wine in frosted silver goblets; a delicate scallopini with mushrooms and tiny peas; *puntarelle,* a grasslike salad served with an anchovy dressing; and, especially for John, an English syllabub, a lemony cream with sherry and brandy.

"You're trying to sink us," said Max. "We can't possibly swim again after this."

"Let's see the picture first," said Linda. "It's comfortable in our suits. Then we'll go in again before you go back to Rome, it's so hot."

Later they settled down on chaises in their suits.

"The only way to see movies," said Claudia.

"It's downright obscene, it's so comfortable," said John, settling back among sailcloth cushions.

Max moved toward Claudia as the picture ended.

"Max," she said, "I wanted to talk to you."

"Claudia," Max said, "I wanted to talk to you."

Their words met and married against the flat marble of the wall.

Both laughing, they arose.

John stood a moment breathing the cloying air and dived into the pool. He avoided the area where Linda was, and came up spouting on the other side of the pool.

He looked about. She was gone. He was alone.

He paddled, head above the ripples, enjoying the cool privacy of the moment.

"There's something I wanted to tell you," said Claudia as she and Max walked along the garden path. The gravel cut into her bare foot, and she winced.

Max took her hand and guided her to the lawn.

They turned into a door. He, too, had guest rooms in that corridor.

"It's about Linda," said Claudia. "Maybe it's the role, Max. She's growing up. She's a woman. She wants to be loved. She doesn't know how it happened. I knew this was going to happen. But she's afraid her situation in the picture has disturbed her. You see, she wants to be really loved, and she wants to know if . . . I mean, if that's what you want of her in the role. Oh, I'm not saying it very well. . . . She's afraid . . ."

Max closed the door to the garden.

They stood in the corridor. He pulled the straps from her shoulders and put his arms around the cool whiteness of her body.

"She wants to be loved," he whispered. "She is a warm woman. She is afraid; oh, Claudia!"

He opened the door to her room, for he knew where it was. He had passed it before on lonely, puzzled nights.

Together they were on the red-velvet coverlet.

He peeled the suit from her as if it were a cold, frightened skin. He pulled off his own bathing shorts, and she was astonished that her skin felt as cool as ice, and his was equally cold, as he kissed her neck, her breasts, and suddenly, with a caress, and a slow loving thrust, became a warm part inside of her which thawed her. She became the adored and the adoring, and everything that moved within them was beautiful, and there was no holding back. She was lifted with him into an ecstatic ladder climb of feeling that ended in a gasping explosion.

Scalding tears poured down her chilled face, and he kissed her eyes, and they clung together, and it was warm and cold, and magnificent and ridiculous at once, and there was no past—no age—it was now and right.

◆◆◆◆◆◆◆◆

John came into his dressing room in the marble pool house. Like all pool houses, as elegant as it was, it still smelled of chlorine, fresh-ironed towels, wet bathing suits, and soap.

He stripped off his suit and walked across to the marble shower cubicle.

As he moved into it, and turned on the water, he almost let out a cry. There stood Linda. The water was cascading down her hair and body, jutting in little points off her breasts. She looked up at him, dressed only in the transparent veil of water. She put her arms about his body.

"Oh, John, John," she said, "love me, love me."

He turned off the water.

She stood in her dripping nudity, her palms now turned up, proffering herself.

For a brief moment her complete and trim beauty dazzled him, and then he pulled away.

"Go get some clothes on."

She moved closer, and put her face up to his.

"I want you," she said, "and I know you want me. You do. . . . You do."

He looked toward the open door.

"You don't know what you're talking about!"

He walked out of the room and into the dressing room.

She followed him, and threw herself down on the couch.

"You know you want to," she said.

She looked up at him and leaned on one elbow.

"The door is locked," she said. "It latched when you closed it."

He sat down on a chair and pulled on his shorts.

"Get out," he said. "Please, God, get out."

She looked at him, and stood up. She put her hands on her hips. She knew fully well how beautiful she was.

"You can't say that to me," she said.

She moved to him, and her breast touched his arm.

He jumped up as if it were hot.

"Goddamnit," he said, "this is no silly child game, Linda."

He saw the hot anger flush into her face.

"Look, ducks," he said, "it isn't rejection. It's just . . . not the time. Not the right time. You're too bloody young. Don't you understand?"

"You don't want me?" she said, unbelieving.

"Christ, yes," he said, "but not the way it is."

Tears started to run down her cheeks.

"You see," she said, "it all turned out right in the picture. Why not us?"

"Look," he said, "dry your tears. I guess I have to talk to you. You're such a trusting little fool. Do you know what might happen to you?"

"I want it to happen."

He stood up.

"Get the hell into your bathing suit. I'll meet you, and we'll talk. Where?"

"Well, there's the amphitheater," she said, "where you saw Claudia and me recite Sophocles once."

Maybe that would suit him better, she thought. It was way out beyond the garden, and it was her place. She saw his eyes seek her body. He was not impervious to her beauty, only fearful.

She returned to the shower and got into her wet suit. At least he hadn't walked out. She felt awkward, and for the first time in her life, humiliated. But he would meet her; there was a chance.

She draped a towel like a chiton around her shoulders and walked off toward the amphitheater. Where was her aunt? Where was Max? . . . She had an instinctive feeling that they were making love together. Oh, this was such a night for lovers. . . . For her and John, too.

"And now," said John Graves, leaning against a marble pillar, "it is all a part of the idiot symbol of the world you grew up in. Like that carefully cultivated pap we see in films. You young American girls have no fear of the jungle. Of course, it is inhabited by bugs, birds, and wild animals, but a white hunter or skin-clad muscle-rippling super scout counselor will swing out of the trees at the 'crucial moment.'

"Good guys never get eaten—the ravenous creatures of the wild apparently savor only the bad guys' innards.

"And when it comes to sex, ah, nature has again provided a satisfactory solution to the inner twitching of innocents. In spite of dire peril and narrow escapes, at the end one gets raped by the 'man of one's choice,' repeating the process forever after, it is indicated in the script, with endless smoldering excitement and ecstasy on an altar of mutually moral concupiscence."

He could see her white teeth in the dark. She could not help smiling.

"You see," he said, "how silly it is when you pause to reflect. Kiddie, as a sailor I saw girls pregnant, girls dying aborted, girls with the clap. It isn't a happy-ever-after world. And I blame the flicks for the poor dreams that have to take the place of a group morality that got shot down in the late international conflagration."

He stood up and pinched his cigarette between his thumb and forefinger, arching it like a small rocket into the air.

"Blimey," he said, "but I'm no moralist. If you'd been older, with experience I'd of cocked a deaf 'un at any bogus cries for mercy, and I would have really had a go, to show you what a man is supposed to do with a beautiful thing like you. But I can't do it on the shadow of a celluloid lie that has given you such fake promises.

"My god, Linda, films function to brew imaginations of titillating peril with a built-in takeout. You scared the hell out of me when you used that film we just saw as an alibi for a boff. What an abyss you are hanging over!

"You think only the bad pay for sins. With you and me, I suppose it would not be sin, but 'living happily forever after'? Well, don't be a goose, my girl. You adolescents are totally unprepared for the possibility that the Great Plot Writer may go awry. There is not always a walking into the sunset hand-in-hand with a reformed Jack the Ripper."

"You're no Jack the Ripper," she said.

He smiled.

"Thanks for the compliment. But I've been about quite a bit, and I find it most nauseating to be lecturing you when this unfortunately innocent affair could be so misconstrued. Claudia would murder me." He grinned. "So, for Christ's sake, before I get another hard-on, as I did when we did our scene this afternoon, let me out, and let's get back to headquarters. That is, if everyone else is out of the kip. I dearly fear that, believe it or not, your aunt and Max have caught the fever."

"Oh!" said Linda. "I hope so."

John could see every part of her face in the glow of the evening. He put his hands to her cheeks, and slowly kissed her lips. She responded, her lips soft. He drew back.

"God," he said, "I'd like to be there when it's time."

He turned and walked along the path.

She followed.

"Maybe someday you'll marry me," she said, "and then it'll be all right."

"You just don't learn, do you?" he said sadly. "Dear child, some men are just not the marrying kind."

The stars seemed to dissolve as she followed him to the pool. The night was dark, the sky mucous, the heat a smothering blanket. He lit a cigarette, knowing he had dampened her spirits. But it had to be.

"I'm a bloody ass," he said. "I'm going to smuggle it out of here."

"What?" she said.

"Skip it," he said. "Just an incredibly lousy old joke."

After he was gone, she tore a rose off a vine and threw it in the pool. The shimmering night became a melancholy ripple, and she went into the villa.

She had never felt so alone. Even Ubaldo was at the port of Rome; a Delphic Line shipment was coming in from Greece for the party. The party, too, was ashes in her mouth.

She went upstairs and left her door open.

Once she thought she heard Max's voice.

Why hadn't he come to say good night? He usually did when he stayed at the villa. He and Claudia likely had been to bed. Claudia was probably lying there now. Nobody worried about her; older people just made love when they felt like it. It seemed once you had experience, you had a sort of a kings ex, anybody could do it. Well, that was it. If she could find someone who thought she was a woman, then she could say she had experience, and anyone she liked would be delighted. How does it work? Does it feel as good when you do it with anyone—or is it better if you love somebody? If it was in the dark, what difference would it make who it was?

You just had to give up the idea that the first man in your life would be the only one.

◆◆◆◆◆◆◆◆

The toothless gorgona, Zoë, brought the infant to Martha as she had brought Pericles Niadas to his mother when she was a young midwife. But this was a girl. It was not the same.

Martha stared at the baby. It was an ugly creature; the body was swaddled tight, which made the wrinkled face and frowning brow seem gross. It didn't look at all like the fat infants she had always admired with sparkles in their eyes in toilet-tissue ads.

"Take it out of here!" she cried, turning her head away. "Take it away. I don't want to see it again!"

Standing in the doorway, Niadas tried to hide his disappointment. This girl infant had taken a heavy toll on him these last hours.

Martha's high-pitched voice approached a wail.

"Just get me out of this place! I don't want to see it, or anybody here again. I want to go home!"

Her throat worked as she swallowed her tears. Her belly hurt when she sobbed, so she stopped.

"You may go home," said Niadas, "as soon as the doctor says you may travel. I presume home to you is Hollywood."

"Where else!" said Martha.

"Where else indeed," he said.

He moved into the room slowly, and sat down on her Louis XIV chaise, overladen with lace cushions. He was weary and dispirited, but he pitied her; she was so poor of spirit, and now, he knew, cheap of body.

"Martha," he said, with his most gentle tone, the one he reserved for important decisions and private allurements, "many women are depressed when they have experienced childbirth. It is a tearing asunder. Postpartum depressions are usual. I am sure you will feel better after you have slept. And babies are not always beautiful at first. They must unfold like a tight little bud. They grow beautiful later."

"Don't try to con me," she said. "I haven't seen a pretty Greek baby yet. I should have known."

"You didn't mean that," said Niadas quietly.

There was only sniffling.

He hoisted himself off the slippery lace pillows, which fell to the floor.

"You have answered me," he said.

"I didn't know it would be like this," she said. "Rome was so much fun. We had such a good time, all those pretty clothes and parties. Everything was different. And now that little teenage bitch is giving a party for that bossy Chloë Metaxa. Don't think I don't know. Your precious Chloë'd like to be having this baby for you herself."

Niadas moved toward her.

"Shut your rotten mouth!" he said.

The midwife still stood holding the infant.

With rigid control, Niadas stifled his anger.

"You are supposed to nurse your baby," he said. "That is why Zoë is standing there."

"Nurse it!" said Martha. "Oh, no!"

"Very well," said Niadas. "I expected that. I have a wet nurse standing by, a young countrywoman."

"My breasts hurt," said Martha, "and I don't want them to sag. Isn't there a breast pump or something in this terrible place?"

He nodded toward the old midwife.

"Zoë will suckle your breasts dry," he said. "She has no teeth. She knows how to dry you out. It is only routine medical care here."

He saw the look of disgust on her face.

"Let that old hag suck me!" she cried.

"She will tie a napkin under her chin, and be most clean and efficient about it," he said. "You have no choice. Unless you prefer me to do it."

"You keep away from me!" she shrieked. "Wouldn't you just like to!"

"Wouldn't I just not!" he said.

He saw an accusing glance cross her blotched face, as if she were thinking: There was a time. And he winced, wondering how he had become so entrapped.

"Martha," he said, "your child will be well cared for. You may safely leave her here with her own people. I don't need you, you don't need me. I have taped recordings of your little plots to get away from me—alone, and without your child—so you can't say I terminated this marriage. Never try to bribe a member of the Niadas staff, my dear, for, you see, aside from loyalty, I have more power or money than you could ever conjure. Since you have been my wife, there will be a proper settlement, and a proper divorce under the most instant and suitable conditions. So you may go home to resume your life a very rich woman."

"That suits me fine!" she said.

He left her room, hoping he would never see her again. He was more disturbed about what she had said about Chloë Metaxa than he was about his own situation. For again he thought of the young Greek girl on the island long ago who had stanched his wounds, saving him from death, while she herself was hemorrhaging from the violence of rape by the bearded men from the north. It would be more difficult to face Chloë on the trip to Rome than anything in life, because of this female infant in the nursery.

The meltemi was blowing, whipping a salt spray on his face as he escaped the house and walked out on the jetty by his Grumman widgeon landing. Caïques hauling produce from Santorini passed like a covey of seabirds on the glistening horizon. He thought of his beautiful villa, Kalliste, tumbled into the sea, and compared it with the wreckage of his marriage, which had given him hope for a while that he would die with a son to carry on his line. What good was it for him to have lived his vigorous and meaningful life, without his seed passing on the essence of his body and heart?

A twinge of pain attacked his chest. Instinctively he groped in his pocket for the nitroglycerin that he always kept in a little golden box. He popped one tablet under his tongue, and stood awaiting the release from pain. It soon came. How thoughtless of him to have started this new life with a common woman who had bilked him for a few weeks with an autumnal resurgence of his sexual powers. What a stupid escapade. . . . There was nothing he could do now. . . . But there was. And with a sense of guilt that lay heavily in his heart, he turned in his mind toward his lifeline, Chloë. She would be the only one who would take care of this life when he was gone, the one it would pain the most, and the one he should have married, even if war had deprived her of the right to motherhood.

His Grumman widgeon swooped in. Out of it stepped Ubaldo. For a few hours Niadas had forgotten this meeting, even the celebration preparing in Rome. But now, as he greeted his majordomo, he felt a weight lift from his shoulders. The man always had such understanding of his desire to re-create the golden legends of his country. He was a strange one, this hairless, yet aristocratic and handsome man.

The pilot stepped on the dock with a film canister in his hand. Niadas looked at it, pleased.

"Good, Stavros," he said. He turned to a deckhand who was securing the seaplane. "Take the film to the projection room, Hector. Come with me, Signore Ubaldo, and let us look at our little Alethea."

He led him to the villa.

"I will share this beauty with you, for you have seen her in the flesh. I am almost jealous of you. Is she as beautiful in life as she is on film?"

"She is a legend," said Ubaldo.

The servant passed drinks, and they settled back. Ubaldo was disturbed more than he cared to show at the thought of seeing his flesh-and-blood Phryne moving in a celluloid world, for he resented this duplication of the girl he worshiped in the flesh.

But as she came on the screen, and he saw the illumination of Max's direction, and the beauty of the photography, he thrilled. It was as if his dreams of the past, the books he had read, the art he had adored, the treasures he had unearthed, had come to an incredible being. His Phryne was walking and moving in a life he could live over and over again in this film.

He was startled at himself, but an emotion that overwhelmed him seemed to have taken over his senses.

Niadas, forgetting his personal sadness, watched her. When the reel was finished, he ordered it run again. While it was being rewound in the projection booth, he turned to his guest.

"I am very satisfied. You see why I am willing to put a fortune in this production?" he said. "Everyone thinks I am a fool. But a dream is a dream, Ubaldo. You know that. I am fortunate to be in the position to have the one whim of my life realized. To me it is far more exciting than building a museum, or founding a school, even though I've had my hand in those, too. This filmmaking is a fairly new art; criticized by some, because the larger part of it has been exposed to the whims of commercial men with questionable taste. But who ever mentions the mediocre painters, or cheap popular writers, in assessing the arts? We only hold up the exceptional as our cultural heritage. With a talent like Ziska, and the underestimated skills of the craftsmen of Hollywood and Rome, they have created the glory of the past. And with this magnificent girl, I feel it is my privilege to sponsor it. Perhaps it is all I shall ever be proud to have existed for."

As Niadas spoke, it seemed to Ubaldo a passionate outburst, as if he were seething within, and reaching out for some denied fulfillment. He wondered what disturbed him.

"I have watched them planning at the villa," Ubaldo said, "and marveled at the immense dedication to every small detail."

Niadas buzzed for the film to be run again. When it ended and the lights came on, it was startling to find themselves in the modern world.

They both sat silently a moment with their thoughts.

"One wishes, sometimes, that such a treasure should be protected from the world," said Ubaldo. "No doubt you saw the unfortunate publicity she garnered when she first came in conflict with Graves and the press."

"Yes," said Niadas, blinking, "and I was distressed until I analyzed it to myself. Then I was pleased. She became a blood-and-flesh woman. I'm glad she is not a puppet—glad that the obvious vulgarity of Graves irritated her."

Ubaldo thought him more than forgiving—more likely permissively enchanted. For these pictures in the papers had disturbed him deeply. But this was no time to discuss it. Fortunately, Niadas plunged on.

"Do you, knowing her, think she is up to the caliber of treasures that the Albini family gathered at the villa?"

"She is Phryne," Ubaldo blurted out. His emotions had betrayed him into mouthing the secret he thought he had locked in his heart.

Pericles jumped up.

"By God, you are right!" he said. "I wondered what seemed so familiar to me. I thought perhaps she had come out of the past world to me. Now I know. . . . How very astute of you."

Flushing, Ubaldo regretted the fact that this man could not know his proud heritage, and the fact that he himself had uncovered the statue from the earth where she had been sleeping, awaiting him.

"We will rejoice in this beauty, we shall drink deeply of the waters of Lethe—the forgetfulness of all sorrow and the remembrance of all joys."

Pain flitted across his face, and a faint smile replaced it. Ubaldo wondered why emotions were so close to the surface in this usually phlegmatic man.

"Indeed," he continued, "let us create new joys, a celebration such as our times have not known."

He opened up the French doors and looked out upon the turbulent sea.

"Even if it's the last thing I ever do."

He turned with a sudden smile to Ubaldo.

"With our expertise, it should be something to remember."

Later, the two dined on the sheltered terrace overlooking the sea. Ubaldo, looking at the Greek, could not help but admire him. He was a brigand, not an aristocrat, but he had a keen way about him, an economy of words, a rejoicing of the spirit, even though today there was a sadness in his eyes.

In the study, Ubaldo brought out sheaves of paper,

as carefully prepared as an archaeological report, detailing the master plans for the oracle festivities.

Niadas listened, agreed, amended, and lost himself in the re-creation of his dreams. At the end of the evening he said a warm good night. Ubaldo could see he was not only satisfied, but intrigued with the plans.

Ubaldo went to his guest room, his own mind occupied with his blueprints of the oracle party. Tonight he had met the Greek on grounds of common interests, gentleman to gentleman.

He was disturbed about his own emotions regarding Linda on film. He wanted to see more. Reflecting on her beauty, and thinking how he could arrange to have a portraitist paint a miniature of her, to own as a treasure, he was startled when the manservant who came in to turn down his bed and leave fruit and a carafe of water by his bedside paused to attract his attention.

"Forgive me," he said, "but we are very happy that you are here with our master on this sad day. You have lifted his spirits."

"Yes?" said Ubaldo, interested.

"Today his wife has given him his first child. Yes, unfortunately a daughter lies in the nursery. No son to carry his name."

Ubaldo saw the distress on the face of the servant. And knowing the Niadas pride, he understood why his host was so vehement about his fantasy—the great festival honoring, presumably his great friend Chloë Metaxa, but obviously the host of his dreams, Linda Barstow.

"And now, also," said the man, "this Martha Niadas has already ordered her trunks packed, and will leave as soon as she is able—alone."

The servant left, shaking his head sadly.

Ubaldo reflected that Niadas had not said a word. The only rejoicing in the house had been Linda Barstow—on film.

8

Along the wave-lapped shores of the Aegean Sea came the halcyon autumn days, combing the winds through the fingers of the mountaintops. Small flowers made a last small cry of color as they blossomed in sheltered valleys.

Demeter's treasures of spring and summer were usually stored against the sleeping winter. But some were not to stay. Bearing the insignia of the silver laurel wreath, the Delphic fleet of Pericles Niadas gathered the bounty from sea, earth, and sky.

Out of these far-flung places came bounty, to excite the whims of a young girl who would never realize their worth, from a frightened man who felt empty and must fulfill his desire for immortality.

Linda Barstow, whose only dream was to seduce a cockney actor; Pericles Niadas, who was disgusted with a marriage to a fading film star and birth of a daughter. Both coming together through a strip of celluloid. Hence this unusual commotion, disturbing the normal pace of the Hellenic world.

Skiffs, dories, launches, caïques, steam trawlers, drifters, seiners, packet boats, car ferries, yachts, inter-island schooners, mailboats, cruisers, tankers, dry-bottom cargo ships, hydroplanes, helicopters, amphibians, and freight and passenger planes rearranged schedules to gather and deliver their cargo.

Ships came from the northern Sporades, graveyard of Xerxes' fleet. They swept along the Anatolian coast, seizing harvests in the scattered god-fistfuls of the Aegean islands. Treasures were sought along the Peloponnesus, in the warm blasts of the Ionic islands, moving into the Roman world, passing the whirling Strait of Messina, legendary haunts of Scylla and Charybdis. Crafts cruised as far north as the fabled island of Circe, now no longer a mystic isle, but joined to the Pontine marshes by the alluvium of the Siste River.

Boats halted for donkey trains threading an endless chain along rocky bluffs, men stumbled, cargo-lamed, along quays and frail wharfs, balancing bruising burdens on their bones. Blue-lit harbors, sugar-frosting villages, olive-tree-crusted valleys, pine-crested mountains, and the pebbled berms of ancient roads surrendered treasures. Seas were speared, hooked, seined, and dredged methodically, from pale shadow-sanded blue-green shores, to the secret silences of purple waters beneath the swirling tides.

Tired men stood bereft, by empty stands, watching the wakes of ships, on which a year of their lives sailed away to an unknown place, while their pockets hung heavy with coin.

At Lemnos, a mailboat loaded dark-blue-velvet prunes, anchovies smoked with fragrant herbs, and the sharp-sweet liqueur mastic.

Honey was shipped from Kalymnos, Thassos, and Hymettus, every one of these places taking pride as purveyor of the best.

Two hydroplanes rendezvoused at Thassos, to transfer an iced cargo of golden Iranian caviar from the Shah of Iran's private store.

Plump olives, sweet chestnuts, and cases of ouzo were transported from caïques to an Athens-bound passenger boat at Lesbos.

At Skiathos, alongside a beach of stone pines, figs, almonds, and quince boarded an Italian freighter, wending homeward.

Oysters and lobsters packed in iced kegs were loaded at Salonika; the mail bound for Rome was thrown off. At Cos, watermelons and casks of wine were deck-loaded on a private yacht headed for Naples.

At Chios, white cheeses wrapped in herbs were

packed on an Italian cruiser Civitavecchia-bound, along with several barrels of fruit preserve, sugar-encrusted loukhoumi flavored with rose essence or violets, spiked with almonds, and a rare chewing mastic which was famed as the favorite of the women of the old Turkish harems.

From Cyprus came special barrels containing beccafica, tiny fig-picker birds preserved for a year in vinegar, to be finger-eaten delicately, bones and all.

Casks of a strong red wine from Crete were set into the hold of one of the old Liberty dry-cargo ships of the Niadas fleet. It also picked up blood oranges and tangerines, white mounds of Misithra cheese, raki, raisins, and quince jelly from Carpathos.

At Santorini, men loaded thick clusters of grapes packed in sawdust, fat juice-bleeding figs, bundles of fresh, fragrant herbs, sparkling wines, and succulent vegetables from the gardens of the Niadas estate. The repairs on the earthquake-gutted buildings seemed to be ignored, as if they were forgotten dust of the past, while a new life and strange exodus flowed in a constant stream away from disaster to some new lifespring.

The last ship to take on cargo was a cruise ship that had disgorged its human complement at Piraeus. Shipping notices announced that it was forced to take its next cruise five days late, due to engine repair. Passengers were diverted to another craft.

As soon as it was emptied, it had its holds and salons packed with produce from the mainland, gleaming fresh vegetables, preserves, and salted olives of various sorts from Amphissia, mountain cheese, a bakery full of breads made from the wheat of the Lake Kopais region, baked partridge from Thessaly wrapped in bacon and herbs, still cooking in their own stamnos, packed in cradles of hot rocks.

There were dozens of sheep from Thessaly, some to be roasted whole, or fileted for roasting, hare to be jugged, kegs of retsina, all wine and pine in fragrance. Mastakeria, Ionian jelly, ice-packed barrels of kaimaki, the sticky ice creams made under the shadow of the Parthenon.

Baklava, cakes of honey, flaky crust, ground almonds, and cloves, loukhoumades, halvah, pastries swimming in cheese, mountain butter, and honey. A white mastic jam from Thebes, bouquets of mountain mint, thyme, rosemary, oregano, sage, and laurel, dolmades, grapeleaf-wrapped bundles of cooked rice, herbs, and lamb. Greek cigars, and packets of pale strawlike Papostratos cigarettes.

As the cargoes were heaped upon docks, and loaded throughout the day and night, it seemed as if there would be no food left in Athens.

Filling the cabins of the passenger ship was a corps of waiters, sommeliers, chefs, sauciers, pantry men, bakers, and even some displaced skilled peasant women from the tavernas and *kaféneons* in out-of-the-way places.

One airplane, bearing the laurel insignia, made its last stop in the Greek hegira that moved toward its old enemy, Rome. It loaded on crushed ice at Corfu, and packed a fresh-caught cargo of the magnificent local lobster, to add to its garnering of red mullet, bream, tuna, jade-boned garfish, crabs, mussels, oysters, octopus, and squid. Baskets of fragrant wildwood strawberries, sykopita, fresh-baked fig cake, and Syphnic honeypie were piled in last.

Several days before the festival, an afternoon plane arrived. The nightclubs and theaters in Athens and Piraeus were stripped of entertainers, performances bought out, and the best of Greece went winging.

Every singer, dancer, entertainer, and musician of distinction would perform in an endless, glittering stream among the many tables set in the gardens, and small tavernas would be set among trees along walks.

◆◆◆◆◆◆◆◆

The day of the banquet approached. The *Oracle* company had worked well into the scenes with the principals, Max was engrossed in Linda's characterization, constantly refined his script, and the unit flowed into a rhythm of work that seemed more real than the interruptions of the world away from the stages.

From time to time he heard reflections of the great arrangements being made at the villa. Once or twice he complained that more attention was being paid to the damned banquet than the picture, which was beginning to look like a small-budget affair in contrast. So it was secretly decided in whispering conferences among Leslie, Claudia, and Linda not to bring up the party in front of him during working hours. But they all planned costumes, hairdresses, and surprises. Claudia shopped in Via Condotti and bought a magnificent silver frame, and Linda selected her favorite colored photograph as the oracle, dressed in a white chiton, her hair wreathed in gold and silver leaves, her face partially shadowed by the mysterious vapors of the adytum. It was to be set in Niadas' guest suite with a note that he would find on his arrival.

Strange, thought Ubaldo, that Niadas, having given up his master suite to Linda, would return as a guest. The rooms he would occupy, having served high officials and kings who had accepted his hospitality, were on the upper landing at the other side of the double stairs that flanked Phryne. But no matter how elegant his baroque rooms were, with their priceless furnishings, Ubaldo knew his thoughts would have to be in his own rooms, even as Ubaldo's had been before this, when he abandoned his villa to the Greek.

◆◆◆◆◆◆◆◆

Pericles Niadas sat in his study. Before him was a paper from his doctor in Rome. He stared at it, and slumped.

No longer was he what he had been. Now he knew that the long path he had followed to the top of his world was finishing; for the first time, he felt defeat. The man he was must be remembered in the past; the swift-moving mountain fighter, courier for Greek intelligence, was gone. The man who battled great odds after the double tragedy of war against the enemy, and then war against his brother, was not there. He had struggled to resurrect the remnants of his fleet. He had battled long to establish dummy corporations, to buy Liberty ships, to make contracts with rich Arab nations for oil shipments and franchises; the man who had paved the way for the golden Greeks was gone. Instead, a weary middle-aged man arose, his breathing stentorian.

Now that he reflected on himself and his plight, the drive that had fetched him millions of dollars had vanished. He tried to analyze what had sent him on his singular path. And now that it didn't matter, he saw it clearly. Lost in the center of his philoxenia, his Greek desire for respect, admiration, and kudos, was a measuring machine that computed in spite of himself. Whenever he had met anyone, some pangenetic gemmule in his head flashed an analysis of the worth, homology, and possible alliance to his needs.

But now his agile mind rewrote the script. The fates had organized him; all he could do was make a satisfactory *pou sto* within the short time that was left.

As a younger man, he would have questioned the doctor's decisions and sought other experts, but he knew that no great physician would be such a fool as to tell the richest man on earth that soon he was doomed to die unless it was written in the sky.

For years, although he had suffered an eternal nostalgia for the past, and perpetual haranguing with himself, he had been a dedicated hedonist, excusing his personal whims of luxury with the alibi that he was creating employment, sponsoring many crafts, and aiding a growing economy with his personal expansion of power.

Although he had given fortunes, built many jewel-encrusted shrines, and worshiped at the great dome where St. Sophia became the ancestress of the hundreds of cubicles erected in the iconic image, all celebrating personal victories over death and disaster, he had not been fulfilled.

Like many of his kind, he had suffered from a loneliness and yearning of the spirit wherever he was.

There was no home for him in his vast shipyards at Piraeus and Melos, in his cement and pumice industries, in the rich vineyards of Santorini, in the tobacco warehouses at Kavella, or his sponge fleets of Kalymnos; instead, he sought an echo of what had been.

A thousand years after the battle of Salamis, the oracle at Delphi gave forth a cry of despair, and spoke no more. But to Pericles Niadas, from Delphi to Leros there was the faint taunting cry of the lyre of Apollo, born on a wind that laughed at a modern world.

From Athens to Zia he was challenged by a wail for aid to the disillusioned spirit of the postwar world. Niadas wanted to reclaim a mystique, a beauty that he had prayed could be. Perhaps because his own personal life had crumbled to ashes in his wretched marriage, he was startled by the vision of beauty when he saw the film test of Linda Barstow. And when he read the inspired script of Maximilian Ziska, he felt that at last a dream had fallen into his hands, which might be made real, to exist after he was gone, to prove that he had properly used his wealth and power to create what had lain dormant in his heart and mind—a legend come true of his country, and the spirit that still dwelled in it.

The last thing he possessed, the Greek *philotemo,* love of one's honor, respect for one's place in society, and obligation not to lose face, even in death, motivated him. He would be forgiven for his vulgar marriage to Martha Ralston and the girl infant who lay in his nursery, a pitiful heiress for a great fortune.

The wind was lowering. . . . Good. A phone call on the ship-to-shore line from the yacht *Circe* informed him that his seaplane was en route to pick him up. In a moment he had concluded his arrangements.

His valet appeared with a suitcase and an overnight bag, and his ever-present attaché case. Niadas unlocked a vitrine and examined the treasures within carefully.

On the top shelf, brilliantly lighted, lay an octopus of beaten gold. Folded into the writhing tentacles were suckers of fabled matched pearls and uncut emeralds. Rare plunder from a Mycenaean tomb, it was the treasure of his collection, having been appraised at a half-million dollars. He wrapped it in his handkerchief and put it in the attaché case. He insisted on carrying it himself. The seaplane landed beside the spidery dock, and he settled in; soon he would be transferred to the *Icarus,* and would be on his way to Rome, to his favorite villa, to Phryne, and to the beautiful young girl who had given him the courage to face each day, nourished by her transcendent beauty.

The only thing that sickened him was that soon Chloë Metaxa would be with him. She must not know, at this festive time, what his doctor had revealed. He had not seen her in the several weeks since his daughter was born, and he would have to face the masked sadness of her face, as if she had erred, not being able to give him a son herself.

9

Chloë Metaxa was seated in the main cabin of the *Icarus* when Pericles came up the ladder. She noted the stoop of his shoulders, and she knew by the color of his face that he had had a heart attack. As in times before, she made a silent prayer for him. There was hardly any of him that she did not know well, although she owned no part of him save the great relationship he had given her, as a *Koumbaro* would have for his godchild, which had bound them for over a decade.

He sat down on the lounge of the private plane heavily, dark glasses masking his eyes.

"You heard?" he said, speaking in English, as they did whenever the Greek steward was around. "The marriage is finished."

The man set out ouzo, glasses, a plate of mezothakes and went forward.

"I heard," said Chloë.

"I am relieved that Martha has gone away. The divorce is arranged. The child, of course, is with me, and will be well cared for."

"I will always care for your daughter. You know."

She wondered if he could read her eyes and her voice, he was so bound with her life. If he did, he would know that in her heart, although she disliked herself for it, she was glad that Martha Ralston had not given him a son. And she would always grieve that she, Chloë, had not been able to have been his love, his wife, and the mother of his child.

"Now I will never have a son," he said. "My own name will die with my flesh."

He seemed shrunken to her, defeated. He finished his milky ouzo as she peered below at the fast-moving, dome-shaped cumulus clouds. He settled back and closed his eyes.

About time, she thought, to forget the past, to make other decisions. Only his dream of creating his masterpiece of ancient Greece brought her to Rome to this swelling-breasted American film child.

Whatever she was, this Linda Barstow could not be worse than Martha Ralston. And when she thought of her, she thought of the first day she had seen Pericles Niadas, who seemed more dead than alive. Even then, like an evil omen, she had pulled the picture of Martha Ralston out of his pocket. Was it more than ten years ago?

As in many transient moments, her memory snatched back at the time she had been in complete control of Niadas' life, the hours that had fashioned her own life.

◆◆◆◆◆◆◆◆

The young girl and her mother lay in the cave, as the low gray fingers of the dawn reached Santorini from the sea below, and made long shadows of the dead men, the fierce marauders from the north.

They had been held hostage and raped. As the men left, a hidden avenger in the cliffs had shot them, some falling at the mouth of the cave, others shot down as they prepared to launch boats in the sea below, with their cargo of children stolen from the village.

She gasped as she saw the stream of dark blood flowing from her mother, who turned her pale face to her daughter, reached her hand out, and gently touched her.

"Mother," said Chloë.

Her mother tried to rise. She fell back.

"Hide from the ones who killed our men. They know who we are, and they will still avenge. Never say your father's name again."

Those were her last words. Her breathing was fast and shallow, and finally faded like a gentle west wind.

The girl lay quietly. She could feel the blood seeping along her legs, and the pain clenching at her groin.

Soon she would be dead, too. She longed for it.

She was awakened by the sweet scent of sage on a fire. A man sat facing the opening of the cave. A British Enfield rifle gleamed across his knees. He was dressed in black, and his longish hair hung on his bent neck. She could strike at him with a stone and bash in his skull.

She picked up a rock, and inched forward cautiously. Her hand was raised for her attack when he toppled over as if her blow had struck. She waited for a moment, her breath rasping in her throat, and then turned him over. He was wounded, a deep gash between his ribs oozing blood. He must have fainted as he sat guard.

In a rucksack by his side she found a pamphlet printed in Greek, a pencil, a bottle of Metaxas brandy, a stub of cheese, and a heel of bread.

Panic was replaced by reason. This man was a Greek; he must have been the one who shot the Reds. He had saved her, and if she did not help him, he would die.

She warily crept out of the cave. The invaders all had gone. Hundreds of feet below lay the calm blue-green sea. No one was in sight. Pulsing with pain, she left the wild rocky glen and walked stiffly over the cliff-edge steps to the cluster of deserted white sugar-icing houses. She must do as her mother had taught her. She found a small earthenware bowl in an empty house. She moved laboriously among the shrubs gathering spiderwebs. From a garden she plucked oleander branches, and let the milky juice drop into the nest of fine-spun silken webs.

She limped back to the cliff and the labyrinth of the cave.

The stranger still lay unconscious. Cautiously she moved him on his back, bathed his wounds, and embrocated his body with her medication, kneading the squamous clots of dried blood, so they would dam up the little life that was still in him.

She washed off his hot, sweating face with the hem of her skirt as the night passed. She relieved his pockets of a goat's-foot knife and a packet of currency, and unbuckled his worn ammunition belt. Folded in his breast pocket, and encrusted in blood, was a picture, one of the dozens that had floated down from an airplane one sunstruck day. Strangely, the same that her dead brother had carried. It was a photograph of a woman in a bathing suit. It was the American motion-picture star Martha Ralston. She remembered how, months ago, they had all laughed at the propaganda of an American star dropping from the sky, when what they needed was food and medicine.

Many of the men had carried them as a talisman. Little good it had done. All of them who had pocketed them were dead. Annoyed, she put the picture back in the man's pocket.

At dawn the sweet fragrance of a cleansing breeze arose as the day came alive with swiftness.

The rest of the day, she dragged the dead men from the mouth of the cave, and shoved them, one by one, over the lip of the cliff, where they fell into the boiling surf below.

"May the earth not receive your body!" she cursed, as each one fell below.

She washed out the bowl and collected water at the seeping spring in the glen and cleaned the man's wound. When he still did not respond to her attentions, she took a Kalymnos sponge from her mother's bundle, moistened it with brandy from the bottle of Metaxas, and squeezed it in his mouth. He came to life with a shudder.

He tensed against her, and she had to hold him tightly, wrenching her own sore body to keep him from tearing open his wound.

His eyes opened, and he stared at her, a slip of a girl who stared back with wide-spaced eyes.

From then on the cave became her dwelling, her place, for they had both come from death to life in it. And this man who would die without her gave her a *pou sto* to go on, with all her family dead.

"Oriste," she said to him with dignity, as any Greek woman would. Make yourself at home . . . come in. . . .

As he came into reality, his lips parted with a faint smile.

"I am not yet gathering letters from the dead."

He spoke few words to her, but sometimes she could see him watching her reflectively, and several times he smiled and patted her shoulder as she tended his wounds. He seemed to live in a world of deep thought. He brought the stub of pencil out of his pocket, and scribbled innumerable notes on pieces of scrap paper she filched for him in her meanderings.

She gathered cooking vessels, fetched water, scraped up wheat from threshing floors, garnered a little harvest of half-dried figs and grapes, discovered salted fish in deserted cupboards, and found a treasure hoard of lentils and honey. She stoked a filtered fire in the back of the cave, and stirred a caldron constantly, making nourishment from scraps.

One day a patrol of armed men passed by the entrance of the cave. She prayed silently, and got the man to his feet, helping him to hide behind the boulders. The men halted, talked, peered into the cave, obviously looking for someone. They decided to move on.

Then the girl knew it would be necessary for them to abandon their cave. She helped him pack his rucksack.

They awaited the night. She shouldered his Enfield rifle, he took the rucksack, and with her support they climbed out of the honeycomb cave, through the glen. Resting often, they followed a footpath among some ruins. Before dawn they stopped to rest before they entered the sugar-cube town of Thera.

She reconnoitered into town while he sat on the white steps of a mariner's chapel and watched sunrise reveal the bubbling caldron of underwater volcanic fissures in the sea below.

When she returned, he was breathing hard, his face tight with pain. She uncorked his bottle of Metaxas and handed it to him.

He drank from the bottle, wiped the neck with his

sleeve, and handed it to her as if she were another soldier.

She took a sip ceremoniously, relishing the moment. It was one she would always remember, a bittersweet brew, an astringent bistort; from then on she was destined to love him, to forget she was a girl of fourteen, and feel she was a complete woman.

As if he read her thoughts, he spoke.

"Perhaps someday we will make a heaven of this hell, when this is all ended. Perhaps, little *koré*, you and I will bring sons out of this place of death. That is, when you are a woman."

I am a woman . . . I am, she longed to say.

"You have given me the rest of my life. You will have anything you want. You will go to the finest schools."

He stopped short and looked at her.

"We will plan a great dynasty. . . . Although I do not even know your name."

She remembered what her mother had said. Too many knew and hated her family name. This stranger did not have to know who she was. She could put him in jeopardy.

She glanced at the bottle that she was still holding.

"Metaxas," she said, her eyes flickering.

She corrected, to make it seem true. "Metaxa."

He glanced at the bottle.

"As you say . . . Metaxa. A good name."

She did not know his name, nor did she ask. But she knew he was a man of importance.

They cautiously walked through the deserted white streets of Thera, the windows shuttered against the dust whirls of the meltemi. This man was in hiding, a rich catch for any Communist band that might be marauding. She led him to a blue vaulted underground room that had once been part of the old Venetian town of Skaros, and settled him on a straw pallet.

Away from him she absorbed herself in the busy life of the town, hoping people would not suspect her secret life. She worked, winnowing, gathering crops, weaving, cleaning, and nursing the old and sick. She was another thin sparrow of a young girl, her head bound tightly with ragged black cloth, another laborer where manpower was so short, striding with the awkward agility of a goat, sparse, unadorned, and seemingly born to serve.

But the villagers knew her secret.

One day an old sponge fisherman who had been a friend of her father came to her.

"I have followed you in the night. You are as kinfolk to this man you tend."

She was startled, but she knew she must answer.

"We gave each other life," she said.

"It is something, then, to have in your hands the life of Pericles Niadas."

She hid her surprise. Then she felt she had known it a long time. Her own father had worked in his dockyards, the other side of the island, and as a child she had been shown a picture of him in a paper.

"Fate spins the thread and cuts it," she said.

The village was both proud and fearful of what could happen to them if Niadas were discovered in their midst. Sometimes she would arise in the night and see a sentry standing guard on their little vaulted house perched on the cliff.

She became his messenger. Now at nights groups of men came to confer with him. They met in a fraternity of plotting. Sabotage and diversions, and the constant movement of food and supplies to vital points of defense, were ordinary conversation.

She knew Niadas depended upon her and trusted her. She was anonymous, patient, and never tiring.

So when he went on a mission to Crete, their neighboring island, sixty miles to the south, in a battered fishing caïque, she was taken along. Niadas established her as a *Dienstmädchen* at a German officers' club. In her unobtrusive way she became an important courier for Greek intelligence.

It was here she first learned what it meant to play a role, to bury the *philotemo,* her native Greek pride, and be the stupid slavey. Germans came and went, Italians moved in, and still she worked at varied roles, protected by her chameleonlike talents.

The day the struggle was ended, Niadas called her to his quarters on one of his freighters moored in the harbor down the hundreds of steps of Santorini. She found him in the master's cabin, in an elegance of polished woods and brasses. She sat, ill-at-ease on a fine leather chair, facing his desk.

"*Koroula mou,*" he said, "your apprenticeship is ended. You will go to my house in Athens and accept the place in my life you have earned. There will be several years of schooling. Then we will make our life together."

Her heart pounded so that she felt he must see the pulse at her throat. She wanted to throw herself in his arms at once, but her pride made her know she was not yet ready to be a *kyria* of so great a man.

He came around to her, took her in his arms, and kissed her brow.

"I am proud to have you in my life. But now I must leave you, for no longer am I an individual alone. I am part of a greater pattern. You will go to Athens and take your rightful place in my house."

For the first time she faced the confining restrictions of a society that was not based on daily survival. She was appalled at the richness and waste of food, many servants, and unending luxuries. Theater and music became her escape, and she devoured books, thinking all the time she must be a woman of exceptional education to be worthy of her future with Niadas.

She was groomed, gowned, and admired; suddenly those about her discovered that she had beautifully spaced gray-green eyes, a straight, classic nose, and abundant, glossy hair. It sickened her, save for her desire to be elegant for Niadas.

Rarely in residence, he was busy resurrecting the remnants of his fleet, establishing dummy corporations to buy Liberty ships from the United States, and augmenting contracts with the new rich Arab nations, for shipment and franchises of oil, refrigeration, and air-conditioning of government buildings.

Niadas' life as a wealthy young man had been forgotten during the war years. Now he was the apotheosis of the best in Greek men, the new breed. Hero, statesman, and tycoon, a kinetic force for his country, evolving the new image of Greece, and shaping his own burgeoning destiny.

As Chloë entered her eighteenth year, she was put through the rigors of a complete physical examination, in preparation for her betrothal to Niadas.

She insisted that she see the findings. For her there would be no children. Her lacerated breasts would never give milk to an infant; her destroyed body must be relieved of its painful flow and ebb of womanhood, along with the scar tissues and displacement of one night of mass rape.

So there was no reason for Niadas to mate with her; she could not bear him the sons he wanted. She could not found a new dynasty. She knew now that she could never be his wife.

She threw a cloak over her silk gown and walked out of the fine estate in the Kolanaki, down into the seething hubbub and humanity of the Plaka. Above, the Acropolis in its ageless nocturnal dignity seemed to refute the truth that so many young men had so recently fallen prey to snipers within its marbled, once sacrosanct glory.

She listened to the babble of voices, the singing in the tavernas, the pluck and whine of string and woodwind, and watched the *seryani,* the mass wanderings of the young and old.

She saw a group of young women as they came out of a factory, squinting into the evening lights. Their heads all turned in wistful unison as a young couple, arm-in-arm, sauntered by, to disappear into one of the *kaféneons,* which poured music and laughter like a gay banner into the night.

Out of the depths of her own grief, Chloë felt their sadness, a mass emotion, as dark and breathless as the evening heat. Thus she would have been, had she not met Niadas. None of them had a *prika;* no father, brother, or family existed to protect them or to give them a dowry. Fruitful or not, there would be few marriages among them. They would work for bread alone until they were all gorgons.

She walked along the streets until her feet bled in her custom-made shoes. She removed them and climbed up the rock to the Parthenon.

It was dark. Sounds drifted upward, a babble that would have sounded the same in the age of another Pericles. But she knew she would not play Aspasia to this one. Children laughed and played. The songs of desire, love, courting, infants crying, and snatches of lullabies.

She sat underneath the porch of the caryatids. Had the stone maidens waited here so long for her to come and throw her problems at their feet?

Hours later, she sat at her desk. By the dawn she had put her message on paper, coldly and logically.

She was sorry, she wrote; although her heart was breaking, she realized now she would have to follow her own path. Now she needed to sing, to dance, to act, to find life for herself after so much sorrow. She could not bargain for an enclosed life. She knew he would understand.

Along with her letter, which he received on his yacht at Cannes, Niadas also received the doctor's prognosis.

He understood.

A great burden was lifted from his shoulders. He would have honorably paid for his life with his life. Now he did not have to do it. Ashamed of himself, he admitted secretly that he wanted a more spectacular beauty to be the mother of his children.

He wrote her that he was grieved she did not want to marry him; he would always consider her as his own, and do anything in his power to see she had the training she needed.

But as time passed, he was dismayed when she chose to be one more dancer in Dora Stratou's dancing group, shocked when she sang in the streets to raise money for her charities—dowries for young women without families, clothes for infants, training schools for young orphaned girls. He was secretly delighted when she became a talented actress.

Little by little her love for him seemed to become a living family relationship. She laughed at his amorous escapades; that's what one expected of a man.

But when he fell under the spell of Martha Ralston, she was bewildered. She was outraged, and felt duped. For the first time it entered her mind that if she had been a wiser person in her youth, she would have married Niadas, and arranged for the birth of his children elsewhere, to be raised in the protection of their mutual love and prestige.

Returning, with a start, to the present, on the airplane she saw that Niadas had fallen asleep. His mouth slacked open; she recognized his weariness, and something she had not known in him, defeat. She looked upon him with pity.

Before they landed at Ciampino Airport, she carefully made up her face, braided the crown of hair into a coronet above her wide-eyed face, and donned a simple dress with its girdle of laurel leaves. She would make a triumphant entrance as the leading actress of Greece, with her sponsor, Pericles Niadas.

As Chloë peered out at the apricot, scarlet, and russet pattern of Rome, bisected by the silver Tiber, she knew what her next move would be.

It would be aimed once again at the tantalizing image of stardom. Time was passing. If she did not hit it soon, she would never have the idolatry and cachet of stellar significance, but instead presently become one of those gifted character actresses playing Hecuba and Medea for the tourists at Epidaurus in the summer theater.

The fire and fury of an unexpected sexual encounter was what she needed. Life had dealt her no reason for permanence. And it was time for a new love affair.

All her mature life she had sought men of consequence to be her lovers. It had been her way of showing Niadas she was of value as a woman.

"It is time," she said.

He arose and stood by her side. Like men of wealth and power, he moved without encumbrance.

They stepped out into Ciampino Airport. An array of photographers stood, flash cameras in hand.

Chloë licked her lips, and stood, head erect. A curl strayed over her brow. She smiled, a dazzling transformation coming over her actress face. She was Greece personified, accompanied by the most important man of her country, making a courteous bow in the direction of expectant Rome.

10

◆◆◆◆◆◆◆◆

Claudia and Linda, watching the incredible activities at the Villa Madonna della Rosa, were delighted to notice that Jessica was too busy with the Roman society she had invited to the bash to take much part in their activities.

Having realized that Ubaldo was a master at arrangements, she left the party to him. Then, dashing off to get a set of individual false eyelashes put on in Rome, she informed Claudia that she knew she could take care of Linda's wardrobe with a whole studio staff at her disposal, and left them to their own devices.

Linda led Claudia to the amphitheater. They had planned to show it to Niadas as the last surprise of the evening. Linda would do her reading from Sophocles. Ubaldo had arranged with the studio electricians to set up a lighting effect. As Linda stepped on thc stage, a pin spot would reveal her white face in the darkness, and lights would slowly spread to reveal her whole figure in her simple white chiton. Claudia had rehearsed her for the lighting cues, and with a thrill, realized that she alone, a small figure on the dark stage, which was edged with magnificent banks of roses, would make the scene memorable.

"He'll never forget it, and it's just far enough away, ducks," said Claudia, "to get away from all that music and screaming of the *finocchi* that your mother's dragging in. Niadas will no doubt be enchanted to get away from all that crap!"

"I'm getting scared," said Linda. "What if he doesn't like me?"

Claudia laughed.

"Of all the things I've ever worried about in my life," she said, "my dear child, this is the last. So let's just run through this once more. I don't want any Hollywood Boulevard in your diction."

"Let's take a look at the action," said Linda. "I know my lines. . . . Please!"

She wore slacks and a gingham shirt.

"Just don't let Pericles Niadas meet you in that outfit, or the game is lost," said Claudia. "Remember, you're his Greek wet dream."

"What's that?" asked Linda.

"Button my lip," said Claudia.

Ubaldo came by, followed by a phalanx of men moving trestle tables. He smiled at them.

"Will you let us know when Niadas is arriving?" said Claudia. "I wouldn't much like to have him meet my niece looking like Huckleberry Finn."

Ubaldo smiled.

"I shall receive a phone call from Ciampino Airport, and will alert you," he said.

As he moved down the path, Claudia stared after him.

"Even in an old jacket, he looks elegant," she said.

"He's a prince," said Linda in such a tone that Claudia turned and looked at her quizzically.

Since the party was on Saturday, which was not a shooting day, most of the technical staff was free to be at the villa, and eager to get in on the excitement, planning makeup, hairdresses, decorations, and arranging electrical effects and sound systems in the villa grounds.

The day was flawless, and already police, clear to the Appian Way, were arranging security against crashers and uninvited flocks of photographers.

A corps of Ubaldo's skilled footmen and butlers set up the tables in gleaming white and gold along the marble loggias of the gardens. They overflowed onto silken Persian rugs that had been laid on the green lawns.

Two curators from the Niadas museum staff checked

out each item as the centers of the tables were ornamented with ancient cult vases and Tanagra figurines. Florists and gardeners followed, lacing them with clusters of velvety grapes and fragrant fresh-cut flowers and fern from the Italian gardens and estate greenhouses.

Candles and wax-filled bronze urns were set about to light the evening scene. Electricians labored rearranging wiring in the trees, blowing out fuses, and causing general consternation at the last moment, as they disturbed the refrigeration devices in the kitchens and pantries. Hurried calls from Ubaldo, with threats of violence, brought out the department of power, including top officials who obviously came along to gape. Order was made out of chaos at the moment that ice sculptured figures of the pediment of the Acropolis were threatened with extinction in the refrigeration room, where artists sent in from Paris were at work sculpturing with hot irons, dressed in fleece jackets.

All Rome babbled. Jewels had been taken out of vaults; there were two spectacular robberies involving prominent courtesans who announced they had planned to wear their jewels to the affair. It became a common gamine's game on losing a pin or ribbon to say, "Oh, I intended to wear it to Perry's party at the Villa Madonna della Rosa!"

Every woman, in spite of her shape or age, wanted her peplos to be exclusive, her sandals the most jeweled, her hairdress the most towering. Friendships were made and lost, courtships launched and forgotten, bedmates exchanged, and business deals based on an invitation to the Niadas gala.

Jessica was in her glory. It was stunning to have Rome figuratively at her feet. She invited everyone who had hosted her in Rome and many who were anxious to get on the bandwagon. Even those with papal titles were willing to forget she was not only an American but also a Protestant. She reached the sublime pinnacle where she had snubbed a few social leaders who had snubbed her. She had even received a few nods at the opera from royalty and one deposed king.

The guest list had grown to 750, and now Grace's press list had added sixty more.

So the press had come winging in from all the important spots: Philadelphia, Boston, Chicago, Cleveland, New York, New Orleans, Mexico City, Dallas, Kansas City, Los Angeles, London, Buenos Aires, Paris, Brussels, Madrid, and Athens, of course, to see the mighty glamour of Pericles Niadas in action.

And since Martha Ralston had just arrived in London before taking the *Queen Mary* home to Hollywood, gossip was rampant about his next move.

Niadas had flown in twenty evzones, great strapping fellows over six feet tall, who were bristlingly moustached and garbed in stocking caps, fustanellas, tights, and pom pon shoes, all a burly bundle of good-looking legs, muscle, and costume to astonish both men and women. They stood at proud attention inside the villa driveway.

"Lord," said Effie, peering out the driveway, "I never saw so many big bouncers in my life, nowhere!"

Linda, looking out on the order forming out of chaos, began to be disturbed.

Was the party really for her, for Chloë Metaxa, or for the vanity of this absent tycoon? How could a man give a party that cost hundreds of thousands of dollars, and walk in on it like he was another guest?

And now that she was facing it, and the unknown Chloë Metaxa, she wondered how she would make herself seem conspicuous and startling to the sophisticated society of Rome.

She began to fear her guests more than she had feared her work on the studio stages, for there she had Max and Claudia to guide her, and here, as a personality among personalities, she was on her own. She felt a little queasy, and was sorry she had started the whole enterprise. Maybe the most spectacular thing she could do would be to miss it. It had all become so much larger than the classic feast she and Ubaldo had dreamed about, that it was staggering.

Max, embroiled only in his picture, complained that the banquet took up too much of everyone's time.

It was Claudia who placated him. She walked him away from the confusion of the gardens surrounding the villa to the amphitheater.

"Look, Max," she said, holding his hand, "can you imagine the fantasy of Linda, in the flesh, standing on that stage in the beautiful night, reciting Sophocles to the man who is making your dream come true? This is really what it's all about. It's to be her surprise. No one knows about it. Not even Jessica."

He took her hand.

"I guess all of the drama is not on my set," he said. "If you say it's all right, I trust you. It means a lot to you, doesn't it?"

"How could it not?" she said. "After all, she's the last of us."

He watched an electrician who was lining up the spots for the lighting of the stage.

"Perhaps," he said, "when the nonsense of this is all over, and my picture finished, we might charter a Greek caïque, and find our own paradise through the Greek islands. Would you?"

She smiled up at him.

"This is the first proposition I've had for years, and I accept."

Late in the afternoon Claudia set out her strategy with Linda.

"We can see Niadas and Chloë from your terrace here as they drive in and step out of their car. But they must not see us," she said.

"Why not?" said Linda. "I thought I'd have Ubaldo give me some roses, and I'd greet them with a bouquet."

"Never," said Claudia.

Linda glanced at her, surprised. She had expected her to be merry and impulsive about the party, as she had at the Cavendish. But of course, it was not that way; in London she had been under the euphoria of the grape; now she was more a general rallying her forces.

"Presentation is half the victory," said Claudia. "You must not meet Perry Niadas until you descend that staircase in full costume after the festival is well under way. Ah, I remember once when Gloria Swanson was the reigning queen of Famous Players Paramount. We were both in such competition! It was at a Mayfair dance, the social event of the season. Well, we both waited it out to make the final grand entrance, and outsat each other so long that when I made my appearance, the band was playing 'Good Night, Sweetheart.' Of course, we won't go that far. But he must see you for the first time as his dream of ancient Greece. That's really what he's paying for."

"I guess you're right," said Linda. "After all, Max did that with me on the set. Nobody met me until I was in costume."

Claudia stood off and looked at her niece.

"Now, we begin with your makeup. You certainly don't need much, but I'll make you up myself, none of those troglodyte numbers that irked Orville. You must be a little more sophisticated tonight. And the hair! That can make you real, or a hairdresser's catalog. There is a magic. Garbo liked to do hers herself, for her own look."

She raised Linda's blond hair off her shoulders, twisting it in a thick knot on top of her head. A few curls fell on the nape of her neck.

"Oh, god," said Claudia, "you couldn't pay enough to have this happen if you had all the money in the world. I'll pin it up like this, twist it securely with several pearl pins, and let the rest just do what comes naturally."

"What about my dress?" asked Linda. "I wear a lot of white in the picture, and they sent over my wardrobe. I guess everybody's told to wear white. Of course, I'd rather just look like Phryne. Nude."

She struck a pose and smiled.

"You would!" said Claudia. "In my day, I went to a few affairs that would have been suitable. But not now, and not for a couple of years. Right now, dear, the best thing you can do is to be Niadas' dream, not a nightmare. If your sainted mother tries to introduce him to her circle, or someone attempts to interview him about

Martha Ralston's decampment, that'll be it. Let's just try to remember we're here to make him happy. After all, we're making a picture on his bank account."

"Help me choose the right costume," said Linda.

"They're all wearing white, you say?" said Claudia.

"Yes," said Linda, "it's an all-white bash."

"That's what they think!" said Claudia.

"I wish David was here," said Linda. "It would be great to have him backing me up."

"He's in Africa again somewhere, no doubt hiding in the bush. I guess the film he's making is his alibi for avoiding this party. He's not much for confrontations."

For the first time Linda brought up a delicate subject.

"I might as well tell you, I heard some people gossiping on the set that Mom was Fergus Austin's mistress. Maybe that's why his son avoids us. Is that true?"

Claudia froze; it was no time to open up this Pandora's box.

"I wouldn't know," she said. "I was in London when your mother worked at Titan."

"And I noticed Fergus Austin didn't show up," said Linda.

Claudia laughed. "Fergus isn't happy anyplace but Hollywood. His favorite landscape is that back lot he started over forty years ago. Who needs him! Let's think about the present."

There was the faint ring of a house telephone. Linda picked it up. Ubaldo informed her that Mr. Niadas was on his way in the driveway from the Appian Way.

They both rushed out on the balcony, peering out between bougainvillea blossoms. A silver Lancia pulled into the driveway.

Linda watched a slim, dark-haired man step out. Of course, he was Niadas. She'd seen pictures of that craggy, handsome face. He turned to put his hand out as Chloë Metaxa stepped out of the car.

Linda studied her, the simple girdled gown, no wrap, the hair braided across the crown of her head, the wide-eyed face, illuminated by a smile as she took Niadas' hand. The very gentle way they held hands a moment, and the authoritative manner in which they strode to the marble steps, spoke more clearly of their kinship than any words could have expressed.

After they vanished inside, Claudia and Linda looked at each other.

"Well," said Claudia, "that is elegance. She is what I would call a worthy adversary. Study her."

As she looked at Linda, she saw a shadow of fear on her face. How could a young girl compete with a classic actress and beloved national personality like Chloë Metaxa?

"Don't fret," said Claudia. "Just remember, you look like no one else in the world. And remember that long parade of gifted ancestors who were waiting for you to claim your place."

She stood a little straighter, and chose the moment to make one of her expressive gestures. Chloë Metaxa had triggered her, too.

"Now, have Effie shampoo your hair and towel-dry it. I'll return after I get dressed; you know, it takes me a bit long to put on the old face, and we'll get you done up by the best makeup artist in the world—me."

Linda smiled.

"And if your knees shake," said Claudia, "just think of your father and how proud he'd be of you."

♦♦♦♦♦♦♦♦

Linda stood nude in the dressing room, drying her hair. Effie had been sent to the garden to bring her some fresh white roses. The door was open, and she looked up.

There stood Chloë Metaxa. Her eyes opened wide as she looked at the girl.

"Oh, forgive me," she said in her deep voice. "The door was open. I thought . . ."

Linda noticed she had a silken scarf with something in it in her hands.

"Effie must have left it open," said Linda. "You're Chloë Metaxa, aren't you?"

"Yes," said Chloë. "I have something for you. Pericles asked me to give it to you himself. . . . You are beautiful, as I knew you would be."

Linda sat down on the hassock in front of her dressing table.

"Thank you," she said, "but I'm scared. . . . What if Mr. Niadas doesn't like me?"

Chloë laughed. Linda thought she'd never heard anything like it. Even her Aunt Claudia didn't have the arresting musical voice of this woman.

"Don't be afraid," said Chloë. "Pericles Niadas, as well as myself, has never seen anyone like you. And he is in love with you already."

She sighed. Linda smiled and rubbed her long curly hair. This woman made her feel as if she'd known her always.

"Oh, if he only had seen you," said Chloë, "he wouldn't have fallen for that plastic bitch Martha. He would have known how fake she was."

"I hear she's run away."

"Yes," said Chloë, "and left him a puny little girl child. How he wanted a son!"

With the innocence of a young girl, Linda looked up. "Why didn't you marry him?"

"Because," said Chloë, "I loved him too much. . . . I . . . I can't have children."

Linda looked at her in surprise.

"Don't let it bother you," said Chloë. "That was long ago. I love him in a different way. I just want him to have everything I couldn't give him. . . . Oh, I'm a poor messenger. The reason I came is to give you this."

She handed her a note and the folded scarf.

Linda opened the letter, written on parchment stationery with the silver-laurel-leaf insignia. It read tersely, "To my sibyl. Pericles Niadas."

She unfolded the scarf, and the ancient golden octopus with pearl tentacles and two uncut emerald eyes was revealed.

"Oh!" she said. "How beautiful!"

"Beautiful!" said Chloë. "It is worth a king's ransom. I do not put a price on things, but a museum with five hundred thousand dollars to pay for it was denied this Mycenaean treasure."

She laughed. "I rather hoped he'd sell it and give me some of the money for my charities."

Linda held it up to her breast. Two of the tentacles seemed to curl over her nipples.

"Too bad I can't wear it like this tonight," she said. "*That* would cause a stir."

"Indeed," said Chloë. "You make me wish I were from the island of Lesbos, and named Sappho, several thousand years ago."

Linda looked at her questioningly.

"Forget it," said Chloë. "I really prefer men. And speaking of men, how about that John Graves? Is he really so sexual?"

"Indeed he is," said a voice.

They both turned. Claudia stood in the doorway smiling. Her hair was pinned into a tower of curls with a silver fillet holding it, and she was draped in fine white chiffon. Her little feet were encased in silver sandals.

"Hello, I'm Claudia."

"Of course," said Chloë warmly. "I would know your lovely face anywhere. Ah, what a family of beauties."

"You should have seen her father," said Claudia, "speaking of sex appeal. But that John Graves is not bad, either. As you no doubt know, I practically weaned him."

"I know," said Chloë. "I saw your motion picture with him six times. Will you introduce him to me?"

"I shall," said Claudia, "provided you see that I personally introduce my niece to Pericles Niadas. It shouldn't be any other way."

"Fair exchange," said Chloë. "Now, as you see, I have delivered Pericles' most treasured jewel to your niece."

Linda picked up the golden octopus. Claudia gasped.

"I've seen it in some of Ubaldo's art books!" she said. "It shouldn't be out of a museum!"

"I'm wearing it tonight," said Linda. "I want to surprise him."

Chloë looked out upon the gardens past the terrace.

Footmen dressed in simple chitons and leather sandals like Greek servants of the golden age were lighting large bronze urns filled with oil. Hundreds of little lights twinkled throughout the grounds, and in the distance the first sounds of bouzouki music began to fill the flower-laden air.

She stood entranced a moment, and then turned to Linda.

"I hope he is happy tonight," she said. "You are very young, but I know you will never in your life meet a man who is as valuable and as full of dreams as Pericles Niadas. He has had great sadness, but this night is the world for him."

A strange, quizzical expression passed across her face. Then, with a faint wave of her hand at Claudia, she left wordlessly.

Linda broke the silence.

"She isn't exactly beautiful, is she, Aunt Claudia? But just the same . . ." She waved her hands, at a loss for words.

"True, she isn't beautiful," said Claudia, "but believe me, that's the sort of woman you remember in a room full of beauties. She's a personage."

"I know what you mean," said Linda. "When the time is right for me to make them change my name back to Belinda, I guess I'll have to be a personage."

She picked up the ancient treasure of the golden octopus. It was as wide as the span of a man's hand.

"I should be a personage to get a gift like this."

"Niadas sees you as a personage," said Claudia. She stood behind her niece, looking at her in the mirror. "I'm glad I'm not your age. I don't think I could bear to go through it all again. Sometimes it can be rewarding to be an onlooker."

"*You* an onlooker?" Linda laughed. "With Max around! Don't think I'm so dumb. As Grace Boomer says, don't try to hoodwink me."

Claudia tried to outstare her, but she flushed.

"Mind your own affairs, miss," she said.

She picked up an ivory-backed brush and began to brush the girl's rope of curly hair.

"Ouch!" said Linda. "You're pulling my hair!"

"Stay still, you brat," said Claudia, "or I'll use the back of this brush on your bottom!"

As the evening embraced the Villa Madonna della Rosa, the music of Greece blended with the elegance of Italy. The multitude of white-gowned, jeweled women, some of the men in black-and-white evening dress, others in Greek chitons, cloaks, and gilded girdles and sandals, suited the marble splendor of the spacious chambers. Music, and the sound of many voices, seemed to cry forth an excitement, which gained momentum and heightened in pitch. As Linda prepared to leave her suite, and make her entrance, she felt that if she were blind, she would have thought that the babble of voices was a cascade roaring as it crashed into a ravine, and as she peered through a crack in the door before she descended, she felt that if she had been deaf she would have looked at the people as a forest of leaves, moving slowly this way and that in the vagaries of a faint wind.

Linda's hair was twisted up into a Psyche knot with pearl pins. Claudia had smoothed out her face with the proper maquillage for the dim evening lights. Her eyes were artfully framed in lilac tones, the lashes full as they were, thickened more with cautiously applied makeup, and her young mouth made fuller and more voluptuous with a scarlet pencil.

Claudia had carefully selected a silken fabric woven on the island of Cos in the ancient tradition. It was fashioned of a weave of scarlet and purple that shimmered in a different hue however the light fell upon the folds. Claudia had knotted it artfully over each of Linda's shoulders and draped it around her nude body, belting it with a silken cord, knowing that her perfection of body was such that no dressmaker could improve it with folds and tucks. She looked translucently wicked in the draped garment.

Upon her breast, fastened from her neck with a gold chain, was the Mycenaean treasure, the gold and bejeweled octopus. Claudia had arranged it so the tentacles curved around the girl's breasts, keeping her upper torso from being too nude in the filmy garment. The gigantic uncut emerald eyes of the ancient cephalopod seemed to stare balefully at anyone who would approach her.

"No one should be nervous who wears that ransom of kings," said Claudia.

On her feet were gold sandals with wings, and as she stood at the top of the stairs, Claudia had arranged to be standing with Pericles Niadas, Chloë, and John Graves, who had attended wearing his hoplites costume from the film.

On a signal, Ubaldo had directed all folk singers to be silent. A hidden string quartet moved into the strains of *Orpheus and Eurydice* as Linda walked down the stairs. At the landing she paused for a moment and put her hand cautiously on the marble foot of Phryne, as she always did for luck.

She became aware of the change in the crowd below. First, the cascade of sound became a trickle, and the forest of people ceased moving. Remembering that her aunt had told her to move slowly, and seek her out, she came down the stairs, and as she approached her, she realized that people were stepping back to give her room, as if she were royalty.

In a second of panic she put her hand to her breast and touched the emerald. It gave her courage. She saw the flash of Claudia's smile, noted with satisfaction that John Graves, standing close to Chloë, looked at her, grinning affectionately.

She saw Chloë admiring her, and then looked into the face of Pericles Niadas, who was transfixed, gazing at her.

Somewhere, as if at a distance, she heard Claudia say, "Mr. Niadas, may I present my niece, Belinda Barstow."

Belinda, flashed Linda's memory. She put her hand out, and Niadas took it, bowing slightly, but not allowing his eyes to leave her face, until he noticed the octopus at her breast.

"Thank you, Mr. Niadas," she said. "I know it's too precious to wear, but I had to do it for you tonight."

"It was made for you," said Niadas.

The silence was broken. Conversation began again. Those who stood close by became self-conscious and stopped staring. As Niadas guided her, they walked through a crowd that seemed to melt away. He met friends, introductions were made. It was all a haze to her. Linda peered at John Graves, who walked closely behind her with Chloë.

"You have really done it," whispered Graves. "I never saw you look so sophisticated. Who would believe it!"

He smiled at her teasingly.

Annoyed, she looped her arm into Niadas'. What had Chloë said? "I know you will never in your life meet a man as valuable and as full of dreams as Pericles Niadas."

As she noted the awe in the faces of some of the beholders, a new dimension struck her. She was walking with a man of great importance. The very fact that she was with him seemed to change everything. With a slight flush of annoyance she remembered how John Graves had tried to put her down. And how Max had kept her in line. Thinking of Max, she noticed that he had joined the group that headed toward the main table, where he and Claudia, Chloë, John Graves, and even Leslie Charles (who had pushed in with a pale chic lady introduced in ringing tones as a contessa) formed a nucleus around Pericles Niadas. This ought to make John take notice of her.

But when they were seated, she noticed that he was in deep conversation with Chloë. They started laughing together at something she couldn't hear.

She turned her attention to Niadas, who was at her right. Max sat at her other side. He complimented her, and told her both she and Claudia were wicked to dress her in bright colors when every woman had been asked to dress in white, but the startling effect had certainly worked.

Somehow it wasn't necessary to hold a conversation, there were so many interruptions. Every time Niadas started to draw her out, someone interfered. She was attracted by his gentleness, and by his warm brown eyes, which gazed upon her with an expression she had never seen on anyone's face. Not even Max's. She felt adored, and witty, and knew she was dazzlingly beautiful.

As course after course was presented, and wine after wine was passed, the currents swirled around Linda.

John Graves, comfortable in the apparently casual and convivial presence of Chloë, felt the burdens of his guilts being released. Here was a mature woman, attractive, alive, and not an impatient young virgin whose unfulfilled passions had disturbed him. Here was an intellectual, someone to share wit, laughter, sophisticated leisure time, and he had heard, in spite of her long and potent relationship with Pericles Niadas, an uninhibited bedmate. It was rumored she selected only first-rate men as lovers, and to be chosen by her was a triumph. After his psychic disturbance of the past few weeks, Graves wanted to get into a romping bed of mingled desire, laughter, and lack of responsibility. He had damned near become a hermit, concerned with Linda's situation, and facing the eagle eye of his longtime friend Claudia.

Graves was pleased to find his emotions reacting with his normal quickening to the charms of Chloë. He anticipated, along with that eye-to-eye look that such confrontations usually started with, that before a few hours passed it was inevitable that he and this remarkable Greek woman would be twining their well-matched bodies against each other in a passionate release. He knew instinctively that she, too, had a need for the sensual joys of life.

"Let's get away from here as soon as we are able," he said, "and forget all this bloody pomp and circumstance. I think we both need a little uninhibited relaxation."

Chloë smiled at him. "Oh, how I need concern only for the moment."

"I'll show you what the moment can be," he said, leaning closer to her. "Perhaps together we can achieve that fabled promise of Pierre Louÿs, 'unendurable pleasure, indefinitely prolonged.' "

Aha, she thought. Listen to this man lifting his little tickle from a superheated French sensualist. How naïve. But he appeals to me.

Under the table John put his hand on her thigh.

"Never promise anything you can't deliver," she said.

The pact was sealed.

Claudia, taking Max's hand, whispered to him, "This is very heady stuff for Linda. I'd like to get her away from this endless banquet. She must have been introduced to a hundred people. Do you realize, we've been sitting here hours? I've counted twelve courses. Don't forget the surprise we've planned—for Linda to recite Sophocles for Niadas in the amphitheater. That poor tired electrician has been ordered to stand by, ready to use that spotlight."

"Sophocles," said Max. "What is she reciting?"

"You know. Yeats's translation of *Oedipus Rex*. She thought it suitable,

" 'Yet an ambitious man may lift up a whole state,
And in his life be blessed, in his life fortunate.
And all men honor such; but should a man forget
The holy image, the Delphian sibyl's trance . . .' "

"Et cetera," said Max.

Grace Boomer came by the press table, headed by Andrew Reed. In her hand she carried a large silver goblet of fine vintage bourbon.

She articulated so carefully that Andrew Reed knew from long past experience that soon it would turn to mush. She wove her way to the table of foreign correspondents. They were not as alert as he, and he knew that somehow in this nest of celebrating personalities, when the time came, he would be the first to make it to that press room. He needed a good gossipy item.

Jessica was in her element. She had invited a distinguished gray-haired Prince Carlo Bonavente, known by his adoring friends as Bo-Bo. He was her newest conquest, of a long lineage, a short bank account, and a large palazzo that badly needed restoration. She dreamed of a liaison and a title, and he dreamed of a new roof and modern plumbing. They both seemed suited to each other.

Jessica was relieved that Max had latched on to Claudia. It had made it much easier for her to pursue her new course. She decided to abandon the vulgar film connections as soon as her ownership of the film came into fruition as Max's partner with a percentage of the gross. She would establish residence in Rome. Perhaps eventually she could even get Linda to marry into an aristocratic family, and they would all forget the Barstow beginnings. But for now, having graciously accepted to hostess a table filled only with members of various aristocratic and governmental connections, she felt like the newest member of an exciting society. She glanced with dismay at the flamboyant costume of Linda, and of course blamed Claudia, but seeing how enchanted Niadas was with her daughter, she indicated to her intimates that Niadas was mad for the girl, and considering everything, should have his whims about her costume fulfilled. The octopus decoration was noted with an impressed amazement, its worth being known in higher art and archaeological circles.

Leaving the chatter and music of the grounds, Ubaldo walked into the empty hall. He was thinking of Linda, disturbed by her dress and the incredible gift of Niadas, and yet relishing the few words he had spoken to her before the festivities had begun.

"Phryne wants you to see her tonight," she had said, smiling.

It was her way of telling him, he realized, that she was ever grateful. Ah, if she posed nude on this miraculous night it would be worth all the effort he had put forth for this gala.

For the first time since his youth, there were many people in his villa he had known well. No one had recognized him, the hairless recluse, as the handsome young prince of over twenty years ago. Some of his inamoratas were now fat, most faded, and some he noticed obviously no longer in love with the partners who had become their husbands and lovers. Looking at all of them, he smiled to himself with gratitude that not one of them had become his. It was good to have stepped out of life, observing unseen the wreckage of other people's lives, wondering which one might have entrapped him.

He was far from trapped. He was in the happy service of a young goddess who was his confidante. With a little twinge of envy he thought of the priceless treasure Niadas had given her, and was amused that, as a goddess, she had decked herself with it, and then seemed to have forgotten it. How he would have liked to have presented her with the golden goblet of Sheba, with the beautiful green nipples of zinnebar, which he had worn smooth with his loving caress. They would have drunk from it ceremonially.

He must not be jealous of Niadas. The man was finished, suddenly old. He alone knew that in the private catacombs below his villa were the treasures he had amassed and hidden in addition to the golden goblet of Sheba. They were his. Bless the old pirate Hadrian, who had collected them. Ubaldo alone knew what it meant to assess and possess them.

He stood looking up at his marble maiden, Phryne, so serene, so splendid in her moment of perfection, suspended in time, immortal beauty forever preserved by the genius of man. Phryne, Praxiteles, I love you, Linda Barstow, embodiment of beauty . . . I love you. . . .

Several hours later he saw Jessica Barstow and her social group assembling in limousines to go into Rome. They had plans for a sortie in costume at the Hosteria dell'Orso. Obviously they would preen about the city's late spots until after dawn, so every observer would know they had come from the Niadas bash.

He was not surprised when he saw Sidney Keyes escorting a staggering Grace Boomer from one of the tables to the security of her quarters. He immediately ordered a footman to send a brioschi and mineral water to her room. Later the resident nurse could check in, as she would undoubtedly do for many of the guests. There would be plenty of hangovers and curative drinking tomorrow morning, as well as calls for the five masseuses he had standing by.

Perhaps if he were in Niadas' shoes he would have done the same thing—put his wealth at the feet of a phenomenon like Linda and of course the genius of Maximilian Ziska. Perhaps strips of celluloid must be accepted as an honorable art form. The world was changing; the ways of presenting the arts were having their metamorphosis, too. As an anthropologist, he must be prepared to evaluate progress.

As Andrew Reed observed Grace and Sidney's exit, he knew he could approach the main table without Grace running interference. A nice juicy personal quote from Niadas was exactly what he needed. He had noted that the Barstow child had tried to leave the table with the Greek several times, but they had been blocked by the endless stream of guests who had come to pay respects and rub off some of the magic such a confrontation would bring about. Each greeting had the potential of a quote that could be used in business and social circles for some time to come.

Chloë Metaxa and Graves had moved away from the periphery of main action. Andrew had noticed them; out toward the hill where the amphitheater was set, among the white statues and roses, was a small orchestra and tables. He had watched them as they merged together on the dance floor, and once he strolled by to see them at a ringside table in amused conversation, hand-in-hand, leaning toward each other in rapt attention.

But now his interest was on bigger game, although God knows they'd be the romantic item of the affair.

He approached the main table, nucleus of all attention.

"Mr. Niadas," he said, "I'm Andrew Reed. I think we met at the Harvard Club in New York. May I congratulate you, you certainly are giving the bash of the century."

Having identified himself as a man of culture, disarming Niadas, who put out his hand, he shook it, and then daringly threw his dart. There wasn't much time to lose; he could already see Max Ziska and Claudia moving in on him.

"I am a journalist," he said, "and while I have you, could you give me a quote on your marriage? Have you filed for divorce from Martha Ralston?"

Niadas, taken aback, was startled. Linda, seeing the suspended shock on his face, turned imploringly toward Claudia.

She stepped swiftly between him and Niadas.

"You must fogive me, but this is my niece's evening. Mr. Niadas has given her a debut worthy of a Barstow, and I will not allow our host to be disturbed by a scandal-seeking news-hawk. I think this interview should be terminated right now."

"Claudia," said Max, taking Claudia's arm, "I shall handle this."

Andrew saw, to his amazement, that his old buddy, Leslie Charles, had stepped forward and was looking at him angrily.

"*I* shall take care of this," he said. "Mr. Niadas, I owe you an apology. It is due to my insistence that I had Andrew Reed invited to this affair. I should have known after a long acquaintanceship that Andrew would abuse all human values for his own ends."

"I can't believe you!" said Andrew. "You ingrate—why, your whole career was dependent on my influence! Acquaintanceship! You call *our* long association acquaintanceship!"

"That's what it seems to be," said Leslie.

"Listen, you two boys," said Claudia, "fight it out between yourselves. Don't embarrass Mr. Niadas. Kiss and make up—or something."

"Come along, Claudia," said Max. "This is not our

affair." He led her away. Amazingly, she found herself meekly following him.

Leslie took Andrew Reed by the arm firmly.

"Forgive the American prcss, Mr. Niadas," he said. "I shall escort Mr. Reed to the door, and return to make my apologies."

As he spoke, from nowhere six of Niadas' evzones, the tall men in their fustanellas, caps, and bristling moustaches, moved in.

"If you need help, be my guest," said Niadas.

He turned to Belinda.

"There's always some sort of an incident at an affair this size. I wouldn't want it to spoil our first meeting."

Linda felt relieved from the tension of the moment.

"Thank you," she said. "I guess Max will take care of my aunt. I've been waiting. I have a surprise for you. Come with me."

She took him by the arm, leading him to the distant amphitheater. En route perhaps she could find Chloë Metaxa and John, and have them come along. She felt insecure without Claudia.

As they passed the dance floor on the outskirts of the rose garden, she noticed that the music was ended in the little garden café. A few people sat at tables, but Chloë and John were gone. In the distance, in another glade, there was the faint sound of a charalambys being sung plaintively. Perhaps they were there. However, as she looked at Niadas' face by torchlight and saw his quizzical and adoring glance as he smiled at her, she realized her growing power; she had seen it in Max, in Ubaldo, and now again it appeared full force in a man who was a world-important person.

They left the light and sound of the festivities. When they came to the brow of the hill, before entering the amphitheater, she realized that Niadas did not even know of its existence, since Ubaldo had just unearthed and restored it.

It would be wise of her to see that the electrician had the proper cue, even though she had planned with Claudia to have him respond to a sound on the stage.

"Now, you wait here," she said to Niadas, seating

him on a stone bench in company with a stone faun among the white clustering roses. Way in the distance she could hear the faint strains of Greek music. It would be a perfect background for her.

Niadas glanced at her, puzzled, but enchanted.

"I will come and get you in a moment," she said.

She entered the dark, silent circle of her amphitheater. It was a moonless night, but she knew the great half-circle of stone seats, and saw dark against dark, the columns where she would stand on the stage. A marble bench had been placed stage center.

High above, in the last row, she saw the gleam of metal, where the electrician stood waiting. When he heard her first whisper of a line, he would be alerted to find the focus of her blond hair, and flood her with light slowly, revealing her full figure. He had waited up there a long time, she realized, but that was his job. Everything was perfect. She must go get Niadas.

But as she moved, she realized that something was wrong. There was a sound on the stage, a deep small woman's cry. Reacting to the awaited signal, the small pinlight spot flickered on a patch of white. It became a nude shoulder and breast, the gown fallen away. It enlarged slowly, focusing slowly on the marble bench that she and Claudia had set up for her presentation.

As it widened, Chloë was revealed lying on the bench. Graves was over her prone body, the two glued together. Paralyzed with astonishment, their faces blinked in the sharp light as their moment of fusion was pinpointed with all the drama that theater could present.

Realizing after a startling moment that the tableau was not what he had been ordered to illuminate, the electrician flashed off all the lights. Linda found herself in the dark, blinded, shocked, frozen by the scene she had witnessed. She put her hands over her eyes. She stood trembling, the scene still impressed on her mind, with all its fleshy undertones against the darkness. John Graves! Chloë Metaxa! After all she had dreamed. . . . They had just met, they didn't even know each other. And then she recollected how quickly he had aroused her when *they* had just met on the set. So that's all it had meant to him. That's what he did with any woman.

It seemed as if she stood an eternity. She could die of shame. The glasses of wine she had sipped during the evening made her feel giddy. She felt nauseated.

In the distance she heard Chloë's distressed voice.

"Who could have done such a dreadful thing!" she whispered, the perfect acoustics of the natural theater bringing each tone of her voice sharply to Linda's ears.

"At least," said John, "there was no audience. Let's get out of here and go someplace else."

"I . . . I don't know," said Chloë. "My God, I'm so upset! We *did* have an audience. That electrician or whoever it was who handled those lights."

"The SOB," said John. "I'd better sprint up there and see who did this to us. Wait here."

Linda heard his steps as he clambered up the stone aisle, and also heard a flurry as the electrician fled. She moved swiftly in the cover of night to the side of the amphitheater.

Then she thought of Niadas, awaiting her. Thank god he had not come with her. Out of her own shock, she suddenly realized the long relationship between Chloë and Niadas. What a shock it would have been for him.

She had to get away before Chloë and John found her. And she could not bear to be alone another moment. She rushed down the steps she knew so well, hoping she'd never have to come back to this place again.

At least they did not know she had seen them.

Niadas was waiting.

"I was concerned," he said. "I was coming to you."

She took hold of his hand and held it tightly. He was surprised, and put his hands on her shoulders.

"Is something wrong?"

"I was going to recite Sophocles to you," she said, "but it was . . . was dark there."

He laughed at her childishness.

"Another time," he said. "This is not an evening for Sophocles. My dear, you seem so upset."

"Maybe I saw a ghost," she said.

She sat down beside him in the warm night. The music had ended. They heard the distant sound of cars leaving.

Linda had to get away from what she had seen. This was to have been her night. This man was important to her. She would have to prove now what an actress she could be. It was time to stop being a scared girl, to try to be a woman.

"Tell me about Greece," she said. "Because I'll be there soon on location."

"Perhaps one day, aside from location, I'll take you to *my* Greece," he said, and amended his suggestion: "Not on my yacht. A crew of forty-four . . . twenty-five guests. . . . It is just an enormous and glittering machine. . . . No, no. I want to show you *my* Greece of whitewashed houses, pots of flowers, seaside shrines, a place where people bless you and say, 'May you live.' On my island, blue sky and sea are framed by ancient ruins. Would you like that?"

"I would," she whispered.

He was conjuring up scenes that were beginning to take the place of the nightmare on the stage to her.

"I would like to swim, and see beautiful things, and not have to think about what I am supposed to do."

He stood up and shook his head. "I am afraid I have strayed very far from my aims."

She was gazing up into the sky, where a faint wedge of pale blue was filtering against the edge of the hill. Her profile was of such beauty that it seemed to him a moving cameo.

"It's dawn," she whispered, "the beginning of a new day. It reminds me of a cinquain my aunt taught me. I think for now it's better for me to recite than Sophocles:

" 'These be
Three silent things,
The falling snow . . . the hour

before the dawn . . . the mouth of one
Just dead.' "

He bowed his head a moment, took her hand, and lifted it.

"Back to life," he said.

Hand-in-hand they left the amphitheater, passed the garden, and strolled slowly along the flower-bordered paths. In the distance, as they entered the loggia, a few men were rolling up the priceless rugs, and tables and chairs were being loaded into trucks. The music, the voices, were ended.

As they entered the hall, a shaft of early-morning light struck across the head and breast of Phryne, the massed flowers sending out their dawn fragrance. Everyone had gone to bed. She alone stood sentinel.

They walked up the stairs. At the entrance to her salon doors, she stood looking at him.

"I don't want to be alone," she said. "Will you come in with me until I get my little dog out of the dressing room?"

He opened the door and closed it silently. It was strange to see his familiar rooms under these conditions.

As they entered the sitting room, she stood for a moment, looking at him. She saw in him all the loneliness she felt. Her whole world—Claudia, Max, John, her mother, everyone—had gone their way.

Not knowing why, she came to him. He put his arms around her. He kissed her. Smothering her pain at the betrayal of John Graves, she allowed a strange feeling to encompass her. Suddenly she did not think of John Graves, or anyone. This man excited her.

"Ah, that I met you so late. If only I could have possessed you . . . once," he whispered.

Wouldn't it be wonderful to be possessed tonight? To have this evening, this night of excitement and tears end in making her a woman? She was sure he did not know how young she was.

"Pericles," she said, "will you make love to me?"

He stared at her in astonishment.

She led him into the bedroom. The wisp of Cos silk fell from her. He lifted the jeweled octopus from her beautiful breasts. He took her into the bed; how easy to forget that it had been the bed of his marriage to Martha Ralston. This young girl wanted him. He caressed her, kissed her with the growing excitement of a groom, sensitive to the young body of his bride—a virgin bride. Slowly and cautiously he moved her into an area of passionate excitement that made it possible for her to want the final thrust of his body, which would give her, first, pain, and later, he prayed, ecstasy. He saw tears on her face and heard the uninhibited cry of her fulfillment as he made love. He was grateful to the gods that she was able to experience an ultimate release and joy—it would have been fearful if it had been only his own pleasure.

Later they slept, embracing; she fitted beautifully in the circle of his arms. To his delight, she awoke him, caressing him, and telling him by her childish pleasure that she wanted him again.

"I didn't know it would be like this," she whispered. "Now it won't hurt me, and I want you to love me again."

He kissed her madly and possessed her again, delighted that she had stimulated him to more excitement than he had known since he was a young man.

She arose and went toward the dressing room, stretching. He rushed after her, and embraced her, running his hands along her shoulders, down to her hips.

"I have never seen such beauty," he whispered.

She looked ruefully down at her thigh, where blood had fallen.

"I'm sorry," she said, "I have to sponge away what you did to me."

He bent and kissed her inner thigh.

"I would like to hang the bloodstained sheet on my balcony to show the world my prize!"

She flushed and opened the dressing-room door. Sarge jumped out, and halted, staring at the interloper, and barking. Linda lifted him up and brought him to Niadas.

"You'd better be nice to him, Sarge," she said, "because he's just been nice to me."

She set the dog down on the chaise, rushed to the bathroom, and threw Niadas a terry robe. As he donned it he heard the shower running. In a moment she returned, nude.

"Oh, I have to show you something," she said. "It will be our ritual. Come with me."

She opened the doors to the hall. No one was astir.

Then she led him by the hand down to the landing, facing Phryne.

"Stand there and close your eyes," she said, "until I tell you to open them."

She rushed to the head of the stairs and struck the pose of Phryne. This morning she felt that she had a right to be the beautiful courtesan; she was a woman.

"Now," she whispered.

Pericles opened his eyes, and let out a gasp as he saw her in the flesh, breasts, golden hair, pink-nude, his woman.

"My god!" he said, marveling.

There was a cry of anger behind him.

He turned, to see Ubaldo rushing up the stairs. All night and into the dawn, after the chores were ended, he had awaited the vision that Linda had promised him.

Ubaldo paused, shaking in anger.

"My Phryne! You have desecrated her!"

Ubaldo moved swiftly toward the statue. Linda let out a scream, and the little dog rushed after him. Ubaldo reached for the statue, and raging, pulled at it. Pericles lunged at him, but Ubaldo shoved him away, pulled at the neck of Phryne, and for an endless moment the statue wavered, then toppled. She fell, and crashed, breaking, scattering head, torso, and arms on the stairway.

Linda let out a cry of anguish and rushed down the stairs.

The torso of the statue had fallen on the little dog. He lay crushed and bleeding on the marble steps. She picked him up and cradled him in her arms. He was dead.

There was another sound, as Ubaldo and Linda stood, staring at each other. Niadas lay gasping on the steps. His face was white.

Ubaldo looked down the stairs. Thank god no one was in sight.

"I must get him to his room," he said, shocked out of his anger at the plight of Niadas.

Linda held her dog, staring from his broken little body to the Greek.

"Linda," he said, "I am sorry; nothing can help your little dog. Please help me. Niadas is very ill."

He gently took the dog from her and set his body on the steps.

Together he and Linda helped Niadas up the stairs toward his suite.

"Now," said Ubaldo to Linda, "go to your room, and remain there until I decide what to say about this."

Linda picked up the body of the dog and took him to her room, sobbing.

Ubaldo led Niadas to his suite. He noticed that the bed had not been slept in. Stifling his anger, he got him out of the terry robe and handed him his silk pajamas. He noted that he was reaching for the gold pillbox at the side of his bed.

Ubaldo handed him the box, and watched him, his hands shaking as he put a pill under his tongue. Ubaldo placed water by him, and then bowed correctly.

"I shall be gone when you awaken," he said.

Niadas glanced at him, his face twisted.

"I know who you are," he whispered. "You, who have served me. Principe Giovanni Ubaldo Albini. You think I have not known all along?"

"What satisfaction you, a Greek, must have had to be served by a Roman prince."

Ubaldo smiled mockingly.

The two of them, linked in hatred at what they had lost this night, stared at each other. Then Ubaldo left.

Linda set the dead dog on her bed, where a spot on

the sheets revealed the loss of her maidenhead. Although her whole life had been changed in these last few hours, her pet was the one thing she mourned.

Ubaldo knocked at her door. There was no answer. He entered the sitting room slowly; the door to her bedroom was ajar. He found her in her robe on the edge of the bed, staring at the crumpled body of her pet. He was overwhelmed at the thought that the loss of this little dog was as great to her as was to him the loss of his Phryne.

"Forgive me," he said, "but this is urgent. When Effie comes to you this morning, you must tell her that servants moving furniture were responsible for your little dog's death."

She looked up at him, he felt, almost unseeing.

"Believe me," he said, "this night is the most terrible of my life, also. But we must go on. You are all that's left of . . . of Phryne, and you must make her be alive."

She bent her head; her tears were falling. Like a child, she lifted up the collar of her robe and wiped her cheek.

There was nothing he could do. She was so vulnerable, so young. He wanted to smooth her hair, to weep with her, to take the little dog away and try to relieve her of the pain. Perhaps before he left the Villa Madonna della Rosa he could help her.

"We might bury Sarge in the amphitheater," he said.

She jumped up.

"No!" she cried. "Never there. I don't ever want to see that place again!"

Startled at her outburst, he was silent. She looked up and saw the affection in his warm eyes.

"I'm sorry," she said. "I didn't mean to be rude. You have been my friend."

"I would always like to be your friend," he said, "although I am afraid that is impossible."

He looked at her tearful young beauty with a pang. She needed a friend. The hurt of this night would be a scar on her. And what was going to happen to her? She could not possibly sustain the role of being the woman of this aging Greek, even if he could face the consequences of a young love. Young love! With contempt he thought of the recent fiasco with Martha Ralston, and now this child!

She was so sunk in her own sadness that she did not even ask him why friendship would be impossible. Ubaldo realized that it would not even have reached her consciousness if he had told her that he must leave the house before Niadas appeared.

"I must go," he said. "Soon you will have to see Effie and your Aunt Claudia. Now, please, Linda, remember what I told you. About how your dog was killed. We must bury the secrets of this night. You will hear that Phryne has been shipped to Greece."

He had to walk away. He could not face her without tears. He must leave her and her problems, and be gone from this house of his lifetime before Niadas awoke.

He closed his ears to her sobbing.

In the early hours before the villa was awakened, he carefully picked up the pieces of his Phryne and put them in boxes. He put pieces of the arms in one, torso in another. When he had swept up a few small fragments, he picked up her lovely face which had seemed to gaze in serene beauty on admiring humans for so many centuries. He held it tenderly cupped between his hands. Tears coursed down his masklike face.

He cautiously swept the landing and stairs of every speck of marble chip. The household would be told that the Greek had ordered the statue shipped to its homeland. Niadas, when he awoke in the morning, would not dare deny this legend.

He carried what was left of her to his room. He knew he would use all his archaeological skills to restore her, even if no one ever saw her patched body but himself.

⬥⬥⬥⬥⬥⬥⬥⬥⬥

It was Effie's custom to enter Linda's suite early in the morning and take the dog out of the dressing room into the garden. Linda, she knew, would be sound asleep after all the festivities of the night.

She tiptoed past the sitting room into the bedroom, and as her eyes adjusted, found her curled up at the foot of the bed. Then she saw the dog's body. She let out a cry, and as she did, Linda raised her head, her hair hanging over her face.

"B'linda!" cried Effie. "What's happened?"

She saw that her eyes were swollen and red, and rushed to her. Linda started to cry again.

"He's dead!" she said. "Sarge is dead. . . . He's dead!"

Effie got a wet cloth, wiped her face, and settled her on the bed. She picked up the little dog, and saw the blood on the bed.

"Something . . . heavy fell on him," said Linda.

Effie wrapped him in a towel and took him to the dressing room, where she placed him in his basket.

"My baby. My poor baby!" said Effie to Linda. "Do you want me to take him away?"

"No," said Linda. "Ubaldo will bury him for me later. But I . . . I want to see Aunt Claudia."

Effie straightened up the room and got the sheets off the bed, believing the dog's blood had soiled them. She called down to Claudia, who rushed upstairs in her peignoir.

Claudia put her arms around her niece.

"Oh, my darling, what a dreadful thing!"

Although she knew, and Max had told her how the dog was her emotional trigger, she was shaken to see Linda's deep despondency.

"We must bury Sarge," said Effie. "You can't keep him upstairs."

"Call Ubaldo," said Linda. "He said he'd do it."

For a fleeting moment Claudia wondered how it was that Ubaldo knew about it.

As Claudia rushed downstairs to dress, she paused for a moment. The statue of Phryne was no longer in its place. But in the distress of the moment it only seemed a fleeting puzzlement to her.

◆◆◆◆◆◆◆◆

Ubaldo himself used a shovel to dig the dog's grave under an olive tree. It would likely be the last thing he did here, so it was no longer a time to be discreet about his past.

"When I was a little boy, I buried seven pets on this gentle hill overlooking the garden," he told Linda. "Your little dog will rest in good company."

Gardeners placed fresh-rolled turf over the grave. Linda picked some roses and laid them on the gravesite. Ubaldo discreetly walked ahead. Claudia took Linda's hand, and they moved slowly down the path. Linda began to cry. Claudia set her down on a marble bench.

"I want to go home!" sobbed Linda.

Claudia held her hands.

"Listen, ducks," she said, "I know you loved the darling dog because your father gave him to you. Sarge led a long life. He was loved. What happened last night is another step in life. It's hard. Now you must be adult."

"If you only knew . . ." said Linda.

"What?"

"Nothing. It's just that I don't want any part of all this. I want to go home."

"You can't go home," said Claudia. "Don't you know that what you think of as home is gone? What you were doesn't exist anymore. You can't be bobbing about in a middy blouse and skirt, toting schoolbooks. There *is* no apartment. There *is* no going back. Someday you will understand that change is growth."

She took her hands away and tried to be lighthearted.

"My god, I should think you'd be glad to know you're not going back to a duplex ruled by Jessica."

Linda smiled faintly at this.

Good, thought Claudia. She'll be all right.

"You must do what your father would do. Forge ahead. I love you, you know, and we are Barstows. You have a wonderful role to play. We'll make it come off. Then together we'll make a home together, somewhere, somehow. You must do what *life* intends you to do, not death."

Suddenly several people came running out of the villa. As they approached, they recognized one as Niadas' Greek manservant, and Kykkotis, his lieutenant, the liaison man who perpetually ran errands for him. As they rushed to Ubaldo and began to babble, beyond them on the balcony outside the guest suite, a woman's keening cry rang out. They looked up and saw Chloë Metaxa, her hands raised in a gesture of despair.

As Claudia realized what had happened, the whole memory of the death of Simon Moses in her arms struck her like a blow. She let out a scream and put her hands to her face. Strangely, it was Linda who, trembling herself, pulled Claudia's hands away from her eyes, her own knuckles white.

"My god! My god!" Linda cried.

Claudia was shaken out of her own trauma, for it was the voice of a woman that came out of her niece's lips. For a moment their eyes met, each with a memory unknown to the other.

Hand-in-hand, not yet realizing what had happened, and what it would mean to their lives, they both followed Ubaldo as he moved toward the house.

Ubaldo, feeling guilty in his lighthearted relief, knew he would not have to be gone this day from the Villa Madonna della Rosa, for Niadas would not awaken again.

11

By ten o'clock, Rome was buzzing with the news of Niadas' death of a coronary occlusion at the Villa Madonna della Rosa.

Andrew Reed rushed from the Hassler to the villa to use the press-room facilities. What a story he had! The glamour of the great party; Niadas' sponsorship of the young star Linda Barstow; Chloë Metaxa's sudden interest in John Graves, which might have triggered Niadas' attack; Martha Ralston, rushing to New York. Was she or was she not the widow? Had a divorce been started? Had papers been signed? If not, she was one of the richest women in the world. What was going to happen to the multimillion-dollar film of *The Oracle?* What would happen to Titan studio if this co-financed film was halted in mid-shooting?

Grace Boomer was in bed with a hangover, her phone switched off. At eleven she arose, looked in the press room next to hers, and to her astonishment heard Andrew Reed on the phone.

"Yes, it's true. Pericles Niadas, the Greek billionaire, was discovered dead in his bed this morning, after giving the greatest and most expensive party anyone had ever given in this century. I interviewed him personally a few hours before he died. His last interview . . ."

Grace tried to wrest the phone from him.

"What kind of gag is this!" she cried.

Discovering it was true, she immediately got on another line to Fergus Austin in Hollywood. Sidney was already sending messages to fetch David from Africa.

The panic was on. All paths began to converge toward Rome.

High in the blue skies of Greece flew Niadas' private plane, carrying his body back to Santorini, with Chloë Metaxa as his escort. Light, foam, rock, sky and sea, terra-cotta earth and white sugar-icing villages, glittering mountains and opalescent seas awaited one more body to be laid to rest with pagans and saints.

Long after the priests, statesmen, kings, bankers, villagers, and beggars had left, Chloë stood on the cliff by his quake-ruined villa, Kalliste, looking down upon the sea at his yacht, *Circe,* moored far below, its white-and-blue Greek flag flying so low it almost dipped into the blue-green sea.

She wondered why she did not throw herself, as Sappho had done, from the Leukas Petra, white cliffs of Lesbos, but knew she could not until Niadas' dream came true.

Chloë did not weep, for she had lost Niadas so many times in life that her only comfort was in knowing that this was the last time. All that was good in him would remain hers, and she would do anything to create a monument to his memory.

Meanwhile, Fergus Austin landed at Ciampino Airport in Rome vowing that he would choke his anger and try to reason. He felt as if he were walking into a nest of enemies who had laid waste to everything that was his, with heedless glee. He had a dossier on all the pictures abroad that had gone wrong because staff and actors looked upon location as a carnival, but he could not understand a pro like Max Ziska allowing things to get out of hand.

The death of Niadas was a body blow, not only to the studio, but to the financial world. Titan stock took a nose dive on the market. What would happen and how the financial structure to finish the film would be arranged, he did not know.

Martha Ralston, as widow to the deceased, had attached everything, including Niadas' *Oracle* payrolls, which were now tied up in litigation. Fergus could thank that bastard Andrew Reed for publicity that gave her and a battery of lawyers a big handle.

Every film Titan made these days was commissioned by financiers, and without this epic, Fergus knew he was a dead duck in picture circles.

Sidney met him at the plane, bone-weary. Weary of being a front-runner. He had joined David's microcosmic film company after the war, deliberately seeking a world of nonreality. Since David had rescued him from the shock of discovering his wife dead in an air raid, in the equally dead arms of her lover, he had skated along with David, feeling that his only escape in life was to have no ambition, no talent; there would be nothing to lose. Thus he could deal serenely with difficult people and situations. Everything would be make-believe, except the paychecks, which could be stowed away for a comfortable old age.

But it wasn't so easy. He had taken sides with David, he was engulfed with everything from Grace Boomer's drinking problems to the ultimate sadness of the gifted offspring of Jeffrey Barstow. And now he was going to face what apparently would be a confrontation between David and Fergus Austin, and he wondered whether he would get off riding that horse to Banbury Cross and assert himself, or take off on the equivalent of another safari to escape reality again.

The unfortunate thing about that feudal democracy loosely called Hollywood was that no matter how much nepotism was involved, at some point the strength would have to take over, and the weak would fall out of the picture. Sidney found himself hoping it would not be David who lost, for if he did, it would be the end of himself as an entity. And thinking of David's unstable mother, who was in an institution, he wondered what might happen to him.

"Where the hell is David now?" was Fergus' first remark to him.

Of course, thought Sidney, no word of courtesy about Niadas' death.

He decided to be polite and apparently nonchalant; his armor was in presenting his flip side, as usual.

"On his way in from Kenya," said Sidney. "We had to send messengers up into the bush for him. He saved us on that one. Among minor little problems, our million-dollar star insisted upon sex with the local jet-black maidens, and massive doses of penicillin had to be brought in for use before and after, to keep the picture going."

"Disgusting!" said Fergus. "And what in God's name is wrong with Max Ziska? Doesn't he realize that but for me and Titan studio he'd be peddling his coffee-stained script at Schwab's drugstore?"

"He's doing his best," said Sidney. "He's a little involved with Claudia at the moment believe it or not, but that doesn't seem to affect his efficiency."

Fergus glanced at him swiftly, settled back in the limousine, and lit a cigarette.

"How about her drinking?"

"None at all. She's been marvelous with Linda. God forgive me"—Sidney made a pretense of crossing himself—"I'm afraid the miscreant in slowing down production was Mr. Pericles Niadas, who almost started a new cult with Linda Barstow before he died. The last two weeks, half of our craftsmen were called off the set to the villa to make a proper Grecian setting for his party. Of course, it slowed down production. Ziska was furious; he muddled along with pickup shots and intimate scenes. We're behind schedule. But there was nothing he could do, for the moneybags was calling the shots.

"It was all turning into a massive jubilee, which I think helped do him in. We hear rumors now that he was not in very good health even before he launched this new saturnalia."

"And Jessica?" asked Fergus.

"Not a problem," said Sidney. "She's up to her arse in Roman society, and since we had the mechanicals under control, she had plenty of time."

"How about Linda?"

"She is absolutely morbid. You know, the dog was killed by some stupid furniture movers the night Niadas died. This disturbed her more than anything. She won't even accept a new pet. It hasn't been easy for her."

Fergus snorted.

"Easy! A kid gets the plum role of all time. And being a Barstow, I should think it would suit her down to the ground to be an instant film star."

"I guess it should," said Sidney, "but you know, while all the young people in Rome and the whole world, including Princess Margaret, are flipping over this new singer, Elvis What's-his-name, singing 'Blue Suede Shoes' and 'Heartbreak Hotel,' and jiving to 'Rock Around the Clock,' this kid is either on a sound stage, or acting with John Graves and Leslie Charles, or between scenes drooling over John Graves and getting nowhere."

"It was a mistake to use her," said Fergus. "I smelled trouble the minute another goddamn Barstow came into the studio. And the whole industry's in enough trouble. I suppose you know that when we let NBC buy Olivier's *Richard III* for half a million dollars we really screwed up our picture industry permanently. We should have subsidized it, to keep it off the air. Listen to this, fifty million, mind you, *fifty million* people tuned in on it, while our city theater ushers could have played baseball up and down the aisles."

"Maybe everyone doesn't like television," said Sidney.

"Well, if they don't," said Fergus, "they read. And I have news for you. Paperbacks are selling by the millions."

"There's only one solution," said Sidney. "Make better pictures. And I think this is a winner. At least, it started out that way."

Fergus glanced at him as if he were a fool.

Didn't the man realize that although today migration to a foreign country saved moviemakers money, it was true that no studio could afford a blockbuster like *The Oracle* without the sort of co-production deal Niadas had offered him?

Aside from this, he and his board of directors had

counted on the distribution fee of thirty percent to save the neck of Titan as a producing company.

And now that Niadas was dead, Fergus was going to face a reality more bitter than anything he ever dreamed could happen in his life.

"You don't seem to know why I'm here," said Fergus.

"To straighten things out?" said Sidney.

"Look," said Fergus, "you look at your call sheets every day. You know, aside from the massive cast, how many our camera crew, our special photographers, our technical staffs, wardrobe, property, transportation, and production staffs number."

"Of course," said Sidney. "At the moment, about a hundred and seventy-five people. And two hundred next month on location with second unit."

"I have news for you," said Fergus. "There isn't going to be any next month. I have come to close down production."

◆◆◆◆◆◆◆◆

A meeting of Greek financiers, lawyers, Roman production men, Swiss bankers, and experts from London had flown in for the moratorium on *The Oracle,* which was scheduled in the large library at the Villa Madonna della Rosa.

Beforehand, Sidney had waited for the car that drove David Austin in from the airport. Ubaldo had alerted him of David's arrival, and avoiding the nervous men who clustered in the halls and sitting rooms, he and Ubaldo greeted David at the entrance to the villa.

David had conferred with the Roman many times when the villa had been taken over by the *Pallas Athena* company. He had instantly liked him, recognizing him as a gentleman. He asked no questions, knowing well how the war had changed the destiny of many.

"Perhaps," David said to Ubaldo, "you can tell us where a quiet place would be where we can talk a moment before they all ace in on us."

"I suggest the gazebo outdoors near the loggia," said

Ubaldo. "It is a pleasant evening. I shall bring you refreshments myself. You'll be beset the moment they know you're here."

David and Sidney retreated to a table and chairs inside the leaf-covered treillage retreat. Ubaldo brought a silver tray with drinks and sandwiches. How fortunate that this conference had fallen into his hands. So much was at stake for him. He stood behind the screen of ferns and bougainvillea. He had heard, but listened again to the panic in the Mediterranean world that had been buzzed about among various conferences in the villa these last few hours. Sometimes it was good to be an invisible majordomo. No one paid any heed to him.

Conjecture on world problems had been rampant.

Due to the Suez crisis, Niadas' fleet of tankers was being routed more than eleven thousand miles around the Cape of Good Hope from the Persian Gulf to Western Europe. Jordanian and Israeli raiders were at each other's throats. Egypt barred Israeli ships, or ships under charter to Israel. Nasser's credit rating was gone; his sterling assets were frozen in London and Washington. Port Saïd was running out of water and food. Greek crews and captains were sent back to Haifa. The world was in deep unrest. DC-4's flew French colonists out of Morocco. Cypriot terrorists killed a compatriot with bombs intended for the British. The British carrier *Theseus* headed for the Middle East. Portsmouth British Red Devil parachutists also embarked for the Middle East. Three British aircraft carriers steamed out, ready for action.

At a conference in London's Lancaster House, America's Dulles and England's Eden assessed the remote possibility of building a peaceful world.

"This situation of world affairs makes the fate of our studio and our epic film seem like small potatoes," said David.

"Your father is all for folding the tents and stealing away," said Sidney. "You're going to face hostility in every direction. What are you going to do?"

David set down his drink. He arose and looked into the garden. Claudia and Linda were walking along the path. Even from the distance he could see Linda's sad demeanor. Claudia stopped, took her hand, and they continued walking toward the gazebo.

Claudia saw David before he could move back into obscurity, and she rushed toward him.

"Oh, David, thank God you're here. The sky has fallen in! It's dreadful . . . dreadful." She spoke quickly, before Linda joined them. "I'm so concerned about her. I can't seem to shake her out of her depression about the death of that little dog."

Her words were halted as Linda joined them. She smiled faintly at David. She seemed so young and frail, he put out his hand, pulling her to him.

She crumpled, putting her head on his shoulder.

"I'm so glad you're here, David," she said.

He found himself drawn to her, an emotion that he didn't often allow himself.

"We'll do what we can," he said. "You're a real trouper, Linda. Our best hope is the fine footage on the film. We'll get on with the meeting, and see what the Greek interests have to say."

Linda looked up at him gratefully, unshed tears in her eyes.

"You know," said Claudia, "I guess we just accepted *The Oracle* as something that would obviously be made. Now that it's in jeopardy, it seems the most important thing in our lives. Don't you think so, Linda?"

David felt that Claudia was attempting to lead Linda to this conclusion. She only nodded mutely.

"Well," said Claudia, "we mustn't disturb you. I know you and Sidney have lots to talk about."

"We'll meet tomorrow," said David. Claudia kissed him on the cheek, and they left.

He watched them, Claudia linking her arm in Linda's.

"Who would believe Claudia," he said, "after the ruckus she caused all her life!"

"She dotes on the girl," said Sidney. "She should. My god, what a transformation for such a kid, and Claudia did it. They're a clannish lot, those Barstows."

For a moment David could not help thinking of Jeffrey Barstow. Now that he was far removed from the shock of Jessica's marriage to him, he had only memories of a kind and somewhat wistful man, in spite of the general studio legends on which he had been nurtured, legends of a wild and difficult alcoholic who had always managed to crash through with splendid performances on film.

David remembered meeting him for a brief moment, swimming in the summer sea at Santa Monica. Jeffrey had walked with him on the beach after they had waited for the first star to come out before they left the water. Jeffrey had seemed so interested in him when he was a young boy. He even remembered the tone of his voice when he had said that David's mother was lovely. So few people had remembered her since she was in a sanatorium. This kindling warmth had remained in David's memory, for with his mother away, and his father busy, he had been a lonely youngster.

He remembered that there had been a few precious special editions that Jeffrey had sent him at various Christmastimes. Dana's *Two Years Before the Mast, The Golden Bough,* the *Odyssey,* the *Iliad,* Shakespeare's sonnets, collections of Masefield, Gibran, Omar Khayyam, Byron, Pope, Donne, a strange little assortment of books from an old movie star.

Childlike, he had accepted them as just one more tribute a Moses grandson received among many in the lush days of Titan's supremacy. It bothered him now that he had never properly thanked Jeffrey. And the thought carried over to Linda and Claudia. Yes, Jeffrey and Claudia had love in them, and Claudia had proven her devotion, guiding her niece carefully into a magic world of acting, doing a much better job on this child than she had with her own career.

With a pang he thought of how wonderful it must be to be cherished like this. It had never happened to him.

David and Sidney sat for a moment discussing the logistics of what was to come, before walking back to the villa.

"To continue meeting our payroll and the cost of location move will cost a million, even before we establish a solid financial future." David shook his head. "Thirty thousand a day plus, at least, considering our loss of all the private benefices Niadas handed out on his golden platter."

"Fergus will never go for it," said Sidney.

"Let's get on with the meeting," said David.

The rich baroque decor of the Villa Madonna della Rosa library, with its sixty-foot-high ceilings and three galleries of books, dwarfed the dozen men who sat at the conference table.

Notepads, pens in holders, and coffeecups ceremonially marked the places. Fergus Austin greeted David with his usual formal handshake and took his place at one end of the table. Nikolas Kykkotis, Niadas' portly, moustached lieutenant, sat at the other end. In between, men whose presence involved millions sat awaiting a verdict of some sort on this meeting. All of them considered *The Oracle* the folly of a man who could afford such a whim. It was even more complicated than building museums, churches, or colleges, and as a half-finished project, would undoubtedly have to be written off. They looked upon Fergus Austin and his son, David, as opportunists who had victimized their personal Midas.

Kykkotis arose.

"We have discussed a world that Pericles Niadas faced for many years with understanding beyond ours. We realize this project was dear to his heart, for he felt the film would glorify the sacred past of Greece. However, without his skills and diplomacy and finance, we feel we cannot expend estate funds on such an expensive project as he desired in his wish to create beauty. A giant like Niadas is no longer here among us to make his dreams come true."

Kykkotis sat down.

Fergus decided the meeting was at an end. He thought of Great Britain quitting after a loan of four hundred million to Greece and Turkey, and Truman taking over. He thought of the one billion two hundred and nine million dollars that had gone into Greece through United States companies. He thought of the vast wealth that had been garnered by the Greek's purchase of United States Liberty ships. Niadas had had it good, he thought. He always had had the first pressing of the grapes. What rotten luck that he had to die, and now the three million dollars Titan needed to finish this picture would not be in his hands to give.

Fergus arose.

"Gentlemen, what can I say? I understand the tragic litigations surrounding the death of such a man as Niadas. My company is not prepared to continue to sustain our payrolls the additional months needed to finish the picture. That would be folly without your continued backing. However, you should certainly realize that this film has a potential of millions of dollars. A large part of the profits would be included in the Niadas estate."

Kykkotis spoke up.

"Can you guarantee a profit, Mr. Austin?" he asked. "I understand that quite often even large films—as you say—lay an egg."

He tried to smile at his American colloquialism.

"Perhaps you would be able to tell us your plan. Since Mr. Niadas' death, the arrangements he so generously—and to our minds, foolishly—made from his private purse for both *Pallas Athena* and *The Oracle* must of course he abrogated. Miss Ralston—pardon me, Mrs. Niadas—has attached the production and is now asking for interest on the widow's portion of the investment."

He cleared his throat delicately.

"That would amount to a fortune alone, I should think. And of course any plans for the future would be on your own. But on the other hand, perhaps a corporate writeoff for all of us would be the solution."

Ubaldo, directing the footmen to pour more coffee, stepped behind Kykkotis so he could watch Fergus' face. He saw him flush.

A new voice came from the side of the table. David Austin arose.

"Gentlemen," he said, "we are not going to jettison

The Oracle. I will personally guarantee a million dollars."

There was a surprised gasp from Fergus.

"You can't put your Titan stock on the market in a large block. You know what that would do to the company!"

"It is not my intention," said David coolly. "It will be my own personal funds."

"That is very dangerous," said Kykkotis. "The world situation is against you. What if the problems in Cyprus spread? We had already warned Niadas of this danger with your location plans."

"My prime asset," said David, "will be the cooperation of the Niadas interests in helping me to get proper permits and clearances to film with my full equipment at such shrines as Delphi. I consider it not only your debt to me, in continuing this ambitious dream of Pericles Niadas, but also your responsibility to his estate, as I said profits will flow in to you when this ambition becomes reality."

Seeing the flicker of several eyes at the way he had couched his demands, he continued in a more practical vein. He was getting to them, for he had forced an obligation into their consciousness, which he must remember to record on paper. They, too, had a moral responsibility. And that was most embarrassing where money was involved.

"This situation has been considered," said David. "I have been in charge of the foreign production of Titan since the war ended. Plans have often been altered with film companies. We are, as they say, a portable art. We can move to the Ionian archipelago. We can borrow the assets of wealth from other patriotic golden Greeks, as much as we deplore the fact that a man like Niadas is no longer with us."

He bowed his head. He was silent a moment.

Sidney wanted to chuckle. By God, his old pal was putting on a show! It was the first time he had seen David shuck his shell, and he was delighted

"There's Livanos' Coronis near Nauplion, and of course we can make arrangements with Niarchos'

Spezapoulis off Spezia, or Onassis' Scorpios if we must change location."

The Greeks were impressed. This young man knew his way around their Hellenic world.

"And your equipment?" asked a Swiss banker.

"I imagine your companies would allow us to charter the Niadas yacht, *Circe.* It has a hydroplane and two thirty-seven-foot Bertrams, which would be excellent for camera platforms and intercom work in action scenes. It also has, as you know, a projection room, which would aid us in showing rushes, doing our cutting and rough assembly, thus saving time and money. Our film can be processed in the laboratories here in Rome and flown to us easily."

The men began to listen. The organization intrigued them. Fergus sat back and nervously lit a cigarette.

"We have generators, barges, and equipment in Rome," continued David. "The generators are mountable on trucks. Top stars and staff will live on yachts part-time. We will throw together temporary dressing rooms, commissary facilities, and camping equipment. We'll have trailers and tent cities, and move in honey-wagons for adequate sanitary needs. Our Italian and Greek crews have worked together before."

Fergus suddenly seemed to be the enemy, instead of the financiers.

"You're taking one hell of a risk," he said to David. "Not that I can tell you how to spend your money. But you have to locate in rugged weather and do complicated sea battles. You have all those shots in Delphi and Itea, not to mention that temple on a primitive island. Altogether you have at least three or four months' grueling location. And you know how costly and unstable sea locations can be."

"You were willing for Mr. Niadas to take a chance," said Kykkotis, tugging at his moustache.

"I was only being the devil's advocate," said Fergus lamely.

David felt like smiling. The first retraction from his father.

"We'll do the best we can, naturally," he said. "What have you got to lose, Kykkotis?"

"Nothing," said the Greek, "as long as you guarantee interest on our loan so far, and legally express no further obligation on the part of the Niadas estate, we will cooperate."

The meeting ended. The men filed out, to gather in groups and discuss the startling turn of events in their native languages, gauging the situation in terms of their personal interests.

Fergus lingered over his cigarette. The vast study suddenly seemed incredibly large as the two Austins faced each other. Sidney had the good taste to leave. Ubaldo dismissed the footmen, and stayed discreetly in the background.

"You're out of your mind," said Fergus. "The charter of the Niadas yacht will be at least seven thousand a week. And the payroll! My god! You won't be able to raise two million more fast enough to go on. With Niadas' estate owning a large portion of it, you have no collateral in this picture, and how are you going to raise money for the finishing bond?"

"On my Titan stock," said David.

"You're bankrupting us!" said Fergus. "If this goes wrong, you can use your Titan stock for toilet paper."

"May I say, as Kykkotis did," said David, "you were willing for Niadas to take the risk."

"You are not Croesus," said Fergus. "He was."

"My grandfather Simon Moses took risks in the early days that were bigger to him, I'm sure, than this is to me. What the hell have I got to lose?"

He stood looking down at Fergus, noticing the slightly trembling hand and nicotine-stained fingers. He wondered why he had been in his shadow so long.

"All my adult life I've been the recipient of insults from you," he said. "You've never given me a decent word for what I've done for Titan abroad when the home company was ailing. I have denied myself all personal relationships because of what you deliberately did to me with Jessica. I don't care anymore. Now I'm taking the risk on my own terms. And for the first time,

I'm advising you, I'm the major stockholder of Titan films, and will remain so. If you in any way undermine what I am attempting to do to save our necks, I shall see that your position is in jeopardy. Remember that."

Fergus stared up at him in fury.

"You *would* tie in with the Barstows," he said.

"And why not?" said David. "They at least have talent. It seems to me they were the cornerstone of your own career and money."

Fergus wanted to open his mouth and tell him the truth. Perhaps it was time for him to know that he was the bastard son of Jeffrey Barstow. But his pride would not allow him to betray the secret that had festered in him all these years.

"I wash my hands of this," he said. "I'm returning to Hollywood tomorrow morning. Don't forget, stockholders have a share in this film, with its co-production funds, no matter where you go from here. And it had damned well better be the right path, or you have destroyed your own studio."

He walked out.

David sat for a moment. He realized what a tangled web of economy lay in this half-finished picture. His father was right. He could not use any of it as collateral. He had put himself way out on a limb. To make good on his daring plan was going to take some doing.

"Forgive me, Mr. Austin," said Ubaldo. "I could not help but be witness to this meeting."

David looked at him.

"Sit down and have a brandy with me."

Ubaldo poured two, and sat down. It seemed natural for the two men to sit together.

"How much will you need to complete the picture?" Ubaldo asked.

"To keep production flowing, a million more than I guaranteed. Then I will have to raise more for laboratory fees, prints, publicity, promotion, but of course the finished product will make that more feasible."

David was puzzled. Ubaldo certainly did not seem a

movie buff, but you never could tell what motivated anyone.

"Why do you ask?"

"I think," said Ubaldo, "that if you keep it most confidential, I could raise some funds. You were mentioning that finishing bond. What would that be?"

"A sort of insurance against the film running over the budget allowed by investors."

"Would you give me an opportunity to invest?"

David smiled. Perhaps this man could raise ten thousand dollars or so.

"What did you have in mind?"

"With good fortune," he said, "and connections, I think around a million."

David sat back, speechless.

12

David sent chits to Max, Jessica, and Sidney to meet with him in the morning. He wanted to avoid the disturbance of private prejudiced meetings until he worked out a master plan himself.

He went to bed, but not to sleep, with facts and figures whirling in his brain, Ubaldo's astonishing promise still ringing in his ears. In the night he heard the sounds of trucks in the driveway. He wondered what was happening. Once he arose. Peering out the window, he thought he saw Ubaldo, the light shining on him as he stepped into a car carrying a small suitcase.

The next morning, as he sat on the terrace eating melon from Africa, and in spite of himself, enjoying the beauty of the perfectly tended gardens, he knew he must have seen Ubaldo leaving, for he was not hovering about. Suddenly he realized how often the man had attended to all the small details that made this villa function so perfectly.

For years David had listened to the dreamers who came up with fanciful ideas of raising money so they could belong to what they considered the magical world of picture-making. Likely Ubaldo was another. Perhaps some treasure, an ancestor's portrait, or some fragment of an ancient past would fall into the hands of a dealer, who would quickly shatter his overestimated fancies, whatever they were, and send him back with several thousand dollars. He was obviously a sensitive, educated man, no doubt of a noble line, who had fallen on bad times. Now that the villa was no longer to be run as it had before, what would happen to him? But how could a majordomo to Niadas expect to raise a million dollars? If he could, obviously he wouldn't be doing what he was. Too bad, thought David, for he liked him.

His thoughts were interrupted by Claudia. He noticed how fresh and vital she was, her dark hair bound in a white ribbon, her print dress fitting her trim, still lithe figure. Even in her sixties she was lovely; and an important man, Max Ziska, loved her. For a moment, remembering his grandmother Rebecca, who had always seemed an old woman to him, he understood how his grandfather Simon Moses must have adored this piquant woman so long. She must have been something. And she still was the vital hope of Linda; the slender vessel on which rested his future with the picture. He was pursuing an impossible dream with as much fervor as Ubaldo, the man he was criticizing in his mind.

The only difference was, he knew all the pitfalls, the mechanics, the blood, sweat, and tears that went into making a film on location. As an architect of such an undertaking, he intended to do it. If he didn't make it, he was a loser; Hollywood, the board, and Fergus would go down with him.

"I wish I could help you," said Claudia. "I've heard a dozen rumors of what is going on. Oh, David, times change. If only we could do like John Graves and I did when we made our *very* free-lance picture in London. Ah, it was such a mixture of penny scraping and excitement. I remember how we rejoiced in the bracken and purple willow in the bomb craters. And how we used *new* war ruins for effect, nujol spray for fog, a baby carriage instead of a proper camera dolly, and sprayed our sets gray to hide the pasteboards. . . . And here we have the wealth of the world, and likely can't use it."

"Don't be too certain," said David. "You may find yourself and John Graves being technical advisers on how to save a buck. Tell me, how's Linda?"

"I'm going to block out scenes with her now," she said, frowning. "I just have to keep her going, David. I might as well keep up the pretense until we hear the final bell. I'm trying to make her believe that what she is able to project on film right now is more important than what has happened to her in life. Someday, I tell her, she will stop sorrowing about her pet, and what exists on film will be the permanent evaluation of this time."

"That's a big order," said David. "I wish you luck."

As she left, he marveled at her spirit and wondered what he was going to have to go through with Jessica, much less Max.

"Stick with me, Sid," he said. "I want to have a witness when I talk to Jessica."

Again Sidney was delighted at the positive attitude of his friend David.

Jessica sat across the desk in the conference room.

"Jessica," said David, "we don't exactly know what is going to happen. I have to fly to London to meet with bankers and my British solicitors. It will take some massive organization to keep this show on the road. Meanwhile, I want you to cut the staff down to the nub. One secretary for you, you'll have to double in conferences. I'm certain you will be very efficient. You seemed to know more about the logistics of this film than Max did when the project got started.

"As you know," he continued, "Fergus Austin has left. I am in charge. We are given two weeks to finish at Cinecittà and Anzio and vacate the villa. Max will have to work with me paring down script and cutting budget with Sidney. We must cut to the bone, or quit. From here on out we will not experience such luxuries as we had planned, and I expect your complete cooperation."

"You will have it," said Jessica. What else could she say? This picture was her lifeline.

"One more thing," said David. "I prefer you leave Linda pretty much in the hands of Claudia. She seems to be handling her psychologically much better than anyone else."

"I think Linda is getting away with murder, sulking

all the time," said Jessica. "Sarge was an old dog, and she ought to be ready to face reality."

"That old dog was given her by her father, don't forget," said David.

Jessica opened her mouth, and then said nothing. She arose.

"I am dismissed," she said ironically.

"If you wish to put it that way, you are dismissed," said David, "and incidentally, no more limousines. They have been cut off. If you choose to go into Rome after our conferences, you can call a taxi."

As she left haughtily, David felt finally cured of all the feelings of hatred from her betrayal of him that he had carried so many years. Now she was only a rather unpleasant but efficient business associate. And since he had the upper hand, and could use her expertise, her unpleasantness didn't matter. He was slightly amused at the fact that in this whole upheaval, probably the thing that irritated her the most was taking away the privilege of her status symbol, the limousine.

The rest of the day, in between international phone calls, David and Sidney worked with Max, Jessica taking notes. They cut scenes, eliminated as much staff and crew as possible. Supers and mob scenes were eliminated. Even some of the long shots at the studio would be jettisoned, as they revealed more extras and more props than would be possible in the real locations. To take their place, Max came up with new scenes that incorporated character instead of pageantry. He was excited. Somehow the tightened script would be better, have the thrust of more personal drama. He was stimulated. He liked creative challenge. Imagination was a most vital factor in filmmaking.

Pros and cons of location equipment were discussed. Most of the cast would live on land, sometimes even in small hotels or houses. Additional yachts and luxuries were cancelled.

It was decided that Claudia, Max, Sidney, Jessica, the chief cutter, Dick Schute, and naturally Linda and Effie would live on the yacht, *Circe,* with visits from David when he was on location. Some of the staterooms, which had housed twenty-five guests, would be working rooms.

This would be wise, as the yacht would function as floating headquarters, more than a luxury platform. Laboratory, theater, projection room, offices, ship-to-shore communication center, and conference headquarters, as well as business office, would be contained aboard.

Late that night, utterly fatigued, after having helped Max hopefully cut five weeks and seven hundred thousand dollars out of the picture, David retired. Again he thought he heard trucks leaving the rear gates of the villa during the night.

Again Ubaldo was not around the next day. But in the evening, while David was on the phone in the study, he looked up and saw him standing there.

"Mr. Austin," said Ubaldo, "I have found it fit to dispose of a rare treasure that has been in my possession many years. In case you think I am a thief, I must explain to you, what I have sold was mine. You will soon read in the papers that a certain well-endowed private American museum has purchased an incredibly valuable golden goblet that is authenticated as having belonged to Makeda, the Queen of Sheba, and King Solomon. It is worth a fortune. And this is only the beginning. There will be more in two weeks."

He handed him a money order.

David stared at it. Three hundred thousand dollars!

"Will that help?"

David looked up in astonishment. Enough money for the picture to wind up in Rome while he made the financial arrangements in London and New York.

"My god!" he said. "This is incredible!"

"You must not reveal the source," said Ubaldo. "I am choosing to carry out Niadas' dream of beauty. One rarely has a chance in life to be a patron of the arts."

"You will have a proper contract and part of my ownership of the film, of course. But I don't understand. Why?"

"I began as an archaeologist," said Ubaldo.

"Well, isn't this a pretty plastic world," asked David, "for an archaeologist to take a risk on?"

"For many people, your fluid plastic world is a shelter from reality," said Ubaldo. "I think I knew it for the first time when I sat with Niadas in Greece and saw the living film. Then I realized my snobbism had accepted art and books as culture, and rejected this new world with your strips of film, because it was considered commercial. But so were the other arts; either economically, or egotistically to the gifted ones. You are capable of capturing beauty, history, and man's dreams. I decided to change one dream for another."

"You are taking a risk," said David.

Ubaldo only smiled.

David felt that this man was indeed a strange one. His explanation of his interest must be a cover-up for some other, more personal motive. So he had seen rushes of the film in Greece?

As Ubaldo settled down in his room, the small flickering light on the table beside his Napoleonic campaign bed no longer reflected itself in the golden cup of Sheba. His hand reached automatically to caress it. All these years it had been his talisman. Now it was gone from him.

He went to a corner of the room, where neatly stacked boxes held the remnants of his equally precious Phryne. He opened the top carton and lifted out Phryne's head. The eyes and smooth forehead, tendrils of marble hair clinging to her smooth brow, moved him close to tears. He set it on the table, where the vigil light flickered, seeming to make the eyes alive.

His days were ending in this villa, this retreat, where he had hidden from the world. It was just as well Phryne was in pieces. He could not have borne to part with her to a museum. Then he thought of the flow of treasures that he had hidden in the catacombs below him, which even now were on their way to make a film, *The Oracle,* come into being.

Knowing that in his hands had been placed the possibility of a reprieve from tragedy to the young girl asleep in his cherub-ornamented bed upstairs in the master suite, he settled back on his pillow, a slight smile on his face, as he closed his travel-weary eyes.

◆◆◆◆◆◆◆◆

Several weeks of hard work, finishing at the studio in Rome, passed swiftly. A moment of silence on the set because of the death of Niadas was the only tribute that was given by the company to the man who had made the whole multimillion-dollar picture possible.

"That's the way it is," said Claudia to Linda as they sat in the cocoon of her dressing room. "Just a moment of silence. It happened only twice in my experience at Titan. One way back in 1918 when Simon Moses lost his son in World War I. That's how Fergus really got started. They needed someone, and he'd been his chum and worked with us from the beginning. And the second time was when Simon Moses died. That's when Fergus took over. Well, that's ancient history. And Niadas wasn't known by anyone on the set, anyway, excepting several of us. So don't expect anyone to be grieving. Except maybe Chloë, who isn't here."

I should be grieving, thought Linda. After all, I didn't know him very long, but I should be hurting, I suppose. Maybe I'd better get one of those stills of the two of us they shot at the party, and keep one. Nobody'd ever suspect there was a reason of any importance except that he made my whole career begin. Then, as time passes, I can remember what he looked like, the first man . . . first lover in my life.

Linda was forced to shake out of her lethargy. She did short bits of scenes with Leslie Charles. Some of her closeups were done again. Claudia became her tuning fork. They played back soundtracks, corrected small mistakes, Claudia still trying to give her an overall analysis of Alethea, and her own creative self.

Leslie Charles, as usual, was very gracious in his scenes. But several matters of great concern bothered him. Having been in the ill-fated *Pallas Athena,* and then facing changes in this film, disturbed him. He heard rumors that important scenes were being cut, and he knew well from experience that secondary plots got lost when money ran short. And also, having lost his long-time relationship with Andrew Reed, and his syndicated columns, he knew he would get the short end of a great deal of publicity.

The Roman gaiety was gone.

He feared, and right he was, that this film would end any chance of his continuing to be a star. Henceforth he would be a character actor; and that meant less money and fun. But being a trouper, he would stick it out, and get every inch of footage possible.

The first time Linda faced John Graves, she felt she must despise him for what she had seen in the amphitheater. Fortunately, Chloë was still in Greece. But Linda was surprised that she could face him so easily. Again memories of Niadas haunted her. That last strange night of Niadas' life had changed everything. She thought of him far more than she did of John. He indeed had been a remarkable man. And it was he who had stirred her for the first time in her life. She wondered now if she had really fallen in love with him, those few hours in bed. She tried to evoke the excitement he had brought to her. And her own secret weapon, which she brought into play facing John, was what his astonishment would have been if he had known how that evening ended for her. What a triumph!

She did her few scenes at Cinecittà with him, following the guidance of Max, who had been kind and gentle to her, knowing of her sadness about the dog. After all, he had triggered her whole sensory reaction with the death of Sarge. Now, in a sense, he was stuck with it. He wondered how he was going to move her out of an aura of sadness, when scenes calling for other emotions would be played in the future. But he relied on Claudia; she alone had the key to this young girl.

After the scenes with John were finished, he kissed Linda on the forehead and embraced her.

"These have been growing days," he said. "I'll remember them when you're a great star."

"But I'll see you in Greece!" she said, fearing the ominous threat of the company being broken up.

"Of course, of course!" said John. "We'll hike and swim and listen to bouzouki music, and have a ball!"

But she was still apprehensive about Chloë.

Chloë returned from Greece. The forty-day period of mourning over Niadas was not finished, but she had her work to do, for him, of course.

She did her scenes splendidly, those of the flamboyant courtesan Diotima who rescues the priestess Alethea, when her lover steals her away from the sacred adytum of Delphi. She was lambent, flame, movement in the grand style, flashing jewels and color and spirit. She reacted with respect to Linda's performance, and seemed genuinely fond of her.

Linda admired her, and watched her closely.

She noticed that Chloë avoided John Graves. She felt that the death of Niadas had made her flee him. No doubt, Linda thought correctly, she felt guilty. Watching her made Linda forget her own sorrows. Oh, if Chloë only knew that she, Linda, had lost her virginity with Niadas! She would have been shocked. Even more shocked than Linda was when she saw her and John Graves glued together in the amphitheater. At least Niadas had not witnessed that scene. And perhaps, if he had seen it, she and Niadas would never have been lovers. Life was strange and complicated. She realized that in this close world of work and living together she had to think about other people and her relationship with them before she could attempt to understand herself.

The location of the Anzio beachhead finished the production in Rome. It was the most expensive part of the picture, and the most trying. An extra staff of fifty was enlisted. Two thousand extras were costumed, cosseted, and fed, kept in line by a squawking loudspeaker system and multilingual assistants.

First-aid tents, a corps of nurses and doctors, and ambulances stood by. Horses and wranglers, and props, chariots, spears, banners, and shields were brought from nearby jerry-built edifices to the core of action before the scene began. Two extra camera crews were stationed to cover from many angles.

Fifty members of the international press stood on bleachers, some with binoculars or cameras, as if they were witnessing a football game.

Max, his white hair covered with a straw hat, his nose white with zinc ointment, impervious to how he looked, but moving like a piece of machinery, sometimes rode with the first camera crew on a dolly, in a moving camera car, and once even in a chariot, camera crew at his side in another, as they plowed through the crowd to show the mad excitement of a mob on the shores of Piraeus, looking for the sacred oracle, who had been kidnapped from the holy shrine of Delphi by Leslie Charles as Hermocrates and John Graves as the footsoldier Diodynus.

Between scenes Linda was kept in her trailer, away from the eyes of the curious press and extras.

"We'll just say, dear," said Grace, "that out of respect for the death of Niadas, you are not giving out interviews at this time. There's nothing you should say just now. This is not the time for chitchat, and why should you be forced to talk to people when you have such a heavy scene to do?"

Grace had a staff of ten press people and twelve interpreters working with her. For the first time, Linda saw behind the social image of the hard-drinking little woman, why she was selected for this important job.

She was efficient, her excellent press releases were handed out in the proper languages skillfully. Her organization was perfect to the last letter. Every reporter from whatever part of the world had someone who could speak his language, and was given a slant on the production that best suited the conditions of the home audience. The press was treated to deluxe box lunches and soothing flagons of red wine.

Linda was protected from the crowds and the confusion by Hank, Sidney, and two guards.

As the fleeing oracle, she was swathed in the folds of a yellow *hematron*, her head wrapped in a *kredemnon*, a hooded kerchief which folded to hide her face.

For the first time, Linda stood on a nearby camera platform and watched a double wearing a duplicate of her yellow cloak and gauzy *kredemnon* playing her role. It was intriguing and disturbing to her to see how easily she could be doubled. She felt she was looking at herself. The crowd moved in, absorbed the double, and then fell back so the camera could catch the movement of the brilliant yellow robe among the carefully calculated effect of the blues and reds and whites of the mob.

"You should be grateful," said Claudia, "that somebody can take the rap for you in all that heat and dust."

On call, a horse reared up near the double, and the girl in the yellow wig had to jump aside to get out of the way.

"And danger," postscripted Claudia, as the girl was pulled up by John and Leslie and lifted out of the way.

"Why don't *they* have a double?" asked Linda.

"Because the camera has to see their faces; they can't disguise them so easily. Now, watch how that happened, because you'll have to duplicate it in medium shots and closeups later."

She was right. Later Linda got into what seemed to be the fray. Only in medium shot, instead of two thousand extras on film, there were only a hundred milling around her. And later, in closeup, there would be only ten. But the whole pattern would fit together in a dramatic flow in tension and movement that would be one of the most exciting sequences in the picture.

She was pulled through the waterfront crowd, waded into the sea, and lifted into a boat, which took her out to a trireme with Hermocrates, to safety from the angry citizens of Athens, to an island retreat.

There was only one day to film the establishing shots of the whole panorama on the new budget.

The press, satisfied, left with copious notes and souvenirs provided by Grace of *causias,* duplicates of ancient Thessalonian traveling hats, which had protected them from the sun, and also given them memories of the day. Grace knew from experience that such a gift would trigger them to memories and extra copy regarding the filming of *The Oracle.*

The next few days, with dwindling staff and the mass of extras gone, Linda worked at the Anzio location, intrigued with the fact that the smaller shots, with the soundtrack of the babble of the big mob, would make the whole scene, down to the last closeup with John Graves, seem part of the massive panic.

Max was excited, exhausted, and wrapped in an inner life of planning. After a shower and change of clothes at the villa, evenings he managed to meet with Lloyd, the unit manager, and Hank, his assistant, for a quick dinner and the meetings that went on until midnight.

One evening, as Linda walked upstairs with Claudia, fatigued, to crawl gratefully into bed, she turned to Claudia.

"Why doesn't he go to bed?" she said.

"He'll toss around all night," said Claudia, "and wake up raring to go. This is the time he's dreamed of for many years."

And so it was.

As the great scene was finishing, it seemed to Linda the whole excitement of the film began to dwindle. She was no longer the princess with a court around her. The inevitable catalysis occurred when the crew knew that their paychecks were ending. Some would go on a rough location to Greece with extra golden pay. The exciting comradeship of a long-lasting picture had been chopped. The fiesta was at an end. Every day, comrades were jettisoned, privileges denied; even the customs of generous midmorning and midafternoon refreshments and a drink passed out with weekly paychecks were whittled down.

Unions began to squabble about benefits. Underlings grumbled who had previously fawned.

David was in and out of Rome the last days. There were midnight conferences, troubled faces; Sidney was perpetually on the phone. Sometimes Ubaldo was in conference. He seemed happier and more involved socially than he had been when the villa belonged to Niadas. It was as if he were in charge again.

"Well," said Claudia, "these are the last days we'll live like lords in a villa like this. Let's live it up!"

Deliberately she began to make jokes, to sing, to do the foolish happy imitations they had first done when they were limbering up on acting exercises in the early days of pre-production. Claudia imitated various members of the staff, Grace tiddly, Max euphoric, Jessica's overwhelming efficiency, Leslie being piss-elegant to a titled woman, and John Graves throwing his masculinity around to a female reporter.

Slowly Linda began to smile again. Soon she and Claudia were joking and clowning together.

"It's a good thing," said Claudia, "you know we can't afford to have Max's beautiful picture the story of a sadsack girl. Let's try a little Greek dancing!"

They danced around the pool in their bathing suits, laughing and deliberately tumbling in.

When they surfaced, Ubaldo and David stood applauding them.

"Too bad," said Ubaldo, "that the men do most of the dancing in Greece."

"Wouldn't you know it!" said Claudia.

David handed them towels.

"Enjoy yourselves," he said. "Location won't be like this."

"Even better, maybe," said Linda. "Imagine swimming in the sea off a Greek island!"

Claudia warned her, "Don't be too sure. I remember when I was a kid, we shot for a week in Catalina, and I didn't even get a chance to go on one of the glass-bottom boats. It won't be so easy from now on, kiddo. You had controlled conditions of glamour here. The big wide world isn't so easy. I've been through the whole round robin. You'll run the gamut if you're worth your salt. It's what happens in the running that matters."

Later they sat on the terrace together sipping lemonade while David and Ubaldo had one of their conferences, which Claudia called "the closing-down doodaddies."

Claudia was still in a thoughtful mood.

"You know, I think you mean a great deal to Ubaldo. How he has reacted to you has been on my mind. I've been trying to analyze what brings about fame—what it is that makes *you* famous, for example."

"What is it?" asked Linda.

"I think the faceless multitude, which has missed its grab on life, seeks involvement, for example, in your image. If you can really touch people, then you are their idol. Of course, when you lose your grasp on this mass hypnotism called fame, then you have to have something else to cling to, or you are lost. Thank God I have you. . . ."

She took her hand.

"Yes," said Linda. "And Max."

"And Max," said Claudia, smiling. "He's working awfully hard, and accepting much of his script being pared down wonderfully. But that's what real talent is. Flexible, no matter what."

◆◆◆◆◆◆◆◆

Again a dream was being folded away. Effie packed most of Linda's pretty clothes and trinkets for storage. A few beach togs, simple cottons, slacks, and jeans to wear on the yacht. Mostly she'd be in wardrobe during the day.

The last day she was in the villa, she knew she had one sad task to perform. She walked through the gardens, up the gentle hill where Sarge was resting under the olive tree.

It was going to be difficult to leave him here asleep in this strange land so far away from home. She sat on a marble bench nearby and allowed herself the comfort of tears, with no one to console her or attempt philosophical overtones. She was tired of Claudia drumming courage into her, tired of David being overkind when she had expected him to be the one severe person, tired of Max looking at her with his warm eyes, trying to make her be Alethea. She was just a girl, and she was saying good-bye to her childhood as she left the little dog in this garden.

She felt someone nearby. She looked up. It was Ubaldo.

He handed her his handkerchief.

"History repeats itself," he said.

She looked at the linen. It was plain.

"That is ended. No crest," he said. "Forgive my intrusion. I had to speak to you away from everyone."

She wiped her eyes and blew her nose.

"I told you you had my friendship," said Ubaldo. "I want you to bury all the sadness you found here. It will be the secret we shall keep. Do you agree?"

He put out his hand.

She took it.

"I will try," she said. "Sometimes it is hard. I almost told my Aunt Claudia about . . . about Niadas."

"It would only disturb her," said Ubaldo. "Since he is gone, perhaps it is better not to burden her. I want you to know that I have . . . become somewhat involved in your production, doing research, shall we say. My work at the villa will soon be done. Niadas has willed it to be a museum. You will be the last guest in these rooms. I am glad of that."

Linda looked at him, surprised.

"Aren't you sorry you won't stay here?" she asked. "After all, it was yours."

"Life moves on," he said. "I am very glad to say good-bye to many memories here myself. Now, we are friends. I shall see you on location. But now let us walk away from here without looking back."

She stood up.

He took her arm, and they walked down the path together.

It was hard, but she did not look back. If Ubaldo could do it with all he was losing, so could she.

IV

GREECE:
1956-1957

1

The *Circe* was moored at Itea. A short jetty jutted out from the shore, and Turkish tunes could be heard coming from the little cafés lining the sea. The olive groves and mystic mountain of Parnassus lay beyond wreaths of clouds obscuring it.

"I wish we could go ashore," said Linda wistfully as they sat dining on the afterdeck in the evening.

"That's the hell of being stuck on a yacht," said Claudia. "You'll get plenty of shore when we start tomorrow morning."

Linda thought Claudia was being critical of the fun on shore just to placate her. But the next morning the reality of location in Greece was the end of the dream for Linda.

First of all, the tossing of the boat at anchor had made her feel queasy. She was awakened early by Effie, who also wore her seasick smile.

"I hope I get off this thing," she said. "My cabin's about as big as a closet and has a porthole like a lifesaver. And that generator buzzes in my ear all night long."

Effie rarely complained, so Linda realized she must be miserable. The quarters that she herself shared with Claudia had two sleeping staterooms, a little private salon, and a small deck with steamer chairs on it overlooking the land.

"You can use this while we're away," said Linda.

"Just get me some of that yarn from that village down the way called Arachova that those Greek sailors were telling me about," said Effie, "and I'll start to crochet. At least, that will be something."

Once shore boats deposited them on land, Linda and Claudia boarded a chartered bus, along with Max, Sidney, and other members of the company. No more limousines. The bus churned through the hairpin turns of the Salona valley. The meltemi, a cool northern wind, blew up dust-laden gusts. From time to time the bus stopped, while country people with their beasts of burden cluttered the road, some scowling with their xenophobic dislike of foreigners, as they passed on the narrow highway.

Linda opened up the window to watch the beasts of burden, some of them carrying so many bundles of cargo that they looked like moving haystacks. As some of the natives brushed by, in their dusty black clothes, she smelled the odor of unwashed, labor-hot bodies.

"Ugh!" she said, making a face.

"Don't be too hard on them," said Max. "After all, they're not playing a role in those wretched rags. They live in them, very likely sleep in rude huts or caves, and cook over an open fire. Just be glad you have your own room to yourself."

Linda slammed the window shut. She felt put down by Max, even though she knew he was speaking the truth.

They stopped at Kastri, the modern Delphic town, picking up crew members billeted in the Hotel Delphian Apollo. Graves and Leslie were among them, both sleepy and surly. Leslie got on the bus, goggles, sun hat, and a large cologne-soaked handkerchief protecting him from the dust and heat.

The bus pulled up in the parking lot leading to the shrine of the ancient Delphi.

Already the crew had set up generators, cables, cameras, sound equipment, trucks, trailers, honeywagons, and a lunch wagon, busy dispensing gallons of coffee and dozens of sweet rolls. Paper cups, napkins, and cardboard boxes littered the trestle tables.

Nearby megaphones called out orders in English,

Italian, and Greek to the multitude of craftsmen who were setting up the scene.

The sea, the nearby temples, and the pastoral solitude had been wiped out by the modern chaos.

Linda was assigned her mobile dressing room, makeup and wardrobe people assembled for the usual ritual, while Claudia opened the script and began where they had left off in Rome.

Before long Linda heard the rumble of buses coming into the parking space. When her makeup was finished, she stepped out of the trailer in her terry robe to see what was happening.

A group of tourist buses had lined up, visitors poured out, gaping at the excitement of "movie people," turning their backs on the glory of Greece they had traveled thousands of miles to see.

A wave of them descended on Linda, talking in all languages. Japanese, Germans, Swedes, Italians, and good old Americans (as some identified themselves) thrust out pamphlets, airplane tickets, guidebooks, checkbooks, even passports for her to autograph.

Sidney rescued her. He led her and Claudia back into the trailer, slamming the door shut for privacy.

"It's a bloody bore," he said, "but we'll rope this section off, and you'll have to stay in it during visiting hours or you'll be pestered to death."

So Linda spent the first hours at the sacred place of Delphi hiding from tourists. The only Greek she saw nearby was a man busy with a sack and a spiked pole, stabbing up dozens of chewing-gum and candy wrappers and soft-drink containers that had been dropped near the holy grounds of the ancient shrine.

Again she was protected in an organized cocoon, a motion-picture-location community shielding her from adventure and any chance of reality.

It was a pleasure to retreat to the boat, take a shower, and change into comfortable clean clothes. But again she was restless, as evening settled, and the shore took on the beautiful aspect that land always seems to have when the erasures of petty details are seen over a stretch of water.

Max, as producer as well as director, was overwhelmed with details. Jessica, as associate producer, struggled with Sidney, trying to cut expenses, fighting for her own career and ownership. Endless hours were spent with unit manager, staff, and crew, coordinating the elements of the massive location; assistants worked with second units on the sea battles, setting up villages of transients who made up the core of this make-believe world. It was akin to moving and directing an army that had to be at the right place at the right time. Each hour ticked off golden dollars. And each day moved closer to the bottom of the pot of gold at the end of the rainbow.

There was something—in spite of talent, ambition, and all the goodwill in the world—that loomed over the company, and it was money cut off; its genesis, after David's and Ubaldo's contributions, was a rising Wall Street storm.

Without complaining, Claudia realized that this enforced togetherness on the boat was going to play hob with her life with Max. After the panic was over, she'd have to talk to him about a little privacy ashore. Poor darling, he had so much on his shoulders.

Guides, sailors, fishermen, and government personnel who worked at Delphi gathered in the tavernas of Kastri in the evening to drink ouzo and the local Fix beer, and watch the girls parade by. They were mostly Americans and Swedes, who, under the proper conditions, could be very enthusiastic temporary companions, especially when their escorts spouted their lines about ancient Greece and the glories of the free life.

"Let's get a shore boat and go up to Kastri for dinner. Wouldn't it be fun to have roast lamb and baklava and all those things?"

"I'm game," said Claudia. As usual, Max, Jessica, and Sidney were in conference.

Claudia and Linda found a vintage taxi and drove up to Kastri.

By the time they arrived, the evening was well started. John Graves was sitting at a table with two pretty long-legged American college girls who were wearing French bathing suits. They laughed at every remark he made, nibbling plates of mezethakia and liberally drinking the ouzo he kept ordering.

After a warm hello, John asked Linda and Claudia to join up, but it was no fun. The remarks the girls and John made seemed out of context, and Linda felt more of a stranger than ever she had on the set. Finally Claudia rescued her.

"Obviously," she said, "you people are never going to eat, so I think we'll have our dinner. We're starved. You'll forgive us."

They were graciously forgiven.

The only other event of the evening, aside from a lamb-and-bean casserole, spicy eggplant, and sticky sweet baklava, was the emergence of Leslie Charles from the sea with a handsome curly-headed boy who was a diver.

"I'd introduce him to you," said Leslie, "but actually I can't pronounce his name."

They went off to a candlelit table, and Leslie handed the musicians some bills. They were engulfed in music, hand-clapping, and rounds of drinks. Soon the men very enthusiastically began to dance the syrtos.

"Well," said Linda, "we might as well go back."

They rattled down the road in their taxi—it seemed endlessly—and boarded the boat.

The wind was whining in the rigging. If the meltemi kept up, there would be only sporadic shooting. The second unit could not film the sea battles. The white villages would be shuttered.

This was the beginning of the first shooting in Greece. To Linda, the rest of the Delphi location also turned into a nightmare. Dust, winds, bad timing due to the time the *Pallas Athena* company had eaten up for Titan bugged them weatherwise. Even when days were good, there were mike-boom shadows, shifts in key light, and interference from the sound trucks as tourist buses and cars bombarded them. Boom squeaks on trucks, lint in camera apertures, braying of donkeys, cawing of birds, and occasionally even the sad, ancient screech of an eagle broke up lines, and held up production.

Max fought for reality. Sidney fought for time. Linda fought to be in character; that's all she had to cling to. Claudia fought for serenity; Jessica fought for her position; David fought for more money; Leslie fought for publicity; Grace Boomer, established in a hotel room in Itea, fought for location news. John Graves forgot his intention to lead the noble life, and had no trouble fighting for the most attractive women who came through town. The whole crew, Italian, Greek, British, and American, fought out production during the day, and often fought each other at night.

Chloë returned from Santorini, where the fortieth day of Niadas' death had ended in a memorial service. The last icon kissed, the last lamp flickered into darkness.

She had waived weekly pay on her contract—her work to be finished last, in order to attend to the many problems that had attended Niadas' death. The evening she returned, she boarded the *Circe* and dined with Max, Jessica, Claudia, and Sidney. Afterward she asked if she could have coffee with Linda and Claudia in their salon.

They sat on the little private deck.

She shook the pins from her hair and let it fall over her shoulders.

"Oh, it's good to breathe the sea air. It has been a difficult time," she said. "I wanted to tell you all about it."

Linda listened, wide-eyed, wishing she could tell Chloë some of the things that were pressing on her. It was hard to keep the secret about Niadas.

"Well," said Chloë, "he was put to rest in the little chapel he built in Thera. And he has left a great monument in my keeping. He left me as conservator of the Institute for Hellenic Women. It was left in a corporate trust fund aside from his personal funds so no one can touch it but me."

"You mean," said Claudia, "Martha Ralston."

"That is right," said Chloë, flashing her an appreciative glance. "She has tied up everything else. Including this picture, I understand."

"What have you heard?" asked Claudia.

"I have heard from bankers that we are over budget, all sorts of bills were laid in that the trustees refused to pay, and David Austin is up to his neck trying to raise more money. Not that he didn't get plenty. Someone, somewhere handed him almost a million dollars. And that's aside from a million and a half he raised himself on his own personal securities. With more to come."

"What's the big problem, then?" asked Linda. "That sounds like a lot of money to me."

"The trustees, pressed by Martha Ralston, are asking him to pay her interest on the massive loan for *Pallas Athena* and this picture. I think Martha Ralston is trying to break us."

"I'd like to break her neck," said Claudia. "Jeffrey loathed her. She was always late, and pouty. He had to make a photographic sitting with her once, and drank a pint of Scotch so he could stand to pose with her."

Linda smiled.

"From what I've heard, didn't my father often drink a pint of Scotch?"

"Shut up!" said Claudia. "You're getting too smart-ass."

They smiled at each other.

"What is your Hellenic Institute all about?" asked Claudia.

"It is mostly a scholarship fund to aid young women without any family support. Also it helps orphans and unwed mothers. Niadas was very generous. But I have a staff working to investigate their needs, and help them as soon as possible. It is a great responsibility to my country."

She turned to Linda.

"I am looking forward to my new scenes with you. I have seen the rushes. You will be a star. You know, I had always wanted to be one, but my life has changed. Trying to be a star around you is like bringing owls to Athens."

"Oh, that isn't so," said Linda. "You're a wonderful actress."

"That isn't being a star," said Chloë. "Pericles Niadas has given me the funds to do the thing I wanted to do on my own. Help my people."

She smiled at Claudia.

"Don't our patterns change, Claudia? I would be an obscenity if I did not use my life with meaning. Sometimes the dreamer must mature without falling victim to desires."

"Yes," said Claudia, "patterns change."

Before the Delphi location was ended, David returned once more to the *Circe*. Claudia and Max had taken a car to drive along the roads, their excuse a search for an ancient berm where the footsoldier Diodynus would flee with Alethea.

David found Linda sitting on the stern deck, in the late afternoon, watching Effie finishing a sweater.

"That's dull stuff for a young actress," he said. "How about taking a walk with me?"

Ashore a car awaited. It carried them up the olive-dappled hills to the mountains. They got out at Delphi.

"You know," he said as they climbed the path, "I haven't had much time for such jaunts lately. But by now all the tourists will have taken their buses off to various taverns. How would you like to see the real Delphi with me?"

The phaedriades . . . the Castalian springs . . . the rock of the sibyl under the Pelasgian wall . . .

"Here. . ." said Linda, her voice echoing, "this is where I would have prophesied in another time."

She walked into the fissure, and shuddered. The mystery was all gone—but what had happened here!

She came out, arms crossed over her breasts.

"Am I magic, David?"

"You're magic, Linda," he said.

She came to him and put her hand on his arm.

"Maybe *you* are," she said. "Chloë told me what you've done to make *The Oracle* come true."

He started up the path to the amphitheater. Jackdaws cawed at them. She followed him.

"It's my job," he said. "I hope I can make it come off. They're falling on me, Linda. What will you do if we can't finish the picture? Have you thought?"

"Jump off the shining rocks," she said.

"I'll go with you." He laughed.

High up above, an eagle circled in the darkening sky.

"Oh, look!" she cried, waving her arms wildly.

They climbed onward. Soon they were at the amphitheater.

"This is where echo was born," said Linda. "If you face a certain way, a whole line will come back to you. Let's try."

She turned toward the cliffs and called out.

"Echo! Echo! Echo!"

When the word came back to her full force, she turned to him and laughed.

"Wow! It hit me in the face!"

"What are you going to say to it?" David laughed. "It had better be pretty memorable."

As she looked at him, the memory of the first time she had seen him in London hit her. It seemed so long ago. The eyes. The brows, the way his hair grew, and even the back of his neck as he turned away from her. So neat . . . so right. Suddenly, with a surge of joy, she realized that she'd rather be with him than anyone else in the world.

"Shall I really say it?" she said.

"Why not!" He smiled. And when he did, it was with his eyes, not just his lips.

"David Austin, I love you," she said.

"Love you . . . love you . . ." echoed back.

He put his arm around her and faced the same way.

"Linda Barstow, I love you!" He laughed.

"Love you . . . love you . . ." echoed back his voice.

He released her and turned toward the sea.

"It's the most beautiful view in Greece," he said.

Streams, groves, mountains, plains, the sea, and the sky, backed by the shining cliffs, and the white ruins of temples blended into a silent, serene kingdom.

"I never thought it could be so peaceful," she said, looking.

They passed upward to the stadium and the stone tubs where the ancient athletes with their ring of admirers bathed after the games. Life was timeless; they could have been two ancient Greeks coming from a festival to the sacred portals of the shrine, to sight see and to peer down at the total splendor of Delphi.

"This is my best day," said Linda.

"Mine too," said David. "I'm glad we talked."

She couldn't remember that they'd said much, but she was happier than she'd been since . . . since she was a woman.

◆◆◆◆◆◆◆◆

It was a small island, one among many of the scattered god-fists of the northern Sporades.

An ancient seafarer who had dredged wealth from the seas and had been rescued from a storm had built a small temple to Poseidon on a flowering hill looking down into a sheltered bay. A stream mothered by a crystal spring had called to its borders willows. Nearby some olive trees had wound their roots into the rocky headland. Shrubs and flowers had edged the little grove. On the slope of a hill someone had planted a little vineyard.

The *Circe* moored in the crescent bay, and as Linda looked out upon it, the company's next location, she hoped all the phantoms of her nights would go away. Here, even with the two hundred of the company a temporary confusion over the hill, she could swim and read and dream and wonder what was to happen next.

It was a time of sun-struck white pillars at dawn, the pure sharp glare of Greek noon. In the clear Aegean daylight Linda could see the acanthus pattern on a sculptured pillar half a mile away over the water. And then came the rosy evenings with their faded light, before the first stars became lamps in the sky.

With the *Circe* settled into the crescent of the harbor, Linda swam in the sea following the daily shooting or on days when the company worked with John and Leslie on the other side of the island filming the difficult and laborious sea battles.

Two of the younger Greek crew members out of the complement of forty-four, Yannis and Fotis, dived with her and explored the underwater glories of the bay. Claudia watched, for the first time seeing her nièce sporting and laughing with boys her own age.

The handsome, curly-headed youths, having seen her aboard the yacht for weeks, accepted her as a young American girl, not the least self-conscious about the fact that she was the star of *The Oracle*. Busy about their chores on the *Circe*, they paid little attention to the film company's activities.

Captain Petroulis, watching the blond girl and his nephews diving off the Boston whaler, which he had lowered for their sport, smiled. It had been a long time since such larking had brought about laughter to the waters lapping against the hull of the *Circe*.

Effie, perpetually knitting sweaters, scarves, and afghans for Linda with her multicolored peasant wool, smiled along with Claudia as they sat on deck watching.

"It's a good thing," she said. "This is the first time that B'linda's had fun with any kids since she left school."

"Wouldn't do her any harm to have a lighthearted romance," said Claudia.

Privately she heaved a sigh of relief that the mad crush her niece had on John Graves seemed to be a thing of the past, or at least was no longer surfacing so obviously. Through the years she had seen too many women breeze in and out of his peripatetic sex life to think there was a possibility of anything but unhappiness coming out of any woman's affection for him. That is, of course, save her own. She had been his mentor and his teacher. She was proud of what he had done with his career. He was the sort of man it was good to have only as friend and co-worker. Perhaps someday Linda could work with him on that basis. They were good chemistry together.

For a moment she reflected on the short spate of admiration that Niadas had given Linda. It had seemed almost like a cult worship. Perhaps it was just as well for her that the man had been in her life such a short time. It was not good to be worshiped like that. And with Ubaldo, it was almost the same, save that his gentle attendance, as far as she could see, had put him in the position of cicerone. She had heard that in some way he was involved with this production. Conferences late at night on the boat as he had come in briefly to meet with David proved this.

Being an old hand at motion-picture production, Claudia noticed the thinning down of staff, the cautious elimination of frills. Here on location all sorts of doubling up could be done, which none of the unions would have accepted in the United States or on the Continent. For example, she had seen makeup men doing body makeup, hairdressers pinch-hitting with wardrobe, and she noticed David even flew in on commercial airlines and traveled on public carriers. Truly, she thought with a smile, the last platform of luxury in this whole film company was the yacht.

And this was only because it was the crowded but usable nerve center of the picture. It had taken a great adjustment for her to accept the fact that Max was nearby, yet not with her. She felt he was as happy as a man could be to have conditions center completely about his work. When he was not directing, he could practically roll from his cabin to the cutting room or projection room. Several times she had laughed to catch him at the moviola in his pajamas. He had a captive nucleus of craftsmen literally living with him. Fortunately, young Schute, the cutter, was a dedicated technician and enjoyed working with the master. The projectionist doubled getting film off to Rome, arranging transportation, and helping the cutter keep the film shipshape.

The men who conferred with him boarded early in a shore boat, and sometimes after a hasty dinner worked late into the night with Max, who seemed tireless; then they were motored back to their digs, waiting to start the next session.

Once, Linda heard Ubaldo, visiting, say they were akin to the youths who lived and labored with the great artists like Michelangelo and Da Vinci. He deeply admired the skilled craftsmen on the production.

It made Linda realize more sharply what dedication existed on a picture. She was only a part of it.

"It's an art form," he said, "as complicated as a fine Byzantine mosaic, made of a million parts, intelligently assembled to create this work of art."

Jessica had sweated it out on script and story, using all her expertise, for her future depended on this film. She occasionally took a few days off to go to Athens "for a breather." The breather, rumor had it, was when her escort at the party, Prince Carlo Bonavente, came into Athens at her urging to spend several days with her. No doubt, Claudia thought, each was making a grab for what the other one could offer; if they ever got together each other's true vital statistics, it would be more than interesting.

Late one afternoon Linda came on deck, after showering the salt from her blond hair. She brushed her hair, her white jumper fresh against her suntanned skin.

"Let's do a little voice placement," said Claudia. "Why don't you do that lovely cinquain you know— 'These be three silent things' and so forth." She sang out, " 'The hour before the dawn . . . the mouth of one just dead . . .' "

"No!" Linda cried out. "Not that one."

She went to the rail, looking at the sea.

"I don't want to hear that ever again!"

"Well, for god's sake, what did I *do?*" said Claudia. "We've done that a dozen times!"

Linda burst into tears and rushed below to her cabin. She slammed the door and sat on her bunk. The hour before the dawn . . . the mouth of one just dead . . . Niadas, that night, the nightmare that awakened her. . . .

There was a knocking at her door.

"Linda, Linda, are you all right?"

She opened the door to Claudia.

"I'm sorry," she said. "I was just thinking of . . . of death."

"Of course, I understand," said Claudia.

But she didn't. It was a puzzle. Linda had refused to go back to the amphitheater at the villa. Now this. . . . Her young womanhood perhaps was not as simple as it seemed on the surface, just the problems preparing to play a make-believe role in a film. What personal turmoil was going on behind that young brow?

Later, as she stood with Linda at the boarding ladder of the yacht, she was glad to see David getting off the caïque that was delivering fresh produce to the boat. With his slim briefcase in hand as always, as he boarded, she thought he looked grim. For some reason, seeing his worried face gave Claudia a personal concern. She was glad that he had turned so affectionately to Linda. They seemed to have a comfortable comradeship. It was good for both of them, perhaps melting all sorts of glacial fears inside them. She would try to talk to him after Linda was in bed.

◆◆◆◆◆◆◆◆

It was very dark on the aft deck late in the evening. Everyone had retired, save Claudia and David. The only spark was the brightening of their cigarettes as they puffed on them. And when David threw one overboard, it made a little sparkling arc as it fell into the sea below.

"What's bugging you?" she said.

"Things are getting very thin," he said. "I can talk to you, Claudia, because you saw Titan grow from the most rudimentary beginnings."

"How's that old son-of-a-bitch behaving in Hollywood?" she asked.

"If you're referring to Fergus, which naturally I think you are, he has settled into a glacial silence and lack of cooperation. That was to be expected."

"Are you scraping the barrel?" asked Claudia.

"Yes," said David, "I am. As with most schedules on location, this is endless. We've got at least two more months."

"I wish I could help," she said. "Well, anyway, you don't have anyone to support. I suppose your mother's well looked after. That's one thing off your back."

"Yes, she is, with a good solid trust fund," said David. "The only thing is, I worry about her. What's to become of her? You know, every once in a while she runs away. I remember one time about eight years ago. Fergus doesn't know I know, but he had to go down to Mexico, Baja California of all places, to some out-of-the-way hotel to get her back."

Claudia felt a chill that climbed up into the back of her neck. Fragments of a puzzle. Jeffrey's note, what did it say? And the remark of Belinda. She had faced her aunt before her father's funeral, denying that her father had died in the house.

"Well," she said to David, "life is complicated, isn't it? I think I'll turn in. See you in the morning. Maybe you can help Linda get over her depression."

Once in the cabin, she opened the envelope that she always carried with her papers. The chunk of amber came into her hand, and she clutched it, thinking of Jeffrey, the little insects forever imprisoned in the smooth lump of amber, and his fascination about them.

It was a time, long, long ago. She unfolded Jeffrey's letter and read: "I'm running away with the one I love."

Then, thinking of David's age, she remembered that night; it must have been over thirty-seven years ago—she usually dated happenings with her films. It was at Arrowhead Springs resort. They were on location, she hadn't known that Esther Austin was coming up to meet her husband, when they had been hotel-bound by a fierce storm, and Claudia had literally seduced Fergus in his suite at the hotel. It hadn't entered her mind until this moment, for it didn't seem important then, that all of a sudden the next morning the young bride was in residence. She must have been there all night; the road was so washed out the next morning that nobody could get in, even on foot. She could have come in, she could have seen them. They had laughed later when they found they hadn't even locked the door, and had made love like crazy people on the floor of the sitting room. Esther could have fallen into Jeffrey's arms that night. Her brother had told her that Esther was his ideal of a beautiful and tender young woman.

And then she remembered when Jeffrey, out of context, had asked her if she ever saw David Austin in London. Even then she had almost stumbled on the truth.

She scribbled a few figures recalling dates and years.

Before she turned out the light, she knew she would not sleep. She thought of David's blue-eyed glance, his innate elegance of body and movement, the way he turned his head, how his hair grew in a widow's peak, and most especially those small, flat ears. She knew David Austin was a Barstow. Looking at a small silver-framed picture of Jeffrey taken in his youth, she realized there was no other possibility. They were peas in a pod. She marveled that no one caught on to the resemblance.

A Barstow! A Barstow! Claudia was torn between deep disturbance and pride that Jeffrey had a son, a man she admired, a man who seemed to be breaking away from some trauma that had disturbed him when she first had met him.

She smiled to herself. Oh, the difference between having Fergus or Jeffrey for a father! She was sorry David couldn't know his heritage. And most of all, she was sorry that he couldn't know that the career he was protecting was that of his own half-sister, Linda. No, not Linda really, but *Belinda*.

She suspected that no one in this company aboard the *Circe*, but herself knew what a family affair this picture was.

◆◆◆◆◆◆◆◆

By the first of December, minor characters had been finished and were off salary. With no facilities for the press on the primitive island, Grace Boomer gratefully returned to set up the press book in Hollywood. Between the still photographers and Sidney, any news on location could be sent in. The major glamorous and spectacular sequences had been done under controlled conditions in Cinecittà.

But when she arrived in Hollywood, she faced a problem that eclipsed even the most difficult days of Claudia's and Jeffrey's shenanigans.

Letters had poured in from stockholders, asking how a failing studio could spend so much money on a film that had as its potential a young girl who was the possible destroyer of the morality of young Americans.

Linda Barstow was potential dynamite, a child-woman sex symbol. Her introduction to London press at Claudia's tacky alcoholic debut, the scandal about her supposed liaison with John Graves, and the final drama in Rome (with pictures), the last public hours of Niadas' life in her company, at a party so lavish that the Hellenic world had cried out in horror at its heedless luxury, times being what they were—all these were enough to cause intense criticism. Also many parents suggested that the glamorous excesses of Linda made every young girl in America consider having an equally exotic carefree sexual experience.

Now the publicity and advertising campaign would have to be directed toward her "magnificent portrayal of a beautiful virgin beset by the pressures of a corrupt society."

Grace's first revelation of the problems facing Fergus came when he called her into his office. She saw a haggard man, ridden by a phantom of impermanence in his hitherto ordered life scheme.

"You realize," he said, "that an account of your shenanigans, all of you . . ."

Grace immediately felt guilty, as if she had been the very matrix of some orgy paid for by dear old Titan.

"On account of the goings-on which you allowed to get into the hands of the eager press, we have the potential of the whole Bible Belt being up in arms."

"Listen," said Grace, "aside from all these problems

after Niadas' incredible party and his dramatic death, any other publicity, aside from what we can get from the normal production values of sea battles, is an anticlimax. Now, our immediate job is to prove to the public that it's not the sexual shenanigans, which we hope will be played down, but the film, the talent of Max Ziska, the performances of John Graves and Leslie Charles, the brilliant introduction of Chloë Metaxa, one of the great actresses of our times, and the amazing gifts of the young star Linda Barstow, that are the elements that make this production so exciting, so meaningful, and so extraordinary, that anyone, from highest levels of international society to Midwest farmers, will be out of things if they didn't see it."

Fergus turned to her with a sudden rather touching wistfulness.

"I've known you a long time, Gracie. We've gone through this studio together since that water tower was put up."

They both looked out of the window at the tower, with its fist holding lightning bolts between the fingers, the Promethean thought hitting them both. Symbol of the Titans, who no longer were the earth giants they once had been.

"And if the board and stockholders so decide at the next annual meeting, I'll be out of things, too. And likely, you too, for you know how it is around a studio. The new guard sweeps clean. Young kids we've never heard about will be doing things a new way."

Grace shuddered. She too had her nightmares. It didn't do any good to try to look younger. She'd been around so long, everyone had her pegged.

"I'll do the best I can, Fergus," she said. "You know how the press and publicity can ricochet. It's never controlled. We're always at the mercy of the freak thing we never expected."

Fergus agreed.

"Well, get on it. Advertising campaigns which are slanted under our control will help. Get out all your stills and check every picture that might have innuendo. Keep Linda clean."

"But, Fergus," said Grace, "the public flourishes on innuendo. You were worried about the Barstow kid having sex potential. You don't have to worry about *that* anymore."

"Walk the tightrope," he said. "I'll trust your judgment."

After she left, he returned to his private worries. It seemed to him that when he was younger his time was taken up with creative problems. Now he worried about abstract things that he could not control.

For the first time in his life he feared David. No longer was he a pushover. He was stunned that David was taking the part of his income that was not involved with Titan stock and spending it on a chancy investment. Yet if it didn't go, the studio was shot. He was appalled at the enormous costs of the picture moving, as if it were a small army on location, with the massive expenses of second-unit sea battles, as well as land scenes.

Prints and advertising would loom up after the last scene was shot. Titan would have to handle that. The only takeout was that distributor's fee from the first dollar. But that was long, long off. There was only a continuity cut on the picture. Nobody could tell yet what it really would be. The close cut would emerge at least three months at best after the production was finished. That would mean that the stockholders' meeting would come in May, before the picture was released. The image of himself stepping down after stormy sessions inhibited his sleep, his rest, and influenced the quality of his work.

Titan was starving in Hollywood while a banquet went on in Europe.

◆◆◆◆◆◆◆◆◆

The teeming portable city that had blossomed on the sparsely settled island was now gone. A small primitive hotel, a little *taverna,* and a cluster of native white houses where fishermen lived remained, along with several temporary buildings that had been thrown together for the company.

The skeleton crew, unit manager, essential camera, still man, sound, makeup, wardrobe, various assistants, script girl, boom crew, and a few gaffers were all that was left of the company that at one time had numbered a staff of several hundred.

The island had all the tattered sadness of a vacation village, deserted, out-of-season.

The temple of Poseidon and the nearby olive trees alone stood solidly against the wind, rain, and sun, clean remnant of the past, which would outstay any evidence that a film company had settled for several months in this desolate place.

Leslie Charles had one more important scene at the temple, having finished the last covering shots of the sea battles. Then he, too, would go back to Hollywood, knowing well as he flipped through the pages of the original script that his role had been deeply cut.

Linda, John Graves, and Chloë, with a handful of supers who would double as slaves, servants, and citizens of the ancient town, would remain to finish the dramatic scenes in the beauty of the Greek seascape that were the core of the film.

Chloë had been invited to stay on the *Circe*. At first she had balked; she would rather stay on land, in a little vaulted villa overlooking the sea. But Claudia took her aside one morning.

"I think I know why you don't want to stay on board; no doubt because of your memories of a happier time on this boat. But I need your help, Chloë. Linda is in a most depressed state. She doesn't even want to swim with the boys anymore. She has a boat take her ashore, and walks alone up and down the beach. It's going to be her birthday December 4. Will you help me cheer her up?"

"I will," said Chloë, "if you'll let me keep my little house to retreat to on the island. I'm not used to living within such thin walls anymore. And perhaps it would do her good to come to my place occasionally, to get away herself. We'll have to give her a little party there."

"That's a good idea," said Claudia. "David is coming in for dinner. Will you join up? I think Ubaldo's coming also."

"Where do you put them all?" said Chloë.

"We make out. Sometimes Linda and I double up." She looked worried.

Chloë glanced at her sharply.

"You are disturbed."

"Why shouldn't I tell you," said Claudia. "I guess you know that *The Oracle* has its own special account, outside Niadas' other interests. Well, Martha Ralston's attached everything to do with it. David's having to dig up money, and I think he's running out."

"How much will it cost to go on?"

"Don't ask me," said Claudia. "I have no idea."

Staying on the boat did not please Chloë, but she felt sorry for Linda and she admired the valorous fight Claudia was making to protect her. Thinking how Niadas had protected her through the tender years when she might have had the most tragic of lives, she felt that the least she could do would be to help this young girl, and to help make Niadas' dream come true. So she settled in her stateroom.

David and Ubaldo arrived, having arranged a meeting, one from New York, the other from Rome.

They had a pleasant dinner, and after the company had dispersed, David and Ubaldo spread out papers on the brilliantly lighted salon table. Chloë went to the stern, pretending that it was Niadas who was inside, as he had been many times with his lieutenants while she sat on deck.

Tonight the northwest wind was again whining in the rigging, and the sea churned. The moon shone on the little white temple ashore, nestled against the dark olive trees. It seemed as stark and cold, somehow, as she felt, knowing that Niadas would never be on his boat again. It was no use grieving for him. He had embraced her with his protection, and left her as much as one lifetime could handle.

After a while, tired of the wind whipping strands of hair against her face, she retired to her room.

And then she heard them through the walls. She didn't care to eavesdrop; she could not help herself.

"I have had a most fortunate experience," said Ubaldo. "As I confessed to you, I excavated my antiquities throughout the years before I sold my villa to Niadas. I feared them being confiscated by the Germans during the war, and hid them well in catacombs no one but myself knew existed. And now, a large shipment of my antique marbles is en route to London. Now I can give you that last two hundred thousand dollars."

Chloë's eyes opened wide. So this was who Ubaldo, Niadas' majordomo, was. He had been the mysterious man who owned the villa and its treasures.

"You have done more than I ever expected," said David. "If I hadn't had your immense help, I couldn't have gone on this far. I am in the middle of complicated financial exchanges. Need I tell you how grateful I am?"

"It is my pleasure," said Ubaldo. "Now what do you do?"

"We'll finish with two months' shooting to go. The most important scenes still to do are with Chloë and Linda," he said. "It's incredible that Max has worked as quickly as he has. He cuts with his camera, and his cover shots are impeccable. But uncontrolled conditions on location are always a bugaboo, and as you know, we were forced into bad weather with our late start due to the *Pallas Athena* fiasco."

The men talked on into the night. Chloë turned on a small bedside unit that was connected to a sound system throughout the yacht. She didn't want to hear anymore. She had heard too much.

The next day she moved ashore to her little white house, with the blue vaulted ceiling. It would be convenient to visit the yacht occasionally, but she had to walk by herself, think by herself, of what she had learned about Ubaldo.

◆◆◆◆◆◆◆◆◆

Ubaldo sat at the terrace of the little *taverna* and drank milky ouzo. Linda and Leslie Charles were shooting a scene at the temple. He had been invited to visit by Max, but he decided against it. He wanted to see it on film, full-blown and beautiful.

"May I?" a voice said.

It was Chloë. Her dark hair tumbled loose on her shoulders, and she wore a simple black dress like the local peasant women.

"Look, may I call you Ubaldo? I did before—before things changed. I don't know much about you, but I know you are not what you seem to be."

He turned his glass, looking down.

"Who is?" he said.

That made her smile.

"Right. . . . Now, I could not help but overhear your conference last night. I know what you have done. Why?"

"Perhaps I believe in a dream too," he said.

"That doesn't mean you can make it come true."

"Niadas tried," he said.

"You're staking your life's worth on this," she said.

He did not nod, but just looked at her. After a moment he spoke.

"When you have no family or home, to be able to believe in something is the ultimate experience."

"The same with me," she said, "but I think we are both interested in one person. Linda. She seems to be deeply sad."

He looked at her, appreciating her sensitivity.

"Will you help me give her a marvelous birthday? One she will never forget?"

He smiled, looking at the selfless joy in her face.

◆◆◆◆◆◆◆◆

Leslie Charles's last scene was with Linda at the portico of the temple. As Hermocrates, the physician, he was to tell her that the seizures she had as the oracle were induced not only by her own illness, which he had cured, but by the clever induction of hallucinogens from Pargas into the vapors of the underground adytum.

As the price for uttering apostasies against the age-old sacred rituals, Hermocrates' life was imperiled; he was leaving his own world of fame and riches, to a voluntary exile. Now that she was healed, she must find a fate of her own making.

The last two words of the scene were his. He was to quote the famous words that were graven in stone at Delphi.

"Know thyself," he was to say, and then, shaken, she was to watch him as he was rowed out to a waiting trireme that would carry him away.

Due to the miracle of cutting, the shot of his exit to the sea had been filmed weeks before. Closeups and medium shots on land would make this magic all of one piece.

It took imagination for Linda to look off to sea in the direction of what was supposed to be the trireme, but was in reality a speedboat tied up to the jetty with Leslie's elegant luggage piled high on it.

Max had promised that he could catch the inter-island boat at the last moment, which would connect with his flight to Rome, his eventual destination Hollywood. If he stayed a day longer, the company would have been penalized ten thousand dollars for an extra week's work.

Sidney was grateful that Leslie was enough of a trouper to suggest that if they could get him off on time, he'd do a quick change on the speedboat, discarding his costume and getting into trousers and shirt en route. For all his elegancies, Leslie's foremost vanity was that he was a trouper. But inside his apparently cool facade, he was quivering, for he instinctively knew what was happening to him. The first of the principal actors to leave the film, he was attempting to be casual about the fact that many of his important scenes had been cut for economic reasons.

As he and Linda awaited camera adjustments for the last take, they looked at each other. He saw the perfection of her flawless youth, and remembered how handsome he had been when he was young. She saw the furrows that sun, age, and makeup made in his face; he seemed ancient to her.

Sensing her appraising glance, he picked a paper out of the pocket in his set chair.

"Well, dear," he said, "I guess this is it. I shall soon be dashing. Here we are on paper, all in a nutshell."

He read from the Xeroxed breakdown: " 'Exterior temple. Scene 538. Hermocrates warns Alethea that the oracle is really a dupe; she has been chosen to be priestess because her seizures induce faith in people. He flees.' "

He set the page back in the holder.

"He flees," he said. "How very convenient."

He lifted an eyebrow.

"What do you mean, Leslie?" she asked.

"There's not always a trireme waiting off-scene for a takeout. Don't let them try to make you a box-office oracle, Linda. I see everyone pouncing on you all the time. Well, they did that to me when they saw I was box-office magic."

He sighed.

"On reflection, I guess that wasn't as bad as what happens later. Probably, next time we perform, if I'm fortunate, I will be your father or some elderly character—no more a star. I'm afraid this picture has done it for me."

"Don't say that. You're a wonderful actor," she said, putting her hand on his arm.

"There are lots of supporting actors who are great performers," he said. "And there's always one picture that demoted them. I guess the worst thing that could happen to an actor is to resist slipping into a secondary position. And we never seem to realize it until it's too late."

Linda didn't know what to say. She tried to understand, but it didn't come into focus. Acting was acting.

"I just hope," he said, "that you will put your money safely away, and enjoy your success. Otherwise, it isn't worth it."

He bent over and kissed her forehead. She clasped his hand. He was the first man she had acted with.

"Okay, Leslie," said Max, "if we can get this last shot in the can, you're a free man."

They found their marks in front of the camera. The hot sun shone down. Action had to halt while the makeup man powdered the sweat off Leslie's forehead. A vagrant wind billowed Linda's chiton; the wardrobe woman rushed in and pinned it. They were ready.

"Action," said Max, almost a whisper.

They played the scene. The noble Hermocrates took the hand of the young oracle, made his pronouncements of her cure, and after a pause touched her cheek tenderly, whispered, "Know thyself," and without glancing back, walked toward the sea. In the silence a seabird dipped into camera view and made its sad cry. Max was excited; such fortunate accidents enhanced the scene.

The camera moved in on Linda's face, Hermocrates forgotten. Her eyes wet with tears of gratitude to her savior, she stood watching him leave, waving wistfully.

Later a scene would be shot by helicopter, moving from her face until she was a small figure. John Graves, as the soldier Diodynus, would come to her from the hill, and the two would be standing side-by-side until the temple and the sea were almost lost in the vast Aegean world.

The crew stood silently, taking in the emotion of the moment.

"Cut," said Max. "That's a wrap. Beautiful, Leslie. Thank you."

He turned to Sidney.

"He'd better run."

But without farewells Leslie had fled. He stepped into the nearby speedboat, out of context in his Greek costume, perched on his Vuitton luggage. The engine revved, the boat took off, almost toppling him.

Linda rushed to the jetty to wave him off.

He was crying as the boat pulled away from the shore.

2

Twelve gathered the evening of December 4 to celebrate the birthday of Linda.

The party was held in front of Chloë's icing-sugar white house, with candles flickering against the blue vaulted ceilings.

Outside, the trestle tables were set up with food and flowers that Ubaldo had assembled on his return from Athens, where he had done some banking chores.

They would dine well on the food of the country. Lettuce, fresh mint, cucumbers, and plum tomatoes with a lemon dressing, calamaraki, fried squid, moussaka, rice pilaf. The traditional lamb on a spit, stuffed with crumbled feta cheese and parsley, was roasting, the scent of garlic and oregano ascended as an old woman from the village turned it. Wild wood strawberries were sent in from Corfu, kaseri cheese, and semi-sparkling wine from Paxos.

The shore boat was crowded as the *Circe* complement left for the jetty. Captain Petroulis carried an ornate cake, which the chef had baked; Claudia clutched her prize gift in her purse; Max carried a package long ordered from Bulgari in his pocket; Effie a bulky package. En route, the two boys, Yannis and Fotis, presented Linda with an enormous shell that they claimed had belonged to Triton. They blew it with ear-splitting blasts.

Jessica seemed particularly affable.

"Well," she said, "my little girl is growing up. And what a marvelous year's ahead of us."

Glancing at her smile, Claudia wondered what was up.

As they approached the shore, they saw the lights of a jeep coming over the rocky road from the village to Chloë's little house. Out of it stepped John Graves. He had brought the musicians from the hotel with him. Playing pipiza, flute, and violin, while Chloë beat on a defi, a primitive tambourine, they greeted them at the dock.

Chloë crowned Linda with flowers. Ubaldo handed her a bouquet, and she was seated ceremonially by the table. Toasts were drunk, glasses were smashed haphazardly into the firestones, and the celebration began.

The two Greek boys started dancing the syrtos, the slow, dragging island dance. In a few moments John Graves, the heavyset Petroulis, who was nonetheless light on his feet, Ubaldo, laughing and expert, and even Max joined in, to the applause of the women.

Chloë, apologizing that the women had the worst of it with their demure dancing, eyes downcast, insisted on showing them a few steps. Linda, Jessica, Claudia, and Effie, who was urged to join and not be a spoilsport, followed in a few steps, to the immense cheering of the other guests and the musicians.

"David ought to be in any moment," said Max. "You know, he went back to London with Sidney, who's taking over the office chores."

"Oh," said Jessica, "is David going to be here?"

"I hope so," said Linda. "It wouldn't be so much fun without him."

Jessica gave Linda a strange look, and at once Claudia realized that Jessica also knew that David was Jeffrey's son.

The thought that David was coming seemed to galvanize Jessica into action.

"Well, dear," she said to Linda, "I was waiting for your eighteenth birthday for this, but time has moved so swiftly, I'm going to give it to you now."

She reached in her handbag and drew out a long morocco leather jewel case.

"Your father gave me these pearls the day you were born, and now I want them to be yours."

She clasped the pearls around Linda's neck, and kissed her on both cheeks.

"Oh, Mom!" said Linda. "What can I say! Your pearls!"

"Your pearls now, dear," said Jessica.

Claudia hated herself for it, but she wondered what was going to take their place. Jessica just didn't do those things.

Everyone admired them. John Graves came up to Linda, took her hands, and looked at her admiringly.

"I wish I had a camera," he said. "Firelight and flowers and pearls, and your face—it's just too much."

He dropped her hand; she smiled. Claudia saw she was not clinging to his words and glance as she had before.

Next, Ubaldo came to her and gave her a package. Before she opened it, she embraced him. It was the first time she had done such a thing. As she clung to him, she said, "Thank you, my friend."

She opened the package. It was a small icon—the virgin, surrounded with emeralds and chip diamonds.

It was passed around reverently by the Greeks. Chloë came to him.

"I recognize how valuable that is," she whispered. "You are a generous man."

"Look!" said Linda. "It's David!"

A helicopter hovering like a giant dragonfly soared in over the hill and landed expertly on the white beach.

David stepped out carrying a hamper.

"David!" she said, rushing to him. "What a dramatic entrance! What have you got there?"

He put an arm around her, smiling as they walked toward the fire.

"None of your affair until after dinner! This surprise will have to wait." He disappeared into the house and came back without the hamper.

The music, the soft night, the toasts, all blended into one. The sumptuous meal was served, and Claudia felt the world was all theirs on the island. She held hands with Max. It *was* a happy birthday. She wanted to end it by giving Linda the one gift she thought would and should mean the most to her, a token of what she was.

John had a moment to talk with Linda.

"It's been a busy and growing time, Linda," he said. "You have come a long way. I may have been beset with my growing, too. I don't have a gift for you, but I do have a promise. Someday—and I hope sooner than we think—I'm going to have my own company, my own way, my story, my direction, do it my way. It will be on a budget. No super release like this. I have a friend in London, Victor Epps, who did a film with your aunt and me a long time ago. He's a fine playwright now. Well, he's working on one, a beauty, and I vow to you on this, your birthday night, that if you'll do it, I will offer you a marvelous role. You would think he tailored it for your talent. Will you accept this as my present and wish for your birthday?"

She could not believe it. His compliments overwhelmed her.

For a moment she stared at him. His face warmed in an admiring smile. He took her hand in his and kissed her cheek. She felt warm and happy inside. She had to struggle to hold back the tears.

"Now, now, this won't do. Do you want them to think I'm being a beast?"

He made a face.

She smiled.

"There's nothing would mean more to me," she said. "It's . . . it's a wonderful present. Do you really mean it?"

"I shall show you the script soon," he said.

"Don't monopolize her," said Max.

Chloë had given Claudia the lighted cake. With careful hands she helped shield the flickering candles; it was put in front of Linda, and with cheers and applause she blew them out in one breath.

"I hope you made a wish," said Claudia.

"Of course," said Linda.

She seemed suddenly sad.

My god, thought Claudia, don't tell me this beautiful creature is going to be a clod. Where is her spirit?

Max presented her with a box from Bulgari. In it was a gold-and-ivory bracelet, like the one she wore in the picture.

"Brings back our early days at Trancas, doesn't it?" she said, thinking how long ago and far away that had been.

She looked at the eleven people who had come into her life these last few months. All of them were on this island because she was.

Effie presented her with a sweater made of wool from Thracian sheep that had been covered with skins, so their fleece was soft as down. It was an explosion of colors, red and orange and mauve and blue.

"Joseph's coat!" said Max. "It would blind an entire camera crew."

The sound of their laughter filled the quiet of the night.

Linda wrapped it around her.

Jessica glanced at her watch impatiently.

"It's getting late," she said, "and we do have a working day tomorrow."

Claudia knew from the crowded life on the boat that she must be expecting that phone call from Rome over the ship-to-shore lines.

At that moment David came out of the house. "Here you are. Happy, happy birthday," he said.

He put the hamper in her lap. She opened it. There was a Yorkshire puppy, sound asleep. She picked it up, stunned. As he awoke, his little button eyes and baby black fur were exactly like the dog she remembered so many years ago when her father gave it to her on her sixth birthday.

She cupped her hands around it and burst into tears. She set it back in the basket and jumped up. Then, as fast as she could, she ran away, past the trees, along the beach, into the darkness of the night.

"Linda!" cried Jessica. "Linda, come back here!"

"Oh, my god," said David. "I . . . I'm sorry."

He started after her.

"No!" said Claudia. "I'll go speak to her."

No one interfered. Claudia had taken over.

"I guess this is a family affair," said John Graves. "Anyway, it's time to take the musicians back to the hotel."

They got into the jeep and left.

In a few moments Claudia found Linda sitting on a rock, in the darkness at the edge of the sea, sobbing.

She sat by her for a moment.

"Now, Linda," she said, "stop acting like a child. This is your festive day. You're being utterly selfish. Everyone did everything they could to give you a happy birthday. You were downright cruel to David. You've been so wrapped up in your own private world that you've spoiled all that's been offered to you. You've got to learn to give, not just to take."

Linda hung her head, trying to stop her sobbing.

"I know," she said, "I know, but I can't help it!"

"You must," said Claudia. "Now, for God's sake, go back there and apologize. You're supposed to be an actress. Just pretend, for all of them."

Linda wiped her tears with the back of her hand. But she still cried.

Claudia's patience ended. For the first time, she was severe. She realized the time was not right for Linda to be given Jeffrey's precious amber, which she carried in her purse.

"I've been a bloody goody-two-shoes, trying to make you come out of yourself. I had a present for you, but now I don't think you're ready for it. You're acting like a crybaby, and I'm damned sick of it! Measure up, my girl! You have so much to be thankful for. Now, for the love of heaven, what's your big problem?"

Linda looked up at her, and drew in her breath sharply.

"I'm pregnant," she said.

The stars and the sea and the darkness whirled around Claudia. She opened her mouth; there were no words, only a gasp.

"You're what!" she said finally.

"I'm going to have a baby," said Linda in an almost inaudible voice.

The words clicked into Claudia's head. Ah, that bastard John Graves, somehow he'd gotten to her. Linda was so eager to be in the adult world. Claudia had tried to watch over her. How could it have happened! She tried to stop the terrible trembling in her gut.

"Are you sure?"

"I've missed two periods." Linda sobbed.

"I'll kill the son-of-a-bitch," said Claudia.

"You can't," said Linda. "He's dead."

And so it was that Claudia found out that Niadas was the father.

◆◆◆◆◆◆◆◆◆

Breakfast was always casual on the *Circe*. Max had his early. When Linda was working, she joined him, followed by a sleepy Claudia, who nonetheless rose to battle the day's work with her niece.

If David was visiting, he usually was up early to talk to Max before the day absorbed him with its many problems on the set.

But this morning when Max came to breakfast, he was surprised to see Claudia sitting alone. She was drinking coffee with an unsteady hand. She seemed tired.

Finding her alone, he came to her and kissed her.

"We'll be off this platform soon, love," he said. "I'm going to take you to some little hotel away from anyone we've ever talked to in our life. We'll just read, and walk, and sleep, and be together."

But as he looked at her, her eyes welled with tears. She fished for a handkerchief in her purse.

"What's wrong?"

She tried to speak, but couldn't. She just dumbly shook her head and mopped her eyes.

At this moment David came in to discuss a few production problems with Max before returning to close down the last studio business in Rome.

"Excuse me," he said, realizing he had walked in on a personal drama.

Claudia held up her hand and gestured for him to stay. She had to wait while a steward served fruit juice and ceremonially poured coffee and went back to the galley.

"You might as well know now," she said. "I . . . I don't know how to tell you."

"What is it?" asked David.

She got up and went to the porthole, looking out.

"Linda's pregnant," she said.

There was a moment of stunned silence before Max cried out. "My god! How did it happen?"

David stood up. He looked sick. He came to Claudia and brought her back to the table.

"Who is the bastard?" His lips were pressed together with anger.

Max and David looked at each other.

"I know who you're thinking it is," said Claudia. "Well, it wasn't John Graves. It was Pericles Niadas."

The steward came in carrying croissants.

They sat at the table without speaking. They had hardly settled after the man left when Jessica came in. She wore a glowing smile and sat down briskly.

"Good morning, gentlemen," she said, looking across the table directly at David. "I have some news for you. As soon as the picture is finished, I'm going to be married. To Carlo, of course. You know, Prince Bonavente."

She looked down modestly.

"I guess none of you are surprised," she said. "It's been in the wind."

She looked up, expecting congratulations. Instead she received only stares.

"Well?" she said. "I guess you *are* surprised. It'll be quite a change living in a villa in Rome."

"Jessica," said Claudia, "stop the crap. We couldn't care less. While you were racing around Rome with your *società del materasso,* it seems your daughter got pregnant."

Jessica stared at Claudia.

"What dreadful thing are you intimating!"

"I'm intimating nothing. She's going to have a baby. That explains why she's been so damned difficult and moody, poor kid! She's been lugging around this secret for two months."

"Two months!" said Jessica. "I thought you were taking care of her. She was in *your* custody. You should have kept her away from John Graves."

"Two souls with but a single thought," said Claudia. "Poor John. Unfortunately for you, for the picture, for all of us, it wasn't John Graves. It was Pericles Niadas. It happened after the party, the night he died."

She shook her head. There was a moment of stunned silence.

"Nobody thought about Linda. The load of responsibility she had carried on her shoulders at her age. The way we all, consciously or not, allowed her to fulfill the fantasy of a man who was making a last grab for love and life. It's our fault."

"What are we going to do?" said Jessica.

"What is *she* going to do?" said Max. "My poor Linda!"

"Well, she'll just have to have an abortion," said Jessica.

David arose, despising her.

"We're talking about her like merchandise," he said. "Has anyone asked her what she'd like to do?"

"She's utterly miserable," said Claudia. "Effie is with her now. I sat with her a long time last night. She finally slept. She's young, and healthy."

"I'm going to see her," said David.

"Never mind," said Jessica. "I'll talk to her myself first."

"I don't think so," said David. "She's in no condition for your suggestions."

He turned to Claudia.

"Come along," he said.

Jessica angrily watched them go.

Max shook his head. "How stupid I've been all these months," he said. "How can I help her now?" he said.

Linda was in her salon in her robe, sitting on the

couch, her feet curled under her. Effie, concerned, was standing by, handing her a pill and a glass of water.

"Well, now that you know," said Linda, "I guess I wasn't seasick. I guess it was just morning sickness."

She looked up at David and started to cry.

"I'm so sorry," she said, "I'm so sorry. It seemed right at the time. He was very dear to me. He wanted me, I wanted to be grown up. I was sick of being treated like a child."

Effie handed her a Kleenex. She blew her nose.

David sat down beside her.

"You're not the only one to blame, Linda," he said. "We must look after you, and decide what to do. . . . What do *you* want to do?"

"What do you mean?" she said.

"He means, dear," said Claudia, "do you want to have this baby? How do you feel about it?"

Linda, not grasping what they were implying, went on. "I don't think about having a baby. Now all I can think is what a terrible thing! *Pallas Athena* was ruined because Martha Ralston got pregnant. And now the same thing is happening all over again. Will *The Oracle* be ruined too, because I'm having a baby?" Her voice rose in desperation. She turned to David.

"Who would believe it?"

"I hope no one does," said Claudia.

"I want to finish the picture, no matter what, Aunt Claudia. You told me how Belinda Pierce Barstow, my namesake, went on playing till the last moment when she was pregnant. Do you think I could get by for several months?"

Claudia was astounded. This is what she had been thinking about, not her own condition!

Jessica came into the room. She sat next to her daughter on the sofa, obviously ready for a verbal set-to.

"Linda," she said, "I have heard the news. I cannot tell you how shocked I am—"

"That will do," said David brusquely.

"*I'm* her mother," said Jessica. "What in the world

are we going to do about the production? There's a lot at stake."

"You will be happy to know," said Claudia, "that your daughter had that first in her thoughts. I'm proud of her."

Jessica saw David take Linda's hand. Suddenly she remembered how he had looked at her that way so long ago, not knowing that she had been Fergus' mistress. For a moment Jessica was stripped of everything she had fought and scrapped for. No one would ever look at her like that again. Slow anger welled up in her. This child was magic by her very existence. She had charmed everyone who stood around her, always the center of attention, the stellar attraction. As if from a distance, she heard David's words.

"Linda," he was saying, "will you marry me?"

Claudia turned pale as she heard Jessica's taunting laugh.

"That's more absurd than you know!" she said.

All the venom, all the hatred and frustration Jessica had carried with her through the years came to the surface.

Quickly Claudia came up to her and grasped her shoulders so harshly that she winced.

"That's not the best way to put it," she said. "I'm sure you don't know what you're saying!"

They stared eye-to-eye. Now Jessica realized that Claudia had the secret she thought only a couple of people among the living possessed. Could Jeffrey have told her that David was his son?

Claudia turned to David.

"It isn't my place to tell Linda what to do," she said, "but, David, we must be reasonable. The whole fate of Titan studio depends on this picture. Linda is barely fifteen. The scandal would be disastrous. You are old enough to be . . . well, to be her father yourself."

She wondered why he flushed, not knowing that he *could* have been her father, but she went on.

"You can't sabotage your life and the lives of so many people with your gallant gesture right now. At least, not at the moment. I think we all should sit down and think the thing out."

"*Sit down!*" she cried out as Jessica started to rise up to interrupt. "Unless you want to torpedo your career, your child, your future bank account, and incidentally, Titan studio."

Jessica sat.

"Well, Linda?" said David.

Linda came to him.

"I love you dearly, David, but my aunt's right. It wouldn't work."

"That's right," said Jessica. "We could fly you to Rome. I'm sure we can find a doctor—"

Effie stepped forward.

"Nobody's going to take my B'linda's baby!" she said.

"What right do you have to interfere?" said Jessica.

"Would you like me to bring up the night she was started in this world?"

Effie spoke softly; only Jessica heard her words. The debauch in the projection room. The hormone shots. Effie had been there and had known and kept her counsel all these years.

Jessica settled back, deflated.

As Claudia looked at Jessica, the solution hit her. Of course, Linda came first. There had to be a way. Her mind moved along.

"You know," she said, "this wouldn't be the first time that a grandmother has pretended to be a mother. Especially one who prides herself in looking as young as you do."

"What do you mean!" cried Jessica.

"I mean," said Claudia, as if she were playing out the next sequence in the script, "Linda can get through the next few months, finish the picture. She doesn't stop now, take off a month, get an abortion, and wobble back weak and feeble under rugged conditions. With care and protection, she does it pregnant. She gets by with it. We protect her."

She smiled sardonically, and framed her hands as if she were a cameraman setting up a scene.

"During this time," she continued, "you, Jessica, stroll around Via Veneto with a growing pillow strapped to your flat stomach. Next sequence, you disappear for a while. Lap dissolve, after the picture is finished, dubbed, looped, and scored, all Max's post-productions done, *Linda* gets away for a so-called rest with her aunt, because *Mother* is pregnant and can't get away."

She moved around, setting up camera angles with her hands, enjoying Jessica's growing fury.

"So the baby becomes her brother or sister. Fade out," Claudia said, sitting down.

"That's insane!" said Jessica.

She turned angrily to face David.

"Don't tell me she means for *you* to marry me."

"I wouldn't," he said, "under any conditions. Not even to save the picture."

"Well, then," said Claudia, "I'm sure we can find someone who would, at least until this picture is made."

At this moment Max appeared in the doorway. He rushed up to Linda.

"My darling," he cried. He turned to Claudia. "Nothing matters but this child."

"Well, here's your chance to prove it," said Claudia. "Do you really mean that?"

"I do," said Max.

◆◆◆◆◆◆◆◆

"I do," said Max.

He and Jessica were married by the grace of Claudia, Linda, and David, who stood by next to Linda, and for the grace of Titan studio. A large corporation can and does cut through red tape, arrange legal affairs, and make a short cut of such emergencies as weddings.

At the end of the ceremony those immediately involved gathered in the salon of the *Circe*. While stewards poured champagne, Captain Petroulis, delighted with a wedding on the yacht, provided a wedding cake. Kourambeides and mezethes were on the festive board.

Koufeta, sugared Jordan almonds, expressing a wish for nothing but sweetness in the bride and groom's lives, were passed ceremonially.

"*Hronia polla*—many years!" the Greeks called out.

The couple stood smiling while proper photographs were made to be released by the press. Linda, the only attendant, stood smiling, kissing her mother, the associate producer of *The Oracle*, and her new stepfather, Maximilian Ziska, her beloved director-producer.

David did not remain after the ceremony, as business took him elsewhere. The Greek officials involved in the happy event left with him in a chartered Delphic hydroplane. The proper wires were sent, one to Prince Carlo Bonavente, canceling the bride's engagement to him; one to Fergus Austin, informing him of the occasion; and another to Grace Boomer, with the proper press release. The couple retired, Jessica with a raging headache to her stateroom, and Max to his, where he sat smoking, his hand shaking, as he looked over the script and rearranged Linda's shooting sequence, figuring on a double for some of the long shots, which would be filmed on the last location in March. It was planned that in April Jessica would join him in Rome, properly garbed in maternity clothes, to make her bow to a few people who had known her previously when she lived at the villa under different circumstances.

Claudia sat on deck with Linda for a while. She tried to hide the sorrow that engulfed her. It was incredible to her that she had sabotaged her own happiness. Linda seemed to grasp her thoughts.

"I know what this wedding means to you, Aunt Claudia," she said, "but it won't last forever. What would I do without you . . . and Effie!" she added.

"It's going to be all right," said Claudia. "As soon as the picture is over and all the dubbing is finished, you'll get away, and we'll both be with you when the time comes. You'll just have a little brother or sister, as far as the world knows. It will still be yours, your child. It can still be with you."

"*It's* going to be a he," said Linda. "I have decided. Just think, another Barstow. He'll be like my father. Handsome and gentle and gifted."

"My god," said Claudia, "I hadn't thought of that! After your father had murdered the man responsible for knocking you up, I think he would have been terribly pleased to have a grandchild."

"I'm going to bed," said Linda, standing up and stretching. "It's been a big day."

After she left, Claudia stood in the dark, listening to the soft plop of water against the hull of the boat, and the little splashes of a school of tiny fish. The land seemed far away and quiet. Her heart was as heavy as the darkness. She thought of what Max had said about their running away to be by themselves when the picture was done, and she knew with a deep and aching feeling that now it would never be. Even if the marriage was just a pretense, the need for it to seem real would make their public appearance impossible.

How about that? she thought. It was my own damned idea. I really did it to myself. At least she had scotched that bitch Jessica, who had been ready to tell Linda and David Austin they were brother and sister.

She thought seriously of taking a drink, but then she also thought of the plight of Linda, and decided instead to take a sleeping pill, and try to sleep out the honeymoon night of the man she loved.

She went to her cabin, carefully removed the makeup she had put on for the wedding photographs. What a farce, her smiling face! She slipped into her nightgown and turned off the lights.

Once more she looked out on the moonlit water. Honeymoon . . . honeymoon . . . she thought, as she opened the porthole to the breeze, and slipped into her berth.

There was a knock at the door.

It was Max.

"Let me in," he whispered. "I couldn't spend my wedding night with anyone but you."

She held out her arms.

3

The next few weeks Linda was adrift in a celluloid sea. Everything else seemed only a rhythmic accompaniment to the film. Strangely, there was no threnody for her. Now that her secret was shared, and she was wrapped in the cocoon of love and care that Claudia, Effie, and Max gave her, she plunged into her work relieved, resigned to let the future take care of itself.

Fortunately, the important American designer who had done her wardrobe in Rome, was gone, and the last of the wardrobe women did not notice the inch or two her waist expanded. Effie stitched and adjusted her clothes so that no one would notice the difference in her figure.

The nearest she came to being exposed was when John Graves said to her one day as they were walking up the trail in one of their last shots, "You're getting more womanly every day. What's happened to you?"

She laughed. "I guess this Greek food is just too good."

"Oh, no," he said, "it isn't that. You seem to have an inner glow. Where is the schoolgirl I used to tease?"

"She is gone," said Linda. "Gone . . . gone."

He looked at her, puzzled. Just then, Max called out, "Action," through his intercom below by the camera.

For a moment she allowed herself to be sad. Where was the mad crush she had had on John? Was it gone because this child was growing inside her? Did it make that much difference? Why couldn't she love John; she had no man, no husband or lover to be true to. Was she being true to the child, was that why she didn't love John anymore? After the scene, wondering, she drifted off and sat alone. She didn't want anyone near her. She had to think.

Later she spoke of it to Claudia.

"It can't be very big yet," she said, "yet I feel like I owe it something. What do you think? Did you ever have a baby, or an . . . abortion?"

"I had several abortions," said Claudia, "and I'm sorry I did. I'm not being sentimental, but I'm awfully glad you're having your baby. It ought to be special. You know, Niadas was a most remarkable man. How proud he would have been."

Linda bent her head.

"I know," she said. "But if he were here, I'm not sure I would have loved him. That would have been terrible. But anyway, I think I'll love my child."

Claudia wanted to cry for her; there was a special, rather innocent dignity about her attitude. She felt that she never would have been so free and happy about having a child, all by herself. Perhaps it was because Linda didn't know what she was getting into.

Chloë had again been away on the island of Santorini looking after her institute, which had settled in a cluster of white barrel-vaulted buildings, in the cliff town of Thera. Now it was time for her to do her last scenes, with Linda and John, on the shores of the sea, and at the little temple.

It was comfortable for Linda to sit in the little garden by Chloë's villa between scenes where the birthday party had been held. One afternoon, while the cameras were being moved for another setup at the nearby temple, she drank a "submarine," a glass of icy water with a spoon of berry jam to be stirred in it, and looked at Chloë. She was lovely, in her violet robe with gold and green palmettes embroidered on it.

"I wish I had your style," said Linda.

"That from you!" Chloë laughed. "Everything you wear has style. Even that simple white peplos you're wearing."

"Tell me," said Linda, "you know that beautiful octopus Niadas gave me?"

"Yes," said Chloë. "What about it?"

"I was thinking," said Linda. "I ought to sell it."

"Sell it!" said Chloë, paling under her makeup. "Whatever for?"

"Well, I might be needing some money. You know, everything I have is put away for me, and I might be needing my own funds."

Chloë laughed.

"Are you planning to run away?"

"In a way, yes," said Linda.

She rose and stretched, turning. Her back ached.

"I think you should keep it. It was the gift of a most wonderful man. If I did not love you, I would be quite jealous of you," said Chloë.

If she only knew the whole story, thought Linda.

"I have a surprise for you," said Chloë. "Ubaldo is coming in. Let's have dinner here. Bring Claudia."

"I'd like it," said Linda.

Linda hadn't seen Ubaldo to talk to for almost two months. These days, when he came in, he stayed at the little hotel in the town. Often she saw him with Chloë, walking and talking, and for a moment, as Chloë mentioned him with a lilt in her voice, she felt a little twinge of envy. Everyone seemed to be making relationships, and she was alone.

She had told Claudia all about that evening that had changed her life so dramatically. The destruction of the statue, and how Sarge had died. Now, although she cuddled the new puppy when Effie wasn't caring for it, she still missed her beloved Sarge and had to stop the tears at the thought of him.

Now that Claudia knew what a large part Ubaldo played in the evening with Niadas, she alerted Linda.

"You must be very careful around him," she said. "He's the one person who might notice something unusual about you and connect it with Niadas."

"I'll be careful," she said. "Although I trust him. I know he's my friend."

But Claudia had not counted on the fact that Chloë

was curious about Linda's comment about needing money. And that, as those close to each other do, she had confided it to Ubaldo.

For the first time since she had been a young girl under the spell of Niadas, Chloë was drawing close, emotionally, rather than physically, to a man.

She and Ubaldo had not touched bodies. Their interest so far was in Greece, in the picture, in discussion of archaeology, and most of all, Linda. She unburdened herself about the institute; he helped her plan various fund-raising ideas, and promotional schemes to make the institute a functional, important force in Greece. So far she had been insular in working with the Niadas staff in Santorini.

"Perhaps," said Chloë, "when this film is ended, you will join my staff. I need you."

Ubaldo smiled.

"Those are exciting words, to be needed. Take care. I may accept."

But when she told him about Linda wanting to sell the jeweled octopus, he was concerned. More than anyone else around her, he watched her move, the way she kept herself wrapped in the multicolored bulky sweater that Effie had made for her, calling it her shield against the winds, how cautiously she draped her wardrobe, how she had avoided swimming while others bathed on the lovely beach when they had the opportunity. He saw with aching heart that she was pregnant. My god, he thought, that night with Niadas! How he hated the memory of that man.

He kept the secret behind closed lips, but he longed to tell Chloë. By now she had confided in him the whole story of her long relationship with Niadas, the complicated *koumbaros,* a familial, almost blood bond of devotion, the responsibility he had left with her to care for the lost and homeless ones of his country, and the sadness she had felt for his ill-fated marriage to Martha Ralston. How sickly and frail the infant from that marriage was, the only one to carry on the Niadas bloodline. The infant now was in the hands of qualified staff in his house. Later, as was provided in the will,

Chloë would take the child and look after her education. The big house in Athens was to be her headquarters for the institute.

How strange that she would take care of Niadas' daughter in the house where she was to have been his bride.

As he lay awake nights in the little hotel, Ubaldo thought of his Linda, his Phryne, and then, to his surprise, of his blood-and-flesh Chloë, a woman, giving and vital.

Claudia was torn between future plans and current distress about Linda's coming trials. Jessica, of course, had been a perfect bitch, furious about the role she was forced to play. Her drive to get the picture finished was the only outlet to the frustration of her shattered dreams, and on this she worked tirelessly.

David, on his visits, had plans worked out for the coming months, and explained to her what she was supposed to do to make the plot come off. In her mind she accused him of reveling in his power over her, and whenever he came to the island, she managed to disappear in her cabin on the yacht. Claudia and Linda rejoiced and joked that after her neglect and harshness to Linda, now she had to carry her burden.

February passed, closeups augmented long shots, a slim young girl on the island was dressed in a blond wig and doubled for Linda when she had to climb down the rocks and swim in the sea.

Claudia elaborately explained to the girl, who passed the news on to all, that she had this chance to be in the film because the star was suffering from her period.

Claudia was torn between annoyance and gratitude that John Graves was so involved in his role and his life that he looked upon Linda with an unseeing eye. Only once or twice did he seem a little irritated that she no longer clung to his every word and glance, as she had in Rome.

Early March was the end of the picture. Everyone had been sent away but John, Chloë, Linda, and the last of the crew.

Linda stood in the sun awaiting a long shot, with

Chloë dressed in the brilliant robes of the courtesan Diotima. She glanced at Chloë, said, "I don't feel very well," and fainted.

In a moment Max rushed up, and she was carried to her jerry-built dressing room nearby. Claudia was on the yacht arranging the packing of their possessions with Effie.

"It's all right," said Max with relief as Linda came back into consciousness. He added to reassure himself, "I'll call the set nurse."

"No," said Chloë. "I'll take care of this. Leave us alone."

When Linda opened her eyes, Chloë was staring at her.

"You are pregnant," she said. "I have suspected it."

She handed her a glass of water. Linda sipped it and looked at her.

"I thought maybe you knew," she said. "I wonder what you think of me."

"I wouldn't ask you questions," said Chloë. "I have helped too many young girls in your condition to want to know why. The deed is done. The question is, what is next, and what do we do about it?"

Linda shook her head.

"That's why my mother got married to Max," she said. "Everyone is going to think it's hers."

"Oh!" said Chloë. "I wondered why they married. Are you glad you're going to have it? What does the father think? Will he be with you? That is very important if it can be arranged."

Linda looked up at her. There was no way she could avoid telling her now. Almost fearful of what would happen, she blurted it out.

"No, he won't be with me. I know he would want to. Because, you see, it was Pericles Niadas."

Linda had never seen anyone react as Chloë did. She went rigid, then put her hands over her eyes. She let out a cry, and slowly sank to her knees. She sobbed, and for a moment was as still as a statue, then slowly took her hands away from her tearstained face and looked at Linda with a dazzling smile.

The actress in Linda tucked it away. What a wonderful expression of a woman, what a gamut of emotion. She must tell Claudia. Then she was ashamed of herself for dissecting a soul in such a way.

Chloë came to her.

"God has been good!" she said. "I am rejoicing."

Her cry had brought Max to the door.

"What is it?"

"My god!" said Chloë, smiling through her tears. "Nothing, nothing is wrong!"

Max left, knowing that now Chloë, too, knew. The circle was widening.

The protection of Linda in the last months of her pregnancy was the most important thing, thought Claudia. She would have to be in a place where no one would know her. Rome was impossible, London was out. Of course, she could not set foot in the United States; she would immediately be spotted. She must stay away from Jessica, who must carry on the false pregnancy. As a matter of fact, Jessica had arranged to go to a very private body-and-face clinic in Switzerland—gift of Titan studio, one more of her little shakedowns, which David accepted happily to hush her up and get rid of her—and go through a three-month renaissance in return for her cooperation, and the fact that she really couldn't get around much the last few months. All the patients there were incognito.

In the end it was Chloë who worked out the plans with Claudia.

Linda, Claudia, and Effie were to be established in a comfortable house on Santorini. Nearby, at her institute, there would be at least eight young girls who were having their infants under her protection. One more wouldn't even be thought about. Blond, redheaded, brunette—they all went by first name. It was a healthy, busy place to be. There was a great deal to do. The girls led a normal family life with each other, instead of grieving in some alley with their burden, or being forced to live in a society that looked down upon them.

And Chloë stressed the fact that the baby would be

born in Niadas' village, Thera, near the little chapel he had built, where he was laid to rest.

The white village would be as good a hideaway as anyone could find. With Claudia and Effic with her, she would not be marooned. God willing, if her spirits were high it could be a time of reading and learning, which she could use the rest of her life.

Leave-taking of John Graves was almost swallowed in the busy exodus of the picture. He said farewell to the crew, whom he had worked with so many months, at the *taverna* at a festive gathering the night before. In the morning he came out to the yacht on a launch before the helicopter dropped down to get him.

"I just wanted to say good-bye," he said.

Linda, swallowed in her voluminous sweater, embraced him.

"I can't believe it's finished," she said. "I wonder when I'll see you again?"

"A bad penny always shows up," said Claudia.

"Are you going back to the States?"

"Of course," said Linda. "Probably we'll see you at the premiere."

"You'll see me in front of a camera," he said. "Don't forget my promise to you on your birthday. You'll be getting Victor Epps's script from me soon. Where shall I send it?"

"Care of David," said Claudia. "He'll find us. Victor Epps, huh? History repeats itself."

"Let's hope so," said John.

He looked fondly at Linda.

"I think I gave you a bad time at the beginning of the film."

"Maybe I needed it," said Linda. "Maybe I've grown up a lot since the picture began."

Her eyes filled with tears.

"So much has happened. . . . I . . . I'm going to feel lost without *The Oracle*."

"No sad farewells," said John. "Every picture you really care for is like this. It's a sign it has been good. Then, the next one you do, you'll fall into emotional relationships all over again, and forget the last one."

"No I won't," said Linda. "This one I'll remember."

John turned to Claudia.

"Good-bye, old girl," he said. "You did quite a job."

"So did you," she said, touched.

He quickly grabbed Linda and kissed her on the lips.

In a moment he was gone, already occupied on the shore boat, his mind on where he was going instead of where he had been.

Linda had a twinge of regret; the old memory of the crush she had on him returned. Wouldn't it have been wonderful if he had been the father of her child? After all, Niadas had just been a sort of glamorous accident.

Claudia, noticing her sadness, realized that one more fragment of her life was gone. Obviously, she'd had a mad passion for John. She was grateful that the situation with Niadas seemed to have stifled it.

"Don't let this breaking up of the company bother you," she said. "There's a danger of this temporary world affecting you. The next thing you know, you'll cry when they load those stinking noisy old generators on a barge and tow them away. You must remember that actors must learn to walk a tightrope between the world of imagination and reality. And now we have to face our reality. A beautiful film was made during this difficult time in your life. You've been so absorbed in your own problems that you've forgotten why we're here. Can you imagine how desperately Max has worked against all these personal problems to make it come off?"

She came to Linda and smiled.

"You know, I'm always trying to drum optimism into you. Maybe it's because I'm not so damned secure myself. And don't forget David, striding through the money world trying to be Goliath, getting the funds together to keep us afloat. You know, *The Oracle* will be shown years after our personal problems, as difficult as they are, are solved. So now, let's play some records before we pack them away."

"Okay," said Linda. "Here's the new Doris Day."

They listened. The words came over. Claudia wished she hadn't chosen this one. How would Linda react?

When I was just a little girl,
I asked my mother, "What will I be?
Will I be pretty? Will I be rich?"
Here's what she said to me:
"Que Sera, Sera, whatever will be will be;
The future's not ours to see.
Que Sera, Sera!
What will be will be!"

When I grew up and fell in love,
I asked my lover, "What lies ahead?
Will we have rainbows day after day?"
Here's what my lover said:
"Que Sera, Sera, whatever will be will be;
The future's not ours to see.
Que Sera, Sera!
What will be will be!"

Now I have children of my own,
They ask their mother, "What will I be?
Will I be pretty? Will I be rich?"
I'll tell them tenderly:
"Que, Sera, Sera, whatever will be will be;
The future's not ours to see.
Que Sera, Sera!
What will be will be!
Que Sera, Sera!"

Claudia glanced at her sharply, wondering if the song would trigger her to tears.

Instead Linda took off the record and put on another.

"I guess that answers our questions," said Linda. "There isn't any answer, is there? Here's another good record."

Lightheartedly she put on "Mack the Knife."

Claudia, listening to the perfect tones of the sound system, and looking around the private salon which had belonged to Niadas, with its lapis-lazuli fireplace, Persian rugs, comfortable down-filled sofas, masterpieces splendidly lighted on the rich mahogany walls, wondered how the girl would react to the primitive settings of a Greek island without this elegant platform. This last year she had been carried on such a fantastic magic carpet of adulation and luxury.

From what she had heard of Santorini, Linda would live in a simply furnished house overlooking the deep volcanic boiling depths of the sea below. She shuddered, wondering how Linda would take it, much less herself and Effie.

◆◆◆◆◆◆◆◆

In the early summer the Etesian winds blew from a northerly direction, flowing across the pure whitewashed main street of Thera, where no animal was allowed to tread. The island of Santorini had gone through its quiet months of comparative calm. Fishing boats, which had been hauled out for the winter on the eastern shallows of the island, were now put to sea again. Crops had been planted, rich fields and vineyards tended, and the daily chores of native life had taken over. Women in bright-colored kerchiefs had cleaned and scrubbed, and the white-and-blue town sparkled. From time to time the high clear silence of Thera, perched like a frill of white atop the black-lava cliffs, made it seem like a place in a surrealist dream, the Cycladic architecture walls and streets all blending together with whitewash.

The tourists were again flocking in on cruise ships, interisland steamers, and chartered caïques and yachts.

Linda, Claudia, and Effie settled in a barrel-vaulted house. The main room overlooked the sea, the cliffs of Oia startling with a band of arsenic green. The three small bedrooms, a tiny courtyard, and a modest kitchen made it a great house by village standards.

Effie kept house, trying to make American-style food for the table, using the simple vegetables, fruit, fish, and dairy products that were available. Sometimes the meals were augmented by goods ordered by a letter to David, who kept Fortnum and Mason busy sending parcels to an unknown Greek institute on the improbable island of Santorini in the Greek Cyclades.

Late afternoon, when the daytime commerce of the bustling little town had subsided, and the donkeys with their bales of fodder and firewood, their casks of wine, and their produce had been stabled, and tourists were resting their weary feet in the *tavernas*, Linda and Claudia would stroll along the spine of the island toward the ruined Venetian town of Skaros. Linda wore a full smock made by Effie, and bound her head in a Greek kerchief. With her sunburned face, she might have been any young wife taking an awkward, pregnant-laden walk with a relative.

Often when they approached this deserted old town the cry of a bird and the sounds of cicadas, which echoed against the courtyard walls, were the only proof that aside from them, there was any life in this vast world.

"The crickets sound like watches being wound," said Linda, rubbing her rounded stomach. "I'll be glad when my time is finished with this."

So will I, thought Claudia. She smothered her thoughts. It had taken all her courage to seem cheerful these months.

Max had returned to Hollywood now that the picture was readying with opticals and scoring. There was excitement in the air, everyone was convinced that Titan had an epic that would lift it out of the doldrums.

Max wasn't the best letter writer; he was so deeply involved with the picture, and his scribbles only promised that there would be times together to make up for this separation. As soon as he could get away and the child was born, he and Jessica would arrange, as had been contracted, a divorce. But now, he could only say, he loved Claudia, missed her, was terribly busy, and the future would take care of itself when the time came. Not much poetry in his letters, thought Claudia, but no one had ever promised her anything like a future, and she treasured every scribble.

It had been difficult enough for Linda. The eight

other pregnant girls, wards of Chloë's institute, one even younger than she, had a cultural affinity. They talked another language, their hours were involved with sewing, knitting, weaving, and housekeeping skills that they hoped would make up their future lives. Even their cooking, which they did with considerable enthusiasm in the institute kitchen (for most of them were always hungry), had little to do with the life that would be Linda's.

Sometimes she saw them as she visited the clinic during checkups, or several social evenings as they clumsily danced to the lilting songs of Chloë, local wind and string instruments accompanying them.

Chloë had spent many hours with Linda, taking her around the island, trying to imbue her with the feeling for Greece that made this place so dear to her and her memory of Niadas.

She took her to the ancient Greek temple, considered the most perfectly preserved in Greece, near Pyrgos. They traveled on a sun-struck Sunday with a picnic hamper, cautiously driving slowly over the bumpy terrain in Chloë's prize possession, a jeep with a canopy, usually housed in Niadas' shipping center on the east side of the island.

She showed her the crude cave where she and Niadas had hidden during the war, and she had nursed him back to life. Together they stepped into the half-earthquake-destroyed Niadas Villa Kalliste. It had not been restored before he died, but Linda could see how lovely it had been.

She even slept on a bed and used furnishings in her house that Chloë told her had been salvaged from there. She was much more comfortable than the richest merchant in the village; wood was rare, and furniture was crude. Some of the citizens even sat and slept on slabs carved out of cave walls.

And last of all, one day Chloë took her to the chapel, which seemed so simple in its whiteness outside, but which within was a treasury of jewels. It was here Niadas had been laid to rest.

"Now," she said, "this is the place you must always think of with joy, for Pericles would have been so happy to know you would be here bearing his child."

"It will be a son!" insisted Linda. "Oh, Chloë, the world will never know it's his!"

"That is the only sad thing," said Chloë.

◆◆◆◆◆◆◆◆◆

As David's interisland steamer approached the great circular bay between Santorini and the smoking island shape of distant Therasia, observing the boiling water from volcanic depths breaking the calm surface of the sea, he was depressed. Looking up into the cliffs and seeing the sugar-cube houses clinging to the edge, he wondered how wise it was to hide Linda out in this primitive island. What a hell of a place to have a baby.

It took him half an hour to climb the endless steps, a mule laden with his gifts following him, a young muleteer whacking its rump to make it move. A miserable trip, but necessary.

He found the house more comfortable than he would have believed, certainly better than the Hotel Atlantis, where he had checked in.

Linda seemed cheerful enough. He was disturbed at her pregnancy, her body unbalanced. It was such a cruel trick that fate had played on a young girl who right now was having a corps of publicists making every effort to make her the new, exciting female star of Titan films.

"I'm so glad to see you!" she said, embracing him. "How is it out there in the big world?"

"I was going to ask that," said Claudia. "How's Max? What goes with the picture?"

David handed out boxes of chocolates, magazines, and paperback books. Then finally a large box for Linda from Harrods.

"Open it now," he said. "I hope I got the right things."

As they untied their gifts, he went on.

"All is well. The picture looks wonderful. We have a

fine musical score. I'll send you a wax for your battery record player. Now is the usual final organization of prints and advertising. I talked to Max, he sent you love. We'll have the premiere in December. It's all going to work out."

"Oh, wonderful!" cried Linda. "I won't miss it, and I'll be free."

"Not exactly," said David, "and you'd better be strong. There will be months of interviews, travel to key cities, and finally we're having major openings all over the country—and you'll have to do a P.R. tour to end all of them."

"Not that!" said Claudia, remembering. "My god, what a grind!"

Linda looked desolate.

"Do I have to?"

"Remember London?" said David. "I gave you a chance to get off the bandwagon. Do you remember what you said?"

"Yes," said Linda. "I said, 'I don't want to run. I'm going to be a star.' "

David and Claudia looked at each other. That settled it.

As they exclaimed over their bounty, Claudia, picking up a book on child care, grinned.

"That reminds me," she said. "How's our little mother, Jessica?"

"She marched up and down Via Condotti, appeared briefly in maternity clothes at several social events in London, did her final angry bow in Beverly Hills at the Bistro and Chasen's, and even once had a conference in the Polo Lounge."

They laughed.

"I can just see it," said Linda, imitating how she looked, only with a real baby in her stomach, exaggerating her off-balance.

"Now," said David, "she is in her resort in Switzerland, getting a complete retread."

Linda opened the package. It was a layette.

"Oh, look!" she said, holding up a tiny shirt. "Do you think my baby's going to be that small?"

"I hope so!" said Claudia.

David signaled that he wanted to talk to her.

While Effie set down her knitting and looked over the baby clothes with Linda, David stepped outside with Claudia. They walked along the cliff, gazing down on the darkening sea.

"Look," he said, "do you think it's all right for her to stay here? It's so primitive. I don't much like it. It isn't going to be easy for her, you know."

"It's better than you think," said Claudia. "I was scared myself. I'd heard so many superstitious things about country people sitting pregnant women in chairs without bottoms to have their babies, using boiled-bran poultices, and wearing garlic and blue beads around their necks to ward off evil spirits. I went to Chloë and told her I wasn't ready for my niece to accept the old ways. You know what happened?"

"She got angry, I suppose, and said they'd done very well the last thousand years," said David.

"Not at all," said Claudia. "She took me to her headquarters and showed me an excellent operating room, all sorts of equipment, oxygen, incubator, all run with its own generator. They even have a ham radio station that one of the two doctors can use. And three trained nurses. Niadas set it up for her several years ago."

"Well, I'll be damned," said David. "I feel better about it."

He still seemed concerned.

"What's on your mind?" she asked.

"We have a problem," he said. "Everyone wants to know where the hell Linda is, and why she isn't around. The studio is screaming for a sexy portrait sitting of her. My suggestion that she's with her mother isn't much of an alibi. Unfortunately, Fergus is right. Wherever she is, we could send a photographer and wardrobe for a sitting. How are we going to get around that?"

"I'll tell you how," said Claudia. "It just so happened, you recollect, that a dear chum of mine, Orville, made a fabulous sitting of her in London. He held back many, at my request, and just gave a few to Grace Boomer. They're all quite different and in costume. Except, of course, a few nude ones that have to be under lock and key."

"My god," said David, "you're playing with fire. How could you ever allow such a thing?"

"He did sittings of all of us Barstows nude through the years," said Claudia.

She smiled as if it were an innocent prank.

"I don't know what to do with you Barstows," he said. "Linda's publicity is building her up as the beautiful virgin. We're ordering five hundred prints of the picture. We've had an immense rush of advance orders, cash guarantees. But the whole thing can be blown if word gets out about this baby. The censor's office would be right on our necks."

"I haven't seen anyone from the *Hollywood Reporter* snooping around these parts." Claudia smiled. "Don't be rough on us, David. Effie and I are doing the best we can."

"I know," said David. "I guess I'm just apprehensive. The information we're passing out is that Jessica's having a bad time holding on to her baby in a famous maternity clinic in Switzerland, and that Linda insists on being with her mother. All the bullshit you have to go through. Poor kid, I'm worried about her."

"I'm trying not to be," said Claudia. "I hope to God they won't have to scar that beautiful body with a Caesarean section."

"I hadn't thought of that," said David, shocked. "Well, anyway, you've solved my current problem about the sitting. I'll get to Orville immediately. Fergus is due in, and I can hand him the portfolio."

"So far things seem to be all right. Two months to go," said Claudia. "Let's go in. Wonderful of you to bring that layette."

"Well," said David, "I never thought I'd be bringing a movie star a layette up the endless crooked track, that thousand feet up Santorini. I think it would be easier going back to get a parachute and jump."

◆◆◆◆◆◆◆◆

Several weeks passed. One evening, as Chloë shared dinner, eating Effie's peach pie, she had an idea.

"I think you ought to teach my pregnant girls how to do some of your good cooking while you're here," she said. "Maybe it might help some of them to catch a husband when they get back into their life. Why don't you come over to the institute kitchen and show them how?"

"It's a good idea," said Effie. "I've run the race on knitting. I'd be glad to show them some simple dishes."

The next morning when Linda awoke, Effie had her breakfast set out on the table overlooking the sea.

"Honey-bun," said Effie, "Miss Claudia and Chloë went to the institute together. I'm going to shop for some stuff for my cooking class, and then show them how. Would you like to come along?"

"No," said Linda. "I'll just take it easy. I wish everybody'd tell me when they decide just to wander off."

"Now, now," said Effie, "come on over and sample my batch later. I'll set out your lunch and be back in plenty of time to get supper ready. All right?"

"All right," she said absently.

When Effie came back in the late afternoon, she found the puppy asleep in his basket. Linda was away.

Disturbed, she went back to the institute. There had been a tragedy there; one of the girls had lost her baby, and to keep the girls occupied, Claudia had joined forces with Chloë, serving them Effie's new baked pie and playing records.

Effie signaled her.

"Is Linda here?"

Claudia shook her head.

"I don't know where she is," said Effie. "We shouldn't have left her alone so long."

Claudia rushed out into the street with Effie. All the nearby places were searched. Then she knew that something was wrong. In a panic, she called Chloë.

In a few moments fishermen, muleteers, and several youths in the street were commandeered to alert everyone. The search was on. First, any house she might have gone to was visited. Then men with torches and flashlights searched up and down the streets, climbed the thorny spine of roadway that led along the cliffs to Merovigli and the ruined Skaros. The runners spread out toward the nearby terrain on the lower side of the island. When dawn came, the search began anew. Half the six hundred inhabitants of Thera looked; the rest stood on street corners and talked about what might have happened to the young American girl. Many speculated that in her condition she had likely gone for a walk and toppled to her death off the cliffs into the sea. All of the *gorgonas* gossiping through windows and on street corners agreed that it was expected that one of Chloë Metaxa's young girls would end up such a way.

◆◆◆◆◆◆◆◆

Fergus met with David in London. It was the first time since David had taken the reins from him in Rome. It was almost time for the Titan board of directors meeting in New York. He had decided to resign before he was asked to step down. He had skated by on thin ice while David had salvaged the company. He had met a worthy adversary in this man who was supposed to be his son. For months he had fretted, and then settled on a decision that was facing many of the old tigers who were competing with the new blood in the business.

He would resign from his official capacity at Titan and ask for a contract as an independent producer. His new corporation, financed by Titan, would own twenty-five percent of the profits. He would settle his contract with Titan for a five-year payment of one hundred thousand per annum. There were properties to be had, he had a solid reputation in the industry, and no one would ever realize the problems that were gnawing at his insides, giving him an ulcer, and causing him sleepless nights.

Now, for the first time, he was the man in the visitor's chair sitting opposite David, behind the executive desk. The Titan office on Wardour Street was far from his eyrie in Hollywood.

He had just settled into his chair and lit his cigarette when David was buzzed.

"No more calls, I told you," he said. "What!" He looked startled.

The secretary reported that the office had received an emergency message from the ham radio station at Santorini.

"My god!" he gasped.

Fergus looked quizzically. After David had listened for a moment, he answered.

"Get in touch with the institute immediately. Get me a plane. Send the message. I'll fly in at once. Have my car waiting downstairs."

He hung up, agitated.

"What is it?" asked Fergus.

David had to tell him.

"Linda Barstow's missing in Santorini. The whole island is hunting for her."

"What in god's name is she doing there?"

"Hiding," said David.

"What do you mean, hiding? I thought she was in Switzerland with her mother. We can't crap around with this publicity pending while she's sightseeing. What the hell's wrong with that kid?"

David said nothing. Fergus looked at him suspiciously.

"What is all this about?"

"I guess you have to know," said David. "Linda is really in hiding. Claudia and Chloë, who are with her, have called me and Ubaldo in Rome to help them. It isn't Jessica who's pregnant. It's Linda. The father was Niadas."

Fergus jumped up.

"And you didn't tell me!" he cried. "Do you know what this could mean to our company. To our picture!"

"I do," said David.

"Not only didn't you bother to tell me, you went on pouring money into it!" said Fergus in white heat. "You think you know so goddamn much. Pulling miracles out of your pocket. Putting me down. I know more about picture-making and its hazards than you'll ever learn. I've sweated it out on a banana peel since I was eighteen. You and your platform of Moses money!"

"Stop it!" said David. "These things don't matter. There's a little kid that we put on a much more important platform which she couldn't handle. We've got to find her. We will, if we're lucky. We played a big game of chess with a little schoolgirl as the pawn."

"She wanted it," said Fergus. "She's a Barstow!"

"Why don't you stop picking on Barstows?" said David. "They didn't exactly hurt Titan in the early days."

"Why don't I stop?" said Fergus, his hands trembling. "I'll tell you why. Because they're my mortal enemies. They have done nothing but plague me all my life."

He paused. David watched him. He had been exposed to his rages all his adult life, but this one, somehow, seemed more of a wrenching inner struggle than any other he had ever seen. Usually he had burst into bombastic vocal angers. This was deeper, and more startling.

All restraint gone, Fergus turned on him and shouted, "Including you!"

"What do you mean?"

David was bewildered. This time Fergus seemed to have taken leave of his senses. His lips were drawn back from his teeth. His eyes were bright with an inner fury.

"You!" His voice was hoarse with emotion. "You're one too. You're Jeffrey Barstow's bastard son. Now do you understand a few things?"

David stared at him, still not taking in what Fergus was trying to say.

"What are you talking about?" he asked. "You must be crazy!"

"I've wished a thousand times I was. Your mother had an affair with Jeffrey Barstow. And you're the result of that ridiculous one-night stand. Now maybe you understand a few things. She was always unstable,

God knows, but her insane infatuation for Barstow finished her off."

David's face drained of color. His mind whirled. That's why Fergus always disliked him! He remembered little things his mother had said . . . the meeting with Jeffrey on the beach . . . the books from him at Christmas . . . a certain way Claudia had with him, of affection. She knew! Now he saw why he had done a terrible thing when he asked Linda to marry him. She was his sister. The night when Claudia suddenly had cut off Jessica when he asked Linda to marry him—Jessica had been about to reveal the secret.

He looked at Fergus as if he had never seen him before. The stranger. The man with horns. No wonder Fergus hated him. No wonder he had disliked Fergus.

"Let's go," he said coolly. "Do you have your passport?"

Fergus nodded dumbly. Now that he had spoken his piece, he knew he had destroyed himself.

Once on the plane, they both settled into silence. Fergus felt David's eyes on him. They were both shattered. The most commonplace gesture became awkward. With the disappearance of Linda, the film, so often teetering on the brink of disaster, was once again on the brink; it was the worst possible time for such a confrontation.

4

For the first time in months, Linda had been left alone. Everyone she counted on to sustain her was intent on someone else's problems. Without realizing it, she had always expected Effie to be with her when she wanted her. Now, even Effie had walked out on her to help some pregnant girls she could not even talk with.

As she had sat in the empty house, she had looked at the baby clothes that had been left by David. Even he was gone far away, busy in the world, having no time for her. She could not understand why her aunt would leave without saying good-bye. What was so important that everyone had left her alone? What if she went into labor? She'd have to walk by herself along the street to the institute, or be helped by a stranger.

As if on cue, the baby in her began to move. It was clamoring for life, too, away from her.

She tied a scarf on her head and decided to go along the streets. Maybe she'd find some Americans; she could at least listen to a word or two of English. She had been warned not to talk to anyone, in case she should be recognized.

Once outside, she saw a cruise ship anchored below, and the usual crowd of tourists huffing and puffing as they finally reached the streets of Thera.

One man with a camera called out to his daughter, a girl about Linda's age.

"Oh, look, Gertrude," he said. "Here's one that's quite pretty—considering she's a Greek."

"Oh, Dad," said the girl, "you think everyone's

pretty if they're young. Can't you see she's just an ordinary healthy pregnant girl?"

Linda stood still, shocked. To say that about Linda Barstow! Linda, who had been adored, elevated to stardom, who had had too much admiration.

She forgot that she had a kerchief tied over her cheeks and chin, Greek style, that she was suntanned and smothered in a maternity dress. She only felt that she was lost, gone, and that any identity she had had vanished.

"Pardon me!" she said angrily in English.

Leaving them astonished, she walked away, down the street, and headed for the institute. She would find Claudia.

As she came near, she saw the little donkey cart of a villager, Demetrios, near the alley. A cluster of people stood by. An American tourist who had been watching took off his hat. And then she saw the small pine box that two men carried from the alley of the institute hospital out into the wagon.

Terrified, she moved away. That could happen to her, too. Which girl had come here, to have this terrible thing happen after all the waiting, the sorrow and loneliness that had awaited her here?

She fled back to her house, slammed the door, and sat, trying to calm the panic in her. Who was she? What did she have to fall back on all by herself? What would happen to her?

On the kitchen table she found the lunch Effie had left her wrapped in waxed paper. Cucumbers, tomatoes, cheese, black olives, and a sandwich of buttered black bread and honey. She pushed the plate aside angrily. She was sick of peasant food. Sick of the load in her stomach, sick of the fake cheerfulness of Claudia, for she had seen the sadness in her face when she was in repose, not doing her act. And as for Chloë, it was evident that she would have given anything to have borne this baby herself. She didn't care for Linda. All she cared for was to have that child of Niadas' in her arms.

As she looked back on *The Oracle* and her year as

an important figure, she felt that she had been used, used by everyone for a reason all his or her own. Claudia had used her to get into the limelight and out of poverty. Jessica had used her to get back into the studio. And Niadas had used her to have his fantasy realized! Max had used her . . . Well, what was the use of listing them all again? David had warned her in London that if she knew what people would seek from her, she'd run.

Maybe it was time to run. To find out what she was. To be in tune with herself, if she could. Try to find out what Linda Barstow was, what she wanted, and what she was going to do aside from all the currents that swirled around her. What if that had been her baby in that little casket? What would she do? What would her life be with or without the baby, always pretending it wasn't hers, living a lie for a corporation.

If she could only believe in something. Claudia had told her she must learn to be secure all by herself. How could she do that?

The walls seemed to press down on her. It would be better to get out under the blue dome of the sky, to wander to some of the places where Chloë had found so much happiness. If she could only get in tune with Niadas and what he had meant, perhaps she would be happier about this pregnancy.

She tied her lunch in a kerchief and left the house. No one was around, anyway. Obviously to her, no one cared. She could do what she pleased.

As she left the streets of the town, she was glad to be free of it. The same faces, the same old toothless gorgons, staring at her and no doubt making remarks about her pregnancy, relishing the scandal. Of course, everyone knew she had no man. She wanted to shout, "Niadas! Niadas! Niadas!" and point at her belly. That would startle them.

Wandering along the countryside, seeing the women in their bright headscarves working among the vineyards and vegetables, she wondered if she could ever be as happy in this place as Chloë seemed to be. She suddenly realized, although she had not thought about it before, that if Chloë had been able to find a joy and usefulness in life although she was alone, perhaps she too could find it.

She headed toward the rocky glen where Chloë had taken her. She and Niadas had hidden there. It was on a lip of rock. It was close to the edge of the water. Chloë had told her how she had pushed the bodies of the vandals over the cliff.

Exhausted after her walk, she found the cave, sat at the entrance, looking out at the sea. Spreading the kerchief out under her head, she lay down and slept.

When she awoke, it was early evening.

She didn't want to return to the house. Let them look. She settled back, in her mind punishing the world for neglect of her. Well, she would try to stay until she had some fulfillment of a sort that made her come back prepared to be her own person.

Why was it that mornings were beautiful, as you woke up with a whole day ahead of you, and evenings were lonely?

Perhaps it was Santorini that made her feel this way. Hadn't Chloë quoted Sophocles, who said Santorini was heaven and hell in one?

Anyplace could be, depending upon whether you were loved or not. Or perhaps whether you loved yourself. What did she have to do to be able to love herself?

She thought about *The Oracle*. She had seen only bits and pieces of it, during the dubbing sessions, but it must be the keynote of her life. She thought of Alethea, the priestess, and she felt suddenly that in portraying her, she had felt power, and beauty, and this would be transmitted to the screen, so other people would feel it.

For a moment she had considered killing herself, for it seemed she couldn't have lived up to her fantasies. Several tourists whose names she did not know had humiliated what she thought she was—magic in person. A star.

But no, she thought, I will wait until I see the picture. Then maybe, somehow, I will know what I am, and what I should be.

She sat in the cave until it was dark. It was the time of the *peripataki*—the little evening—when people strolled to see the sun set and early nighttime turning the sea and sky depths into myriad colors, or gathered to have drinks and dinner in the *tavernas*.

Nearby was the little chapel in the Byzantine style that Niadas had built to celebrate his escape from drowning in the sea during the war, when his ship had been sunk off the rugged shore, and he had swum to one of his vessels in his sponge fleet and been hauled aboard. It was there overlooking the land and sea he loved that he had chosen to be buried.

If she could find this retreat, she would stay there and hope that Niadas and what he had been would give her comfort. She would pray for power and strength for her coming ordeal, and then walk back to Thera.

The night was blacker than she expected. Finding her way over the hilly terrain, she was terrified as her trail led to an edge of a precipice. She turned back, not knowing whether the glitter in the black below was the flicker of a star reflected in the sea or a light from a half-hidden cave dwelling below.

She had always been fearful of nighttime shadows and getting lost in the dark, but she swallowed her terror. She had to be brave or she would panic.

Several times she smelled the fragrance of a fire, and thought of calling out for help, but she went on. Finally a rim of white shone in the distance. She was on the right path. Beyond was the point where the little Byzantine chapel awaited, a beacon, the white dome with its Greek cross silhouetted against dark sky. Inside, its rich gold icons and jewels would beckon by flickering candlelight. Now that she was heading toward it, she felt that Niadas was protecting her.

A faint wind blew the scarf against her face, and a small animal scampered by, startling her. She rushed forward, and pitched into a depression in the rocks in the dark.

She fell in a heap, and lay a moment, gasping for

breath. When she tried to pull herself to her feet, a pain crossed her side into her groin.

Fearfully she lay still for a moment. Another pain accosted her. Slowly she pulled herself up, and arose. Bending over, she managed to stagger to the chapel. Another horrendous pain racked her, and she fell across the threshold.

It was some time later that an old woman, Sophia, came by with her mule. She had been to market, stayed to gossip with her daughters, and was returning to her cave house nearby, where she lived independently and proudly by herself. She always stopped at the chapel, finding comfort in the richness Niadas had left, for her husband had fought with him during the war, and died.

Sophia saw the girl lying across the threshold. When she turned her over, she saw that she was pregnant. Looking at her, she could not remember having seen her; she knew not where she came from, but she was in trouble.

The old woman slapped her cheeks until she came alive, and helped her get on the mule. It was obvious she could not go very far. The best thing she could do was to take her to her hut, which was half-cave, but a fire was in the hearth, and there was a cistern of good water nearby. It was a place where her own children and several of her grandchildren had been born, so any ordeal ahead of her was to be faced with a stoic familiarity.

She barely got her in the house when Linda's water broke. She looked down with a cry of terror as she saw the liquid splash down her legs onto the stone floor.

The woman cried out in Greek, but Linda shook her head; she did not understand.

Sophia stretched her out on her straw pallet on a ledge carved from the stone of the cave. She pulled Linda's dress off, brought linen to clean her, and immediately set to work at her stove.

As Linda went into heavy labor pains, the woman gave her a rope looped to a beam on the ceiling to hold onto, so she could pull against it. She wrapped hot bran poultices in a cloth and laid them on her stomach.

She fished about in her possessions and brought blue beads and a string of garlic to hang on her neck to chase away evil spirits.

She put a wet cloth over her forehead, and held her head with a steady hand when she strained. Greek or no, Linda understood when she praised her for helping. She taught her by imitation how to draw in her breath, and when to press.

The old woman massaged her, rubbed her with oils, freshened the bran poultices, and changed the linens, wiping her sweating face.

Linda cried out in agony. It seemed the pulsing pain was endless.

"Let me die!" she said. "I just can't stand it! Let me die!"

But the old woman smiled her toothless smile, patted her cheek, and nodded that everything would be all right.

Finally, with a gush, more water poured out of her, and with a cry she felt her body heave more than she would have thought possible. Her breath and heartbeat were coming so quickly that she thought she could not bear the strain. She would perish.

And then she fought death, rather than asking for it. She pressed her buttocks, the old woman's hands and gestures guiding her. And then the baby came out of her, head-first. It seemed to rend her in two.

The old woman grasped it under the arms and helped pull it from her body. In a moment she had cut and tied the umbilical cord. Linda looked at the baby. It was beet-red, bloody, seemed creased, and encrusted with some substance, its head covered with something which looked like a veil, not at all what she had expected a baby would be.

The old woman removed the caul from its head, held it precariously by its slippery heels, gave it a whack on the bottom, and it let out a wail. She then set it down on a blanket, cleaned it off with oil, and placed it in the protection of Linda's arms while she turned her attention to cleaning up Linda and the bed and stanching a flow of blood. There was a moment of distress as the afterbirth came out of her, and gasping a sigh of relief, even though she was exhausted, Linda turned to the infant. As weak as she was, she pulled the baby's covering away.

Even if she were going to die, she thought, she had to see her baby.

The gorgon watched her face with her toothless smile.

Strange, thought Linda, the two times in her life that she had known a man, the night that she was made love to by Niadas; the time this child was conceived, it had all been in the dark.

And now, looking at her baby was the first time in her life she had ever seen a penis.

She had brought Niadas' son into the world.

◆◆◆◆◆◆◆◆◆

Dozens of crafts of all kinds pushed among the deep currents, below the beetling cliffs of the island, looking for the body of the unknown foreigner, the young girl who must have fallen from the cliffs.

Effie stood watch in the villa. It was her third day of vigil. Numbed, she awaited any message, caring for the household, the moment any physical need brought anyone to the house.

The baby's layette was still on the sideboard, the little puppy frisked about, and the larder was replenished as villagers brought an abundance of food and sympathy.

Effie's eyes were dry at last. She blamed herself for tending to other matters instead of looking after her B'linda. After all the years of care and love, she felt she had been to blame for this tragedy.

Chloë had not blamed her. She had taken her in her arms a moment, calming her, and saying, "You could not watch her all the time. She followed her own will; she is a woman."

Claudia tearfully took her hand and said, "I know

you could never be to blame. And incidentally, we won't alert Jessica unless we have definite news. Just say your prayers."

Having answered Chloë's call for help, Ubaldo had appeared suddenly, coming up from the sea. They were sitting in the house having a bowl of soup when he entered.

In a moment Chloë had jumped up from the table, upsetting her chair, and had fallen into the protection of his arms. Their clinging, even in this moment of grief, made Claudia realize that Ubaldo had found his woman. With a pang, Claudia thought of Max, wishing he were here. And then she thought how terrible it would be for him if anything happened to Linda.

These personal moments were swallowed by the driving necessity to find Linda. Ubaldo joined in the search, never resting. Claudia put on her stout walking shoes, and waited for the break of day, when she could find her way about the rocky, forbidding trails of the island.

"We'll look everywhere," she said. "She has to be on the island someplace."

Chloë had the support of everyone on Santorini. The elders had known her since she was a child, and respected her as she had worked the fearful wartime days alongside Niadas. The children of Thera knew she was a lady of importance, and had shared in her bounty on their saints' days. They all scampered over the island, looking in caves, talking to farmers and goatherds. It was an exciting treasure hunt to them, with the shuddering overtones of tragedy. Every one of them envisioned her body coming up from the depths, beaten by the tides against the cliffs, or discovered bloody and twisted in some fissure in the rocks.

Ubaldo took the jeep and scoured the windy terrain beyond walking distance. He even searched the Greek ruins for any clue on the lower reaches of the island.

In a few hours Fergus and David were climbing the slippery steps to Thera, Fergus on donkeyback, suffering vertigo, while a youth switched his mount so it seemed to jump along the zigzag path with the treacherous cliffs below. It was hell for him, and for David, who walked on up ahead, trying to unravel the startling facts in his life, while he thought: I must find my sister . . . my sister. . . . And fearing for her more than for Titan or *The Oracle*.

This was no time for a personal vendetta. An unspoken truce took place.

David, being young, followed Chloë, who strode tirelessly in every village lane or ruin on the high spine of the island. She knew of every out-of-the-way place and talked to anyone, from priest to beggar, who stopped her with a suggestion.

Fergus followed Claudia, helping her over rocks and footpaths, walking up and down the streets, never stopping.

What a sad ending, he thought, to the Barstows, and of course, to Titan. He knew that a picture which came out with a newcomer, no matter how brilliant, who had died, was poison at the box office.

Finally a young girl came in from the Niadas chapel, bringing a kerchief. She had found it near the entrance, and her mother had thought it might be a clue.

Chloë rushed to Effie with it. She recognized it as Linda's. It gave them all fresh hope.

Chloë rushed to the chapel with David. There was no other clue. She looked across the rocky vale beyond, and as she did, an old woman saw her, and then fled into her hut, which was built halfway into the hillside.

Strange, thought Chloë. I know that woman, Sophia. Why should she run?

She followed her, and as she approached the hut, she thought she heard the faint wail of a newborn infant.

Sophia came to the door. She held out her hands, halting her.

"No," she said, "you must stay away! No one must enter this house for nine days."

Chloë pushed her aside and rushed in, followed by David.

There on the cot lay Linda, holding her baby at her breast.

"My god, my god!" said Chloë. "You're safe!"

Linda looked up at her.

"He hurts when he nurses," she said. "Oh . . . Chloë. Get me out of here!"

She burst into tears.

David thought she looked like a little girl as she lay there.

"We'll get you out," he said. "Don't worry, Linda."

"I told you," she said, smiling. "It's a boy."

Chloë stood weeping in the doorway. Sophia rushed up to her.

"You must go away," she insisted again. "There must be no visitors in this house for nine days!"

Chloë turned to David.

"There's no use to explain. She's going by the old superstitions. Go get Dr. Lourekas and have him bring a litter," she said. "I will try to talk some sense into her. And for the love of heaven, tell Claudia."

As Claudia rushed across the rocky point to the chapel, tears of gratitude poured down her face.

Fergus followed, stumbling in his leather city oxfords.

"I'm going to make five thousand prayers," she said, "and burn at least ten thousand candles. I may even turn Greek Orthodox if they'll take me, and since I've given up drink, I may be forced to give up cigarettes."

"This is no joke," said Fergus sourly. "You always act like everything's an amusing anecdote."

He took her arm and angrily swung her around.

"Do you know what happens if this gets out? Titan is ruined. Do you understand! I've taken your whims and covered for you forever, Claudia. But this is a different world. Everybody knows everything. There is no privacy. The abandon of this young girl is unforgivable and will have the worst consequences if anyone finds out. How could all of you have been so permissive?"

Claudia pulled her arm away and stared up at him.

"Listen, you sour old son-of-a-bitch," she said furiously, "I'd like to refresh your memory. How did Titan start? Maybe you don't remember. With a young kid, *me*, who got pregnant by your boss, Simon Moses, to whom *you* introduced me. And what happened? Now that I look back on it, you got me out of town, on a train, to Hollywood, because he was a married man and was scared. And who was it rousted up a butcher who gave me an abortion which nearly killed me? *You.* So don't go getting moral with *me* about my poor niece who decided to have her baby, or I'll ring the bell on you."

She rushed toward the chapel, where Chloë stood at a nearby hut, gesturing excitedly.

To Chloë it was a new day, a new life, and she was the happiest woman in the world. Well, perhaps not; she would have to stand in line with Claudia and Effie for that honor.

As for messages, the first one that went out was a wire to Jessica in Switzerland signed by Claudia. It read: "Congratulations, you have just had a six-pound son!"

The infant, installed in the villa, was taken out of his primitive swaddling clothes, bathed, and cleanly dressed by Effie in David's layette. Sophia, distressed at the apostasy of allowing anyone to visit the baby before nine days had passed, much less carry him away, for he was very special, being born with a caul covering his head, relented when Chloë explained to her that these people were foreign, and their traditions had to be observed. The gift of a lamb helped to soften the distress of the old woman.

Claudia was amazed at the healthy baby and at Linda, who seemed to have forgotten the anguish of bearing him in the cave house. She had told of her fearful labor in a torrent of tears, once they had rushed to her side. But now she was placid.

"And when I think," said Claudia, "of my relief that Chloë had a perfect hospital going, and you wouldn't have to be exposed to any superstitious customs of a midwife! Garlic, blue beads against the evil eye, and God knows what else!"

She shuddered.

Fergus held a conference with David as they sat at a *kaféneon.*

"I can proceed now," said Fergus, "since we know where we stand. Linda can stay here the prescribed forty days that seems to be the custom. That will be an excuse to keep her out of the way until she's fit. I will bring Effie with the baby to meet Jessica in Switzerland. I'll charter a plane; it's the least I can do, considering what has happened. Then I'll get them settled in a house somewhere around Beverly Hills or Santa Monica, whichever they prefer. Claudia can take Linda in hand, get her some clothes, which will go on the budget for personal appearances. There's no use to penalize her; she's got to feel like a decent human being before she gets started. After all, at her age, she has been through hell. It was a big world she was pushed into."

David was surprised at his thoughtfulness. These last few days since he knew he was not his father, David had tried to imagine how hurtful it must have been to his pride to know that Jeffrey had sired him. He thought back on his childhood, and it seemed that Fergus, although he had always been busy, had been affectionate to him then. He was curious. He had to ask.

"When did you find out about . . . about me?" he asked.

Fergus looked up at him, lit a cigarette, and drew on it before he answered. He spoke faintly.

"I learned it from that bitch Jessica, the day you . . . saw us together in my office. She was so enraged, she blurted it out. It seems your mother told her one day at Santa Monica."

David, looking at him, saw him in a different light. He had been a scrapper, and he had fought for Titan as long as it had existed. He found himself admiring him. With all this hatred of Jessica, he still was going to pick her up and get that baby back to Hollywood.

"I hope you realize by now," said Fergus, "that what I did with Jessica in front of you was to show you what she was. But since then, obviously, I don't have to draw any more diagrams."

David nodded.

"We'll get the campaign moving along," said Fergus. "Grace Boomer will do a good job. In three months we'll start our sittings, magazine campaign and set up interviews to make up for what we had to cancel out these last months. We'll coordinate with the opening. I think Grauman's Chinese will be the best premiere setting in Hollywood for publicity. We'll draw interest on the nostalgia of the golden days of Hollywood, and Linda's virginal young beauty. After all, both Jeffrey and Claudia's footprints are in cement in the foyer, and we can do a big thing of getting Linda's footprints to follow."

David's eyes flickered at Fergus' bland mention of Linda's virginal young beauty, under the circumstances. Then he realized that Fergus was quoting from the campaign that had been put into motion these last months. He had even hypnotized himself into believing it, and was mouthing the "shtick" on which the campaign was being built. Well . . . that's show biz, he thought. . . . That's what brings in money to repay all the trials and tribulations of this insane, massive caper. Who outside the industry would believe that a motion picture could create so much havoc in so many people's lives, from death to birth?

"You think of all the angles, don't you?" said David, smiling faintly.

"Listen, David," said Fergus, "if you get by on your wits as I have all these years, you become an angle artist. I was not handsome, wealthy, creative, or talented. I only had gall—lots of gall. And in my life, two families put me down. The Moses brothers, Simon and Abe, and the Barstows, Jeffrey and Claudia. It hasn't been easy."

He held up his hand.

"But I'm not complaining. I've had a longer run at Titan than any of them. I'm a survivor. Now, because I'm so involved in the machinations of *The Oracle,* working out the advertising campaign, promotion, bookings, et cetera, I'll remain until the picture is out. Then I will step down. I would like to be an independent producer; that's about the only jackpot left in Hollywood, and of course I'd want a Titan release. Okay?"

"No," said David.

Fergus felt he was being rejected. His face reddened.

"Not at all," continued David. "As Fergus Austin, rather than my father, I need you. I need an old warhorse with guts like yours. Stay on, we'll run the studio flank-to-flank, at least until we clash so much it's impossible."

Fergus looked at him eye-to-eye. David was smiling at him. Feeling ridiculously close to moist eyes, he looked out to sea.

"Okay," he said. "Let's get the hell out of this place."

They arose, and side-by-side along the narrow whitewashed streets, they walked back to the villa.

◆◆◆◆◆◆◆◆

"I can't name him after Pericles Niadas," said Linda, as Chloë held the baby. "You know, I'd like to."

"I know," said Chloë, "but it is our custom to name boys after the paternal grandfather. Pericles' father was named Alexandros, Alexander to you."

"Alexander Ziska," said Linda. "That's pretty good, everything from A to Z."

Chloë smiled.

"Beautiful," she said. "I shall miss you, and you must promise to bring him here when you can. A godmother should not be too far away."

"And a godfather," said Linda.

"Yes," said Chloë, "Ubaldo will be here with me. You see, one way or another, you brought us together. How strange is fate!"

"Yes," said Claudia, coming in. "Here is some mail, sent by way of Grace to your mother in Switzerland, where, of course, you're supposed to be. Already they're clamoring for interviews. You'll have sittings the minute we get back. It's going to be hectic."

David and Fergus came in. Claudia greeted them at the door.

"Mail from Grace," said Claudia. "She's already lining up all of Linda's time. How soon does she have to get there?"

"I'd say three months," said David. "After she feels up to it. We'll have to plan for you to get her wardrobe, perhaps in Paris, and work out something so she won't look quite so young."

"You know," said Claudia, "if I remember my Shakespeare, Juliet was not yet fourteen. Lady Capulet, which I played in the sticks, said:

> " 'Well, think of marriage now;
> Younger than you,
> Here in Verona, ladies of esteem,
> Are made already mothers: by my count,
> I was your mother much upon these years
> That you are now a maid.'

"So there you are, not quite so scandalous as we make it today, and God knows, David, Linda never looked more beautiful."

David smiled and squeezed her hand. Fergus, engrossed in the London *Times*, which had come with the mail, went to the garden to look up stock-market quotations.

Claudia leaned close to David.

"Aren't you proud of her?" she said.

David looked at her sharply.

"You know," she said, "don't you?"

He nodded.

"Yes, Fergus lost his head and told me in London," he said.

"Are you horrified?"

He shook his head.

"Immensely relieved," he said. "It has released such a floodgate of hurt. Does that sound strange for a man to say?"

"Not at all," said Claudia. "Now you know you are

related to the most gorgeous people in the world, and it must be the most marvelous relief not to be related to that old bastard Fergus."

They laughed.

The last days in Santorini were a kaleidoscope of plans, changes, and future maneuvers.

Fergus and David planned a flying trip, one to Hollywood, the other to London. Fergus was to return in a month to carry the baby and Effie to Switzerland and pick up Jessica.

Before they left, Claudia had a conference with David.

"It seems to me," she said, "that Linda and I could establish housekeeping with Effie and the baby. Get a house on the Santa Monica oceanfront for us. Since we know Jessica is going to get her divorce from Max right after the premiere, we can use the excuse that she has business in Rome, to alibi the baby living with us."

"Jessica has business in Rome?" asked David.

"From all indications," said Claudia, "she's going to chase down her prince, and with her share of the picture, she can pay for the plumbing in that broken-down villa."

"To each his own," said David. "How do you know?"

"She asked Max to co-sign a lease for an apartment that she has taken after the premiere of the picture, which he says is to be their last appearance together. Naturally, she asked Max to pay for it. She knows Max and I are eager to get together. So what of it? Who cares as long as we work it out? I couldn't be more pleased."

Claudia glowed.

David embraced her.

"My grandfather was a lucky man," he said.

◆◆◆◆◆◆◆◆

As she said farewell at the top of the steps, Claudia gave Fergus a kiss. He had elected to walk, even if his knees gave out, rather than risk imminent destruction on a donkey that swayed precariously over the zigzag bluffs.

"I figure that I'm smarter than the donkey," he said, "even if he's stronger than me."

Claudia felt a twinge of affection for him. Subdued, and thoughtful, he had tried in his way to help glue together all the pieces of this situation so distasteful to him. She saw a growing relationship, filmmaker-to-filmmaker, man-to-man, between him and David, and she respected him for it.

"Well, old boy," she said, "we've come a hell of a long way from that train ride to Hollywood. As long as you're around, I'm not worried about that Titan water tower."

"You'd better be," he said. "It's running dry."

But he embraced her, holding her close for a moment.

David spoke to Linda just before he left.

"We're asking a great deal of you now, Linda, but we have given you a great deal, too. Now it's up to you to help us. In front of the public you're going to have to put on your false face and be the complete movie star."

He took her hand.

She was pleased that he treated her as an adult. He didn't put on a false face, or pamper her with optimism.

She remembered how he had once told her that they should keep their relationship impersonal. That way they would not have the luxury of hostility or the blindness of affection. Something had changed. There was affection.

As he left, she watched the back of his head, the way he moved, and she felt an emotion, thawing out the coldness of her disturbances of the last months, the feeling that she could care, that she was a person, all on her own.

In the days that followed, she helped Effie look after the baby. He was christened into the Greek Orthodox faith at Chloë's ardent suggestion.

Linda went through the ceremonies, the incense, the

candlelight, the rich ritual; it was all strange to her, but seeing the joy of Chloë and Ubaldo by her side, she tried to evoke Niadas, and think of how happy he would be. Chloë gave a celebration at her house, and the officials and townspeople came to be festive, little knowing who sired the baby.

From then on the baby was Alex, and it seemed to give him a personality, a being all his own.

The day came when Fergus' chartered helicopter landed, to take Effie and Alex away. Their belongings were loaded aboard. Linda handed the baby over to Effie.

The next morning Linda awoke to a silent house. She wondered how Jessica would react to the baby. But it didn't matter. He had Effie.

And Effie, dear Effie, was gone. She wandered about the house in her pink robe. Claudia was asleep, having read late.

The crib, which Chloë had lent her, still remained. The little white-and-blue blankets were folded, to be returned to the institute. Linda touched them.

The emptiness suddenly overwhelmed her. Her baby was gone. The part of her that she had carried through such a difficult time, the flesh-and-blood Barstow, wasn't here anymore.

With a pang she missed him. She sat down, sobbing, not caring that her emotions were flowing over in grief.

In a moment Claudia was at her side.

"Let it out, honey," she said. "Just let it out. You're lucky. You'll be with him again soon. He'll be able to live with you. Under some conditions it would have been impossible."

"I know," sobbed Linda, "I know. . . . It's just so complicated. And I miss him!"

Claudia picked up the puppy, which was barking for attention. She petted him, and went to the door to put him out in the garden.

On the way back, she saw that Linda hadn't even noticed him. Her mind was in a different direction. She was missing Alex.

Well, well, thought Claudia. That trigger that Max

started is gone. She's off in a more real direction. Now it's Alex. She's growing up.

⬥⬥⬥⬥⬥⬥⬥⬥

Ubaldo greeted Linda in the little garden of the villa as Chloë helped the women pack their few possessions.

Engrossed in her own troubles, she glanced up at him, surprised. He had reflected such melancholy in Rome, now his face was alight.

"I wanted to tell you," he said, "that in a most incredible way, meeting you led me to a life I never knew would be possible. I know that time will do the same for you. We do not need our Phrynes anymore, Linda, you, nor I."

"I haven't even thought of the statue lately," said Linda, startled. "Once she was so important."

"That's what I was trying to say," said Ubaldo. "The Villa della Rosa and all that existed there was just a stepping stone along our path."

"I hope so," said Linda, her eyes moist.

"I know so," said Ubaldo.

His smile as he embraced her took some of the sadness out of her heart.

⬥⬥⬥⬥⬥⬥⬥⬥

Chloë strove hard to make farewells as light as possible. In no time the helicopter had lifted Linda and Claudia off, and they saw the island recede. Thera looked like a row of white teeth perched on the edge of the cliffs. As it became smaller, it lost its reality and became a fantasy, its crescent shape a revelation that it had once been a raging volcano.

Once it was gone, Linda put her head back and closed her eyes.

Claudia had the rambling thought that if Niadas had lived, Linda would be one of the richest women in the world. Instead, she was going to have to make her own way. Oh, let that picture be successful!

"You know," said Linda, breaking into her thoughts, "I have such a strange feeling about David. I think I love him. Wouldn't he be a wonderful father for Alex? Maybe I should have married him."

"Nonsense," said Claudia. "It would never work. You must eventually find someone your own age. That's foolish talk."

Linda looked at her, surprised.

"Well, don't get so angry," said Linda. "It was just a thought."

"Forget it," said Claudia. "He's a born bachelor."

Someday, thought Claudia, I'm going to have to tell her. She felt exhausted. It seemed that somehow, after all her careless youth, she had turned into a regular den mother, helping everyone to get out of messes. It wasn't her style. She was tired . . . tired . . . tired.

◆◆◆◆◆◆◆◆

Hollywood Boulevard was dressed in its gaudiest tinsel. Titan had gone all out to make the premiere of *The Oracle* the outstanding motion-picture event of the year. It evoked old days, days of more lush times. Twelve arc lights shot streaks of lights that wove in the sky, announcing a filmic event. The boulevard had been closed off, save for one lane, where policemen allowed cars with special *Oracle* stickers on their windshields to pull up with all their chauffeured elegance to the brightly lit court of Grauman's Chinese Theater, traditional shrine of premiers.

Bleachers had been erected. They were overflowing with people of all ages, who had gathered since early morning to see the circus.

Now, in the dark, ropes held back six or seven hundred more people, and extra police were called in to prevent a crush.

Many in the crowd remembered Claudia and Jeffrey Barstow, as a matter of fact their footprints were preserved in cement in the foyer with other luminaries, but the great excitement, which had been engendered by thousands of dollars of publicity, was the debut of "the incredibly beautiful virgin who was desired by every man in the world."

It had been finally decided by David and Fergus that Linda should make her entrance with John Graves. Since he was the hottest new sex image of masculinity from Europe, their appearance would make good copy. And then Grace Boomer suggested that since they were promoting the virginal quality of Linda, and there had been more than a whisper about a romance in Rome with Graves, it might be smart to have Claudia, who still had a lot of clout with the press, enter with them in her new position as chaperon and teacher to her niece. David was asked by both of them to complete the foursome.

On a platform a clutter of cameras and microphones broadcast the event to the world. An overenthusiastic master of ceremonies who wrote a trade-paper gossip column introduced the famous, past famous, and future famous.

This was only the prologue. The film, the main event, would lead up to a party for six hundred at the Coconut Grove, an industry "must" for Titan. If the picture was a success, the party would be an exciting event. If it was moderately received, many of the tables would be empty, and the large group of guests would leave after courteous free drinks and supper.

Linda was terrified. She was dressed in a white crepe gown fashioned after the Greek style, with a white cape falling from her shoulders. On her breast she wore the gold, emerald, and pearl octopus Niadas had given her. Her hair was tied up in a fillet of golden ribbon.

"Do I look all right?" she asked. "My knees are shaking."

"You look wonderful," said Claudia. "Now, stop jittering. Pretend you're stepping on the set."

"You'll get used to it," said John Graves. "Just remember, they're the public who buys you. Be grateful they're here."

Linda started to paste a smile on her face. The doorman had his hand on the handle of the limousine as they glided to a stop.

"Don't wear that phony smile," said Claudia. "Just look mysterious and aloof and leave them guessing."

The next thing Linda knew, she faced a battery of blinding lights. Up ahead of her was Max and her mother, who rushed back to give her a public kiss on the cheek.

Claudia gritted her teeth.

Linda mumbled a few words of thanks to Max and to the company in the mike. John Graves took her arm, paid his respects to the makers of the picture, and they passed on along the red carpet.

Cheers came from the crowd. If they had become excited before, now they were ecstatic. Linda almost cringed from the force of the crowd reaction.

Somehow she heard David talking into her ear.

"You've got them, Belinda," he said.

She turned, looking at him in surprise.

"What did you say?" she asked.

"Look on the screen," he said. "It's Belinda Barstow."

She opened her mouth in surprise, and turned to Claudia.

"Did you hear that!" she said. "Did you?"

Claudia smiled.

"I nearly perished, not telling you," she said.

In a haze Linda, now Belinda, moved on into the theater foyer. All around, people came to her, pressed, pushed, wanting to be recognized, hoping to seal their image into the mind of the new commodity which was Belinda Barstow. Flashlights popped until she saw only circles of lights.

Seeing them surrounded, Fergus joined up. He and David pushed the crowd politely away.

"That's enough boys!" said Fergus. "See you later at the Grove."

The picture began. Soon the audience was engrossed in it. When Belinda made her entrance, there was a gasp from the audience. She was beauty of a divine sort, vulnerable and innocent, a target for the dramatic conflict in the story.

The magic number of people in the theater, 1,492, held the future of the film in their collective selves.

They absorbed it, became lost in it, and were carried away as the story progressed.

Three-quarters of the way through the picture, Belinda leaned back. The audience knew, she knew, everyone who was sitting near her, that little cluster of people who had changed her life, and now allowed her to be Belinda Barstow, knew. There was no way out of it.

She was a star.

Titan was saved. Claudia had her place in the limelight again. Max was again master of a glittering career. John Graves would have anything he wanted professionally. David Austin would be hailed as one of the new forces in the film industry. Fergus would run his studio. Jessica would be rich enough for princes and plumbing. Ubaldo would be well off. Chloë would be acclaimed an international actress. Alex, in the nursery in Santa Monica, would have a rich life. And Leslie Charles, who was sitting a few seats away with the old columnist Clarissa Pennock, would be as he had feared, a character actor henceforth. But he'd win an Oscar.

Belinda was lost in the cocoon of her own making, her character in the story of the oracle.

Something was pressed into her hand. It came from Claudia.

She looked down. There was the little globule of amber with the two insects imprisoned in it. She remembered playing with it on Jeffrey's desk when she was little.

And so, suddenly, her father was there with her, too. Her throat tightened with emotion.

"What is this for?" she whispered.

"I'll tell you later," said Claudia.

ABOUT THE AUTHOR

MARY LOOS is the third generation of her family to write for the motion picture industry. Her grandfather wrote silent film titles for Lasky Famous Players (now Paramount Pictures). Her aunt, Anita Loos, is the well-known author and screenwriter of *Gentlemen Prefer Blondes.* Mary Loos has been highly successful in both the movie and the television world. She's done publicity for MGM, collaborated with her husband, Richard Sale, on over fifteen films, and was associate producer of *Gentlemen Marry Brunettes.* For television, she wrote and produced with Richard Sale the TV series, *Yancy Derringer.* Together, they also wrote *The Wackiest Ship in the Army, Please Don't Eat the Daisies,* and *Bewitched.* Mary Loos lives in Santa Monica, California, where she wrote *The Beggars Are Coming* and its sequel, *Belinda.*